Also by Alex Abella

The Killing of the Saints

THE
Great
American

A Novel

Alex Abella

Simon & Schuster

SIMON & SCHUSTER
Rockefeller Center
1230 Avenue of the Americas
New York, NY 10020

SIMON & SCHUSTER and colophon are registered trademarks of Simon & Schuster Inc.

Designed by Elina Nudelman

Manufactured in the United States of America

10 9 8 7 6 5 4 3 2 1

Library of Congress Cataloging-in-Publication Data

Abella, Alex
    The great American/Alex Abela
        p.   cm.
    I. Title
PS3551.B3394G74   1997   96-43384
813'.54—dc20   CIP

ISBN 0-684-81427-7

To My Father,

Antiguo integrante del ABC, apóstata del Partido Comunista, conspirador del 26 de Julio, laureado poeta y suprema inspiracion.

¡Cuerpo y figura
hasta la sepultura!

"Am I the only one who really cared for Pyle?"

—Graham Greene

The men have finished loading the heavy weapons into the red van when the pink-cheeked student called José Antonio, whom everyone knows as Manzanita, Little Apple, speaks.

"There has never been anything like this. And if we don't succeed, there will never be another chance like this. Beyond us is the future, overwhelming in its possibilities. Behind us is the past, full of blood and injustice. We are only a handful of men against the thousands of the tyrant. But remember this: win or lose, our names will be written in blood on the pages of the history of Cuba."

No one speaks in the stifling heat of that garage in the heights of El Vedado, for no one is certain if Manzanita has finished exhorting the troops to battle. True, the operation has been planned, nurtured, and spawned by the wiry Spaniard standing in the corner, Carlos Gutiérrez Menoyo, who fought with the Republicans against Franco and with the Free French against the Nazis. But Menoyo has ceded the spiritual leadership to José Antonio, who now turns his deep-set hazel eyes to the exiled Iberian plotter for permission to continue. Menoyo waves his hand horizontally over the group as though to say, Go ahead, their hearts and minds are yours; mine are the bodies and their weapons.

Silence prevails. Not that the men there are other than eloquent in their normal lives. Architects, businessmen, teachers, painters, and poets, on any other day these men would be spouting a cacophony of opinions and impressions. But on this occasion the solemnity of their act has descended upon them. For once there is quiet in a room full of Cubans.

Outside, the drone of Havana traffic fills the warm spring afternoon.

"I know many of you are not believers," continues Manzanita. "We at the Directorio have never made it a condition that free men share our beliefs to join in the struggle against the tyrant. So we ask your forbearance with those of us who follow the principles of Mother Church as we raise our voices in prayer to the Virgin of El Cobre, the patron saint of Cuba. We pray that she may guide us and protect us from harm and that, if harm befall us, we may die like men, remembering the Apostle, who said better to die on your feet like a man than to live on your knees like a slave."

José Antonio then says a Hail Mary, which all the men recite, even those who, like Menoyo, have lost their faith or who through cruel experience have grown to hate the falsehoods of the church. It can bring no harm, thinks Menoyo. Besides, who knows, maybe she will listen after all.

Upon the final words, "and at the hour of our death. Amen," José Antonio looks up, brandishes his 9mm Thompson semiautomatic in the air.

"*Patria o muerte,*" fatherland or death, he cries.

The men look at him in stunned silence, then Menoyo answers the call.

"*Venceremos!*"—we will win!—he cries. And the men, in unison, like the troops of Saint James out to battle the Moor, out to rid their land of sin, ignorance, and oppression, all raise their weapons and shout, not caring any longer who hears—the passing patrol cars, the tattletale neighbors—all shouting the unstoppable cry of a nation demanding freedom and justice.

"*Venceremos!*" We will win! We will win!

"*Venceremos! Venceremos! Venceremos!*"

And the garage doors open and the men drive out to meet their fate.

It is three o'clock exactly.

At that moment in the Presidential Palace, General Fulgencio Batista y Zaldívar is putting the finishing touches on his afternoon agenda.

It has been exactly five years and three days since the brisk early morning when Batista drove into Camp Columbia and staged a coup against President Prío. "The people and I are the dictators," he said then, pledging a new dawn of prosperity for the Cuban nation. He has kept his promise, but he has also turned the island into an abattoir. Not that the Leader of the Country, the Protector of the People, the general in chief of the armed forces, and the sixteenth dubiously elected president of the even more dubious Cuban Republic stoops so low as to pull out molars with pliers, stick red-hot pokers into rectums, or drown suspects in toilets full of feces. Those are things he entrusts to his hirelings, Captain Esteban Ventura, SIM colonel Orlando Piedra, Police Chief Pilar García.

Personally, Batista prefers to collect his monthly one and a quarter million dollars in payoffs from gambling interests, to listen to secret tape recordings of his opponents' sexual liaisons, and, best of all, to play canasta and watch horror films at Kuquine, his country estate outside Havana. Still, occasionally he feels obliged to carry out the ceremonial functions of the presidency, as on this very afternoon, for instance, when he is due to meet, first, with one hundred American commercial airline pilots and, later, with the outgoing ambassador from Uruguay, who is returning to breezy Montevideo. No, by and large Batista has a pleasurable, involving job as the country's leader, *el hombre fuerte de Cuba,* a charge he has held one way or another since 1933.

Having given his final instructions to his adjutant, Morales del Castillo, Batista takes his private elevator to his residence on the third floor of the palace, where his wife, Marta, is keeping an eye on their youngest child, down with a fever. Batista kisses his pouty, chubby consort, then rings the bell for the steward to set the table for their late lunch. On a couch lies the book that kept him up until the wee hours of that morning, *The Day Lincoln Was Shot.*

Outside, a tropical torpor falls upon the sun-swept streets surrounding the ornate Presidential Palace. Misiones Avenue is deserted, the statue of the old hero of the War of Independence Máximo Gómez rising lonesome at its end above the growing mounds of dirt dug up for the excavation of the transbay tunnel. Across from the palace, at the Parkview Hotel, an American couple—she wearing dark glasses and a scarf on her red hair to ward off the piercing sun, he tall and blond, in dark beltless slacks—take pictures of the mansion with their new Leica. A few hundred feet away, at the Beaux Arts Building, gallery employees prepare a photo exhibit called "The Human Family," while at Sloppy Joe's the barkeep dusts the establishment's ever-growing collection of exotic liquors, readying himself for the nightly invasion of visitors out to have a hot time in Old Havana tonight.

Inside the palace, blue-uniformed police and soldiers in white leggings and helmets keep a distracted eye on the comings and goings on the first floor. On the second floor, ministers, officials, and secretaries trawl the corridors in the daily paper shuffling of all governments, legitimate or not. In the press room, dozens of newspaper and radio reporters, who beef up their meager paychecks with cash contributions from the executive mansion, gather to receive the daily news report on the president's many activities.

The time is 3:15

Jorge Boubakis, a descendant of Greek immigrants, is not among those waiting for their handout at the palace. Head writer for the city's foremost news station, he is hard at work in his office a few miles away, preparing the afternoon's newscast. He is an expert at the format of his employer, Radio Reloj, or Clock Radio, where every minute of the hour an announcer gives the exact time, filling out the remaining fifty-seven seconds with commercials and news drafted in telegraphic style.

In the master control room the engineer, Manuel Fernández Morales, also called Bicicleta, or Bicycle, because of his unusual choice of transportation by Havana standards, keeps a sleepy eye on the controls while the announcers read their copy on the air. Normally the night engineer, he has traded shifts with a colleague, and the unaccustomed working hours are proving more soporific than he expected.

In front of the skyscraper housing both Radio Reloj and its counterpart, CMQ-TV, a gaggle of teenage girls dressed in poodle skirts and buck shoes are waiting for celebrities, pink plastic autograph books at the ready. Hunting for autographs of prominent artists has become the thing this year, and some of the girls have scored big stalking Radiocentro—William Holden, Ezio Pinza, Dean Martin. One fortunate girl, Vivian Fuentes, even bagged Tony Curtis, but that was because she saw him on La Rambla and ran out of her mother's car, chasing the handsome actor all the way to the Riviera Casino, where he finally succumbed. He was nasty to her, but just one look at his scowling signature on the pages of her book was enough to make her forget his unbecoming rudeness.

It is now 3:18

Two automobiles come to an abrupt halt before Radiocentro's entrance. The screeching of their tires and the obvious agitation of the dozen or so armed men inside the cars alarm the autograph hunters, who take refuge behind their male cohorts, longhaired boys in tight jeans with broad sideburns like Elvis's.

One of the men gets out of a car, looks nervously up and down the sidewalk, a machine gun in his hands. The youngsters gasp and watch anxiously as the other armed occupants descend from the vehicles. Finally José Antonio comes out, ample smile, lock of straight black hair falling rebelliously on his forehead. Some of the girls smile when they recognize him. José Antonio, used to crowds of followers and well-wishers, smiles back even at that grim moment.

"It's Echevarría," says Vivian. "It must have something to do with the students."

Everyone on the island knows José Antonio Echevarría Bianchi; his chubby, smiling face is always surfacing in the local newsreels and newspapers. As president of the national student union, the FEU, and founder of the Directorio Revolucionario, he has traveled around the world leading the opposition to Batista. Time and again José Antonio has stood on the wide, sweeping steps of the University of Havana urging the violent overthrow of the current unconstitutional government. Now he's about to put his words into action.

One of the cars sweeps around, blocking traffic in the middle of the street, while pedestrians and curiosity seekers, spotting the weaponry, quickly move away.

"Nobody move from their places!" shouts José Antonio. "That group over there, against the wall, hands up!"

All the teenagers comply, quivering with surprise but not fear, for they know they are becoming witnesses to an event they will recount time and again until, in the ultimate retelling, every one of them is a commando with José Antonio, or at least his confidant, patting him on the back, whispering words of encouragement and advice for which the fearless leader is most grateful, even as he strides gallantly into the radio station.

José Antonio and five others sweep past the genuinely frightened—because older—doorman, Maximiliano Estévez, who hasn't seen any insurgent activity since before Grau was last president but who certainly isn't going to put up any resistance. So Estévez waves pleasantly, wishing the six young men a good day when they walk by, as though to say, Go ahead, gentlemen, do our job for us, and do it well, if you please. Once the gunmen are safely inside the elevator, Estévez picks up the phone.

"Oye, Reinaldo," he tells his counterpart at the CMQ studios, where, just a few years before, Senator Raúl Chibás blew his brains out on the air in despair over corruption in the island, "I think you have some angry viewers coming your way—Echevarría, the one from the FEU, and some little friends of his. For your information, they're heavily armed."

Echevarría and his group however, head for the Radio Reloj studios on the fourth floor. The moment the elevator doors open and the band empties out into the hallway, the receptionist shrieks in terror.

"Don't be afraid, lady," says José Antonio, "we're revolutionaries."

A wall speaker broadcasts the final notes of a Fab detergent jingle, then the ticktock of a clock and the announcer's honeyed voice.

"Radio Reloj . . . the time is three-twenty-three . . . exactly."

At that moment, just a few miles away, two agitated young men in checked shirts, carrying automatic weapons, climb on a route 14 bus on Chacón Street. The driver sees them huddle on the runner as the bus wheezes its way past the Presidential Palace, and he makes the instant decision to let them be. One thing he has learned in all the political battles of the last twenty years—the shoot-outs on the street between the Tigres of Masferrer and Emilio Tro's UIR, the Auténticos and the Ortodoxos, the whole panoply of *pistoleros* that have infected Cuba since the fall of President Machado—is that the less attention you draw to yourself, the safer you will be once the bullets start to fly.

A few hundred yards away, up Monserrate Street, a black Buick and a green Chevrolet follow a red van with the lettering *Fast Delivery S.A.* on its side. Over the next sixty seconds, all the vehicles meet on the side of the palace between Zulueta and Monserrate streets. Abruptly, the Buick and the Chevrolet drop away. The van cuts in front of the bus and halts as though it had stalled. Moving ahead of the van, the two cars come to a shuddering stop as well. The bus driver, annoyed to see the vehicles blocking his way, notices his two armed passengers jump off. Then, to his horror, he sees nine men emerge from one of the cars, brandishing machine guns, then five others jumping out of the second car; still a dozen more spring out of the back of the red delivery van; and in less time than it would have taken him to lean forward, turn the steering wheel, and floor the accelerator to fly from this death trap, the leader of the gunmen has let off several bursts of machine gun fire at the stunned palace guard.

"Now!" shouts Menoyo. "Attack! Attack!"

It is 3:25.

Menoyo is first to reach the gate, followed by eight other men. In quick succession they down four palace guards. Within seconds an army machine gun nest posted atop the nearby Church of San Angel swings its .50-caliber air-cooled recoil weapon and begins to rake the street with gunfire, even as the remaining shirt-sleeved revolutionaries toss grenades while negotiating the thirty feet between their cars and the gate.

Swarms of bullets trace figures on the side of the route 14 bus. The driver collapses on the steering wheel as dozens of passengers howl with fear and drop to the floorboards. The conductor, Alberto Triana, collecting fares in the back, also drops to the floor, next to a Chinese man whose head has been blown open by a grenade fragment. On his hand and knees, Triana crawls up the aisle around the dozens of weeping, bleeding passengers, as he shouts at the driver, "Step on it! Step on it!" Reaching the front, Triana realizes the futility of his plea. He heaves the body of the unfortunate driver to the floor; then, with one hand on the accelerator and another on the steering wheel, barely daring to peek above the dash while the fighting flares loudly just feet away, he slowly drives the bus out of the danger zone. At the end of the day, when the bus company inspects the damages, they will count 136 bullet holes in the vehicle.

At the palace gate, Menoyo looks back and sees his second in command, Faure Chomón, take a hit in the buttocks. Yelping like a pup, Chomón drops his gun and runs away, leaving his *compañeros* to save their own souls. Now from the truck Menelao Mora, a former congressman who insisted on being a foot soldier in this glorious deed, races to the gate. A handful of men follow him, among them Nicolás Ramírez y Caballero, scion of one of the wealthiest families in Cuba; they jump over the bodies of six fighters who have already fallen on the sidewalk. The revolutionaries storm the palace, shooting an army sergeant who has placed himself behind a column upon closing the door to the Communications Room. The sergeant falls dead after a few shots—the way is clear to Batista's office on the second floor!

Menoyo looks out to the street, hoping his reinforcements will arrive in a few seconds, then throws a grenade at the phone switchboard and races up the marble stairs. He will never know that the explosion failed to cut off phone service and that a lone American operator stayed on the job, keeping the besieged palace in constant communication with the outside world.

Up on the third floor, Batista looks up, alarmed, as the sound of shooting pierces the thick walls of his sanctuary. His wife puts down the half-eaten slice of plantain on the Sèvres china plate, takes a quick sip of water from the Limoges glass, wipes her bud-shaped mouth with the Irish linen napkin.

"I hope that's not that what I think it is," says Marta. Then she stands, kisses her husband for what she feels could be the last time.

"God bless you!" she whispers fondly, heading for the back bedroom to stand guard over their sick child.

Batista dashes to his desk, picks up the phone, rings for his assistant Major Ramos.

"*Coño, chico,* what the fuck is going on here?" shouts Batista even as the shooting grows louder and closer.

"It's a suicide attack, *mi general,*" says Ramos, reverting to the comfort of military titles. "Revolutionaries have stormed the palace!"

"*Carajo!* Don't hang up! Keep me posted!" Batista puts down the phone, heads for his closet, and eases on the lucky leather jacket he wore during the 1952 coup. He returns to his desk and takes out his favorite, all-chrome Colt .45, making a silent pledge right then and there that they will not take him alive. He'll make his stand by the door to the elevator, his last stand if need be. God damn Fidel Castro, he thinks. I should have never let him out of prison.

※ ※ ※

At that moment, at the announcer's booth in Radio Reloj, Florial Chomón, benighted brother of the revolutionary who escaped with a bullet in his butt, looks up at the barrel of José Antonio's gun. Chomón watches in stunned silence as José Antonio presses down on the telegraph signal on the desk to tap out FLASH in Morse code, then slaps down an open file, out of which spill several handwritten pages. Chomón fellow announcer, Hector de Soto, quicker to react, picks up the pages and reads, prompted by José Antonio's gun:

"Radio Reloj reporting . . . The Presidential Palace has been attacked . . . A group of unidentified civilians have stormed the Presidential Palace with rifles and machine guns . . . The atackers have managed to reach the interior of the Presidential Palace, where Presidente Batista was at work."

Remembering the station's format, José Antonio turns to Chomón, who inserts the commercial:

"Lustre Creme Shampoo, the favorite of Deborah Kerr—Four out of five Hollywood stars wash their hair with Lustre Creme—Shouldn't you?—With its secret lanoline formula—For shiny, lively hair—Use Lustre Creme."

✖ ✖ ✖

Down at the corner of Monserrate, a block away from the struggle at the palace, Menoyo's little brother, Eloy, listens to the broadcast from his car radio. He is liaison between the first wave of commandos and the reinforcements, one hundred men due to arrive five minutes ago and still nowhere to be seen. Eloy hears the announcer cry out, "What is this?" Silence. Then: "Our colleague Luis Felipe Byron reports from the Columbia army camp that soldiers and officers have stripped General Tabernilla of his command."

Then another moment of silence as all the people of Cuba glue themselves to the radio, across the island, from Maisí to Guanahacabibes, in Pinar del Río, in Camagüey, Cienfuegos, Santiago, Las Villas, and Sancti Spiritus, in all the neighborhoods of Havana, the poor in Jesús María, the rich in Miramar, at the sloop in the yacht club, in the well-tended courts of the country club, downing *choripán* and *croquetas* at the corner stand on Obispo, guzzling a cold Polar at La Esquina de Tejas, doing the wash in the Chinese laundry, or selling a tail-fin Cadillac to the engineer in La Rambla, in the Santería altars of Regla and the automobile body shops of Luyanó, even in the hills of the Sierra Maestra (where Fidel Castro listens to his shortwave radio and turns to his handful of men, to Che Guevara and Raúl and Camilo and the others, worried that someone else might deny him the victory he knows is legitimately his and his only, and says, "Something big is happening in Havana"), all over the blessed and befouled island of Cuba, men, women, and even children, home from school and reading Walt Disney cartoons *en español*—*el Pato Donald, Tío Rico MacPato, Tribilín, El Ratoncito Miguel*—or spinning tops down on the broad esplanade facing the spot where the USS *Maine* once sank, all are turning from their everyday chores and lending their ears and their body and their mind to the shoot-out at the palace because they know this could be the end of the world as they know it, and there is nothing most of them can do about it except listen and wait for the bloody end.

Then on the radio, the cry everyone knows has been long coming—

"*Viva la revolución!*"

—and all around Eloy the bullets and the grenades and the explosions are lifting the veil of complicity and rending the air with their sounds of death, and Eloy looks down the street and he has a feeling that the reinforcements will never come and that all the men in the palace will end up burned like the mist of a summer's day.

17

Then more news: the Moncada Garrison in Oriente Province, the one that Fidel Castro failed to take four years before, has joined in the revolt—Tabernilla is now under arrest.

Soto returns to the air: "Due to the gravity of the situation, the president of the Federation of University Students, José Antonio Echevarría, will now address the people of Cuba."

※ ※ ※

In his office, head writer Boubakis hears the broadcast. He is staring down an armed revolutionary. Boubakis tries to get up.

"I can't allow this."

But the gunman coldly points the Thompson submachine gun at Boubakis's head.

"You move and I'll kill you."

Boubakis sinks into his executive leather chair, taps his fingers on the desk.

Down the hall, in the master control room, Bicicleta, the engineer, is also being kept company by a gunman, who shouts, "The revolution has triumphed! *Viva la revolución!* Echevarría is going to speak."

"Oh, really?" asks Bicicleta. "Where?"

"Right here, stupid! On Radio Reloj! Turn on the speaker!"

Bicicleta does so, and Echevarría's voice blares a call to arms.

"People of Cuba, the dictator Fulgencio Batista has received his punishment. He has met his just deserts in his lair in the Presidential Palace. The revolution has triumphed! Young officers and soldiers in the military have—"

But in his excitement, José Antonio had raised his voice, and the relay switch in the control room has taken the station off the air, and only silence flies out of Radio Reloj.

(And it is then that Eloy knows for certain that the backup will never come in time, and he starts to make plans to collect the remaining weapons to start anew in the hills far from the quicksands of Havana.)

José Antonio reads on, not knowing he cannot be heard further, his message of glory and heroism known only to the handful of men around him.

"In this glorious day, next to the Directorio Revolucionario are to be found the Federation of University Students and the commandos led by Faure Chomón, Menelao Mora, and Carlos Gutiérrez Menoyo, as well as hundreds of brave and honest Cubans. It's your turn now, people of Cuba! Rise up! Go out into the streets! Workers, leave your place of employment and support the revolutionary struggle! Soldiers, sailors, policemen, join the struggle!"

The Great American

It is now 3:30.

Inside the palace, the attack led by Menoyo has split into three groups. One has remained down in the lobby to cover the retreat, while two others scramble up the stairs in search of their prey. They can hear the gathering of police sirens and the rumble of tanks approaching the building. Menoyo knows his task has to be accomplished in scant minutes or it will never succeed. He also knows, as he surges onto the second floor, that no one else is coming, that it is all up to him and his handful of rebels.

Menoyo heads for Batista's office at the end of the Hall of Mirrors while the second group, led by Menelao Mora, turns right and goes for the stairs leading to the third floor.

One of the commandos breaks into an office. An ancient executive aide, who has witnessed the comings and goings of Cuban government since the Dance of the Millions in 1919, is trembling behind his desk. The revolutionary, blind with fury at everyone and everything that signifies the dictatorship, rams his machine gun against the old man's chest.

"*Rápido!* Where is Batista?"

The old man hesitates, drools, unable to make words come to his aid. Too frightened to even ask for mercy, he blinks quickly, expecting the fatal bullet, when another gunman runs into the office.

"This way! This way!" shouts the second gunman, and the two commandos fly out to the hallway, where they meet a hail of bullets and fall dead to the ground, even as the old man looks down at his pants and realizes he has voided his bladder.

※ ※ ※

Menoyo and Mora by now have regrouped and have reached Batista's office, which is locked. Signaling the others to stand aside, Menoyo tosses a Brazilian-made grenade at the wooden doors. The grenade bounces back, a dud. Menoyo, exasperated, tosses a second. This one too ricochets off the fancy mahogany paneling.

"This is the kind of shit we get from that son of a bitch Prío!" exclaims Mora, who then drops to the ground gasping for breath, seized by an unexpected asthma attack. Menoyo pulls the cotter pin on a third, U.S.-surplus grenade and tosses it. This time the door bursts into pieces, and in the clamor and the smoke Menoyo, a gasping Mora, and four others enter the office, spraying bullets left and right. Two khaki-suited men fall to the ground, but Batista is not one of them. Menoyo searches for the stairs he was told lead directly from the office to Batista's quarters up

19

on the third floor, but he cannot find them—the plans to the palace that President Prío's people gave him, like everything else Prío touched, were flawed. Frustrated, hearing the blasts and commotion of the other fighters inside the palace, Menoyo leaves the office with his men, not knowing he had been standing just a few feet away from the door to the secret elevator.

The commandos cross the Hall of Mirrors once more to the North Terrace and fire out the window at the police, moving toward the palace. They try to find another way up, but already the counterattack of the palace guard, commanded by Major Alfredo Ramos, has begun. Menoyo and his fighters are forced by the gathering fire to retreat to the winding marble stairs.

In his quarters, Batista, phone in hand, directs the offensive, even as an aide, Major Vargas, hears the news report from Radio Reloj claiming victory for the rebels.

It is useless—to remain would be total slaughter. Menoyo gives the order to retreat. Mora, barely breathing, tries to cover the few survivors. A policeman runs up the stairs and sights Mora. He takes careful aim and with one sure shot drops him. The cop now slides up the side of the staircase. Menoyo is up on the landing, spraying furiously at the advancing counterattack. The cop raises his gun again, fires. Menoyo feels the bullet pierce the back of his head, cutting through his cerebellum like a slap from an old friend. He turns, curious as to who might have greeted him at that moment, and he sees the floor coming up to greet him, and darkness, and he hears the ringing words of the Cuban national anthem, *"A las armas, valientes, corred!"* To your weapons, my brave ones, run!

One of the survivors, in desperation, lights and tosses a stick of dynamite at the regrouped government forces pouring out of the third floor. Six of the attackers take advantage of the blast and reach the first floor, but on their way out they are cut down by Cuban marines, who have arrived from Camp Columbia. The marines have deployed themselves around the palace in spite of sporadic fire from a handful of student sharpshooters in nearby buildings, who on hearing the news of the attack over Radio Reloj, have come to lend their weapons to the fight.

Several surviving commandos run outside but are pinned down behind the red van by enemy fire. The few remaining laggards come out of the building, but they too are mowed down by the now hundreds of soldiers, marines, and policemen who are firing indiscriminately at any civilian in the area.

Only four of Menoyo's men survive.

The battle has been lost.
Batista lives still.

❊ ❊ ❊

At Radio Reloj, one of José Antonio's men comes up to him in the booth.

"You're off the air, something happened. We better get out of here."

José Antonio looks around dazed, nods.

"You two are coming with us," he says to the announcers, Soto and Chomón. The men stand up and walk down the hallway with their hands up, ahead of José Antonio and his band of revolutionaries. The commandos halt at the master control booth and signal at the men inside to come out.

José Antonio presses the elevator button. Just then the elevator doors open and a man in a blue suit, ignoring the weaponry, turns to José Antonio.

"Excuse me, young man, is it true what they're saying over Radio Reloj?" he asks.

"Yes, it is true," says José Antonio simply. The group is walking into the elevator when one of them turns to José Antonio.

"We can't leave the station on the air! We have to destroy the master control!"

And without further notice the gunman lifts his machine gun and sprays the thick safety glass plate window, which shatters into flying shards. The engineer, Bicicleta, dives for the floor as the bullets bounce off the walls, turning the reception area into a free-fire zone.

In the confusion, Chomón and Soto run to the stairs and race down and away from imminent death. José Antonio and his men all crowd into the elevator, which closes its doors to the tinkly tune of "Guantanamera."

Down on M Street, onlookers applaud the revolutionaries when they exit the building. José Antonio smiles again, gives an understandably hurried bow—a performer before his loving public—then climbs into his Chevrolet.

It really wasn't all that bad, thinks José Antonio. At least our message went out. Now we link up with our boys at the university, and by tonight I will make sure our announcement was no idle boast. And if we fail? Then we'll take to the hills, just like Fidel. But not with him, though. That man is crazy, he cannot be trusted. Even if we have no weapons, even if all we have are razor blades to fight, we'll go to the hills if we fail. We can't allow Fidel to be the only leader. But we will succeed. I hope so. I know so. The Virgin is with us. God is with us. We must win. We will win.

Venceremos.

José Antonio's car travels up M Street to Jovellar, then turns right, heading for the university campus. He sits in the front seat, absorbed in his thoughts, the pain of possible defeat drawing deep furrows on his unlined baby face as he makes plans for the future—his future, his country's future. The two other men in the car, Marcos, the driver, and Jorge in the back seat, exchange looks in the rearview mirror. They have their plans too—for once Juventud Socialista and Castro's 26th of July Movement have the same desire. Destroy the Directorio. But is now the time?

Suddenly a police car speeds toward them. Marcos, the driver, sees his chance and takes it. He grabs the machine gun and, before José Antonio can countermand him, fires through the windshield at the patrol car, then swings to the left, plowing the car against the side of a building, leaving José Antonio's side exposed.

Marcos and Jorge open the left side door and slither out of the car even as José Antonio opens his door, hits the ground running, and fires at the police car with his only gun, a revolver. The patrolman fires back with his machine gun, striking José Antonio in the leg.

José Antonio crumbles to the ground. So this is the end, he thinks as the bullets rip open his calf muscles. I will not go down easy. I will give an example with my death. Like Martí. This is my Dos Ríos. This is my fate. So be it.

"*Viva la Virgen del Cobre!*" he shouts. "*Viva Cuba!*" And he rises and fires his gun straight at the patrol car and a hail of machine gun fire slices him apart and he falls on his right side and as he falls he sees his mother and his dead brother and those who died before him and from somewhere he hears a children's song and he's holding hands with all of them in a great wide circle in a golden land under a golden sky and they all sing—

Mambrú se fue a la guerra.
Qué dolor, qué dolor
Qué pena.
Marlborough is off to war.
What pain, what pain
What sorrow.

—and his blood pours freely, mixing with the cigarette butts and the candy wrappers and bus transfer stubs and the piece of half-eaten *churro*, easing down the curb and through the drain hole to the waiting waters of the healing bay.

※ ※ ※

José Antonio Echevarría was twenty-four years old.
With his death the Cuban revolution has truly begun.
It is March 13, 1957.

The time is four o'clock.

Chapter

1

The Cuban whore was thirsty.

The room at the Ambos Mundos Hotel was dank and shuttered, dust balls gathering behind the carved mahogany headboard of the creaky bed. William Alexander Morgan, an inch or two under six feet, blond, blue eyed, and American, lay among the soiled sheets, watching the beige curled smoke of his Pall Malls billow out in the warm air. He hadn't meant to wind up here. It had all sort of happened after getting off the ferry from Miami and not finding Ramírez. But there it was. Couldn't have been in town more than four hours and he was already shacking up.

Shame on you, William, he thought, you ought to know better. Shame on you. You're right, I know. But Nicky would have appreciated it.

He smiled at the whore, a bright-eyed, cinnamon-colored girl with soft black hair who could not have been over eighteen. Pointed brown nipples, caramel legs, insatiable mouth. She had already slipped back into her cotton shift and was now making a drinking gesture. He pointed at his crotch. She smiled back and rubbed her fingers together. Why the hell not?

※ ※ ※

The waiter at the café opposite the Plaza de Armas was surprised that the Americano would actually take such an obvious harlot out for a Coke. Those creatures were good for only a quick tumble in bed and then, *Adios, chiquita*. Nonetheless, the waiter—a florid-skinned Spaniard sporting a pencil-thin mustache and an effusively false smile—dutifully brought out the *refrescos* for the visitor and his lady, setting them on the small marble-topped wrought iron table with the same panache as his Parisian confreres at the Closerie de Lilas. He knew that someone so foolish as to parade his hired bedmate in public would also leave a generous tip for a hardworking man.

Morgan nodded at the waiter and lit another of his Pall Malls, playing with the Zippo lighter—close, open, close, open, close, open, *trac, trac, trac, trac, trac, trac*—while the whore sipped her Coke from the bottle through a striped paper straw.

A late afternoon breeze rose off the bay, which shone like pewter in between the massive gray buildings housing the Navy Department and the Stock Exchange. Crowds of locals and tourists hustled down Oficios Street now that the temperature had eased down to the seventies and the lingering rays of the sun fractured in reds and purples over the mauve horizon.

Nat King Cole played from the jukebox *en español*. Soon there would be another of the famous starry nights of Havana, a city wrapped in music, rum, and sex, where every man was Don Juan and every female a sultry Carmen.

Too bad Nicky isn't here, thought Morgan. I'm going to miss the son of a bitch. But what the hell was he doing at the palace? Since when was he mixed up in island politics?

❊ ❊ ❊

Nick Ramírez, five foot six, white skin, dark hair, with the even teeth and slim hips of a flamenco dancer, was the ballsiest little spic Morgan had ever known. Morgan never figured out exactly how an intelligence officer like Nicky had wound up in the trenches in Korea—a failed mission? a missed contact?—but Morgan sure had been grateful for his help when the Chinese rushed their position, drunk on the mad music of Mao thought. Morgan's A-15 had jammed, and Nick stood alone on the hill, his machine gun rattling time and again, the barrel of his gun giving off steam on that cold day, mowing down the invaders until they pulled back and Morgan scrambled from the forward point and joined the party at the summit and killed and killed and killed. The next morning the Chinese were gone, retreating overnight into the Korean mist with the capriciousness of nature itself, and Morgan knew he would always owe Nicky a big, big favor.

Here in his hometown Nicky became, through the alchemy of geography and culture, Licenciado Nicolás Esteban Ramírez y Caballero, attorney, dutiful son, and devoted husband, the rankest product of Cuban society and not just another Latin G.I. In La Habana Nicky enjoyed the success that Morgan never knew in his own feckless country, where all he had to show for his efforts to contain communism were bruises, curses, and the stockade. So when Nicky had asked him down to Cuba, Morgan had jumped at the chance. Anywhere as long as he was out of Uncle Sam's reach.

Dear Willie,

Come on down to Havana! It sure was fun seeing you again at the ballpark in New York the other day. Sorry about the little trouble you've been having with Uncle Sam, but then, who likes the old fart anyhow? I'm sending you these tickets because I think a change of scenery would do you a world of good, if you know what I mean. I have a job for you down here that I think you'll like. I'll meet you at the dock.

Abrazos (that means watch your butt, buddy),
Nicky.

P.S. Keep this under your hat, alright? I'll tell you all about it when I see you.

That morning, stepping off the ferry from Miami and seeing Nicky nowhere to be found, Morgan had hailed a taxi to his savior's home. The driver, a Caucasian-looking man with glistening chocolate skin, glanced at the return address on the letter Nicky had enclosed with the tickets.

Marianao was the only word the driver would say until the end of the drive, *Marianao* and a grunt. Not knowing Spanish, Morgan assumed that meant, I'll take you there.

"Marianao," repeated Morgan, sinking into the warm leather backseat of the yellow Ford, smelling the oddly feminine lilac scent of the driver's hair pomade.

Tired and thirsty, Morgan did not remember much of his taxi ride, only that the cab pulled away quickly from the dock, down wide white avenues leading inland, and that they passed by a cemetery, where they were held up briefly by a funeral procession, the files of gleaming new American cars moving slowly in the wake of the long black hearse festooned with blue ribbons and white flowers.

The taxi stopped before a Mediterranean villa two stories high, with red-tiled roof, sienna walls, pots of geraniums placed along the walkways, masses of red and white hibiscus spilling over the masonry wall. Morgan paid, got out, pushed open the creaking iron gate, walked hopefully with his cardboard valise to the front door. He pressed the bell button. Deep, resonant clanging echoed inside the house. Morgan smelled gardenias and roses from the yard, noticed the thick, studded oak door, the Spanish barred windows, the small balcony overhead, a stage setting for an opera of some sort.

He heard steps darting to the door. The shutter opened and shut quickly. Then a woman in her twenties jerked open the door, as though seeking combat. Fair, dark haired, deep blue eyes ringed by circles of insomnia, the woman was dressed all in black. Her strong salient jaw ended in a defiant dimple.

"*Qué desea?*" she queried—what do you wish?—the open vowels of Cuban Spanish ringing in the darkened foyer.

Morgan knew four words of Spanish and now he used them all.

"*Sí, no hablo inglés.* Nicky?"

The woman gave a perceptible start, controlling herself by an amazonian effort of will. She replied in a flat New York accent.

"Who are you?"

"Sorry to bother you, ma'am. My name is Morgan. William Morgan. I'm looking for Nicky Ramírez. He's a war buddy of mine. I just got into town. Nicky sent for me. I probably missed him down at the dock, so I took the liberty. Is he in?"

The woman snorted, contempt mingled evenly with grief.

"Yes, he's in a casket."

"Excuse me?"

"I mean he's dead. Nicky was killed during the attack on the Presidential Palace."

"I'm sorry, I had no idea. Are you his wife?"

"No, I'm his sister. His family escaped to the States already, thank God."

"My condolences."

"Thank you. Condolences accepted. Now, Mr. Morgan, I advise you to take the next ferry to Miami. This is no place for the likes of you. If you don't mind, we'd like to be left alone."

Stunned, Morgan had barely mumbled, "I understand," when the woman slammed the door in his face.

Morgan picked up his cardboard suitcase, walked back to the gate, and let himself out. He took a last look at the villa, then muttered, under his breath, lest the grieving woman overhear him: "Damn!"

* * *

Trac, trac, trac, trac. The whore put her hand over Morgan's to stop the nervous flickering. She shook her head *no,* large doe brown eyes full of reproach.

"OK, OK," said Morgan. "Coca-Cola?"

"No, *gracias*," she replied, adding that she would soon have to go back to work. But Morgan simply nodded pleasantly, her Spanish words flowing like so many flowers down a river of sibilant speech. She jerked her head and gave a small impatient frown. Morgan grinned some more.

A hand dropped heavily on Morgan's shoulder.

"Willie? Willie Morgan? What the hell you do here!?"

Morgan turned in his seat and stared into the wildly animated face of a small man with a sharp nose and a sharper smile.

"Who are you, friend?" asked Morgan.

"Willie! You forget? I'm Max, Max Weinberg. We meet in New York last March, remember?"

"Not really."

"Sure! I was with Nicky Ramírez, remember? Ebbets Field, Dodgers play the Cubs. We jump for the ball when Roy Campanella hit home run!"

Morgan nodded, the veil of memory opening onto a day full of sun, beer, and pretzels, shortly after he had escaped from the stockade.

"Oh, yeah. That's right. Max, sit down. Man, it's good to see somebody I know."

Max, thin and agile, in a creased white suit that had seen many fruitless exertions, scooped up a chair and sat nervously on the edge of the seat, hands hanging down in between his legs. He cast a quick admiring glance at the girl.

"You don't waste time, no?"

The girl, knowing she was being talked about, fidgeted in her seat. But Morgan was all business, puzzled by his friend's disappearance.

"When was the last time you saw Nicky?"

"Maybe two, three months ago. I am very busy man here, you know. This is my country. I have a radio program, *La Voz de Cuba*, the Voice of Cuba."

"Nicky was supposed to meet me at the dock and he wasn't there."

"Really? That is a shame. You know we Cubans always make it a point to go to receive the friends and the family when they come. We give them the welcome, a little coffee, make them feel good for coming to see us. Very bad manners Nicky has. Did you go to his house?"

"I did. This girl comes out, says he died during the attack on the Presidential Palace. I want to know, what gives? I had no idea. Was Nicky some kind of revolutionary?"

Max sat up, looked cautiously around him, then bent closer, his surface bonhomie vanished as quickly as his Cuban accent.

"What else did that woman tell you? Keep your voice down."

"She said I should go home."

"Maybe you should. A couple of weeks ago a group of rebels and students stormed the palace on a kamikaze action, trying to kill Batista. They failed. Now Batista's people are taking their revenge. Things are very unstable."

The girl, upset at Morgan's lack of attention, slammed down her Coke and released a torrent of Spanish, then strutted away from the table, crossing the street in a huff.

"What's wrong with her?"

Max smiled. "She says that if you don't want to occupy her services any further she'll have to go get another paying customer because she sure isn't going to waste her time with the likes of you, baby."

Max noticed two men in a green Chrysler Town and Country cruising down the street. Suddenly he loudly relapsed into his best fractured Cuban accent.

"Is OK, my frien'. We haff many *chiquitas* like her in La Habana. Come, I show you the good time."

Max pulled Morgan by the arm.

"Hey, what's going on?" said Morgan, looking at the departing hooker.

Two men had jumped out of the Chrysler and grabbed the girl. One of them, small and thin, yanked her hair, slapped her to the ground. She let out a moan of anguish, not from the pain she felt now but from the pain she knew was coming.

"Let's go while the going's good, Willie," whispered Max, again tugging at Morgan.

"Who are these guys?" said Morgan, angered by the sudden violence.

"Let it be," cautioned Max.

Morgan, with the strength of the righteous, jerked Max aside and in a few strides was next to the girl, who lay sprawled on the sidewalk, whimpering, as the little man in the brown suit beat her with a blackjack. People around the scene pretended to go on with their business, shining shoes, wiping tables, buying groceries, staring fixedly into space, refusing to get involved even though every muscle in their bodies strained to jump in.

Morgan shoved the little man headfirst into a torn poster on the wall of the movie *Vera Cruz*, Burt Lancaster and Kirk Douglas facing off in a manly duel.

"Leave her alone!"

Startled, the hood whipped around furiously and eased a .38 out of his back pocket. Years of combat training burnt into his reflexes, with a swift kick Morgan dislocated the man's left knee while wheeling sideways, grabbing the gun, and wresting it out of his grip. Just then the little mutt's partner, a tall hulking black man in a blue suit, tried grabbing Morgan from behind in a headlock. Morgan stumped on the man's foot, lifted his elbow to connect with the man's jaw, then slammed a hammer fist into the man's groin, dropping him unconscious to the ground with a broken jaw. Morgan turned around to see the little man propelling himself with his only good leg, lunging at Morgan with a pearl-handled knife.

Morgan pulled the trigger of the revolver. The little man flew backward, his arms slamming against the brick wall, then slumped down to the sidewalk next to the girl, his face contorted in a grimace of hate. She shrieked, scrambled to her feet, and ran away barefooted, leaving her black stilettos next to the dead man.

Morgan stood helplessly, as though dazed by his own deadly reaction. Max ran over to him.

"You fucking animal, you know what you did?"

Morgan shrugged, gun still in hand.

"It was self-defense; he came at me with a knife. Call the cops."

A siren wailed some blocks away, and the crowd around Morgan and Max took off running, wanting to put as much distance between themselves and the bloody melee as their legs would let them.

"Let's run!" said Max.

"No!" countered Morgan. "Let's wait for the police. I want to report this."

"You big schmuck, don't you get it? That *was* the police! Follow me, c'mon. Run, run!"

Without a thought, Morgan and Max raced down the cobblestoned streets, darting down alleys and backways, as night fell and the stars of Havana came out and Batista's police cars arrived on the square, looking for their revenge.

Chapter

2

Max opened the peeling wooden shutters of the balcony, peering into the luminous Havana night garlanded with rooftop neon signs and the yellow incandescent lights of many open windows. He turned to Morgan.

"You and I have got to talk," he said.

"Yeah, sure."

Max went to the small rusty Kelvinator refrigerator lodged underneath the tile counter in the kitchen. He took out two bottles of Hatuey beer, brought them back out to the square, high-ceilinged living room. Morgan sat on the mahogany-and-rattan couch, his head on his hands, eyes fixed on the arabesque teal floor tiles.

Morgan looked up, and Max saw for the first but certainly not the last time that Morgan was a man who wanted to please. In his eyes he noted the shock of fresh death and the unrestrained eagerness to make others feel right, to set the world straight, to follow the rules and settle the score. Max had forgotten there could be so much innocence contained within one powerful, overbuilt man, that so much heart could be contained behind light blue eyes now veiled with tears.

Morgan grabbed the beer, gulped down half the bottle, then leaned back on the couch. A cannon shot resounded throughout the city. Morgan jerked upright.

"What was that?" asked Morgan.

"The nine o'clock cannon. They shoot it every night from La Cabaña Fortress to mark the time. It's an old Spanish custom."

"Some city you got here."

"Some country, you mean," countered Max. "Do you have any idea what you've gotten yourself into?"

"What could I have done? He pulled a gun on me."

"I don't mean that. I'm talking about this godforsaken island. It's the biggest wasp's nest in the whole goddam continent, and you've come down to put in your two bits' worth."

"So? It's just like any other country. There are good guys and there are bad guys."

"Bad guys? Let's try ghouls. Let's try crazy. I mean, the whole country's a nutcase. You think things are bad in the mainland with the Democrats and the Republicans. Here they have about a dozen political parties, including the commies, who were legal until last week, when Batista decided to make nice with Washington. But of course Batista is no president like you and me think of it. He's a dictator. Staged a coup five years ago. Never mind that he'd been out of power for only four years; I guess he missed the Presidential Palace too much."

"Who was Nicky with? Was he a rebel like the ones in the hills the papers back home are talking about?"

"No, the guys in the Sierra Maestra are the Twenty-sixth of July people. They're headed by a former gangster named Fidel Castro. He attacked an army fort in Oriente Province on July twenty-sixth, nineteen fifty-three, was caught, pardoned, and exiled. In Mexico he got a bunch of his people together, launched a boat, and landed in Oriente Province last year. They're commies. Or at the very least fellow travelers."

"Was Nicky?"

"No, he was with the Directorio people. Romantics. They believe in violence. They're like the anarchists in Russia during the czar. It's all crazy, I tell you. Sheer crazy."

Morgan finished his beer, set it down on the floor, and sat up straight, preparing for the counterattack.

"So what are you doing here?"

"I live here. I was born here."

"You may have been born here, but, brother, you're no more Cuban than I am. I saw your kind when I was stationed in Japan. You're with the CIA, aren't you? You're a spook."

Max lit a Lucky Strike, the wax match flaring like a torch before he tossed it out the balcony to the dark street below.

"Let's say I have dual citizenship. My allegiance is to both countries. But that's none of your business. You have other fish to fry, my friend."

"Such as?"

"Such as getting the hell out of this island."

"It was self-defense."

"You still don't get it. The man you killed was a sergeant in the Havana police. While they might be likely to give a respectable American citizen a break, I don't think they're going to in your case."

Morgan rolled his shoulders as though shrugging a heavy load off his back, stood up, walked to the balcony. In the distance he could make out the blue Mercedes-Benz sign, the twinkly lights of the Malecón, the searchlight from La Cabaña prison scouring the low clouds. At the Chinese *fonda* down the street someone dropped a nickle in the Victrola; a jarring mambo surged up in the dank night. A bottle dropped and broke; patrons clapped.

"You were waiting for me, weren't you?" said Morgan. "That was no chance meeting."

"I'm afraid you're right."

"What else do you know about me?"

"What Nicky told us. You're from the Midwest, divorced, one kid, career soldier. Or at least you were until you went sour. We don't know why. You're a real professional. A man of his word. And you are AWOL. We don't personally care, but the Cuban authorities might."

Max walked up next to Morgan, leaned the elbows of his soiled white suit on the thick concrete balustrade.

"Down here you'd be considered just a common criminal. So after you served your sentence for killing Silva, which might not be that long—maybe six or ten years because they give presidential pardons everytime there's an election—they'd turn you over to the . . . I forget, which one are you, the army or the marines?"

"Marines," said Morgan, tightening his grip on the balcony railing.

"Well, *Semper Fi,* you see the mess you're in? The one thing you have going for you is the Cuban character. Especially the cops. They're very intense and dedicated, but their dedication never lasts longer than forty-eight hours. Besides, they've got a revolution to worry about. I'd say in a couple of months you'll be able to just walk on the ferry to Miami, but for now I suggest you lay low."

Morgan shook his head, hit the balcony with the flesh of his hand.

"I'm out of money. Where the hell am I going to stay if I can't go back?"

Max smiled. This was the moment he'd been waiting for.

"You can stay here. I can lend you some money. I have to go to the mainland for a few days. When I come back we can talk about a job we'd like you to do for us. In the meantime, stay away from police stations. And casinos."

"Bars too?"

"If you can. Grow a mustache. Get some Cuban clothes. You'll look more like a Spaniard, a *gallego*. Don't talk. Make believe you lost your voice. And smile. Cubans are very cheerful people; they love to sing and dance."

"I noticed."

"Yes, well, that is the other side of the coin, isn't it?. Extreme love of life is just a step away from thanatomania."

"You mean love of death?"

Max hesitated for a moment before answering.

"Exactly."

Morgan grinned at Max's stunned look.

"I did a lot of reading when I was in the stockade. Nietzsche. Schopenhauer. Ortega."

"In that case I'll send somebody over to teach you some Spanish. It shouldn't take that long for a superman like you to get a working knowledge."

"There's nothing special about me, Max. Nicky had me wrong. He was the brave one. I was just along for the ride."

"We'll see about that."

"Tell me one thing. Why are you doing this?"

Max gave Morgan the kind of amused grin he'd find throughout his years in Cuba, the kind that said, You're a fool to trust me, but you'd be a bigger fool not to.

"Let's just say we're good Samaritans. Cast your bread upon the waters."

"I wouldn't know about that. I'm not a churchgoing man."

Max clapped Morgan hard on the shoulders, with more strength than he would have expected from such a lightweight.

"That's OK. After a few years in Cuba, you'll even be a praying man."

❈ ❈ ❈

It didn't occur to Morgan to ask why he would be spending years in Cuba, just as he didn't wonder why he had been chosen or what the job was. He figured Max would disclose his assignment in due time, and at that point he would decide whether to go ahead with it or not. Doubtless it had to do with the FBI or the CIA or some such agency. Morgan guessed it would be a dirty job, but he also knew he was qualified for whatever came his way. In any case, the less he knew right now, the better off he'd be. Hard experience had taught him that often it was best to let life take its course and just follow in its surprising wake. For the time being, that meant staying in Havana with somebody else paying his room and board. Not a bad deal, all in all.

The fact that all this made little sense did not particularly worry Morgan. Long ago he had given up trying to understand why things happened. What counted was today, next week maybe, and the hell with the rest. Who could figure out this crazy existence anyhow? He had wanted to become an engineer, but the family farm had demanded his time after his father's death. Then his mother remarried and he was free, and he enlisted, hoping to achieve his dream, but the best that he could do was radio technician in Germany before shipping out to Korea. The year he spent back in Ohio before he hitched up again, he'd been a plumber's apprentice, hardware store clerk, substitute high school phys ed teacher, holding down a succession of growingly dissatisfying jobs until he finally ran back to the arms of Uncle Sam. The second time he thought he'd finally made good, that he was on his way to being an officer, when one misty morning in Okinawa, waking up in a harlot's bed, he found all his drive shriveled into nothingness. He saw his desire to thrive in the armored links of the corps disappear in a matter of days. It all seemed worthless, futile, a lusting after glories that would never be his. Then started the drinking and the fighting and the infractions, goaded by the haunting thought, which he was reluctant to contemplate, that life must have something else to offer. But what?

So that night, after he had lain out on the rickety fruitwood bedstead, after Max had left him $50 and the key to the apartment, after finishing off half of the bottle of Bacardi Añejo, after smoking all of his Pall Malls, Morgan did not congratulate himself or even thank God or the stars for his luck.

He took it for granted that that was how things were meant to be and that as long as he tried his best, everything would be all right. He had survived worse situations. He was certain he'd have his way with this one too.

※ ※ ※

A long, piercing cry woke Morgan up the next morning, a wail that seemed to invoke all the powers of heaven for succor. Morgan rushed to the open balcony and glared down, convinced he was about to witness another scene of mayhem and uncertain of just what he would do about it. Instead, on the sidewalk he saw a knife-and-scissors sharpener pumping away at his portable grindstone, throwing sparks as a giant butcher's knife was honed back. Two housewives stood around waiting for their utensils. The sharpener, short, plump, with glinty blue eyes that glittered clear across the street, threw his head back as Morgan peered out the balcony, then gave out his sharpener's cry again, a guttural, high-pitched invitation to the *amita de casa,* the little housewife, to the store owners and the cooks, to come have their blades honed back to honest shape, a cry he had learned from his father, and his father from his father, and his father from his, a cry hailing back to the labyrinthine streets of Toledo and Seville during the time of Ferdinand and Isabella.

Morgan smiled and finally relaxed, his tension dissipating in the cool, fresh morning air of Old Havana.

Morgan could not figure out how to light the strange cylindrical kerosene water heater on the shower head, and so he showered shivering and cursing the surprisingly cold spray. By the time he had dressed and stepped outside, the sun had begun to warm the cobblestones, the limestone buildings, the air, and the hearts of the people outdoors. The unflagging Cuban spirit poured through in the resonant, jivey give-and-take of the store owners—steel shutters rolled up, clean aprons on, pencil stubs behind ears—who argued with their customers just for the pleasure of hearing their own resonant voices.

A produce vendor, pushing his cart full of exotic fruit through the narrow street, joined his cry to that of a strolling lottery man, tickets pinned to his shirt and a sign on his hat with the winning number of the previous day's drawing and the word GANADOR! From the chicken vendor's store came the cackling of hundreds of fowl—brown hens, black hens, white hens, and guinea hens, hens for all kinds of tastes and pocketbooks—stacked by the hundreds in their cages, loudly awaiting their fate, unaware how soon they would be picked, plucked, and slaughtered for the ever-chattering housewives, who now took a brief second look at the Americano in his loud rayon shirt and loose linen pants and wondered for a moment who the obviously lost tourist might be, before returning to the chore of keeping a watchful eye on the store's scale.

At the corner, a bug-eyed black boy in torn shorts and striped T-shirt hawked the latest edition of *La Prensa* in an angelic tenor. The high battlements of Morro Castle down the street and across the bay loomed behind him like a picture cutout; he seemed the tropical equivalent of the little shepherd boy singing on the fateful morning before the walls of Castel Sant'Angelo. The boy spotted Morgan and walked up to him, waving the newspaper in Morgan's face.

"*La Prensa,* mister? *Mataron al Sargento Silva!*"

"Sorry, no *español,*" said Morgan, smiling at the urchin. The boy widened his already wide green eyes and pulled yet another paper from his canvas bag.

"*Havana Post,* mister. Nickel, please!" He said it with such urgency that Morgan couldn't help but dig into his pocket. He handed the buffalo coin to the boy, who took it with such flair and good cheer that Morgan felt he had accomplished something special just by buying the paper from him.

"You should be in the insurance business, kid," said Morgan, rubbing the boy's short, wiry curls. The boy smiled even more sweetly.

"Girl, mister?" The boy made a gesture outlining a mound of voluptuous breasts. Morgan shook his head, rubbed his stomach.

"No. Hungry. Breakfast."

"Ah, sí. Comida. Por aquí."

He took Morgan by the elbow and led him to a restaurant fifty yards around the corner and up the street. He waved at the waiter, who nodded, came over, pulled a chair out for Morgan.

"Muy bueno," said the boy, "top banana."

"Good morning, mister," said the pasty-faced waiter, slapping an English-language menu on the marble-topped table.

"Good morning," answered Morgan. He dug in his pocket for a quarter to give the boy, but he was already gone, strutting happily down the street, repeating his melodious cry,

"La Prensa! La Prensa! Mataron al Sargento Silva! La Prensa!"

※ ※ ※

Morgan turned to his paper.

POLICEMAN KILLED IN FRAY OVER PROSTITUTE.
SECRET RESCUER SOUGHT. WHO WAS THAT BLOND MAN?

Authorities in Havana today confirmed a citywide search for a blond man, believed to be an American, responsible for the shooting death of veteran Police Sgt. Armando Silva Ponce. The 22-year veteran of the force was killed last night by the unknown assailant during what officials described as a routine questioning of a lady of uncertain virtue. It occurred at the corner of Remedios and Mercaderes Sts. in the old section of the city. According to police spokesmen, the sergeant was struck from behind by the assailant while acting in his capacity as head of the Vice and Gambling Section. When the heroic defender of the public trust turned to address the unknown aggressor, he was cowardly shot by the unidentified man. Authorities describe the killer as blond, blue eyed, of muscular build, about six foot tall, in his early 30s. He is thought to be an American.

Witnesses to the event paint a different picture from the official version, however. They say the deceased was acting in an abusive manner, slapping the woman, when the American, out of chivalry, intervened in the conflict. Matters soon degenerated, say the witnesses, and the sergeant pulled his gun on the suspect, who disarmed the officer and shot him instead. The eyewitnesses called the man "a brave Americano." When informed of these statements, authorities said they were lies spread by political opponents of Pres. Batista, who try to malign his administration by all means possible. They say they have posted extra manpower at the airport, the harbor, and the city's marinas to prevent the escape of the North American suspect, who they believe will try to flee the island to avoid arrest. When reached late in the day, officials at the U.S. Embassy said the description of the suspect could fit many people. They added they have received no official notification of this event, therefore they would have no comment.

Morgan put down the rest of his coffee, wondering what his next step should be. He was not unused to being sought by authorities; in fact, his whole life he had been in one kind of trouble or another with the law. The news that someone was looking for him did not trouble him unduly. What did give him cause for alarm was the redoubling of manpower to prevent his exiting the island.

※ ※ ※

A police patrol cruised slowly down the street. Morgan stiffened suddenly, ready to bolt. But the police car seemed on a mission to nowhere, the two officers—a black and a white—laughing at some private joke as they drove away. A snatch of song from their car radio drifted out, *"Contigo se fue toda ilusión,"* mingling with the street noise and the rattle of the car's clogged carburetor. Morgan felt his pulse return to normal and he noticed how the restaurant patrons also breathed easier, the pall of fear lifted from everyone's shoulders for the time being.

I got to get my clothes, was Morgan's first thought, as though his garments could disguise his physical presence in Havana. I bet the police have staked out my room already, though. Wait a minute, that's only if they know who it was that killed this—what was his name? Silva. If they don't know . . . I mean, there must be other blond Americans down here. They can't possibly be checking all the hotels in the city, that's too many people. And I do need a change of clothes. There's only one way, then. I have to go see for myself. Maybe there is nobody there after all.

Morgan got up, left fifty cents and a dime tip, then caught himself smiling. If they kill me from this, he thought, it's going to be because I wanted some fresh underwear.

And with that absurd thought he eased out of the restaurant, whistling "Perdito" down the narrow cobblestoned street even as a sudden, brief rain shower opened up into a golden veil. He didn't notice the thin auburn-haired young man who'd been staring at him for the last two minutes from the shelter of a jewelry store entrance. The young man looked up and down the street, then, shrugging, resigned himself to following Morgan in the drizzle.

❊ ❊ ❊

The Ambos Mundos was only a few blocks away from Max's apartment in the crowded, dense hive of Old Havana, but Morgan, threading through the side alleys and courtyards, past the just-opened storefronts, found himself going farther away from his destination, veering off, after a long hour's hike, to the hub of new Havana.

Morgan didn't recognize any of the multitude of streets before him, the trail of shimmering white buildings traipsing through his mind as an inner voice recited their odd, vowel-filled names—Muralla, Campanario, Belascoaín, Reyna, Zanja, San Rafael, La Rambla. Nor did he recognize the buildings that years later would have more solid meaning—the Customs House, the Supreme Court, Navy Headquarters, the Telecommunications Building, the Focsa. He was facing his future and he did not know it, blinded by the immediacy of his quest and by the pressing throng of Cubans—men in light-colored suits or guayaberas, women in bright cotton dresses and pumps, walking, talking, buying, arguing, waiting for the bus, going on with their daily activities with the quiet assurance of the new day. At the bus stops bands of black children in tatters jumped on the back bumper of the outgoing buses, hanging on to the window railing, four and six urchins at a time, laughing and singing like flies hitching a ride on a pack horse.

Morgan walked up to a colonnaded building that took up an entire block, gray and ornate, its entire ground floor lined with shops stocking the same merchandise he had just seen days before on New York's Fifth Avenue. Past a fountain and a horse-and-buggy stand, he gawked at the white-domed replica of the U.S. Capitol. Hearing the honeyed cadence of a Southern American tourist telling his wife to hurry along, Morgan experienced the dizzying sensation of having entered some sort of sci-fi continuum that placed him simultaneously in Washington, D.C., and in

Havana, as though by turning a corner he had gone from Prado and Teniente Rey to Constitution and Pennsylvania. That impression vanished just a few blocks away, when he observed armored cars and sandbags piled around another white building, tanks posted at each corner, nervous men with submachine guns glaring at all pedestrians, daring any other foolhardy revolutionaries to come and try their luck again.

So that's the Presidential Palace, thought Morgan as he hurried away, crossing diagonally at the corner just moments before the claxon-blaring traffic roared down the boulevard. He stood in front of the Sevilla Biltmore Hotel, its walls pockmarked from the barrage of artillery fire of two weeks before. How could they have tried it? It was suicide, what these fellows tried to do. They must hate Batista something fierce. What kind of government is it that would drive them to do something so crazy? What is Batista doing to the Cuban people?

The smiling doorman held open the door to the hotel. Morgan shook his head *no* and slipped back into the flow of humanity down the wide street. A half hour later, finding himself lost in a neighborhood strewn with skyscrapers lifted straight from Miami Beach or Park Avenue, he glanced down at the azure harbor at the foot of the sloping avenue and realized where he'd gone wrong. To find his hotel all he had to do was follow the waterfront. So he wended his way down to the Malecón, ambled past the monument to the *Maine* down to Old Havana, then turned up a street, and suddenly, to his surprise, found himself in front of the raffish splendor of the Ambos Mundos.

He walked around the block carefully, wanting to make sure no one was staking out the hotel. He studied the rooftops and the open windows of the nearby buildings, where an observant secret agent or special cop might have been posted, long-range rifle at the ready to shoot him down, as he was by now convinced would happen in this topsy-turvy country where ordinary appearances were only a thin scrim over a swirling, changing reality. After reconnoitering for ten minutes he was certain no one was surveilling. Feeling somewhat reassured, he crossed the street and entered the lobby.

A few fellow tourists were still lounging on the tufted horsehair sofa, reading the day-old *Miami Herald*. Behind the counter, the day clerk was stashing mail into the row of glistening cubbyholes. Morgan approached the desk, smiling slyly as though he'd just come from one of the all-night baccanals Havana was famous for.

"Key to room five-fifty, please," he said.

The clerk wheeled around, saw Morgan, and in one swift motion reached down behind the counter. Morgan stepped aside, expecting a gun blast, but instead, the balding clerk, with an unctuous smile, handed him an envelope.

"*Buenos dias,* Señor Morgan. This came in for you," he said pleasantly, placing the envelope on the counter.

Morgan thanked him, picking up the ivory linen envelope without return address or name of sender, only Morgan's name written in cursive purple letters.

"A young boy, he left it this morning," added the clerk, more than a little curious himself about the mysterious missive. He slapped the large brass room key on the desk blotter.

Morgan pocketed the envelope, grabbed the key, and walked to the spiral wooden staircase, feeling the eyes of the clerk on him as he took the stairs two steps at a time all the way up to the fifth floor.

Morgan's heart was racing when he arrived at his floor. He glanced down both sides of the carpeted corridor. No one around. Swiftly he went to his door, opened it. He looked in. No one had come into the room during his absence. He took a welcome deep breath. It would all be easier now. Just toss his suitcase out the window, then go out the service entrance before anyone spotted him. He'd already paid five days in advance, so management would not be going out of its way to find his whereabouts. It was just a question of slipping away unnoticed, as he'd done so many times on base.

He was locking the door from the inside when he felt a hand drop on his shoulder.

"Señor Morgan?" asked a man's voice. Morgan whipped around and in a flash saw the slender auburn-haired young man, who must have been hiding in the bathroom, grinning as though to say, The game is up.

Morgan swung at him but the young man, with surprising ease, dodged the blow and stepped back, still smiling. Morgan came closer and swung again, but this time the young man grabbed hold of Morgan's wrist and, using the motion of Morgan's own body, lifted him bodily over his shoulder and flipped him to the floor. Before Morgan had time to react, the young man jammed his forearm against Morgan's throat in a swift move that Morgan belatedly recognized as a jujitsu hold.

"Take it easy, Mr. Morgan," said the young man, smiling hazel eyes inches away from Morgan's face. The intruder's breath smelled of garlic and violet tablets.

"Max sent me. I'm to be your Spanish teacher. Are you hungry?"

"I was a jujitsu champion for the university. I hope I didn't hurt you."

"Just my pride. My neck is a little stiff."

"You have to learn how to fall. It's a trick. Cubans learn it right away. Americans take a little longer."

"I suppose you know the reason."

"As a matter of fact, I do. Americans charge like a bull. You have to learn to be more flexible."

"Like Cubans?"

"Exactly. *Exacto. Repita,* repeat, *por favor.*"

"*Egg-sag-toe.*"

"*Muy bien.* You will learn very soon, I can tell."

❊ ❊ ❊

Morgan couldn't help smiling at the auburn-haired young man, his prospective instructor, who sat wolfishly at the table in the Chinese joint picking apart a pork chop with ravenous satisfaction, as though having downed Morgan was reason enough for a feast. His name was Wilfredo, and he had helped Morgan check out of the Ambos Mundos ("No police around, I looked already," Wilfredo had said with a tart smile, flashing a hand signal at the desk clerk, who nodded and scratched Morgan's name from the register). After dropping off Morgan's battered suitcase in Max's apartment, he had invited himself to lunch at Morgan's expense.

Wilfredo had already downed four beers to Morgan's half a glass without noticeable effect, except for a growing reluctance to speak. Of

course, Wilfredo's reticence was the Cuban kind—the height of elo-
quence in those places up North where people believed in thrift, mod-
eration, and speaking through clenched teeth.

The Chinese waiter set down a plate of golden *tostones*, thick fried
slices of plantain, and asked Morgan a question in singsong, Shanghai-
accented Spanish. Morgan looked dumbfoundedly at Wilfredo.

"El señor no quiere más, son para mí," said Wilfredo, pushing the plate to
his side. He grabbed two *tostones* and made an improvised sandwich with
a piece of the pork chop.

Morgan thought for a moment, then asked hesitatingly, *"Cómo se
llama?"*

Wilfredo smiled, wiped his grease-streaked mouth.

"Mr. Morgan, remember that in Spanish the third person usually
requires a referent, otherwise the sense is lost. You just asked what is the
name. Of what? Me? The food? The restaurant?"

"Sí, Usted."

"All right. *Me llamo Wilfredo Antonio Fernández Larramendi Cáceres y
Vizoso.* But you can call me Willie." He offered his hand. *"Tanto gusto."*

"Tanto gusto," repeated Morgan, exactly. "Me Willie too."

"I know," said Wilfredo. "The two Willies. *Los dos Weelees. Repita, por
favor."*

"Sí, los dos Willies."

They shook hands, smiled once more. Maybe this Spanish thing won't
be so bad after all, thought Morgan. He raised his hand, calling the waiter
over.

"Muchacho, dos cervezas for *dos Willies, por favor!"*

✼ ✼ ✼

The rickety bus clambered up the steep hillside that rose in flower-
filled exception over the flatlands of Havana. Morgan and Wilfredo sat
alone in the backseat as the signs of the tourist city dropped away and
they penetrated deep into the heart of the working-class neighborhood
of El Cerro. Morgan noticed that the buildings were low and square,
with ornate grillwork on the balconies, and that the vegetation—the
hibiscus, geraniums, bougainvilleas—seemed on the verge of invading
the old, beat-up buildings with the insatiable appetite of the tropics.

They alighted in front of a bodega. The tall *gallego* wiping the counter
in the store took a look at Morgan and smiled, expecting news from Vigo
or La Coruña. He was about to greet Morgan in Galician when he recognized the American slouch, the American clothes, the American open

face. He frowned and returned to dusting the bottles of scotch and Spanish anisette on the showcase.

"Our house is just around the block," said Wilfredo, waving at a little boy skating down the middle of the wide street. Traffic rumbled down below, but here on this street there was only the heady warmth of the late afternoon sun in the stillness of a shuttered world, its dwellers still at work in distant places.

"We've lived here for almost sixty years," added Wilfredo, "since the last year of the American occupation. My grandfather built the house. Originally it was for the American who ran the El Telegrafo Hotel. The American sold everything after the First World War, during the Dance of the Millions."

"Your grandfather was an architect?"

"*Albañil*. A mason. He built it himself with no plans. Just from a picture the hotel owner had. What did your grandfather do?"

Morgan remembered the foul-tempered old man who cuffed his ears for speaking out during the long and tedious Lutheran services but who made him his first slingshot and taught him how to skin a deer.

"Same thing as my father and his father before that. A farmer," said Morgan. "We're all farmers. I think that's why I joined the service. To get away."

"Is that why you came to Cuba?"

"Not really. A good friend of mine invited me. Maybe you knew him. He was one of your boys at the palace."

Wilfredo turned a guarded expression on Morgan.

"What was his name?"

"Ramírez. Nicolás Ramírez y Caballero."

Wilfredo blinked repeatedly, as though struggling mightily to remember.

"No, I do not know anyone with that name."

"Wilfredo! Wilfredo!"

A high-pitched wail preceded a boy in short pants and striped shirt who came hurtling into view, running maniacally.

"*Un fuego, hay un fuego. Corre, corre!*" screamed the boy.

"*En dónde?*" asked Wilfredo, sharply.

"*En la cocina!*"

Wilfredo leaped past the boy, up a cracked ornate walkway through banks of oleanders.

"Come along, Willie!" he shouted.

Morgan ran after him.

"What's wrong?"

But by then Wilfredo had run into a two-story white plaster building festooned with hanging plants and surrounded by a rapidly growing black cloud. Morgan followed him through the living room down a long corridor to the large kitchen at the back, filled with the smoke from an old iron stove caught on fire. Two women with large fans were trying to blow out the flames, which seemed to stem from a large roasting pan. Wilfredo shouted at the women, then ran to the water cooler and grabbed the large water bottle.

"NO! Don't do that!!" warned Morgan.

But the warning came too late as the water splashed on the burning pan. The flames soared to the ceiling and the two women and Wilfredo staggered back from the force of the fiery blast. Now everyone was crying. The boy was wailing, and the crackling flames reached out to the kitchen sink window; the lacy curtains burned like a dead leaf in the hearth. Morgan spotted an old wool blanket next to a saddle at the far end of the room. For an instant he asked himself what a riding saddle would be doing in a city kitchen, but the question vanished from his mind as he grabbed the blanket, tossed it on the flaming pan, and held it down, hoping it would be thick enough. In seconds, deprived of oxygen, the flames died down. Morgan turned to the window curtains but one of the women was already snatching them off with a wire clothes hanger. She opened up the faucet and wet them down at the same time that Morgan ran into her.

"Sorry, I didn't . . . " Morgan never finished his sentence. The woman was a girl of about nineteen, with thin, arched eyebrows above almond-shaped brown eyes, waves of russet hair framing an impish smile. Her face was smudged from the smoke, her hair singed by the flames, and her flower-print dress stained throughout with grease, but Morgan knew instantly that he'd never seen anyone as beautiful or as desirable as that cream-colored girl. She's got colored blood in her, he thought. Who gives a damn?

The girl said something in Spanish and laughed, turning to Wilfredo, who got up off the floor. He replied in a torrent of Spanish, obviously annoyed by whatever sarcastic comment the girl had just made. She glanced back at Morgan, her eyes sparkling with the same intensity as the fire that had just raged in the kitchen, then she looked down the front of her dress. She let loose another stream of commentary, shook her head, and smiled again at Morgan. All this in the few seconds it took for Wilfredo to ceremoniously wipe his pants, walk up to the sink, and announce, "Mr. William Morgan, I have the pleasure of introducing my sister, Laura Fernández de Quesada."

Then, to her: *"Es el señor William Morgan, un soldado americano, amante de la libertad."*

She shook his hand. He felt her fine bones, the smooth, hairless skin.

"Tanto gusto," she said.

"Tanto gusto," he repeated, and it was then that he realized he would be in Cuba far longer than he had ever expected.

"What did you tell her?" he asked Wilfredo.

"That you're an American soldier and a lover of freedom. And that I will be teaching you Spanish."

Just then the other woman, taller even than Morgan, long gray hair in a bun, black dress bringing out the crystal blue of her eyes, pale white skin also streaked with smoke and burned fat, strode up to Morgan.

"This is my mother, Doña Susana Larramendi de Fernández. *Mamá, el señor William Morgan."*

"How do you do," she said with a slight British accent. "Thank you for saving our kitchen."

"My pleasure, ma'am. I hope I didn't spoil your dinner."

"Qué dijo, qué dijo?" asked Laura. Wilfredo translated. They all laughed.

"Y yo, y yo," said the boy, who now joined the group, pressing against Doña Susana.

"This is my cousin, Jaimito. Little James," added Wilfredo. "He is staying with us."

"Good afternoon," said Jaimito in his best grammar school style, revealing a gap-toothed smile.

"Hi, kid."

"I hope you will stay for dinner," said Doña Susana. "We don't usually flambé our meal, but I hope you will like it all the same. Right, Laura?"

Laura moved her head up and down, eyes still sparkling.

"Sí, please. I . . . *cómo se dice practicar?"*

"Practice, my dear," said Doña Susana dubiously.

"Yes," said Laura. "I practice the English. *Con usted. Contigo.* With you. OK?"

Morgan felt all of their stares on him, but he could not stray from Laura's swimming brown eyes.

"OK. We practice."

❋ ❋ ❋

"The saddle is all that we have left of the property," said Wilfredo during the commercial on the Gillette fight. Morgan's attention was drawn for a moment to the large Du Mont. The dubbed seltzer jingle played while animated characters downed their sparkling antacid and the lights went out in apartment buildings that looked very much like the New York skyline as the satisfied customers went to bed, the ending three notes matching the product's brand name in Spanish, EH-EHNEH-OH!

Laura came in bearing a silver tray with eggshell-thin tiny cups of the liquid tar Cubans call coffee. She gave Morgan a half-coy smile while setting the tray on the old demilune mahogany table next to the wall-length shutters. Morgan's eyes jumped to Laura as she set down the tray. The top line of her bra showed when her blouse scooped out, and she knew he was watching, and he knew that she knew, and they both knew that she liked that, and then she smiled again and returned to the kitchen in the back to help her mother with the dishes.

Out the window Morgan could see the darkened outline of the palm trees and the oleanders while the smell of night-blooming jasmine wafted his way, penetrating even the smell of the H. Upman cigar Wilfredo had given him. Morgan realized, yes, he was a little tipsy and, yes, he probably could use the antacid and, no, he couldn't think of anywhere else he'd rather be than in that rocking chair right now in that house, with her just a few hundred feet away, unless of course it was in bed, with her just a few inches away. He made a mental note, counted his drinks, came up short by at least six of the number he'd ordinarily need to get drunk.

It must be the weather, he thought. Yes, that's it. This warmth, it's like some gal saying, Don't mind me, as she presses herself against you. Hard to ignore. You get used to everything, I suppose, even that, but it's mighty intoxicating at first. Yes, that is why. But listen, listen, Willie is trying to tell you something. Listen to him, drink your coffee, and sober up. You're a guest here. You're just a guest here.

"The farm had been in the family for quite a while. Many years. Generations. But when this all happened, we had to sell it." Wilfredo let out a pungent mouthful of self-pitying smoke.

"I don't understand," said Morgan.

"Weren't you listening? To get the money to rescue Laura's husband from jail. He was being tortured to death."

"That's right. Sorry, I forgot," said Morgan, also wrapping himself in a cloud of smoke.

Yes, my friend, how conveniently you forget, thought Wilfredo. If I were you I would have forgotten too. Who wants to hear *rope* in the home of the hanged man? Not the way I have seen you looking at Laurita. You showed such tact and concern and for at least ten minutes you tried to keep your eyes away from her and made conversation with us about Miami and New York and with Jaimito about baseball, and you didn't even ask how come her husband wasn't there at the table with us and why, if she was married, she was looking at you the way she did, like I saw more than once with my own two eyes. You will find out in good time, clearly. *She* will tell you. Cuba has a role for you, and we will make sure you play it perfectly.

"Would you like a glass of *añejo?*" asked Wilfredo as the fight resumed.

"I don't think so. The *mojitos* did the job already. Oh boy."

"Rum, mint leaves, lime juice, and sugar. That is all. Very simple but very effective."

"You don't need weapons to defeat Batista, with drinks like that. Just set up a bar before the battle and you will win by default."

"You are right. If we can get them to drink."

The two men pulled on their cigars again, watching distractedly the white fighter clinching his black opponent, trying to stop the kidney jabs and blows to the ribs.

"Tell me about your farm," said Morgan, finally.

"It wasn't too large, by our standards. Ten *caballerías,* that's about three hundred and fifty acres."

"Where was it?"

"Near Bejucal, south of the city. It's very fertile soil there. Red like blood."

"I suppose you grew sugar."

"Produce. Oranges, avocados. We even developed our own brand of avocado, the Fernández Number One. And your family?"

"Dairy."

"Excuse me, a daily farm you said?"

"No, *dairy,* like milk, cream, cheese. Dairy, cow products. Five hundred milking cows. Four bulls."

"They must have been very happy, the bulls."

"Happy enough."

Suddenly Morgan was fed up. He really didn't want to talk about Wilfredo's farm or his parents' farm or the fight or anything that would remind him of the fix he was in.

He got up with some effort, walked to the balcony, stared at the blinking stars in the black crepe sky.

"Something is the matter?" asked Wilfredo.

Morgan turned, leaned against the door frame. He could see inside, past the living room, down the long hall to the kitchen, where Laura paced back and forth, putting away the clean dishes.

"What do you know about Max?"

Wilfredo took another pull on his cigar, rocked himself in the mahogany-and-rattan chair.

"I'm not going to call him a good friend," he said, "he is not. He is someone that I was introduced to at the last employment I had."

"Where was that?"

"Gibraltar Insurance, on Muralla Street. I was an underwriter. The company sent me to the radio station where Max works, and that is how we met. When I was laid off because the company wanted to bring in an American, I ran into Max again. He said he had friends, Americanos who wanted to learn Spanish, like yourself. That is how we met. But you will be my last student. Do not misunderstand me, I like you, but teaching takes a long time and it does not pay much. So this week I start a whole new job and a whole new life."

He took another drag off his cigar, more dejected by the second.

"Would you like to know where?" asked Wilfredo.

On the screen, the black fighter now pranced around the fallen body of his white opponent, who failed to get up after the ten count.

"Sure."

"At the Havana Yacht Club. I, Wilfredo Antonio Fernández Larra-mendi Cáceres y Vizoso, graduate of the University of Havana, captain of the national jujitsu team at the last Panamerican Games, former farmer and landowner, will now become a captain of a different sort. I will be—what you call it?—the maître d' at the restaurant in the club. And my sister, who has never worked a day in her life, will be a waitress. What do you say to that?"

"It's an honest job."

"You do not understand. I was not brought up to be like that. I was not educated by the Jesuits nor did I learn French in the Sorbonne to be a little monkey in a little monkey suit. I was brought up to rule this country. And Batista has taken that away from me."

Wilfredo rose from his rocking chair, puncturing the air with his cigar.

"That is Batista's kindness. That is how he controls people. He brings you down, takes your money, but keeps you alive, thinking that if only you play the game with him right, he will give you back all you had before and even more. Oh yes, he would like to kill us all, but he doesn't dare because of the memory of my father, General Omar Fernández, the youngest general in the War of Independence. So he makes us beg for our living."

Wilfredo made a motion as though wringing out a towel.

"He squeezes you, he wants to make sure you will lick his boots. How I hate the man!"

He stopped, looked around concerned.

"I was not speaking too loudly, was I?"

Morgan shook his head. "Just loud enough for the neighbors to hear."

Suddenly Wilfredo stepped into the window and shouted at the top of his lungs in Spanish, bellowing a rage that Morgan could only watch in surprised detachment. Morgan recognized the words *madre, Batista,* and *Viva Fidel,* which streamed out of Wilfredo like so many colored banners. But there were others Morgan did not recognize, a string of qualifiers and exhortations that at one point included the word *socialismo,* but then Laura and her mother rushed into the main room and dragged Wilfredo away from the window, shushing him like an overexcited infant. They steered him to the rocking chair, where Wilfredo still sputtered a string of insults, but only half as loudly as before.

"Mr. Morgan, you had better return some other time," said Mrs. Fernández, momentarily turning her attention from her son.

"No, *mamá,* he stays!" bellowed Wilfredo. But the old woman made a sharp rejoinder to Wilfredo, who shook his head in overburdened fury and threw up his hands in dispair.

"Laura will walk you to the door. *Laurita, m'hija, acompaña al señor hasta la calle.*"

"*Sí, mamá,*" said Laura, who took Morgan by the arm and away from the high-ceilinged room.

"Good night, Willie. I'll call you tomorrow for the lesson."

"He will call you, Mr. Morgan. He is not himself when he is like this." She touched her temple, then returned to soothing Willie, stroking his hair, whispering in his ear.

"All right. Good night, then," said Morgan, feeling the burning tug of Laura's hand on his arm. As the two exited the room, Mrs. Fernández abruptly ceased to minister to her son, standing before him with folded arms. Wilfredo stopped his fussing and fidgeting and calmly glanced at the door of the adjoining room, then gazed at his mother in a silent question. She crossed her arms even tighter and stared back at him, the silence in the room broken only by the soft ticking of a grandfather clock and the retreating patter of the young couple's footsteps. The distant rumble of the cannon shot from La Cabaña stole into the room seconds before the clock erupted with nine loud gongs.

※ ※ ※

Laura and Morgan stopped by the old iron gate at the end of the footpath. Behind them, the house on the rise, lit up against the dark sky, seemed an illustration from some colonial-era tintype. The masses of white oleanders glowed in the half-light of the new moon and the dim yellow glow of the old lampposts on the property. Somehow, during their walk down, Morgan found himself holding Laura's hand, soft, warm, small, and slender, and now he was reluctant to let it go. She hesitated as well, the half-open gate before them a reminder that their path had ended, at least for the time being. Morgan felt flushed and exhilarated, at odds with himself. He wanted to kiss her but he didn't know if that was right; he wanted to ask her out but did not know how. He cast his eyes around in desperation. He noticed some distance away a mocking statue of Diana in a niche set against a grove of Italian cypresses. A wreathing band of ivy wrapped itself around the goddess, who kept only her head, shoulders, and fine hunter's arms free of the confining vegetation, which fluttered in the soft nighttime breeze. The fragrance of jasmine assaulted Morgan's senses with such violence that for years all it would take would be a whiff of that sweet perfume for him to find himself holding Laura's hand by the gate, his heart racing at a gallop.

He looked down at her, her wide sable eyes, the expectant half smile with the touch of childish impishness he would never forget, as she tilted her head up, her full lips opening up to say good-bye. It seemed like the most natural thing for him to do to bend down to her, but no sooner had their lips touched than she moved her head and his kiss seared her cheek instead.

"*No es posible, mi matrimonio*"—it's not possible, my marriage—she whispered unwittingly in Spanish, secretly wishing that he would pay no attention to her protests and press himself on her.

Morgan understood only her *no*, but he could guess the rest. He stepped back from her, his heart awash in regret. He extended his hand. She shook it.

"*Buenas noches, señora.* You won't mind if I come visit some other time?"

Her look made plain her puzzlement. He pointed at himself and then he touched her shoulder, never suspecting that his fingertips felt like marking irons on her flesh.

"Me go, come see you. *Mañana.* OK?" She nodded, beaming.

"*Sí, como no.* I like very much."

He stood there a moment feeling as useless as a stump, then walked out the gate to the half-lit street. The moment his foot was on the sidewalk, Laura ran down the oleanders, breaking through the boughs to catch a last sight of him, until she reached the corner of the property and grabbed the iron fencing, pressing her face against the rails, staring at Morgan as he crossed the street and stopped under the yellow light of a peeling lamppost.

"Taxi!" shouted Morgan at a green car with the yellow rooftop sign a half block away. The driver flashed his high beams to tell Morgan he had seen him and was on his way.

Morgan searched his pockets for money. He pulled out a $10 bill and the note the clerk at the Ambos Mundos had handed him. He opened the envelope.

Dear Mr. Morgan,

I regret having been so rude when you came to pay your respects. Naturally any friend of my dear departed brother is a friend of mine as well. Please call me so I can make amends for my uncivilized behavior.

Cordially yours,
Violeta Ramírez y Caballero.
Tel. 348–241

"Hey, mon!"

Morgan glanced up from the note, expecting to see the cab driver. Instead a large black man in a blue suit rose before him, standing in front of the open door of a yellow Bel Air.

"Get in the car, mon," said the black man with a Jamaican accent.

Morgan stared at the man, noticing the scar that ran from the man's right forehead to the corner of his jawbone.

"Who the hell are you?" asked Morgan.

"I give the orders around here; you don't talk back, mon," said the black man, whopping Morgan across the face with a blackjack before he had time to react.

Morgan raised his hand to ward off a second blow, then grabbed the black man's blackjack and heaved him against the car. Three swarthy Cubans swarmed out of the car and jumped on Morgan, shoving him to the ground, kneeing him, kicking him, pistol-whipping him, thumping him with pipes and blackjacks, raining blows on him until Morgan stopped struggling and the men hauled him inside the Bel Air.

Laura, who had been watching from across the street, let out a scream of horror. She ran back to her house to fetch her brother, but by then all that could be seen of the Bel Air was its taillights, easing down the darkened side street at top speed, the engine backfiring like gunshots in the expectant night.

In the breeze, Violeta Ramírez's note blew down the gutter.

Chapter

4

Captain Esteban Ventura Novo, chief of Havana's fifth police precinct, had a problem and he was staring at it. He had very little patience to spare at this late hour, the end of a very long day that had started at ten in the morning with a railside chat with President Batista at the inauguration of the new dog track. He had then proceeded to a meeting with the American ambassador, Mr. Smith, who had demanded extra police protection for his personal friend from Martha's Vineyard, the young vacationing senator from Massachusetts named John Kennedy. After a late lunch, Ventura's day had continued with a questioning of suspects from the *La Epoca* bombing, which lasted into the early evening; he had then gone home to change from his blood-and-gristle-spattered clothes into tails for the Spring Ball at the Miramar Yacht Club.

Now, finally, at three in the morning, when by all rights he should have been in the warm embrace of his wife, who had just returned from Caracas with a valise full of cash as a little thank-you present from President Pérez Jiménez for handling the conspirators in the Fierro case—that is to say, when Ventura should have been enjoying the well-deserved fruits of his constant struggle for peace, order, and prosperity, instead he had to deal with this big-lunk-of-an-Americano problem, who now slumped, bleeding from the mouth, hands cuffed behind his back, in the special leather chair in the captain's office.

But this is ridiculous, thought the captain. I am still in tails, my head is buzzing like a beehive from no sleep. Of course I have to deal with it because if I leave it to Piedra or any other of these brutes, all they will do is kill him, which does us absolutely no good. We have to use him, not destroy him. They have no finesse, these men.

"Throw some water on him," ordered Ventura.

A brown-shirted SIM officer emptied a pitcher of ice water on Morgan, who woke up with start, his breath rushing back on horseback. At first he had trouble focusing and he couldn't remember why his vision was so blurred or why he had the ringing headache, then in a flash it all came back, the Jamaican whipping him with the blackjack, the others in a wide circle around him, kicking and jeering as he struggled to cover himself. He tugged at his handcuffs and heaved himself forward to rise from the chair. The two uniformed officers pushed him back down. Through the mist of blood welling up in one eye he saw a thin, elegant man with a pencil-thin mustache, dressed in tails, offering him a Chesterfield from the pack.

"Cigarette?" asked Ventura with a gentlemanly air.

"I'm kind of tied up at the moment," said Morgan. Ventura smiled at Morgan's insolence. This might actually be entertaining after all, he thought.

Ventura snapped his fingers in unwitting imitation of Conrad Veidt. One of the SIM officers placed the cigarette in Morgan's lips, lit it. Funny how everybody seems to speak English like Americans, thought Morgan. Wonder why they don't act like Americans.

Ventura spoke rapidly at the second officer, who nodded and left at a clip. He turned to Morgan, warily.

"My apologies for the beating," he said. "Julián was very afraid of you. That is why he was so harsh. I told him not to fear Americans so much from now on."

"Next time he'll shoot first, right?"

Ventura smiled. "A sense of humor is a good weapon at a time like this. You must have been a very good soldier."

"Matter of fact, I was lousy," said Morgan, asking himself if there was anyone left in Havana who did not know all about him. He wondered how long it would be before they turned him over to the MPs and back to Chillicothe.

"Well, Mr. Morgan . . . that is your name, right?"

Morgan nodded. "Never used any other. Never had to."

"Admirable. Tell me, do you believe in fate, Mr. Morgan?"

"Like I believe in the tooth fairy."

"Well, I do. I had indulgent parents. They always left me an American ten cent piece for each tooth I lost. You see, I believe there is an invisible hand that guides our destiny, Mr. Morgan. It lets us think we are free but secretly points us to where we are supposed to go. Take you, for instance. You thought you were coming down here to visit your friend Nick Ramírez, to have a nice time in Havana and all that. But I'm certain that to your surprise your vacation has brought you in contact with some—how shall I say this?—strange characters. Alien to you. Un-American. Mixed up in this revolution business, no?"

"No. I don't know what you're talking about."

"Yes, you know. Tonight, for example, you have spent a wonderful time with Wilfredo Fernández and his family. I understand the widow is a very good cook. And the daughter, Laura, is certainly very pretty in a Cuban mulatto way, if you like that kind of thing. I have a feeling you do. You probably stole a kiss from her, right?"

Morgan looked away, embarrassed, the ashes from his cigarette falling on his clothes. These Americans are so transparent, thought Ventura. I wonder how they came to run the world. Historical accident, no doubt. I am sure we would have been as great or greater if we'd had their luck and resources. We are so much smarter.

"I hope I don't disappoint you when I tell you you weren't the first to taste that forbidden fruit, Mr. Morgan. She is pretty much what we call light of hoof. You say round at the heel, I believe."

Morgan tried to jump and shove Ventura's smile down his throat, but the remaining SIM officer grabbed the empty water jar and whacked Morgan clear across his forehead with all his might. Morgan's cigarette flew out as Morgan fell back into the chair, dazed, blood running out the open wound in his temple.

"Please, Mr. Morgan," said Ventura with all sincerity. "My colleagues are very nervous around you. Have some consideration for their feelings. No more sudden moves, all right?"

Morgan closed his eyes momentarily, the bruises and ringing in his head demanding all of his attention. The room is slipping away from me, he thought. I'm going down and I'm never coming back. This is the way the story ends, the story ends, the story ends. This is the way the story ends so early in the morning.

"Mr. Morgan? Mr. Morgan? Are you all right?"

The words came from far away, the lilting accent a ghastly perfume of pain, pain to be avoided so easily by drifting to the other side, down the chute, surrounded by a torrent of words, of plans, of tourist brochures showing Old Havana and the white beaches of Cuba, his passport, his sentencing papers, his enlistment papers, his wedding certificate, all twirling twirling twirling down the drainhole of wasted life and used-up memories.

Ventura looked at the slumping body and realized they had made a mistake after all. The Americano was not as tough as he seemed. Ventura glared at the rivulet of blood dripping from Morgan's mouth, at the gash on his forehead, and wondered briefly if they had ruptured something in the man's insides. He was about to call for the night shift doctor when Morgan reopened his eyes, smirked.

"I'll try not to scare you people anymore," he said.

Ventura smiled in relief. The man does have *cojones.* Perhaps we can do some business after all.

The second SIM officer came in with a pot and two cups, which he set on the scratched metal desk.

"The coffee will clear your head, Mr. Morgan. I had them brew it American style."

"How the hell do you expect me to drink it with my hands tied up?"

Ventura gave an order in Spanish. The first SIM officer walked behind Morgan, removed the handcuffs. Morgan sat up, massaging his wrists. The SIM officer removed his .45 from the braided holster and stepped into the corner, gun pointed at Morgan, finger on the trigger.

"Sorry, we're out of cream. Sugar?"

"That's all right."

Morgan took the chipped china mug, inhaled the strong fresh-roast smell, sipped the coffee, and wondered when they would kill him. He hoped it would be quick.

"Strong enough for you?"

"Plenty."

"Good. Now please listen to me. As you know, things are different here in Cuba from the mainland. Even people like yourself, a former marine and all that, can sometimes, shall we say, vanish. Regrettably, you understand. Usually the U.S. Embassy would put up a fuss, but since you're AWOL—"

"All right, all right," growled Morgan. "I got the picture. Tell me what you want."

Ventura lit a second cigarette, walked around the room as he talked, yet making sure he never strayed into the sight line of the officer pointing the gun at Morgan.

"We are in the front battle for the soul of the West, Mr. Morgan. I hope you realize that."

"I'm sure I don't know what the hell you mean."

Ventura smiled patiently at Morgan. So much to teach, so few willing to learn.

"Mr. Morgan, we are speaking of the battle against godless Marxism," said Ventura, his words strung together by frustration. "It's a titanic struggle, sir, one that involves the very soul of the Western world. You will admit that, won't you?"

Morgan took another sip of his coffee, nodded at Ventura, measuring in his mind the distance to the armed policeman. Twelve feet. No windows. I'd have to take that one down and this one hostage. Then what? Better than getting beaten to death down here.

"If you're talking about communism, I don't like it much either. I believe in freedom."

"That is precisely what we believe in, Mr. Morgan. Freedom, precisely!"

Ventura, excited, sat on the edge of the desk just a few feet away from Morgan. The officer in the corner made a show of recocking his Colt.

"The front line of this battle has ranged all over the world, from Europe to Malaysia to Iran and now here to the Americas. They were defeated in Guatemala but they are coming back at us, right here in my beloved Cuba. We are the next front, Mr. Morgan. We are the defenders of the free world. Like our ancestors, we are the defenders of the faith against the heathen. And we need your help. That is why we brought you here tonight."

"Is that so?"

The two men looked at each other for a moment, then laughed at the rejoinder, a gleeful laughter that bounced off the wall, searching the room for its partner, joy, and, not finding her, turned into a rasping noise of pretense. Now, thought Morgan, right now while he's . . . He felt the end of a cold barrel stuck against the back of his head, heard the strained breathing of the man holding the gun behind him. Ventura bit off his laughter, then sat back behind the desk. The man behind Morgan moved to the side, a short strawberry blond man in a bloodstained shirt holding a sawed-off shotgun.

Ventura spit out an order and the man moved to the opposite side of the room.

"I told you, my people are very protective. He must have thought you were going to do something you shouldn't. Never mind them."

"Not at all," said Morgan. "As long as their trigger finger doesn't twitch."

"Twitch?"

"Yes, you know. Shake. Tremble."

60

"Of course. Sorry. I went to school in the States, you know. Fordham. But it's been more than twenty years, and I really don't use English all that much, so at times it is—how shall I say it?—rusty. You know how unpredictable memory can be."

"So I've been told."

"Like you, Mr. Morgan."

"Now, I wouldn't say I'm like that at all. I'd say I'm very easy to read, Mr.—You know, you never told me your name."

Ventura stood up, took a small bow. "Captain Esteban Ventura Novo at your service," he said, then promptly sat back down.

"Right, Captain. Like I was saying, I am easy enough to please. All I want is some sweet rum, some juicy pussy, and a warm place to shit, and I'm OK. Maybe that's why I'm getting to like this country, in spite of people like you."

Ventura shook his head, tsk-tsked. "No, no, Mr. Morgan. Everything was so much better when you were angry at me. It is no use to try to insult me or Cuba. It will not work. However, if I were in your position I might do the same, so I forgive you."

He paused, took a sip of coffee. "Mr. Morgan, as I was saying, we need your help terribly. You see, I find myself in a very embarrassing situation. Let me show you."

Ventura opened a drawer, extracted a sheaf of papers, handed them to Morgan, who took in the seals, the signatures, the official rubrics.

"It is in Spanish, but I believe you can appreciate that it is an official document."

"What about it?"

"It is an arrest order. Do you care to see the names? They are typed in, I believe."

Morgan searched out the names in the middle of the parchment-thick paper: Laura Fernández de Quesada, Wilfredo Fernández Larramendi, Susana Larramendi de Fernández. He glanced up at Ventura, who now leaned back expectantly in his chair, holding his cigarette inward with the first three fingers of his left hand.

"I recognize the names. And?"

"They are going to be arrested for conspiracy."

"I didn't know your government paid attention to such niceties."

Ventura dropped his cigarette in his coffee, the hiss filling the attending silence in the room.

"We do when the people involved are the family of the deceased Senator Omar Fernández González, youngest general of the revolutionary army of eighteen and ninety-eight and personal friend of President

61

Batista. Of course you realize that once they are in—what is the word?—the bowels of our prison system, they are no better than anyone else. Sometimes it is hard to control the overzealous defenders of our government, as you have found out."

"Well, Captain, I know this sounds coldhearted, but why should I give a damn? I just met them."

"Because their life is in your hands. Because if you cannot show me who their associates are, who are the other communist conspirators, I have to arrest them. What do you say to that?"

"You want me to be an informer?"

Ventura shrugged with the delicacy of a probate lawyer or a medical examiner, people for whom loss and death are only more paperwork to handle.

"Think of the lives you are saving. A small price to pay for an indignity to your self-esteem."

"And if I say no?"

Ventura's grin widened further. "Cuba is a free country, Mr. Morgan. You can always say no. Of course you will automatically be considered part of the conspiracy, so you would be subject to trial and imprisonment. Then, if you survive—excuse me, after your period of incarceration—you would be delivered to the proper authorities in the United States to settle your AWOL status. And let's not forget the little matter of that abusive, corrupt officer. What was his name? Solís? No, Silva, that's it. Sergeant Silva. Slain by someone who looks a lot like you, Mr. Morgan. What a coincidence, don't you think?"

Morgan glanced at the two armed men in opposite corners, then back at the droopy-eyed captain.

"What is it I'm supposed to do?" he said at last.

※ ※ ※

The cry of the street vendor came from far away, mingled with the hum of morning traffic, the rumbling buses and nervous, honking cars. The three-vowel cry of *nah-ran-has,* oranges, eased into the room, accompanied by the piercing smell of fresh Cuban coffee. Morgan slowly opened his eyes in bed and glanced cautiously around, taking in the same scuffed chiffonier to the side, the same Virgen del Cobre calendar against the tangerine wall, the same little nightstand with the big Philips radio in Max's bedroom.

For the briefest moment Morgan thought it had all been a dream, the kind of nasty nightmare in which there is no escape, in which one room leads to another to another in the successive confines of a universal prison. He'd had those dreams years before when married to Ellen, but they had gone away once he'd shipped off to Japan and Okinawa and Mariko. He dozed off briefly, then awoke with a start, cold sweat in his armpits. This is no dream, he realized, a spinning sensation of terror gripping his chest. He sat up, fighting off the fear, but the pangs in his body were another confirmation of unavoidable fact. Gingerly he moved to the bathroom, looked in the darkened cabinet mirror, noticing the bruises on his arms and chest, the sutures the doctor at the police station had stitched on his forehead. At least you're still alive, he thought. Barely.

Morgan dragged himself to the balcony, opened the shutters. The salty sea air slapped him awake. Down in the corner in front of the Chinese restaurant a man in a gray cotton suit looked up and smiled, tipped his felt hat at him. No, it was no dream.

He sat at the kitchen table, lit a Chesterfield, and realized, as he put out the match, that he was smoking from the pack Ventura had stuck in his pocket the night before. Morgan put out the cigarette, opened the small refrigerator. Beer, butter, molasses, a loaf of moldy white bread, a shriveled orange. He closed the door, sat back down at the table, feeling the throbbing in his temple accelerate with each passing second. A woman in an apartment somewhere laughed, her peals of laughter floating up the air shaft and into the kitchen through the open window. She spoke rapidly in Spanish, mockery dancing off her words, the tone recognizable even if the content was undiscipherable.

Suddenly it all came to him. Willie, his language teacher, the man he had to spy on, was both the problem and the solution. Willie and Laura were going to be working at a yacht club. What was it? The Havana Yacht Club. Maybe he could sneak on board one of the boats and take off. Anything—a dinghy, a rowboat—whatever would get him off this damned island.

Instantly he felt better and the pressure on his temples subsided; even the salty fresh air smelled sweet. He looked at his watch. Five to eleven. He'd only slept five hours in the last twenty-four, but now the prospect of freedom, enticing as a mirage, spurred him on.

He rose, took another cold shower, still unable to figure out the odd water heater. He examined his face in the mirror as he shaved. Ventura's thugs had busted his lower lip, but the teeth were still firm in their sockets, and even the cut on his forehead, on closer inspection, revealed only four stitches. He looked over his body, still bulky from all the exercising he'd done out of boredom at Chillicothe. Bruises but no internal damage—his urine was clear and his stool bloodless. Damn bastards, I'll get you yet.

He dressed deliberately in the drabbest color in his suitcase, cream-colored shirt, dark pants, the kind of clothing that would let him mingle unnoticed in the crowds. No flashy rayon pants or Hawaiian shirts or open leather sandals. Not that a big Americano would be completely inconspicuous, but he thought he had an answer. As Morgan stepped out into the street, the undercover agent in the gray suit tossed his cigarette to the ground and followed.

Morgan walked down the length of Mercaderes, making sure that the little fat cop never lost sight of him. As he had planned, the crowd of workers and tourists soon filled the narrow sidewalk, the noon sun a tropical spotlight turning everything theatrical.

Morgan stepped into a great white building with revolving glass doors—EL ENCANTO read the large red letters out front. The air-conditioned air was a stateside girl's kiss, cool, dry, with the smell of talcum powder and clean sheets. He walked through the furniture department, stuffed couches and recliners that seemed lifted from downtown Cleveland set next to gaudy lamps dripping with tassels and geegaws. At the escalator he glanced back and spotted the little fat man heading his way through the lounge chairs. Morgan hustled through the couples on the escalator, bumping them aside even as he heard the complaints and insults of the jostled shoppers. He looked back quickly on the second floor and saw the cop elbowing his way up.

The tinkling of an elevator! He ran. The doors were closing just as the huffing officer, his little round face red with vexation, extended his hand to hold them open. Morgan, with a wicked grin, shoved him back out, and the little man fell flat on his butt right as the doors slammed shut.

"My brother-in-law," said Morgan by way of red-faced explanation. The passengers nodded, smiling. An old woman turned to her equally elderly companion and squawked, *"Qué dijo, qué dijo?"*

Morgan tore out of the store through a side door, stepping into an alley crammed full of cardboard boxes stamped *Hecho en U.S.A.* Racing through the adjoining parking structure, he did not stop until he was blocks away from the store, somewhere back in the old town again. Smiling from helpless satisfaction, he congratulated himself on giving the cop the slip, even if none of it made sense—his life, his trip, even this little cat-and-mouse game he'd just played. After all, they knew exactly where to find him. But that did not lessen his pleasure one bit, for he thought, as all warriors do, that there is no war, there is only the battle you're in right now.

He was crossing Obispo Street when he glimpsed a woman with the same milky white skin and bright red hair as Ellen, little Ellen Boyd, and his heart gave a jump. It can't be, he thought, hurrying to the curio shop with the picture postcards and stuffed baby alligators. He smelled the dust of petty business when he entered, then the witch hazel of the woman's companion standing behind her. She turned, her straw hat set high on the crown of her head, saying in a bright voice,

"Oh, Jack, this is just like Acapulco!"

Morgan walked outside, took a deep breath. I don't know what I would have said if it was her. How's the baby? How's your mom? Why did you divorce me? He stood at the edge of the sidewalk, looking absentmindedly at a horse-driven fruit cart, knowing he was truly lost and not knowing where or whom to turn to when he heard the click a fraction of a second before the blast hurled him across the street.

He found himself holding on to the haunches of the horse, its head, neatly severed by flying glass, spewing blood from the mouth. The body, still harnessed to the produce cart, remained standing as though expecting the missing part to be screwed on and the body made whole again. A brief silence, a moment of stunned lucidity when it seemed the whole day hung in the balance, teetering this way or that. Then with a loud thump life fell into the baying deep, and the motes of dust suspended in the air in front of Morgan's eyes turned a bright purple shade, and a great crack erupted from the bowels of the earth as the world trembled unto darkness.

Alarms blared, women screamed. The excited babble of high-pitched Spanish, the keening of dying animals, the feeling that reality had given way to a new era, a new epoch, a storm that hurled darkness at the brilliant sun. The horse collapsed and Morgan with it, and a load of oranges and avocados fell on him like a warm tropical blanket of sweetness and fat, and in the cloying-scented darkness he heard a string of thunderclaps, one, two, three, five, ten different explosions going off all around him like a giant firecracker bursting all over the city, pillars and walls and windows collapsing in the destruction of a world reduced to its knees, shattered by a force too powerful to overcome.

After a second or two Morgan pushed his way out of the covering mound of oranges. Feeling his clothes wet, he looked down, certain that it was blood. It was orange juice. He was soaked with the juice from the fruit slivered by the glass of the shattered shop windows.

He staggered out to the middle of the street, looked dazedly this way and that, noting the slow-moving taxicabs, the shocked faces silently screaming, a blue-uniformed policeman with his mute whistle in his mouth, the trees on the boulevard quietly fluttering their leaves against the slow-moving mauve clouds. Then the sound of everyday life rushed back in, occupying the empty space that had distanced him from death. The hubbub, the heaving, the horns and tooting of reality returned and laid a hand on his shoulder, saying, Beware your turn. He walked back to the colonnade by the gift shop.

The milky white woman lay on the ground, her head resting on the large sombrero, flowered dress raised to her waist, showing pink rayon panties and burly thighs covered with unshaven down. He bent down to help her but her face came off in his hand, the jawbone loosened, a gristly mass where her cheeks had been. He lovingly put her down again, placed the sombrero on her face, lowered her skirt to save her decency, and stumbled away, drunk with death. No one stopped him, no one questioned him, no one thought twice about a man ranging wildly down the street, lost among the crowd of Havana mourners.

He came to while sitting on the wall of the Malecón, the broad sea-side boulevard facing the deep blue between his homeland and his hell. The sun stung like an insect's bite, turning his skin pink from exposure. A wave exploded on the reefs directly below him, and the spray slapped him out of the dreamless reverie he had sunk into. He'd heard other explosions as he walked to the Malecón, but in his mind's ear they could not be distinguished from the disfiguring burst of mayhem that had con-fronted him earlier; that is, he wasn't sure whether he was actually lis-tening to more bombs or if the one he'd been so near to had simply kept echoing unwanted in his mind. (Later he would buy the *Havana Post* to read that fifty-five bombs had gone off that day in Havana, a supply of destruction orchestrated by a group of madmen in love with the Wagnerian music of death—death to Batista, death to the old, death to the gangrenous obscenity in Cuba.)

For a moment the crazy notion of throwing himself off the sea wall, to plunge into the roiling waters below, gripped him with enticing ferocity, not to die but to swim, to swim away from the fragrant hellhole others called paradise. Don't be ridiculous, he told himself. Ninety miles of sharks, stingrays, and storms—who can swim that? The screeching of yet another police siren tore by. Morgan stared dumbly at the patrol car howling down the boulevard. The people of Havana saw the car speed by, and for a moment all was quiet as the chariot of oppression flew by, then everyone returned to their jobs, their jokes, their black beans and fried plantains, to the rhythms of Beny Moré and Celia Cruz, to reading *El País* and *Avance* and *Bohemia,* to the vaudeville routines of Garrido and Piñeiro, to all the daily activities that ruled their days, jubilant that the angel had spared their doorway. A few couples meandered down the sidewalk, arm around each other's waist. A nut brown fisherman tended a line off the wall.

Morgan looked at the giant Mercedes-Benz billboard, the Spanish tiled cupola of the Hotel Nacional, the dazzling white-and-gray sky-scrapers in La Rambla, searching for the sign that was not long in com-ing—a two-man fishing skiff out from Santa Paula dock, tacking into the wind, making its way to the great blue river outside the harbor entrance.

Morgan got to his feet, shooed away the flies drawn by the smell of dried orange juice on his clothes.

Damn simple, he thought. It's not my country. It's not my fight. I'll commandeer a boat and get myself the hell out of here. Let them bury their own dead. I need a shower.

This time, acting on instinct, he had no problem finding Max's apart-ment; this time he even lit the strange gas water heater attached to the showerhead; this time he collapsed in bed, naked, into the nourishing nothingness of sleep. He woke hours later, the sky outside his window glowing with the pinkness of dusk, to the noise of someone knocking frantically at his door.

"It's me!" came Wilfredo's voice, muffled by the thick wooden door. "It's Willie, open up!"

Morgan sat up, his body as heavy as a rain-swollen punching bag. Wilfredo rattled the doorknob.

"Open up, William Morgan!"

His mouth cottony from exhaustion, his muscles aching with fatigue, Morgan stumbled to the door and jerked it open.

"What the hell," he said, then registered the shock in Wilfredo's and Laura's faces. He saw his nakedness, then looked back up, not at Wilfredo but at Laura, who did not seem able to take her eyes off his crotch even as she flushed from embarrassment.

"Let me get dressed," said Morgan, walking back into the bedroom and slamming the door behind him.

※ ※ ※

Morgan lit a cigarette, took another peek out the shutters at the street below. Another man in a cheap cotton suit was posted at the corner.

"We were sure they had killed you, my friend," said Wilfredo, nursing the *añejo* he'd poured himself from the bottle in the kitchen. Laura rocked in the rocking chair, twinkling eyes on Morgan.

"My mother had to call an old friend, who got us in touch with Ventura," continued Wilfredo. "He assured us you had been released unharmed. We came here right away this morning, but you weren't here. Today was a bad day, in any case. You heard the explosions, no?"

Morgan nodded, pulled the shutters close again.

"I got caught in one. Was almost cut to pieces."

"Very bad day. The Twenty-sixth of July people and the Directorio, they shook the city this afternoon. I counted twenty-two explosions. Perhaps there were more."

"Well, good for them."

Laura fired off a question in Spanish at Wilfredo, but he pointed at Morgan.

"Ask him yourself," he said. "You speak enough English."

He took another sip of his *añejo* and leaned back in his chair, happy to be uninvolved.

"What they want?" asked Laura hesitatingly.

Morgan sat on the mahogany-and-rattan couch a few feet away from her. Released by the heat of excitement, her ambergris perfume floated like a veil of desire about her. She stared straight at him, her feet now planted on the ground.

"What they want?" repeated Laura.

They want to know all about you, thought Morgan. He said instead: "They say I killed a man."

"A man. Is true?" she asked.

"Yes."

"Por qué? Why?"

"He was hitting a woman."

"You kill him for that?"

"I didn't mean to. It happened." Like my loving you, thought Morgan, who caught himself off guard, surprised by the sudden emotion that burst fully armored into his consciousness, saying, Dare you not acknowledge me? Yes I do yes I do.

"Yes, like that is life," she said, withdrawing into some inner chamber where her own memoirs played out. She glanced down at the arabesque teal floor tiles.

"Now I ask the questions," said Morgan. She looked up, eyebrows arched with eagerness.

"Yes?"

"Your husband, your . . . help me, here, Willie," said Morgan.

"Marido," came Wilfredo's reply from the kitchen as he downed a third shot of rum.

"Yes, your *marido.* Where is he?"

68

She looked over at Wilfredo, who waved his hand as though saying, Go ahead, the harm is done already.

"In the mountains. He fight. *Tat-tat-tat.*" She made like a machine gun.

"Do you love him?" Morgan heard himself asking, uncertain of the path this fork might lead to.

"Love? Me love?" She smiled, more from compassion than affection, then shrugged.

"Me like. He is brother."

"You mean you love him like a brother," said Morgan, happy to strike emotional gold. Then the the shaft caved in.

"No, no. He brother. Prime brother."

"What?"

Morgan turned to Wilfredo, who by now had his hand wrapped firmly around the neck of the bottle, took a swig, then raised the Bacardi to the ceiling.

"To incest!"

Laura smiled in amusement, then beamed her wonderful smile at Morgan.

"Yes, my prime brother. Yes."

She nodded.

Chapter

5

The heat made the Parque Zoologico, Havana's very own and very small zoo, different from the zoos Morgan had known in his childhood, those ripe palaces of the homesick ocelot, the scruffy lion, and the mangy bear. In Cuba the sun, already blazing at eleven, made the creatures ill tempered yet lethargic, so that if any of the screeching children around the cages, shouting, *"León, león,"* or, *"La pantera!"* threw peanuts or Orange Crush bottle caps at the morose animals, the beasts would only growl halfheartedly, bare a yellow fang or two, then churlishly retreat into their brick-and-concrete dens.

Laura coaxed Morgan into buying her an enormous fluff of pink cotton candy and two paper cones of salty Spanish peanuts. Laughing like one of the many children swarming the grounds, she led him down a flagstone path, past the empty polar bear cage and the orangutans and the chimps and the snake house and the seal lake, all the way down to the aviary, where she made him stand in front of a rookery holding small, piebald birds with a high-pitched song and nervous fluttery movements. Laura spoke excitedly in Spanish, pointing at the small birds and at another cage, holding fat yellow sparrows sitting placidly on their perches. Morgan knew that what she was saying mattered a great deal to her, but neither one of them was able to breach the barrier of language. Finally she threw up her arms.

"They Cuba," she said, pointing at the little squeaky bird. "They Spain," she said, pointing at the sparrows. "They fight, many people die."

"I'm sorry, Laura, I don't understand," was Morgan's only answer.

"Oh, it's OK," said Laura finally, out of frustration. "Is my country, no one understand."

Later, at a hillock overlooking a pond, they sat under an almond tree, its top garlanded with a wreath of white blossoms hosting a symphony of bees. He took her hand more confidently this time. It was the first day since they had met that they were alone together, away from the constant drilling and rhetorical questions of Wilfredo, who seemed intent on teaching Morgan how to speak Spanish before the week was through. All Morgan had retained were a few verbs—*ser, estar, amar*—and the sundry adjectives that graced most conversations in Cuba: *de película,* like a movie; *caliente,* hot; *revolucionario.*

Laura let him take her hand, but when he drew close and tried to kiss her, she pushed him away, letting him know in her uncertain English that Cuba was not America and Havana was not Paris and that decent women did not neck in public in her country. Morgan again wondered at the strangeness of her country, more accepting of corpses in the gutter than lovers trading kisses, but that oddity only made him more determined to reach the cultural core of Cuba so that by understanding it he might also understand Laura.

Certain things were already clear about her. For one, she had not really married her brother but her first cousin, the mistake one of mistranslation, the kind of small error that shatters guilty hearts and innocent lives. Nor was she a teenager, her age being somewhere in the mid-twenties, even if she did keep the joie de vivre of the perpetual adolescent. She was Willie's half sister, although her relationship to the family—whether she was born of Willie's mother and a previous husband or from General Fernández's fling with a girl on the family farm—was too complex for her to explain and for Morgan to understand. The fact of the matter was, Morgan didn't particularly care who her father or her mother or any relation might have been; all that mattered to him was Laura herself, her burning present flesh and smile and spirit, and there was only one question that he wanted to ask and that now came unbidden, flying out of his lips.

"Do you love him?" he asked, still holding on to her hand, aware he shouldn't be prying but unable to stop, testing the limits to find the path to her affections, not knowing she had already built an altar there in his name.

"I love who?" she asked, leaning against him, enjoying the solidity of his flesh, the sweet smell of milk and Mennen and cool, cool things from the North that he always carried with him. She tossed a handful of

71

peanuts to the mallards, who waddled through the grass pecking at one another before grabbing their treat.

"Your husband," he said, drawing her into him, enveloped by the sweet coconut smell of her hair.

"My husband," repeated Laura softly, as though the question came from far away about a place she'd long ago forgotten.

"You know, your *primo marido,*" said Morgan. She laughed, turned, and kissed him on the cheek, enormously amused by his question, and stared into his round eyes.

They're the color of the pool at the Biltmore, she thought. The color of truth and innocence. I wonder what they feed these boy-men up North that makes them so dreamy eyed, so strong. So unsuspecting.

She leaned back into him again, ran her fingers through the thick hair in his arms, trying to choose the right words in her limited English.

"My husband, he is good man. He is poor, from farm. When I know him, he sweet. We like very much but *Papá* no like. We run away, no? Then things change. You understand?"

"Perfectly," said Morgan, drawing her closer, remembering his own failed marriage, the way love's petals are ground to dust by unstoppable change. He caressed her hair. Encouraged by his affection, she darted fleetingly around the barriers of language.

"We going to have baby but he worried. He think no have enough money. I tell him *Papá* is Omar Fernández, *el senador,* he help. But Roberto too proud, he say no want money from nobodys. He say lose baby, we make other baby later. I no want, we fight much. I want baby so much. But in end he win. Man always win with woman, you know that. Is law of life. I go to doctor and he pull the baby out. Is not legal in Cuba and doctor no very good. In house I cry and cry and he think it is because baby, but I hurt so very much I throw the blood, much much blood. I sit in living room and blood comes out of me like wine from broken bottle, from here." She touched her sex. Morgan nodded solemnly.

"I lose *conocimiento,* all is black. I wake up in hospital and Roberto there, *Papá* there, everybody, whole family there. I very happy, everybody happy, but doctor tell me no more babies. Forever. I am a well with no water. I cry much. I hate Roberto then. I go back to *Papá y Mamá,* Roberto he join students against Batista. Papa then is dead and police arrest Roberto. He almost kill, but Willie help him out. Now Roberto is in mountain, with Fidel. We no man and woman long time. He return someday, we divorce. Is end, you know?"

"I know," replied Morgan, "it's the end." He thought of his own exits, the many times the flames of love had been dampened into cinders by the vagaries of fate, and he found himself wanting when compared to this child-woman he held in his arms. He brought her closer, turned her head. This time their lips met, chastely closed, yet he felt as though a current of life was coursing through him, connecting him to another view, another sphere.

They stayed under that tree for hours, talking about themselves in the unquenchable way of new lovers. Morgan told her about his parents' dairy farm, how he would rise early in the morning to start the milking, how the world used to smell new and strong and possible, and how it had all changed when his father died and he had joined the service, and how his wild courage had pulled him out of danger in Korea but only queered his life back in the world of civilians. He did not tell her about Ellen or Mariko or the reckless way he always had of looking for a girl that would . . . he didn't know what, but he knew he had found what he had longed for, and now all he need do was find the key to open the treasure trove of emotion by his side.

Laura suggested lunch at a Spanish restaurant nearby. Walking out of the park, Morgan felt lodged in a hiding place of happiness, certain that this girl he held by the hand marked a new start in his life. For a riotous happy moment he saw himself learning the language, getting a job, settling down in the old city in an apartment with a view of the harbor near the clanging cathedral bells. They would have children, tow-haired and dark-haired alike, and on Sunday they would all go off to their grandmother's in the big old house in El Cerro, and their uncle Willie would drop by occasionally with presents, for he was a hell of a guy too, and maybe someday he would take the whole crew back to Ohio so they would see where Daddy had come from, and won't all my old neighbors be annoyed when they see me with my Cuban wife and my Cuban family arriving at the old farm, traipsing through the fields, mooing at the cows, oohing at the grain bins, and one of the kids will say, Daddy they're just like rockets.

At the squat, tiled-roof building housing the public toilets he gave Laura a kiss and told her with hand signals to wait for him. He made the sign for little, *un poquito,* by putting thumb and forefinger an inch apart, then jerked his head at the men's room. Laura, blushing, looked him up and down, shook her head, and put her hands a foot apart.

"Oh, no, *muy grande,*" she ribbed him.

Once he was out of her sight, Laura cast off her mask of gaiety and allowed her true emotions to surface, despair leaning into her like an old lover.

Ay Dios mío, but it would be so pretty to have another life, she thought. With him, strong and confident of the future. To go somewhere where you can believe in tomorrow, not always be carrying the past like a mule with a pack saddle.

Sometimes I think this country will never change, no matter what we do. It's as though we all carry this sin in our blood, this way of thinking that will never change, no matter who's in power. Look at Menocal, at Machado, even Batista himself. They all started with great plans, and look what they left us, a maimed republic, a trough for politicians to feed on and a poorhouse for the rest. We are all so *exaltados,* so full of the song of our own emotions. We need someone to calm us down, to bring us down to earth. That is why the movement insists on obedience; it's the only way to get things accomplished in this country. We need the cunning of the ant in an island full of grasshoppers. Yes, that is the way, devotion to our ideals and to our cause. If we want to accomplish anything in Cuba, that is what we have to do.

There go the two men who have been watching us since we entered the park. William must know we have been watched, he's an expert at this, he just didn't want to disturb me. They're going into the men's room. I better go pee before he comes out.

Laura walked into the women's room, which reeked of unflushed waste and Pine Sol. She sat at a stall, hiked up her skirt, lowered her panties, felt the warmth of the urine passing thorough her. Finished, she as usual saw no paper in the toilet. She hunted in her purse for a spare sheet of Kleenex, wiped, and moved to the cracked mirror by the washstands, where some lonely woman had etched *Papi te quiero,* Daddy, I love you. Laura dreamed again of a day when venality would not be the rule, when there would be plenty of toilet paper always and towels and clean, unbroken mirrors at all public facilities, a time when the pride of being a free Cuban would show in all facets of life.

Morgan was buttoning his fly as the two men stationed themselves at the door to the rest room, the light shining behind them. Morgan didn't see their faces or think much about them until the man in the urinal next to his caught a glimpse of the arrivals. His penis still flapping out his fly, the man ran to the back window and jumped out.

Morgan felt a tap on his shoulder. He turned to see, aimed squarely at his face, two sawed-off shotguns, held by the two men who just moments ago had been guarding the doorway, one of them the black cop with the odd crescent-shaped scar from the jawline to the forehead. Standing behind them was dapper Captain Ventura, who nodded amiably at Morgan, then raised his hand in command. The cop with the scar lifted a foot and sank it into Morgan's crotch. As Morgan bent over, racked by the pain in his testicles, the cop swung the butt of his weapon, striking Morgan on the chin, sending him flying across the room against the tiled wall, where he sprawled with arms open, a supplicant at the throne of pain.

The room turned dizzyingly indigo for a few moments. When Morgan came to he heard the anxious twittering of a bird on a nearby tree, then the warm voice of a young girl somewhere shouting "Albertico!" and the loud buzzing of a fly.

Morgan opened his eyes. Ventura stood before him, gray woolen suit perfectly pressed, white shirt sparklingly clean, gold-and-jetstone cufflinks on the French cuffs showing only when he moved his perfectly tailored sleeves, black cordovan shoes without a speck of dust, shining like dull mirrors.

"It has been two weeks since our conversation and we have not heard from you, Mr. Morgan. Why is that?"

Morgan spoke through a mouthful of blood.

"I lost your number," he said.

Ventura looked puzzled for an instant, then ventured a smile. His two goons looked down on Morgan, deadly serious, their guns aimed squarely at the sprawled Americano.

"My phone number. Very clever, Mr. Morgan. You are quite the comedian. But I do not think you will find it so funny in the future if you keep acting this way. Please get up."

Morgan staggered to his feet under the watching eyes of the gunmen. Ventura grabbed a paper towel, wet it under the faucet, handed it to Morgan.

"Wipe your mouth," he suggested with sudden squeamishness, as though hating the very sight of blood. Morgan took the towel and at that moment was so overcome by a fit of blinding fury that without knowing it, he had already cast his lot with the other side.

"Have you been able to obtain any information?" asked Ventura. Morgan shook his head.

"We haven't talked about politics."

"You have not talked about politics," repeated Ventura, almost to himself. He came up to Morgan. Even when standing to full stature he still came several inches short of Morgan's chin. Ventura slapped him.

"Liar!" he screamed. "Cubans do nothing but talk about politics! Do not ever lie to me again!"

Ventura turned his back on Morgan, as if defying him to grab hold of him. Morgan raised his hands at the same time that he saw the two shot-

guns being cocked and raised to his head. He put his hands down again.
Ventura took out a lilac-scented handkerchief, dabbing his temple in
short nervous gestures, then pocketed it. He extracted a Lucky Strike
from a silver case. Without needing to be asked, one of the gunmen took
out a flint lighter and lit his boss's cigarette. Ventura inhaled deeply,
bringing his temper under control.

"You will find out what it is they are planning," he said evenly.

"How can I? I have no idea what they are planning," countered
Morgan. "You asked me before to get the names of the other conspirators. Well, I haven't seen anybody conspiring with the Fernández family.
I haven't seen anything, I haven't heard anything. I can't ask because officially and unofficially, I might add, I don't know anything either. See my
point? How can I ask about something I don't know about and they
don't talk about?"

"Fine. Let me inform you then what we know so far, and you will
take it from there. The underground—we don't know who exactly, the
twenty-sixth of July, the Directorio, perhaps some other group of revolutionaries—they are plotting to assassinate one of the leaders of our
government."

"I thought they tried that at the palace."

"Yes. But they never stop. We do not know who it is or where. That
is what you must find out. We have evidence that the Fernández are
involved."

"How? In what way?"

"Our . . . informant did not reveal that information before he died,
unfortunately. He named the Fernández and said they were involved,
that is all."

"You torture someone to death and you expect the truth?"

"You would be surprised how reliable that information can be.
Whether you choose to follow our methods or you choose your own,
that is your problem. Regardless, all we want are the other names."

"How do you expect me to do this?" replied Morgan.

"That is up to you. Fuck the girl, fuck the brother, fuck the mother,
fuck them all or not at all. Whatever you must do, do it. I want my
answer in forty-eight hours. Then, my friend, if I have it, I will personally drive you to the nearest plane leaving for the States. Or the country
of your choice."

"With the girl?"

Ventura smiled again.

"Naturally. I do believe in love at first sight, you know."

✳ ✳ ✳

The moment Laura noticed Ventura coming out the men's room she hugged herself, shuddering as though a winter's chill had blown through. He was flanked by two tall, muscular men in guayaberas, who made no effort to conceal the shotguns by their side. Laura stood transfixed to her spot, hesitating whether to run and hide as a welter of thoughts rushed to her head—her husband's torturing, her duty to the cause, her faith in a new Cuba, her fear of pain. Breathlessly she looked around for Morgan and saw him coming out of the men's room, a wet paper towel to his mouth. She glanced back at Ventura, almost gliding away down the slope, his head bobbing in the thermals of heat rising from the blacktop.

"What happen?" she asked Morgan, touching his broken lip.

"I slipped and fell," he said, with a shrug. *"Estúpido americano."*

"No, you no *estúpido*, William. No how."

They drifted away, going the direction opposite Ventura's, each silently wrapped in individual contemplation of their plight. How should I do this? thought Morgan. How do I tell him? thought Laura.

At the corner across from the park, they saw what Ventura and his people had come for.

A Buick convertible had been stopped by two patrol cars. Three young men, with the white skin and fancy clothes of the upper class, were lying facedown on the pavement, hands spread out in front of them, as though wanting to swim away from their predicament. A policeman kicked one of the prisoners, a red-haired, freckled boy of slight build, barely of shaving age. The boy twitched and said something, his words lost in the clamor of buses and cars flying by, avoiding all contact with the gathering clouds of death. The noon whistle blew at the vinegar factory down the road, the sharp smell of sops permeating the area like the breath of a man on a three-day drunk.

One of the officers opened the capacious trunk of the orange-colored convertible. He took out an old Garand rifle and a Thompson submachine gun, holding them aloft like trophies in the dazzling white sunlight. Ventura shook his head in genuine dismay and raised his right hand, almost like a benediction or a forgiving of sin.

The gunman with the crescent-shaped scar was the first to open fire. The boy closest to him, thin, fair haired, with Botticelli features, had turned to him crying, begging for a mercy that was not to be seen as the blast from a few feet away shattered his handsome face into pieces, gouging out his left eye, leaving the cheekbone exposed, and blowing away part of the jaw, so that the tongue, still moving, lay open to the corrosive sun.

The second man was executed in seconds by the other gunman, who emptied the sixteen rounds of his automatic. The body jerked with each bullet even after the skullcap was shattered and spread out in gristly chunks on the pavement. The third detainee, the red-haired boy, sprung to his feet the moment the shooting started. He ran toward Ventura, perhaps thinking that if he grabbed the leader he would make an escape somewhow. But in a whirring motion Ventura eased out a .45 from the hand-tooled Italian leather holster under his jacket and fired four shots at the boy, who fell howling and holding his crotch. He screamed like a newborn, thrashing his head on the pavement to stop the pain as blood and life spewed out of his bullet-torn genitals. Ventura, somber until then, laughed, enormously amused. He carefully walked around the boy to avoid the gushing spurts of blood, then fired a bullet into the boy's temple, the plug of brain matter blowing out in a gory trail.

Morgan felt his stomach heave. He asked himself what kind of people he was dealing with—in the name of what cause or principle could they murder this way? They're worse than the commies, he thought.

Laura, who had watched mutely, petrified with fear and disgust, lunged forward as though that last act of brutality had broken the spell. She yelled a string of obscenities and jumped down to the street, tiny fists clenched into tiny weapons of hate. Morgan had to hold her close to him to stop her forward movement. She flailed the air, cursing the sun, the moon, the stars, the Virgin, and God, and the whore mothers that had given birth to these killers of the flower of Cuba.

Down the block the killers holstered their weapons, spat on the lifeless bodies, then filed confidently back into their cars. As Ventura left he wheeled around, observed Laura with a deprecating grin. Morgan would have sworn that the henchman actually winked at him before getting into his Ford and running over the bodies, which jerked upwards from the weight of the vehicles, then rolled down to the gutter, their blood already drawing large, bottle green flies.

Laura wailed uncontrollably, her cries of pain as great as if it had been her own flesh and blood she had seen murdered before her eyes. Morgan tried to calm her down, calling her by all the terms of endearment he knew and some that he invented, in English, in Spanish, in Japanese, German, and Korean, reluctant to let her go from his arms. He knew he should slap her to bring her out of shock, but he could not bring himself to do even that little bit of harm to her, so he forced her mouth into his and he kissed her, swallowing up the protests that still convulsed her slender body.

At first she resisted, her fists striking Morgan's back, but soon she

kissed him in return, her body jammed against his, seeking the reassur-
ance of his muscular flesh, so alien from her own troubled, burning kind.
When she broke away, Morgan noticed a line of blood running down
her chin, then he realized it was his own blood she was swallowing from
his broken lip as her glistening tongue licked off the last drops around
her mouth.

"Come with me," she said, "Come to *la posada*," and yanked him to
her with the greediness of a child before the pastry cart.

They were drawn together not by lust but by need, a necessity so intense it was practically an unsurmountable barrier. Even after they received their towels from the surly front-desk hotel clerk—who demanded a deposit of twenty pesos, a week's wages, upon seeing the embarrassed Americano towering over the frail girl, who paid for the room with her own money—even as they ascended the wide, concrete-tiled steps to the top floor, looking down the fancy wrought iron balustrade at the empty courtyard down below, even after they opened the peeling wooden doors and entered and closed the doors and sat facing each other in embarassed silence, and then opened the shutters and then somehow fell in bed, slowly removing each piece of clothing from each other, so that in the end they lay naked side by side, staring at the ceiling, even then they were afraid to touch, their need for each other so strong it lay between them like Tristan's sword.

Only with deliberate effort did they make the first moves, smelling each other's skin, tasting each other's lips, running their hands over each other's body, finding out how well and how naturally he fit inside of her, as though they had been measured for each other long ago by a wiser and now forgotten maker. Not a word did they say, for there was no need for words. Their glances and their gestures and caresses were language enough, and three times he entered her and three times they climaxed in the quiet ecstasy of found lovers, whose world lay between each other's arms, drowning, in the quiet joy of their lovemaking, the buzzing of the chariots of death of Havana.

A gentle breeze picked up in the late afternoon. Honeyed sunlight slanted on the lime green wall, falling on the print of the Virgin of El Cobre, Our Lady of Charity, holding the child Jesus in her hands as she treads a globe while the three Johns—the black, the white, and the mulatto fishermen who found her image floating in the water of the Bay of Nipe—row on in prayerful eternity.

Laura had fallen asleep, the regular rhythm of her breathing like the rocking of the waves of a nearby ocean. Now she stirred, jerked her head, opened her eyes wide from terror.

"They here!" she said, scrambling up the bed, leaning on her elbows, masses of wavy hair falling on her slender shoulders, her smallish breasts puckered up in fright.

"What's the matter? There's no one here," said Morgan. "What's wrong?"

But Laura was seeing not Morgan but her persistent dream, the one where the door always slammed and the killers always marched in with their pickaxes and their hoes, dressed in brown uniforms, bearing the cross of Lorraine, and one of them held a wicker basket with the hacked-off heads of her husband, Roberto, and her mother's and her brother's heads too, and now a third killer walked in and she could not see his face, for it was covered by a cloud, and it was only when he brought the long hoe down that she recognized the aquiline nose, the deep-set eyes, the fleshy lips, and curly beard of the leader in the mountains, and she heard a deep manly voice crying out, The ides of October mean the world, and the hoe came down on her neck and off came her head, which fell into the wicker basket with the others.

She woke to find Morgan shaking her, and the moment the blaring images of desolation had been swallowed again by her unconscious, she wrapped her arms around him, hugging him as hard as she had ever hugged anyone, full of the fear of an unvanquished past. Surprised by her rage, he stroked her hair, kissed her shoulders, but she only hugged him tighter as though never to let him go, as though wanting to meld into him so that they would become the perfect couple, united as one for all eternity.

Laura didn't mean to, she certainly hadn't planned to, but she could not help crying, the sobs starting out small and reluctant and soon growing into deep, racking, cleansing sobs. The pain in her heart—the anguish, the dreadful premonition that nothing she would ever do would ever turn out right—was as barbed as the agony she had endured when her insides were torn out of her. She knew there was this hollow in her, a great big demanding space that she had to fill, a space she had crammed with thoughts of revolution, of change and transformation, but now, in the weakness of the afternoon, she wondered if even the image of Cuba could replace the flesh and blood she would never issue.

She fell back on the bed, facing away from Morgan, tears burning with rage and regret, rage at those who had done this to her, rage at the forces that had twisted her life and the life of millions of others on this island, who saw their hopes shattered, their families obliterated by the cruel, venal men who thought material prosperity was reason enough to destroy the soul of a people.

"It's OK, honey. It was just a dream."

She buried her head in the pillow, thoughts of the future as dark as the shadows she willed herself into. A rumbling bus down on Aldecoa back-fired. Laura sat up fiercely, her eyes red and wide, her hair tangled and thick, framing her overwrought features as though the sheer emotion that surfaced in her was enough to convince Morgan of what she knew he must do.

"I want you," she said, taking his hand.

"I want you too, sweetheart. You're my girl," he added almost auto-matically, even though he instinctively knew that it was not romantic tenderness that she now craved.

"I want you help, you understand? I want you help me, my brother Willie. I want you help Cuba, I want you help we all."

"Sure, baby, you know I'll help you. All you have to do is ask. Anything you say."

She grew grim for a moment, her lips pressed together in firm defi-ance, her eyes narrow and cold. Morgan recognized that expression but could not place it until he recalled his Sunday-school book, and he felt chills when he remembered the illustration, the same high cheekbones, the same tawny skin, the same masses of curly hair, the same cold-steel glint in the half-closed eyes, and the name of the victim eased into his mind, and he knew before she spoke what she wanted, and and he told himself, Judith, I will do it; Judith, yes, I will do it, even before you ask, for that is what I want too, and I don't know if I'm going crazy or if it's my love for you or my hate for these sons of bitches or just my fate, but, yes, I will do it and gladly if you ask me, just ask.

"You have to kill him," she said coldly, without inflection.

"Kill who?" he asked, needlessly.

"You have to kill Batista. He go, everything go. Liberty then for every-body, for all Cuba. You are Americano, nobody suspect you. You kill him easy, everybody else hard. You have to kill him. You must."

Morgan drank from her liquid brown eyes cold with the knowledge of death, and he felt pulled into the kind of madness only love at the crossroads of history can provide. He heard himself saying, "I will do it. I will kill Batista for you."

As they spoke, in the lengthening shadows of the old hotel, a plane buzzed overhead and yet another bomb went off, blasting its heart to pieces somewhere in the frightened city.

Chapter

7

Morgan was letting himself into the apartment when he smelled the coffee brewing. He closed the door, headed for the kitchen. Max stood at the counter, one hand pouring a mass of black foam from a pot into a cloth filter he held with the other hand.

"How do you like it so far?" asked Max by way of greeting, not taking his eyes off the boiling brew that gushed through the filter into a battered tin cup.

"Just fine," said Morgan, glad to see him back. "When did you get in?"

"This morning. Took the first Cubana flight out of Miami. Want some?" Max rummaged through the cupboard, took out a dainty espresso cup with a band of gold along the rim and a cameo of a Watteau hoyden on the side.

"No, thanks. Last thing I need is something to keep me up. I've hardly slept two winks since I got here."

"So I heard," said Max, filling his cup with the inky black elixir and hastily carrying it to his lips. He sipped, let out a sigh of pleasure.

"Just can't get decent coffee in the States, no matter where you go. Even the Italians don't know how."

"What do you mean you heard?" asked Morgan as nonchalantly as he could. He lit a cigarette and suddenly he wasn't so happy that Max had returned.

"I heard from Willie, your . . . Spanish teacher. He came to pick me up. That's not really going anywhere, is it? I mean the Spanish lessons."

Max took another sip of *café cubano,* noticing the circles of fatigue

84

under Morgan's eyes. They have really gone overboard, thought Max. We don't want to kill the goose either.

"Not for want of trying. Willie has been going after me like I was going to be swearing the Cuban oath of allegiance pretty soon."

"That's interesting. You wouldn't expect so much patriotism from a commie."

"A what?"

Morgan flicked his cigarette to the sink, where it sputtered to death in a bowl of soapy water.

"You look surprised," said Max. "I thought he would have told you by now."

"No, he didn't. I never had any . . . " Morgan grew quiet. It all made sense now. But did it really make a difference? Did that really affect how he felt for Laura and how, he hoped, she felt for him? Sure, she prodded, but he would have wound up there on his own anyhow.

"Well, maybe he's not a card-carrying member of the party, just a fellow traveler. I mention it because for someone with your perspective, that kind of thing might not be too copacetic."

"I see. And what's your relationship to him?"

"He's a friend. You know."

"No, I don't know."

"OK, he's a source. He keeps me informed. In this businesss you have to play both sides. Sometimes the middle too."

So where does that leave me? thought Morgan. What is it you want me to do? Are you going to tell me, or do I have to keep playing dumb?

"Isn't Laura a glamour-puss?" said Max, pouring himself a second cup. "Kind of makes you forget that black blood she's got in her. She's only Willie's half sister, you know that, right?"

"I figured it out myself."

"Pretty radical in her opinions, too. Some of the people we'll be seeing today wouldn't exactly approve of her politics, but they'd go nuts for her, let me tell you."

"Who are we meeting?"

"I wanted you to get to know a couple of people that might be useful in the future, especially if somebody figures out who killed that low-life sergeant. Friendships are the coin of the realm in this country. You can literally get away with murder if you know the right people."

"Or if you work for the government."

So he is in already, thought Max. This is better than we expected. I think.

"You've been making your acquaintance with some of Havana's finest?"

"Only from afar. I saw three kids killed right before my eyes this afternoon. I was out by the zoo with Laura and these kids got pulled over. The police found some weapons in their car and they got shot right on the spot."

"Batista justice. They should be happy they weren't tortured to death."

"How can these people take it?"

"They don't. That's why they're fighting out in the hills and planting bombs all over the goddamn place. The State Department thinks Batista has a chance, but I don't."

"Explain this to me, will you?" asked Morgan. "Why is it that we're always backing the wrong guy in these conflicts? We say we want freedom and democracy, then we turn around and support people like Batista. That's not what I was taught. I like to think that's not what we're all about."

Max nodded, assenting, even though his thoughts were coldly dismissive. How naive can you be, William? Don't you know that's the way of the world? We don't have principles, we have interests. Freedom and democracy are privileges we reserve for ourselves.

"Exactly," replied Max. "I keep telling my guys that Batista is making too many enemies all at once. Somebody should do something about him, don't you think?"

Morgan was about to confide in Max when he saw the sparkle of dangerous curiosity in his eyes, and he walked away.

"That's up to the Cubans. I'm just visiting here."

"What does Laura think?" prepped Max.

"I don't know, I haven't asked her. Look, I might as well tell you. I'm in love with Laura."

"Who isn't? Got a cigarette?"

Morgan tossed him the pack of Chesterfields.

"It's more than that. I'm going to marry her."

Max turned on the burner, lit the cigarette from the blue flickering gas flame. Jesus, either this guy's an idiot or a saint. What the fuck have these guys been doing to him?

"Why are you grinning like that?"

It was true, Max's face had lit up with the greatest uncontrollable smile, which Max knew he should repress but couldn't—the very reason why he'd been banished to the backwater of Havana by his superiors.

"I was just thinking it must be pretty hard to communicate with Laura, given her limited knowledge of the English language. And your Spanish leaves a lot to be desired."

"Some things you don't need language to understand."

"I had no idea you were so romantic, William."

The moment the words came out of his mouth, Max realized the mistake he'd made. The last thing he needed was to sound condescending or to alienate Morgan, who now looked on the verge of tears, if such a thing could be believed. The man is really in love. God, sometimes I wish I could bite my tongue off.

"I'm sorry," said Max.

"No need to apologize. So what if I'm romantic? I love her, what's wrong with that?"

"Nothing at all. It's just that, well, you've only been here a couple of weeks. It's kind of sudden, don't you think?"

Morgan looked down on Max, haggard and unshaven, a salesman peddling shoddy goods, and he felt more than anger, he felt pity for him. You little man. There's so much you don't understand, with your bright eagerness and yapping mind. You think only the obvious and you forget the heart of the matter. A week can be the world. A week can be the crowning point of an existence that might thin out for decades after that. But you, you have never even had that week. You have a lifetime of short dreams and small desires. You wouldn't begin to understand what I feel. You wouldn't understand at all.

They stared at each other, Max tense, upright, a tight little terrier of a man ready to scurry away if the blow came.

"A lot can happen in a week, you know," said Morgan finally. "A lot."

"I can tell. Look, fella, congratulations are in order. I'm glad things are working out for you. Just tell me how I can be of assistance. You two are going to be leaving the country, I take it."

"I don't know."

"Well, Jesus Christ, man, what the hell have you decided? As long as you're in Cuba you're on borrowed time. You can't hope to make a living here, and you have to have something to live on. Willie's family lost all its money; they're dirt poor right now. All they have is that big old house in El Cerro. What have you two decided?"

"Lay off, Max. You're not my brother. Or her father either."

"All right, OK, you got a point. None of my business. Sorry again. So, when's the wedding?"

"I don't know. I haven't proposed yet."

The black men in all-white clothes gathered in the president's ante-chamber with their drums, their *keikayus,* their *bambelekes,* even a fiery red rooster with sharp spurs, annoying greatly Señor Boyeros, the only white man waiting in the gilded room.

It was Boyeros's first visit since the failed attack on the palace, and he was surprised that workers had been able to fix everything so quickly. Only here and there did Boyeros spot unplugged bullet holes in the plaster or the odd speckle of dried blood on the windowpanes. Still, enough was enough. He had other business to tend to. Boyeros was about to walk out, knowing that would enrage Batista but willing to endure the consequences, when Batista's secretary, Morales, came out of his boss's office.

"*El presidente* will see you now, Señor Boyeros."

Carlos Boyeros y Ordóñez, lifetime member of the Senate, owner of the largest Cadillac dealership in Cuba, developer of Ciudad Jardín, and majority stockholder in Cubana Airlines, rose quickly to his feet, relieved he didn't have to wait until the *santeros* gave their black blessings to the affairs of state.

In his chambers Batista was surrounded by the usual retinue—his chief of staff, Luisito Pozo, the son of the mayor of Havana; the chief of police, roly-poly Pilar García, who had replaced the dreaded Salas Cañizares, killed in a shoot-out at the Haitian Embassy; the chief of army staff, General Francisco Tabernilla Holz; and other assorted hangers on— all of whom watched wide eyed an old *santero* shake helplessly on the ground, possessed, as they all knew, by the saint of his devotion.

Boyeros frowned. There was always something wrong with these meetings. Why couldn't Cuba get itself a decent head of government instead of this buffoon, someone upright and just, like Franco, who may have been a son of a bitch but who at least rebuilt Spain? This pimp is facing a civil war and he fritters away his time on black magic. All these mulattoes are the same; scratch one, and all that nigger blood comes out.

Batista was dressed in Boston banker pinstripes—setting the example, since he had forbidden anyone to be without a coat and tie in the palace, even if it was a hundred degrees outside. He sighed with relief when Boyeros entered, like the barkeep for a thirsty crowd who spots the beer truck rounding the bend.

"*Chico,* so glad you're here. You know anything about these things? This has never happened to me before."

"Good morning, Mr. President," said Boyeros, choosing his most formal attitude to convey the exact degree of his displeasure. He ignored the *santero,* who thrashed within a few inches of the industrialist's glossy wing tips. "Has Your Excellency decided about the resolution of the match factory trust?"

"*Coño,* Boyeros, that can wait. What are we going to do about this man? He was coming here as a representative of all the *awayós* of Havana when all of a sudden, just like that, he has this fit. We can't allow this kind of thing in here. It besmirches the dignity of our office. None of the boys knows what to do."

"*Mi general,*" said Tabernilla, who always referred to Batista by the rank that had won him the support of the army during the March 10 coup, "I say we shoot him."

"There you go again, wanting to use your gun instead of your head," snapped Batista. "Is that all I have around me, gunmen and yes-men?"

You chose them yourself, Fulgencio, thought Boyeros. Toadies, killers, and parasites sucking our country dry. If you lie down with children, you know you'll wake up in piss.

Boyeros turned calmly and deliberately to look at the *santero,* who arched his back, thumped his head in uncontrollable spasms. He noticed the tribal scars on the old man's cheeks and wondered, given the nimbus of gray curls and the quivering wattle on his neck, if they were dealing with that most wondrous of all Cuban blacks, a *negro nación,* an old African brought over before the end of slavery in the 1880s. Boyeros himself had seen some of those old Negroes at his family farm engendering children well into their eighties and nineties, dancing and drumming the *batá* during the village feast for days on end. Not work, of course; that was too much to ask of these old bodies on a regular basis, but on occasion the blood rose, the music summoned, and an old nigger just had to answer. They're just like children, thought Boyeros. Just like the other fucks here. God, why am I not a Spaniard? Oh well, let's give them what they really want.

Recognizing the red-and-white beads of the follower of Changó, the god of thunder and lightning, power and might, Boyeros decided water might end the trance by springing the god forward, reminding the deity of the veil of rain that always accompanies his appearance. Boyeros filled a water glass.

"No, no, don't do that!" pleaded Pozo, but Boyeros paid him no mind and poured the water on the writhing man. Might as well get it over with, he thought. True to form, in a few seconds the old *babalawo* shook his head, then his shoulders, his torso, and his legs, as though shaking the water off his entire body, like a dog after a dive in the ocean; then he spun around, rising effortlessly on his tiptoes as though someone were pulling a string from above.

Batista took a step back and crossed his arms, waiting. The revelation they all knew was coming did not take long. The old black man, with the deep voice of the gods, raised a quivering finger at Batista.

"*Mujercita!* Little woman! You are a slut who lets herself be fucked up the ass by the white man in the mountain!"

Tabernilla moved for his gun on hearing the lèse-majesté, but Batista held his hand. A secret follower of Changó, Batista had been visited more than once by the fiery god, who loved to make his appearance during the ceremonies in the basement of the Capitol, amid the smoking remains of burnt chickens and goats. But never had the god mentioned politics, no matter how many times Batista had appeased him and implored him. Now here, in front of his cabinet, the feckless divinity was finally taking a stand, almost as if wanting to shame him into action.

One of Cantillo's people must have bribed him, thought Batista, remembering the army general who had been pressing for an offensive against the rebels. I'll have to find out how he did it. I'm sure García will oblige once this travesty is over. But I better wait, just in case it is Changó.

"And you are no son of Changó, no matter how many chickens you slaughter or how much rum you serve me. Because you are a woman, Fulgencio, and as a woman you will cry over what you could not defend as a man. I am gone and I will never return to you."

And with that the old man crumbled to the ground like a rag. Tabernilla took out his gun, walked up to the man, put the barrel to his head.

"Now, *Señor Presidente?*" Tabernilla looked forward to the shuddering blast, the stream of blood that would gush when the brains blew out.

"*Coño, chico,* not here, this is an Aubuisson carpet! Marta will kill me if I get it dirty again!" joked Batista. All the men laughed; Tabernilla holstered his gun. I'll get you yet, *negrito,* he thought.

Then the old man opened his eyes again, and this time he rose clear into the air, levitating before the astonished group. Pozo and Batista crossed themselves as Boyeros wondered how the old man was pulling that trick and Tabernilla thought, I shouldn't have asked, I should have killed him anyhow.

"*Hijos mios*"—my children—said the black man, floating six feet above the ground, arms spread out like wings, speaking in a delicate woman's voice with the precise intonation of the natives of Spain, "I have come to warn you of a great peril if you do not cease your fighting. You must achieve peace, for if not, a great torrent of blood will wash over this fair island and the world will never be the same. Pray to my son, Jesus Christ, that you don't all burn in the final firestorm. Listen to my words. I am Caridad."

And saying those words the old man fell to the ground, the sound of his head hitting the floor like a calabash dropped from a great height.

Boyeros felt for the old man's pulse. The fractured pieces of skull gave under his fingers.

"He cracked it. He's dead."

Batista paled and thought quickly how he could turn this to his advantage, as he did all moments of crisis in his life, a gory collection of silk purses from sow's ears, but he could not find a way. He knew and they all knew the visitation was that of the Virgin Mary, who had chosen this moment, of all moments, and in the body of an old nigger yet!

Batista had never heard of such a thing. And what was that warning about a firestorm at the end, anyhow? He would have to ask Marta. She had gone to Lourdes and Fatima; she would know.

Batista cleared his throat, looked around at his retinue, all waiting for his command. He turned to Pozo.

"*Bueno, chico,* have him taken away. Obviously the Virgin didn't like his choice of words."

A bad joke, he knew, but they would have laughed at anything, and laugh they did, Pozo chuckling with rest as he darted out to the antechamber and signaled at a couple of army officers, who came and removed the body from the room. As the soldiers carried the corpse out, the *babalawos* all stood and stared wide eyed and some crossed themselves, invoking the aid of their particular saint, for the soldiers were removing the body of the oldest and the greatest of them all, Juanito Carabalí of Guinea and Cabo Verde, who had come to Cuba in a sailing ship in the year 1874 and who had been blessed by the gods of Africa since he was born, announcing in stentorian tones upon coming out from the womb the name of his god and how he should be treated and where and how he would die. Now all his prophecies had come true and the great night of Cuba was about to begin.

Ayé, Ayé, Ibarago Moyuba, Ayé, Ayé, Ago, Ago ilé, Ago.

※ ※ ※

Batista sat at his desk, straightening the gilded crystal writing set, lining up the hand-tooled leather blotter to the edge of the table, turning the revolving Cartier clock the millimeter to the left that it was off so that everything on his desk was perfectly aligned in perfect geometrical proportions with the edge of the desk. He looked at his top advisers standing expectantly in a semicircle in front of him. Might as well grab the bull by the balls.

"So how many of you think that I should do what the . . . what that dead nigger said? Who thinks that I should start a dialogue and make peace with the rebels?"

No one raised a hand, made a gesture, batted an eyelash, not even Boyeros, who always thought the best remaining service Batista could do for his country would be to resign. He was not about to bell the cat, not in front of these people, in any case.

"Alright," continued Batista, "then who thinks that I should leave office, in spite of the elections in fifty-four, when I ran unopposed and won ninety percent of the vote? Who says, Batista, get out? Let me see those hands."

Again not a stir in the group. Too many horses in Kentucky, mistresses in Paris, bank accounts in Geneva. Too many deaths.

"Fine. In that case it's steady as she goes. Who knows what evil spirit got into the old man?"

Sighs of relief in the room. Lives were still in place, seals were not yet broken, the chilling sound of revelation again was lost in the clatter of everyday Havana.

"Boyeros, I called you because the boys here have a plan. We want to know if you'll go along."

※ ※ ※

Boyeros was furious when he stepped out of the palace. He was in such a rage that he barely nodded at the captain of the guard, son of a former administrator of his cattle ranch in Camagüey. The young man clicked his heels as Boyeros stormed past, but Boyeros did little more than half raise his hand in a barely veiled imitation of the *falange* salute and exited to Zulueta Street. He dismissed his driver, telling him he'd walk to his offices, and headed for El Prado, the leafy boulevard patterned after the Rambla of Barcelona, with its flowering trees, small cafés, womens' string ensembles playing sweet *danzones* in the morning light.

What Batista wants is outrageous, thought Boyeros, just the sort of half-baked scheme that has caused the problems (for Boyeros refused to call the armed opposition "revolutionaries" or even *rebeldes;* to him those words were sacred, to be used only in connection with the glorious handful of men who in 1898 had waged a harrowing war against one of the greatest colonial powers of the time).

There was no way Boyeros could or would go along with the scheme, even if it did have the kind of warped simplicity that appealed to uncultured minds and to the typical Cuban *exaltado,* the overexcited type who makes a game of dominoes a fight to the death. Like that idiotic senator who had challenged the society columnist over a double entendre about his wife. Boyeros himself had been one of the seconds to the columnist, a second cousin to his wife, Milagros. Swords at dawn—sabers, no less, as if they were still in the time of Lope de Vega—under the royal palm trees. Everyone was reining in their laughter at seeing two overweight middle-aged men lunge and parry and riposte while swarms of *jejenes,* or no-see-ums, from the nearby swamps gathered in noisy clouds around them until the senator drew blood from the columnist's arm and everything was settled in some stupid honorable way as in some stupid nineteenth-century novel by Bécquer or Zorrilla.

What can we do with people like this, thought Boyeros, these romantics? Or these cynics, who are the other side of the coin? We either believe in everything or we believe in nothing. What a country I've been born in, Lord. And now this, this preposterous scheme to smuggle a fighter into Castro's lair and assassinate him in a power struggle and then take over the movement. Do these men think the opposition is that stupid? Do they really think the leaders of any movement, no matter how misguided, can be switched so easily? Obviously they do. And they have charged me, because I own property out there, to find a way to slip the man into their hands, pretending the killer is from my people, my party, my money.

"CIA, Sureté, Interpol, whatever you want to call him, just say he has foreign support and he's independent of you, me, everybody else," says Batista. *Estúpido mulato.* I should have let Cantillo kill him back in the forties when he had a chance. If it weren't for Milagros and Mauricio,

I'd leave this damned island in a minute. God, what a mess. I might leave it at that anyhow.

Just then Boyeros spotted Max Weinberg, tramping down the Prado in a cotton poplin suit that had been ironed so long ago no one would have found its creases even they had wanted to. He walked next to an obviously perplexed Americano, with the heft and posture of a soldier in mufti. Max, thought Boyeros, Max, what are you doing with this Yanqui? Since when does the CIA give tours to GIs?

Max had seen Boyeros a block away and purposely crossed the street to the center island of El Prado so that they might seem to have run into each other just casually on a fine Havana morning. Max deduced Boyeros had just come from the palace, having run into him before during walks like this, from Batista's office to Boyero's newspaper office. Judging by Boyero's demeanor, the gruff way he held his stocky body, legs stretched stiffly out front, arms behind his back, frowning as though contemplating a beggar's outstretched hand or the dread hammer and sickle scrawled on the ground, Max knew his meeting with Batista had not gone well.

When Boyero's meetings with Batista went well, the whole town knew it. Boyeros would board his convertible, order the top put down, and slowly drive down the avenue, waving and nodding at his friends and acquaintances like a triumphant general home from a minor victory in the provinces. But when matters went badly Boyeros would walk. And walk. And walk. Max had heard that one time, after a spectacularly riotous meeting with Batista, Boyeros had walked all the way across Havana, clear out to his beach cabin in Tarará, a distance of about fifty kilometers, followed all the while by his chauffeur-driven Mercedes 230, his wife's Lincoln, and a truck full of army soldiers, who served as protection against bombers or kidnappers, an incongruous convoy for the gray-haired man in the fine English woolen suit trudging through knee-high weeds and mud holes on the side of the highway, unheedful of the slowly moving caravan behind him, hands behind his back, head deep in the clouds, trying to come to grips with the madman who ruled his country.

"OK, Willie," whispered Max to Morgan when they were a half block away from Boyeros, who waved at them in greeting, "this guy here is one of the top five men in the country."

"That old fart?"

"That old fart, as you call him, *owns* the Bank of Cuba, plus the biggest newspaper on the island, not to mention several thousand miles of farmland. He's the richest man in Cuba. He's also the head of the Partido Conservador. He's so far to the right he makes Joe McCarthy look like Alger Hiss. So play it cool."

"Cool? What do you mean?" said Morgan, who had never heard the word used like that before.

"Cool as in, don't blow your top. Make believe you're a visiting reporter. And for God's sake, don't talk politics!"

"Mi querido Max," my dear Max, were the first words that Morgan heard out of the old man's mouth, a deep rumble of conversation that launched into a stream of Spanish sonorities that left Morgan stranded in ignorance. He noticed that the old man was taller than he, unusual among the Cubans he'd seen so far, that his suit draped perfectly on his still-powerful body, and that his fingernails were varnished, that is, he was a complete picture of urbane gentility, especially standing next to tiny, rumpled Max.

Morgan smiled and disappeared into his mind, thinking of Laura and his future and how he had agreed to her scheme, and maybe it wasn't such a good plan after all and he might pull out of it, but then again maybe not, for what did have to lose, and maybe it would work after all, and in any case all his life there had only been one thing he had truly been good at, and that was killing, but how someone could make a living doing that in civilian life was beyond him, and didn't it sound funny to make a living by taking lives, but that's what marines do, and that's what he was, and how will we do it and where will the boat be when we do it, all these plans have to be finalized, she didn't even have any accurate information, and I hope she has it all this afternoon as she said she would because otherwise . . .

"This is my friend William Morgan, *Coronel,"* said Max in English, breaking into Morgan's train of thought. "He's a reporter for the *Albany Times,* here on vacation."

"Mr. Morgan," said Boyeros, tingling with pleasure when he shook Morgan's callused hand and realized his hunch was right and that this beefy GI was no more a journalist than Boyeros was a ditch digger. Morgan was too manly and Max was no *maricón,* so Boyeros knew it had to be agency business. It was perfect, just perfect. What was that word he saw in Hesse the other day? *Serendipitous,* that's it. Serendipitous.

"It is a pleasure," added Boyeros in a clipped Connecticut accent, modulated by the occasional open vowels of Cuban Spanish. "Are you here on a working vacation, or just working on your vacation?"

"The latter, sir," said Morgan, smiling brightly.

"In that case, perhaps you will allow me to show you the nicer side of my country. I am sure you have heard about the little problems we have been having lately."

"Yes sir. Kind of hard to ignore."

"Perfectly understandable. Part of the local color, you know. In Cuba what others settle with ballots we settle with bullets."

He laughed slightly, as did Max and Morgan. What is the old man up to? Max asked himself. I wonder if he's ready to come over to our side.

"I'm not sure William wants to see too much of that, *Coronel.*"

"Of course not. I tell you what. We are having a little ball at the yacht club tomorrow, in honor of the president having survived the fireworks at the palace the other day."

Max was frankly stunned. "Batista? At the Havana Yacht Club? I thought he'd been blackballed."

"Yes, well, this is the mulatto ball," chortled Boyeros. "No, seriously, he has been turned down for membership in the club. This is only a special occasion. As our guest, you understand."

"Not your fellow member."

"Oh, heavens, no. In any case, why don't you two boys come around to my house first and then we can all go in my limousine? Would eight o' clock be all right?"

"Sounds fine to me. Right, William?"

"Yes sir, Mr. Boyeros. Thank you for the invitation."

"Don't mention it. I just want to make sure you go away with a memory of the real Cuba."

Boyeros shook hands with both men and strode away, happily going over the myriad possibilities someone like Morgan could work in his scheme. Abruptly, he wheeled around, looked back at Max and Morgan a few yards away.

"Oh, and Max?"

"Yes, Mr. Boyeros."

"It's a formal affair. Black tie, you understand?"

"Yes sir. We understand."

Chapter

9

Heavyset, with bad skin peeling from sunburn, a scraggly gray beard, and eyes dimmed by one too many daiquiris, the old Yanqui sat at the counter of the bar, noisily crunching fried shrimp heads with his short worn-out teeth. He exuded wasted strength, selfishness, and a misguided compassion poisonously directed at the self. He slurped the inside of the crustacean, only too aware of how the handful of drinkers at the bar looked down on his porcine manners, flipping their attitude back in their faces, growing progressively messier, downing the pitcher of daiquiris as though it were holy water that would expel the familiar demons from his insides.

The old man was making a day out of his drinking, and he felt better for it than he had felt in a long time. He knew that later he'd wind up in one of the cheap brothels down Virtudes, where he'd again attempt to make flesh follow desire, and he was soothing himself ahead of time for the humiliations he also knew he would endure. He thought, without much regret, he might again be reduced to the role of spectator, watching his priapic companion penetrate the three laughing and admiring twelve-year-olds, entering and departing from each proffered pussy like a laughing, shuddering bee lunging from bud to flower to bud until the aging actor reedemed his reputation as the ultimate swordsman of modern film and ejaculated not once or twice but three times, once inside each girl, depositing his yellow wastrel sperm like his offering to the gods of youth and desire, all while the dusky whore was still on her knees, trying to coax the old man into his first erection of the week.

It was all enough to drive anyone to drink, and that's what the Yanqui was proceeding to do, good manners be damned. He had never cared much for propriety, and it was certainly too late to start now, not when he had so little time left to his allotment. Wasn't he the best? Wasn't he the father of modern literature? Had he not won that prize which warped his life, like all enthroning crowns do? He could do what he wanted, and this was what he wanted. He was only one sorry step from God, and like God, he commanded, in his own mind, the old hack to enter through the door so they could really begin to drink in earnest.

The door to the Bodeguita del Medio swung open. The old man swiveled in his seat, expecting the rangy Tasmanian to burst forth. But he saw only yet another American with another Cuban *chiquita*. Country of whores, the old man thought and returned to his pitcher.

Morgan, who had walked in hand in hand with Laura, looked quickly around the small, dark premises, the walls covered with drawings and graffiti left by the thousands of intoxicated visitors. At that hour in the afternoon the place was practically empty, the small, white-cloth-draped tables bereft of their usual company of sunburned tourists and their local hunters. A portly waiter led the couple to a small booth in the back, as Laura had requested. Morgan ordered a Hatuey, Laura a Pepsi-Cola.

"Why here?" he asked her again. Laura, nerves in knots, took out a pack of Regalías, the kind with the cigarettes packed upside down. She tapped out a cigarette, lit it from the small red votive candle at the table, and promptly coughed from the smoke.

"I tell you before, more tourists is more good, no suspicion then. We wait for tall man, black hair. He ask you from Baltimore. OK?"

"OK," answered Morgan, "OK." This sure is nervy, he thought.

Just then he recognized the old man at the bar, who chose that moment to let out a deep belch. At one time in the service, during one of his frequent stays in the brig, Morgan had been left with no other company save for one of the old man's books, the story of a charter fishing boat captain in Cuba and Key West. Morgan had never been fond of reading or writing, for the reality that writers wrote about never corresponded to his own; it was always filtered, distant, detached, those words which mean the author is keeping himself at arm's length from the subject because he doesn't understand him or, worse, he has no idea what his character's reality is all about. But this book of the old man's was different.

From the beginning Morgan understood clearly how the book's captain felt. He could see his dilemma in choosing between his family and his conscience, the tragedy of the things he had to do to get money for his wife and kids waiting for him in that shack back in Key West. He could even see why he had to kill the Chink and why he'd even had to be ready to kill his friend the old rummie as well. This book was like a real man's life, the way things were, not some imaginary concoction by some Brooklyn Heights or Park Avenue scrivener thinking he's telling you the world when all he's writing is tales out of school. It was a life you knew the author had felt and experienced—you knew that he had practically written it at his kitchen table in the cool hours of dawn, when the truth always comes out of the hearts of men.

Later on Morgan had been surprised to hear that the book he'd liked so much wasn't even considered one of the old man's best, that he had written many others, about the First World War, about Americans in Paris, about Spain and Africa, about places where men go to do men's things. He had picked up some of the others and, although he was disappointed that they never came close to the immediacy of that first book, he would always be grateful to the old man for having put him inside the mind of that captain, for allowing him to see through the captain's eyes, hear his voice, and in the spaces in between, telling us of how he had lived and how he had died and what it all meant. In fact, that book was the first time he had heard of Cuba outside of geography class and probably the reason why he had quickly become friends with Nicky Ramírez to begin with.

※ ※ ※

"Excuse me a minute," said Morgan to Laura, getting up.

She tugged at his shirt. "Where you go?"

"I have to pay my respects."

Morgan walked reverentially up to the bar and watched in silence as the old man tore off yet another crustacean head, fragments of batter-covered shrimp bristling from the old gray beard.

"And what do you want?" barked the old man, swilling down the dregs of the pitcher and gesturing at the bartender for a third one.

Morgan felt hurled back to fourth grade, when he had spotted Jack Dempsey buying a pair of antler gloves at a store in Milan, just weeks after beating Schmeling, and all that little William could do was point and stare speechless at that colossus of a man threading his way through the crowd of shoppers.

"What happened, Cuban girl sucked your tongue off?"

That wasn't necessary, thought Morgan. But I am probably intruding. I will make it quick.

"I just wanted to tell you, sir, that I think you're a great writer, sir, and that your books have given me much, many moments of enjoyment, sir."

"Well, that's good, that's why I write, for enjoyment. Everybody knows that. Enjoyment for the people. Never mind death, sin, or conscience. It's enjoyment what counts. Where's that fucking daiquiri, Paquito?"

"Coming, Señor Papa," said the bartender, setting the frosty metal pitcher in front of the old man.

"Where you from, sailor?" asked the writer, filling his glass with his lime green poison.

"Not a sailor, sir. Marine. From Ohio, sir."

"Ohio. They don't have Cuban girls over there, now do they, sailor?"

"Marine, sir. And no sir, they don't have any that I am aware of."

"That's good. Because Cuban girls get under your skin, sailor, remember that. Once they're in, they're never out. You understand me?"

"Yes sir."

"So are you a real man?"

"Well, yes sir, I am."

"Then eat one of these. Head, shell, and everything."

Morgan looked dubiously at the mound of fried shrimp on the platter, grabbed one, and bit into it, the crunch of the shell mixing in his mouth with the iodine of the eyes, the tang of the gills, the sweetness of the flesh.

"You like it?" growled the old man.

"It's different. Never tried them this way."

"Cuba has the best shrimp in the world, sailor. Big fat sweet shrimp living at the mouth of rivers up and down the coast. The best marlin too. Is your father still alive, sailor?"

"Marine, sir. Marine sergeant. No sir, he passed away already."

"What did he die of?"

"Heart attack, sir."

"Did it come sudden?"

"I suppose so, sir. He was doing the books at the farm and he fell facedown on the pages. When my mother came in she thought he'd fallen asleep."

"I hope mine comes sudden too. It's an awful thing to pray for your own death, but that's what I pray for every day."

The old man gulped down another glass, then bent his head down, eyes closed, as though invoking the deity in the potent drink to come end his misery.

"I meant to ask you, sir."

"Don't you think you should be getting back to your girl, sailor?"

"Yes sir. Marine, sir, but I want to ask you why don't you write more about Cubans, sir?"

"More about Cubans? What about that goddamn last book about the fisherman. Where the hell did you think he was from? Ohio?"

"No sir. I mean yes sir, but why don't you write about Cuba today, sir, I mean about the revolution, sir."

"Revolution? What revolution?"

"The one going on right now, sir. I'm sure you've seen."

"What I've seen is the same thing I have always seen since I started coming down here thirty years ago, sailor. A bunch of crazy people shooting at each other claiming to do it for the greater good of the people, only to get big and fat and greedy when they take over, if they take over, and become just like the last people that were in. If that's a revolution, my friend, then maybe Al Capone should write their constitution."

"Al Capone is dead, sir. And these people are different. This is like Spain."

"Spain? This is not Spain. Cubans are not Spaniards. These people live for song and dance, Spaniards live for blood and *cojones*. This is all without consequence, sailor. The future of the world is not at stake here like it was in Spain."

"I don't know, sir. They say this Fidel Castro fellow is different, sir. And then there's the Directorio and the others."

"Castro. The Directorio. How long you say you've been in Cuba, sailor?"

"Two weeks, sir."

"Two weeks. And in two weeks you have become a Cuba expert. Let me tell you something about that Castro fellow, sailor. He is a gangster, he was running around with the Tigres of Masferrer in the nineteen forties. He's a protofascist."

"Do you say that from personal experience, sir?"

"As a matter of goddamn fact I goddamn do. We were in an expedition together, Mr. Cuba expert. I'm sure you've heard of Presidente Leónidas Trujillo, generalissimo for life, protector and benefactor of the great neighboring republic of Santo Domingo."

"Sort of."

"Well, friend, sort of. It sort of happens we sort of went out to invade Mr. God Almighty's country in nineteen forty-nine, Mr. Castro and me. And fifteen others with the Caribbean Legion. But you probably never heard of that either, I suppose."

Morgan shook his head, embarrassed more for the old man than for himself, sorry to see what age, drink, and fame had done to him.

"Well, we lost the boat at Cayo Confites and we were stranded for two weeks waiting to get out. I got to know Mr. Castro very well then.

He wanted to be a pitcher for the Senators, and when the scouts turned him down he decided to go into politics, any kind of politics. You know who his political hero is? Mussolini. And you know who his military hero is? Napoleon. And you know what he said about democracy? That it's for the weak and the base hearted. So don't talk to me about this revolution being any different from the ten thousand other revolutions this country has gone through. They're all a bunch of thieves and they never do anything for anybody but themselves."

The old man slurped the rest of his drink, let out another belch.

"Just like that porker Batista. Now go back to your girl and leave me alone, sailor. I got wiser company from this glass than I get from you."

Morgan towered over the old man and he felt like giving it to him then, just one great big knockout punch that would bring him to his senses, that would shake him out of his self-pity, his whining and complaining. But then he took a second look and he saw just another old man, broken-down and on the ropes, going through the motions but knowing that he's already given all he has to give and what's left is just the shell, like the ones he's eating, and he's marking time until the bell finally rings. But he was great once and he should be given his dignity even if he doesn't deserve it.

"You're just old," muttered Morgan, "and you've forgotten."

"What's that you said?" replied the old man, turning savagely on Morgan.

"Nothing, old man, it's all right."

"Pues, tu madre me hace puñetas, maricón," said the old man—your mother jerks me off, faggot—but Morgan was already halfway across the room, back to the table with Laura. He sat down beside her. She took his hand, squeezed it tight.

"He comes here much," said Laura. "Is sad."

"Yes, it's sad," said Morgan. He didn't envy the old man's wealth or fame or even the many books he had written, for he saw it had all become nothing, and Morgan held the world by the hand while the old man had been left empty handed.

The bar doors swung open again. The rangy actor with the fluorescent grin and the pencil-stripe mustache walked blithely through, heading for the old writer at the bar, vigorously clapping him on the back with the fake vivacity of an old Warner Brothers flick. In the heels of the actor entered a lanky white Cuban with sallow skin, brilliantined hair, and hooded eyes. He was sweating profusely, patches of perspiration spreading up and down his dark blue cotton jacket. He spotted Laura at the booth, then walked to the bar, where he touched the sides of his hair in the counter mirror. Mustering his courage, he ambled over to Morgan's table, unlit cigarette in his mouth.

"Got a light, mister?" said the Cuban, in English.

"Sure," said Morgan, flicking his Zippo open. The Cuban's cigarette jerked in his mouth from excitement. The man swallowed a mouthful of smoke, coughed.

"You from Baltimore?" he asked.

"Yeah," replied Morgan, even as Laura squeezed his hand.

"I thought so," said the Cuban, his cigarette now doing figure eights from nerves.

✼ ✼ ✼

The bar doors swung open again. In the doorway stood three men, two black, one white, in loud sport shirts and dark pants, looking like any other three Cubans out for their afternoon *cerveza* except for the automatic pistols bulking up at their waistbands and the automatic carbines they held in their hand. Their eyes fell on Morgan's table.

"*Oye, tú, blanquito, ven acá—*" hey you, whitey, come over here—said the leading man, short, ebony black, with a round petulant gash of a mouth.

"*Esta noche, el Finlay,*" whispered the Cuban at Morgan's table, then scuttled into the kitchen a few feet away. The three men ran after him. Morgan yanked Laura by the hand, pushed the table out of the booth, and they both ran out of the restaurant even as they heard the shattering of glass, a great bellowing, and the spray of bullets thump-thumping when the men sliced up the body at close range.

At the bar the old man raised a glass to his own reflection, the swarms of bullets flying all around him, while his friend and drinking buddy, the heroic actor, cowered behind the counter, heaving his gin fizz and eggs Benedict breakfast.

"*Viva la muerte!*" toasted the old man. "*Que viva!*"

Jeff Dunphy, Max Weinberg's case officer, sat in his office in the American embassy, listlessly whittling a piece of yellow pine into the outline of the beak-nosed man sitting in the chair in front of his desk. As the shavings fell in the wastebasket between his legs, Dunphy debriefed his visitor, whose nasal twang was compounded by a thick Cuban accent and a magnificent head cold.

"The situation in the hill is like that," said the visitor, blowing his nose into the starched handkerchief no male Cuban was ever without. "These guys, they are very brave men, but they are very disorganized. We lost the supplies you dropped at Caibarién two times already."

"So the guns never got there either?" asked Dunphy, turning his blade ever so slightly to carve out the small bump in the man's nose.

"Never saw them. Who you pay to take them?"

"The usual."

"Martínez Callao and the Old Man?"

Dunphy nodded, proceeding to carve out the man's dimpled chin.

"That's no good," said the visitor. "They work with Castillo. They turn around and sell to Fidel."

The mere mention of the name was enough to shatter Dunphy's composure, his blade going off at an angle, destroying the curve of the nose and spoiling the composition.

"I don't know why he wants to buy them. We send him enough as it is," said Dunphy.

"Not for what he wants. Fidel thinks he got to have an army, not just fifty people up there. He wants to prepare for big fight."

"That will never happen," said Dunphy, taking out another piece of wood from the drawer and starting his carving all over. This time he decided on an easier, more familiar shape. "The fight is going to be won here in the cities, in the plains, not the hills. He's just there for show."

"He don't think so. He thinks he can come west like Gómez and Maceo against the *españoles*."

"He's crazy."

"You know Fidel."

"I don't know why we waste our time with him."

Max entered the room at that moment. As always he was struck by the easy air of collegiality that prevailed in Dunphy's office, with its Ozark quilt on one wall, Miró lithograph on another, potted plants, and blond Scandinavian furniture, as if he had stepped into the office of some tenured department head in some progressive East Coast college, a Bennington or a Sarah Lawrence. Dunphy glanced up, waved Max in.

"Sorry. I was held up by the crush of Kennedy fans downstairs."

"Ah, yes, the senator from Massachusetts. Hopeless liberal."

"Better than Stevenson."

"Anybody's better than that pinko egghead."

Max shook hands with Dunphy, noticing the piece of wood about to be carved. I wonder if he ever keeps one of those, thought Max.

The little man stood up, erect as only short wiry men can be.

"This is Roger Izquierdo. Max Weinberg," said Dunphy.

The men shook quickly, firmly, taking stock of each other. Max saw a little olive-skinned man with darting green eyes, thinning black hair, and a hawklike nose that seemed borrowed from a Florentine coin. Izquierdo saw a haggard, unshaven wreck in a wrinkled gray suit, with light brown hair, deep blue eyes, and a bulbous nose above worried thin lips.

"*Mucho gusto. Usted es hebreo?*"— a pleasure, are you Hebrew?—asked Roger.

"*Sí, Papá era polaco, yo nací aquí*"—yes, I was born here, but Dad was Polish—replied Max, calling himself by the Cuban appellation for all European Jews, regardless of whether they came from Warsaw, Tirana, or Hamburg.

"I thought so," said Izquierdo, switching to English. "When I hear you on the radio, I am always surprised by your *sutileza*, how you say?"

"Subtlety," tossed Dunphy without looking up, carving out the crescent-shaped figure in a few flicks of his wrist, proceeding to the broad indented eastern base of the figure.

"Yes, that is so," continued Izquierdo. "Your analysis of the coming elections, for example. When I heard on the radio how you speculate on the successor to Batista, I say to myself, This is Hebrew thinking, you know, split the hair ten times. But good. Like Salomón."

"Well, thank you, *muchísimas gracias,*" said Max, taking the veiled condescension as a compliment. Back in Washington, where his Brooklyn-born mother had raised him, Max would have taken the comment as an insult, but it was different in Cuba. He knew how Cubans appreciated arcane logic, the music of the spheres being their favorite tune after the national anthem. He never could decide if that was a relic of Roman law, with its endless disquisitions on the degree of consanguinity required for paternal property claims, or if it was a legacy of the large, unacknowledged draught of Jewish blood most Cubans carried unbeknownst to themselves. Max knew that Cuba had been a favorite hiding place for the Marranos, the converted but still-persecuted Spanish Jews of the sixteenth century who escaped the long arm of the Inquisition by settling in the remote balmy island. Such a large influx couldn't help but affect the national psyche, that love of enterprise and learning, that quicksilver wit and droopy sentimentality which all the children of Sepharad had in common with Cubans.

"Roger here just got back from the Sierra del Escambray," said Dunphy, carving still, proceeding now to the southern coast, making a sharp indentation along the heel of a shoe-shaped peninsula.

"As you know, we have been giving a hand to some of the other anti-Batista forces to make sure that Castro and his boys don't get all the goodies when the time comes, if it comes," Dunphy went on. "Like you Cubans say, putting the spoon in the soup," he added, his gray eyes squinting with pleasure.

Max and Roger both gave him strained smiles. What a poltroon, thought Max. The Soviets must be like this, lean, mean, and condescending.

"Who are these men? Why didn't they go to the Sierra with Fidel?" asked Max.

"Some of them are survivors of the attack on the palace. Others couldn't make it to Oriente so they just headed for the nearest hills."

"Do they have any training?"

"That's the problem. While many of them are highly qualified for urban actions, they are all a little lost out in the bush. They took off without supplies or many weapons. From what I understand, some of them had never been out in the jungle before, right, Roger?"

"That is correct. Their morale is very bad," said Roger, shaking his head. "They are not *comunistas* but they think only *comunistas* get support.

From the party, the people, so on. Is a very bad situation. We have to help."

"How many men are we talking about?" asked Max.

"I think about fifteen. Eloy Gutiérrez Menoyo showed up with some weapons, but is not enough. They need boots, uniforms, stuff to be nucleus of the future fighting force," said Roger.

"And if we don't help them, the nucleus is going to give up and come home to *Mami, Papi,* and the *novia,* you know?" said Dunphy, finishing his carving.

"What can we do?" asked Max.

"Well, I remembered that fellow you've been following, that army sergeant," said Dunphy, examining his handiwork, realizing he had carved a perfect likeness.

"Marine. Marine sergeant William Morgan."

"That one. You had him in with the Fernández group, right?"

"That's right. He made a good connection there. I'm not sure how much control we have over the Fernández, but I believe they're going to be asking for his expertise pretty soon."

"What do you mean we don't have control?"

"Just like we had no control over the palace, did we? Sometimes they spring things on us. I'm trying to make sure it doesn't happen again. My contact tells me they're planning some action, he's not sure what. I don't think it's that big, but you never know."

"Well, you better get that G.I. out of there."

"What do you mean?"

"We think he'd be better suited out in the hills. Those guys could use a trainer. Someone to whip them into shape, teach these city boys all about weapons and fighting."

"You want to send him into the Escambray?" asked Max incredulously.

"That's right. Roger here will be his guide up the trail, make sure he finds them. We'll give them a little more support as soon as he gets there."

"And if he doesn't want to go?"

"You'll have to convince him, then, won't you? That's part of your job. I'm sure you'll find a way," said Dunphy.

Max looked at both men, shook his head in wonder at the outrageousness of their plan. Fine. Let them fall on on their own swords, he thought. William will survive. Who knows, he might even like it.

"Ok. You're calling the shots."

"I am. So that's what it will be," said Dunphy, getting up to shake their hands. "Let's get on with it. Let me know as soon as he leaves town."

After the two Cubans had departed, Dunphy picked up his carving, turning it this way and that, proud of the likeness of the island of Cuba he had carved, down to the little westernmost peninsula of Guana-hacabibes. I really should do more of these, he thought, then broke the carving in two and tossed it in the wastebasket.

Morgan drove left onto Galiano then left again onto Zanja, heading for the Finlay Theater. Laura sat silently by his side, watching the buildings go by, the hand-painted Spanish-language signs for beer, *churros, fritas,* stores, and schools replaced by large neon signs in garish yellows, reds, and blues, their lettering half in Latin script and half in Chinese ideograms. The crowds on these sidewalks—for it seemed to Morgan every sidewalk in Havana was always packed with a pressing throng, a restless body of prowlers that never ceased to make its rounds no matter the time of day or night—these crowds now showed other colors in this new neighborhood Laura and Morgan were approaching.

You could still see the usual olive-skinned Cubans arguing on the street, waving their hands like orators on some soapbox, the blacks and mulattoes gliding by as though inviting onlookers to join them for a walk. But there were also many spare, somber-faced Asian men and women traipsing down the narrow streets in silk jackets and black pants, entering and exiting the many small businesses with names like Café La Perla de Cuba, Restaurante Cantón, Farmacia Formosa. Standing out against them all were the ruddy-complected white-suited sailors from American and European ships out to taste the pleasures of the harbor, promenading in groups of three or four, drunkenly standing on the cobblestoned streets, crowding entranceways to houses with balconies where women in slips and nightgowns lingered, waiting for the right offer.

Morgan veered right and down an alley so narrow that pedestrians pressed against the wall to let the Buick pass.

"Is that where the place is?" He pointed with his chin.

"Yes, there," she said, pensively pushing back a lock of her russet-tinged hair that had fallen on her forehead. God, but she is beautiful, thought Morgan.

Morgan looked her over and his love was decked with admiration as Laura stared ahead, calm, as though they had just come from the senior prom and were headed for the malt shop. Yes, Cuban women are different. They're the hope of this country. Maybe even my own.

He parked the yellow Buick in an empty lot on Zanja, two blocks from the theater. He threw a quarter at a black teenager to keep an eye on the car and, wrapping his arm around Laura's waist, walked up the crowded, half-lit street.

"Who is going to be here tonight?" he asked her.

"I don't know," she said, placing her arm around his waist as well.

"Then how will you know you're in the right place?"

"Easy. Is the Finlay. I ask for a person."

"Who?"

"Genovevo," she whispered after glancing around to make sure no one heard.

"Excuse me?"

"Genovevo," she repeated, breathing in his ear, kissing his earlobe.

"Do you know what he looks like, this Henoh guy?"

"Oh yes. Everybody know him. He Mr. Chinatown."

A blue Ford behind them slowed down, letting a blind beggar with his helper cross the street behind the wedge-shaped park. The Ford swung to the right and stopped beneath a canopy of trees across from the old police station a block away from the Finlay. The driver watched Morgan and Laura enter the lobby of the Finlay, then lit a cigarette and settled in for what he knew would be a long, boring wait.

※ ※ ※

The lobby cards caught Morgan's eye as he waited while Laura talked to the ticket seller in the pagoda-shaped booth. Lifted from Clifton's Burlesque in Pittsburgh, they showed a bevy of long-legged bosomy beauties from the 1930s—all white, all American—in a succession of poses with spangles, pompoms, and sparkles for a long complex spectacle inspired by the fleshy extravaganzas of a Billy Rose. Revealing yet chaste, high-mindedly lubricious, they showed the flesh as a field of joy, all bright smiles and big ass, the gifts that God, nature, and good nutrition had bestowed on the young females of the North. Morgan looked then at the flirty mulatto whores posted outside the theater, with their tight dresses that showed no flesh but promised so much lust encased inside, the defiant way they would accost the men wandering down the sidewalk, and he saw as never before the universe of difference between his country's scrubbed, aseptic beauties and Cuba's fragrant women, who lived on the surface of their tawny skin.

Laura returned, jerked her head at the long velveteen curtains framing the entrance to the theater.

"Is OK. They wait for us."

The scrim over the stage read *En la Vieja Rusia,* and even though Morgan did not know that *vieja* meant "old," the few moments he spent in the darkness adjusting his eyes were enough to let him peer into the heart of the piece. Six half-naked girls with fake ermine belts and hats writhed on a large brass bed, where an immense mulatto man— Pushkin's brother?—his ratty fur coat open, serviced each and every one who came near his prodigiously large member. Morgan thought the man's dick must be as long as his forearm, but he told himself that was impossible, nobody could be that big—just as it was hard to believe that anyone could be as unmoved by the fleshy spectacle as that mulatto man, his face as much an expression of bottomless boredom as that of the stamp press operator punching holes in sheet metal.

Out of the darkness a short man with a spotlight approached Morgan and Laura.

"*La luz?*"—the light?—he asked.

"*La escalera,*" answered Laura. The stairs.

"*Síganme.*" Follow me.

The circle of white light danced ahead of them, the man leading their way down the side aisle of the theater. Morgan stole a last look back at the audience and saw a collection of dark, saddened faces, all in utmost concentration on the stage, observing with devotion the sacred spectacles of the flesh. Only in the back were there a few couples, Americans all, jeering and laughing at the incongruous solemnity of the occasion.

The man slid open yet another velveteen curtain. Morgan and Laura followed him down a narrow winding staircase illuminated by murky yellow lightbulbs encrusted with the dessicated bodies of tiny flying insects. The stairs smelled of dampness, wood, and cat piss. At the bottom the man turned to Morgan and Laura. His skin was the pallor of old ivory, his face round and hairless—no eyebrows, beard, or hair, not even eyelashes. His black suit made his face glow, his roly-poly body a sorcerer's idea of a mortician's apprentice. Only the squinty almond shape of his washed-out eyes revealed the dash of Chinese blood in him.

"You know who Gus Hall is?" he asked in a vaguely Eastern European accent.

"Sure. The head of the American commies."

"That's right. You're not a red, are you?"

"I hate communism."

"That's good. We hate them too, remember that. I was born in Shanghai. I saw what they did in forty-eight. No matter what you hear, we don't want commies here."

"I'll remember."

"Tell Uncle Sam we need his help. We are his children too."

"I'll remember that too."

"Good. Everybody's inside."

He nodded at the scratched wooden door. Laura bent down, kissed him on his hairless cheek.

"*Gracias,* Genovevo," she said.

"*Por mi Cuba, todo*"—everything for my Cuba—he said, and he spun on his heels and trucked up the stairs.

Laura knocked. The door swung partially open, revealing a young dark-haired white woman in flats, chartreuse capri pants, white blouse, and sunglasses, the picture of a Havana socialite out for a spin at Varadero Beach, except for the submachine gun hanging from a strap around her shoulder. She pointed the weapon at Morgan and Laura.

"*La escalera da a la luz*"—the stairs lead to the light—said Laura quickly. The young woman turned on a high-voltage smile—canasta time at the country club.

"Come in, come in, you're late," she said, opening the door wide.

Faces looked up from a set of architectural plans spread upon a table. All white, all young, all male except for the other woman in the group, whose gentian eyes sparkled even in the dingy light of the converted closet.

"Mr. Morgan. Small world," said Violeta Ramírez y Caballero, sister of the late Licenciado Nicolás Esteban Ramírez y Caballero, the ballsiest spic Morgan ever knew.

She smiled.

Morgan smiled back.

❊ ❊ ❊

Outside the Finlay, the driver of the blue Ford listened aimlessly to the Vicentico Valdés ballad blaring from the jukebox at the bar across the street:

Voy a escalar la montaña
Hasta la cumbre he de subir

The Great American

Y si la cima es de hielo
Con mi amor
Yo la puedo fundir.
Quizás si escale la montaña
Me querrás a mí.

I will go and climb the mountain
And to its peak I will climb
And if its crest is made of ice
With my love
I'll melt it down.
Maybe if I climb that mountain
You will then love me.

He tossed his cigarette out to the street, watching the big-breasted whore with the long flowing black hair wiggle her butt once more for yet another drunk *yanqui* sailor stumbling by. The driver smiled and was grateful that his days of fishing for sex in the murky waters of Zanja had ended with his marriage to Filomena. Not that he didn't feel temptation—he was a man, after all—but it was so much easier now. One woman, one bed, one job. That was the way he wanted it. Stricture, conformity, devotion. That's how you make your way in this business. Even so, maybe one of these nights he'd give it a tumble again. After all, who would know, anyhow? Just look at that one in the yellow dress with the *café con leche* skin. *Qué rica mulata;* why, she probably . . .

Morgan and Laura came out of the theater. The driver sat up, looked at his watch, wrote down the time. Two hours inside. That was no show. That was something else. He waited until they climbed into a cab, then he started the Ford and trailed them discreetly a half block's distance away, the shadow of death swiftly trailing.

Morgan sank his face into Laura's perfumed hair, splayed out on the threadbare pillowcase. She slept still, her breathing even and regular in the early morning hours. Outside the green shutters, Havana's wake-up traffic hummed and rattled, venting its dull roar. Here inside, all was quiet in the luminous, expectant glow of a new day. On the ceiling, the city's violent sunlight painted patterns of shadow and light from the shutters' slats.

Morgan turned on his back and counted the alternating bands, then multiplied them by two, then counted all the objects in the room of the posada, then multiplied those by two as well, then divided them by ten in a willful attempt to flush out the worries from his mind. It had worked before in the trenches of Korea, in the trembling hours before the Chinese onslaught. But he was younger then and he wasn't in love then. And love can make one's mind stick uncomfortably close to reality.

His eyes fell on the two hand grenades and the .45 with soft lead bullets that he had received as tokens of his loyalty to the cinnamon-skinned obsession by his side.

It was a simple plan, and he had liked it because of its simplicity. The best ideas were like that, so starkly simple that you could see right through them, like a crystal finely carved, and thus quickly detect the fatal flaw, if any. Well, there was none except for one, and that was a beauty. It was splendiferous in its wrongfulness, so big that no one mentioned it, because it wasn't necessary; everybody knew. It was simply there, like the sun, like the moon, like darkness and death, an unavoidable end to an impossible job.

That's the price, isn't it? That's the reason for all this passion, that's how come they're all like this. And you too, Willie, my good amigo, you too are in on this. Oh boy, but have I gotten myself into a good one. Oh boy.

He asked himself how it was possible that he had fallen into this madness, but he knew that the answer was lying right there by his side, softly breathing in the darkened room. He'd fallen for her, all right, fallen in ways he never would have thought possible. He wondered briefly: if their destinies had not been brought together in this pressure cooker of emotions but in a clean, well-ordered country where feeling knew its place and the future sat expectantly with a pleasant smile upon its face, would he have craved her the way he did last night, when he couldn't get enough of her, when he felt compelled to undress her so slowly, teasingly, achingly, that he felt his whole body was going to explode?

Morgan had trembled when he laid the gun and the grenades on the scarred dresser, Laura staring out the shutters at the night scenes in the harbor, the yellow light of a bare lightbulb falling like a golden mantle over her tawny skin.

He had walked up to her, kissed her neck, cupped her breasts with his hands, brought her to him, her buttocks pushed tight against his crotch. Then she had turned and kissed him, her tongue darting quickly into his mouth, seeking the old friend from before who touched and embraced just as their bodies did. Morgan shuddered as she loosened her hair, and he undid one by one the tiny cloth-covered buttons of her dress, which fell to the floor in a puddle of bright fabric, and she stepped out of it and he gloried in her sight.

He went down on his knees and kissed her belly button—the little knob of folded flesh that had fed her in her mother's womb—pressing it to his lips as though he too wanted to draw life from that source. But he knew life was farther down, in the valley down below, under the flowered rayon panties that he now proceeded to unroll, revealing the prominent mound, barely covered by short tendrils of soft russet hair, smelling of sex and brine and the beginning and the end, and he ran his tongue down into the groove and felt the hard bit of flesh in the furrow sticking out, pink and determined to scream out its desire. He ran his hand up to her breasts as she undid her bra strap and he could feel her nipples at fierce attention as he sank his face into her sex which opened up with a glistening sigh. She let out a moan and his tongue darted in and out but then she pulled him up and kissed him and on his tongue he carried her taste to her mouth. They both stumbled on the bed which gave a sigh of welcome and she quickly undressed him and he felt drunk with the smell of their desire as he entered her and the time flew gloriously fast and sometime somehow after they had joined and entwined and felt the light explode inside their head a lonesome boat's whistle blew deep and hollow the sound of its departure and night's sweet sleep fell on them, a robe of kisses on their passion.

But now the light of day pounced irresistibly into the room and only thirteen hours stretched between Morgan and the sealing of his fate. He knew he could back out at any time, that he could get dressed and walk out on their crazy scheme. But he also knew Laura would never come with him, that she would keep to her secret meetings, her plans, her singleminded pursuit of her elusive freedom until she or this government died, and that he could not allow. He knew he was like the bear in the trap, and he wasn't sure he had the guts to chew off his own limb to gain his freedom.

Freedom to do what? he asked himself—freedom to be lost, freedom to be AWOL, freedom to have no binds or relations or anything tying me down to anything? Freedom to be lonely? No, that's a freedom I won't choose. What I have to do is find a way to make it work. It's not true that there is no way out. There is always a way out. Maybe not for everyone, but certainly for me and her. I'm sure there's a way out. I'll find it yet.

So he lit a cigarette and watched the gray smoke rise against the yolk yellow plaster walls while he plotted his way out of the maze of politics and desire.

The main thing was the location. He had been shown the plans of the club, filched by one of the plotters from his father's firm, which had built the stucture twenty years before. Morgan had committed the blueprints to memory, and now he brought the blues back to his mind's eye, pinpointing the exact location of the stage, the path out of the kitchen, the planned escape route.

"We'll have a boat waiting," Violeta had said. "You should be in Miami within three hours with no problem."

"The two of us," said Morgan, pointing at Laura. She gazed at him intently, her look a mix of love and admiration, then stretched her hand and covered his large callused palm with her long narrow fingers. Violeta nodded.

"Naturally. We'll be looking out for her too. There will be chaos, but it will be good chaos. Then we will proceed with the other plans."

"What are they?" he asked, stepping back from the dingy circle of light.

"We take over the government. Camp Columbia, the Presidential Palace, the Ministry of Communications. We have commando squads that will sweep throughout the city, ready to take over in the name of the Directorio. It will be a new day for Cuba. A day that you will usher in. Are you not proud?"

Morgan looked quickly at the motley crew around him, and he wondered if any of them had the balls, the all-demanding passion and drive, to really overturn a government. There was the debutante who had opened the door, who leaned back in her chair, filing her nails, machine gun propped against the wall next to her. Then there were two anemic-looking men in their thirties who smelled of dusty files and long hours at display counters: a short, thin, hook-nosed man who back home would have been mistaken for an Assyrian selling snake oil to lonely farmers' wives; a sandy-haired, beefy, collegiate-sports-star type, the one who'd swiped the blueprints. And then there was Violeta, smiling ever so politely like the hostess at the party when the stripper pops out of her husband's birthday cake.

They're nuts. And I'm even crazier for being in with them. Batista's people will eat them for breakfast before they catch on to what's happened. They really think that to want is to succeed.

"You fellows just tried that two weeks ago. Your brother Nicky was killed then, at the palace. What makes you think this can work now?"

"We are fewer in number, so there is less chance of someone denouncing us to the government. No one suspects it. And no one will expect lighting to strike twice so close."

"You better hope Batista's not a farmer, because any farmer knows lightning always strikes three and four times in the same spot when there's a storm."

The sports captain opened his massive arms, pounded the table. "I told you we shouldn't bring in this Americano," he said in Spanish to Violeta. "They're always the same, criticizing everything we do, like they're better than we are. We don't need this attitude. I move that we eliminate him right now."

Morgan watched the boy make his argument with sweeping gestures and harsh tones, and though he didn't understand the particulars, he could tell they were passing judgment on him. He glanced quickly at Laura, who squeezed his hand anxiously but did not say a word.

"What's on Junior's mind?" he asked Violeta. She looked up with a smile, amused by Morgan.

"He thinks you're less than enthusiastic about our plan."

"You bet I am. I don't know anything about how you're going to take over afterwards, but when it comes to this action, you are dead in the water already. You haven't made allowances for extra security, for an alternate escape route, or for any reinforcements if needed. You are setting up another suicide mission. I don't know that I want to be involved with that."

"That's it, that's it," said the boy in English, getting out of his chair. "See what I mean? You are no good, mister!"

Violeta barked an order at the all-star, who frowned but sat down, fidgeting. She turned to Morgan.

"If that's what you think, how would you make it better?"

Morgan examined the prints, noticed the means of ingress and egress, the number of places where security could be placed, and realized there was no way out of the building by the usual exits.

"It's suicide unless you can get out this way." He pointed at the kitchen. "Where does this lead?"

The boy looked at the plans. "Is a passage to the *sótano.*"

"The cellar," said Ramírez's sister.

"The wine bottles, they are there," added the boy.

"Is that a door?" asked Morgan.

"Yes. It go to the alley next to garage," said the boy. "But this is impossible. It was closed long time ago. Many robberies. A big lock."

"How big?"

The boy made a fist.

"You have any grenades?"

The boy suddenly smiled, truth dawning on his dewy features.

"Por supuesto." Of course.

But it's not as easy as that, thought Morgan in bed. I wish it were. Even if we can carry it out. Of course, who's going to suspect? That part itself is fairly easy, if we manage to get close to him. But if security does the job it should, it will be a touch-and-go affair. From the main ballroom to the service bay. From there to the kitchen. From the kitchen down the steps to the cellar. Finally that door, then go outside and hope the street has not been blocked off. Then make it out to the boatyard. Start the boat. Take it out past the harbor police. Past the coast guard. Past the air force. All the way over choppy seas to Miami. Where I'll be arrested if I slip into port. Either for murder or for going AWOL. Some trip. Some choice. Of course, I could just go and take my punishment right now. I bet you I could just walk into the American embassy right now, turn myself in, and this whole thing would be over. They'd send me to Chillicothe. Do a couple of years hard time, and I'd be out with a dishonorable discharge, but who'd give a rat's fuck? I'd be alive.

You know that's not what you are here to do, said Morgan to himself, while the bells of a church nearby tolled for the morning Mass.

You came here to get away from the mess that you made of your life. Here you have a chance to change history, to be something different, someone new. To bring a ray of hope to these people. A chance at liberty.

Come off it, he told himself. You don't really care for Cubans; you don't even know them. There's only one reason why you're doing this, and she's lying right beside you right now. No, that's not right. Don't try to mix me up with your scheming. I'm not going to think less of what I do because I love her. She was the cause, she was the door, but I think what they're trying to do right now is right. I do. Yes, but it's so much nicer to be righteous when you have a pretty piece of ass to go along with it. Stop that! Stop thinking those things! She is not a piece of ass. She means the world to me.

Laura stirred at that moment. A ray of sunlight crept down the wall and illumined her face. Morgan examined the slender lips, the long narrow nose, the hooded oval eyes, the sliver of eyebrows, the barely visible scar down the middle of her forehead like the sign of a marked woman. Her tawny skin glowed from the warmth of the bed; the headiness of her perfume, mixed with her own smell, made Morgan dizzy with renewed desire.

No, he told himself, you cannot let her down. Or yourself. You have chosen your path. Now walk down it like a man. No matter what happens, it is yours, freely chosen. And if it is the end? So be it. It comes to us all sometime. Rarely do we have the choice of how to exit. And if this turns out to be the exit, you will be going for something worthwhile. Not for a paycheck or a career, but for love, William. Remember that. For love. But don't think like that. You will live. You will live.

Laura opened her eyes, her lips creased into a smile.

"Buenos días, mi amor," she said, throwing her arms around him.

"Buenos días," answered Morgan, losing himself in her hair and wishing the moment would never end.

"Te quiero," she said.

"I love you too" he answered, as the bells of the church sounded once more for morning Mass.

Chapter

13

Still in his bathrobe, Carlos Boyeros y Ordóñez stirred the last of his *mojito,* the crushed mint leaves clumped at the bottom of his highball glass, their aromatic sweetness having infused the clear white rum. He did not normally drink alcohol alone, much less outside his meals, but on this occasion he felt the need to fortify himself for the evening's performance.

President Batista; the American ambassador with the young U.S. senator, Kennedy, and his wife; Prime Minister Conte Aguero; the Hodges and Simmons families; assorted business leaders of the American, British, and Canadian colonies in Cuba—all these and more were gathering for the *homenaje,* the homage to Batista for having survived the attack on the palace. Havana had become a grotesque comedy of manners, and Boyeros had his part to play, which the alcohol made at least a little more tolerable.

Everyone he knew wanted Batista out, but everybody, including Boyeros himself, cozied up to him, like addicts around their supplier. The whole country was like that. Didn't a quarter million people show up in mass at the Plaza de la República to celebrate Batista's survival? It wasn't that he was so loved, decided Boyeros; it was that everyone was afraid of his most likely alternative. If only there were someone else.

Manuel brought the newly pressed tuxedo, which he laid carefully on the French Provincial bed, gleaming patent leather pumps already set next to the nightstand. He lifted his disconcertingly pleasant half-African, half-Chinese face with its wide black smile and narrow Asian eyes.

"Will the gentleman be wearing his truss tonight?" he asked, half mockingly.

"*Chico,* let me see if I dropped those pounds," said Boyeros, putting down his glass and struggling into the sharply creased pants.

"Now that Milagros is in New York, I've been eating less, so maybe ... *Coño, no. Qué va!*"

He tried to button his fly all the way up, but the last two buttons refused to close the gap.

"Oh well, get me the *faja.* Damn it, I feel like a stupid woman with that thing on, but what can I do?"

"*Sí, señor.*"

As Manuel wrapped the corset around Boyeros's middle, Boyeros thought back to the last time he'd worn that contraption, when Senator Aniseto Pin Garay had challenged his wife's cousin to a duel over a column. Manuel smiled at hearing his master's chuckle.

"Am I tickling you, señor?"

"*No, chico, qué va.* I am just remembering that fiasco with Pin Garay two years ago."

"Excuse me, *Coronel,* but that was ten years ago."

"Ten years ago? Are you sure?"

"Yes sir. We had just had our first son and Eremilda was all worried, thinking you might get killed and I would lose my job."

"How would I get killed if I was just the second in the duel?"

"You know women, sir. She worried you might get a *sablazo* accidentally."

"Like a girl alone in the beach with her boyfriend, no?" Both men chuckled at the sexual innuendo, then Manuel warned: "Hold your breath, sir." Boyeros felt the pain from the bones around the middle, then felt his flesh firmly encased once more, as it used to feel when he was young and his stomach muscles still held.

"Well, in any case, there was never that much danger."

"No sir, that's just what I told her."

"Besides, muchacho, you're in my will. Remember that. I never forget my boys."

"That's what I told her too."

"You did? You know me well then."

"It's only been eighteen years, *Coronel.*"

"That long since I hired you in Santiago?"

"*Sí, señor.* Eighteen years ago last February, when you lifted me from the street after you ran over me, and offered me a job."

"Yes, I guess you're right. I was racing to the *finca* because the cane fields were on fire from that freak lightning storm. Four times it struck in the same place."

"Yes sir. That's what you said."

"Oh, well, I don't know about you, but I am glad we had that accident," he said, letting out his breath once again.

"Yes sir, so am I. Anything else?"

"No, that will be all."

As Manuel hobbled away, his left leg still stiff from the shattered tibia replaced by the iron rod, Boyeros shook his head and smiled paternally. *No hay mal que por bien no venga.* No harm comes without some good attached.

❈ ❈ ❈

Boyeros was dressed and was in his library downstairs waiting for the limo to be ready when Manuel came in to see him again.

"Coronel, there's a journalist to see you, a Mr. Max Weinberg, with a friend."

"That's right, I'd forgotten. Send him in."

Max came in accompanied by a tall, red-faced American whom Boyeros did not recognize.

"Nice to see you again, Max," he said in English, vigorously shaking Max's hand. "But you're not dressed! And your friend is not with you, that Morgan fellow."

"I'm afraid I can't make it to the ball, sir," said Max, "and neither can he." Max turned to the tall man next to him. "I took the liberty of bringing Mr. Dunphy, the American embassy's cultural attaché. We wondered if we might have a brief word with you."

Cultural attaché? thought Boyeros. CIA head of station, obviously. He waved at the leather Chesterfield couch, under Zurbarán's picture of Saint Teresa of Avila, then rang for Manuel.

"Naturally. Please make yourselves comfortable. I'm not due at the yacht club for another hour."

The two men eased into the leather couch. Max glanced at Dunphy, who calmly took out a pipe from his jacket pocket, then raised questioning eyebrows at Boyeros.

"I can offer you a Montecristi if you want," said Boyeros.

"No, thank you," said Dunphy. "I'm partial to Turkish tobacco. I have it mixed for me at Dunhill's in New York."

Boyeros smiled genially, thinking the CIA man was as arrogant as Sumner Welles when he ordered Machado out of Havana. Choate.

Choate or Exeter. And Brown, I'll bet. Not smart enough for Yale or rich enough for Princeton.

"What did you want to see me about?"

Dunphy puffed up a cloud of apple-spiced tobacco.

"It's about the rebels, Mr. Boyeros."

"The rebels? What do you mean?"

"The rebels you have been supporting with your arms shipments. We mean the Twenty-Sixth of July and Fidel Castro."

"What arms shipments?"

"The ones you've been sending them out of your sugar mill, La Poblana, in Oriente. We'd like for you to help another group. For the sake of Cuba."

Just then Manuel entered the library with a tray full of drinks.

"I took the liberty of mixing these. I thought you gentlemen might enjoy them."

The men glanced at the tall glasses and laughed at the trio of Cuba Libres.

T his is it. No mistakes or you'll never get out alive. No mistakes.

Morgan silently repeated this to himself as the old GMC van trudged into the parking lot of the Havana Yacht Club. Encased behind the driver, lodged between crates of filet mignon, chorizos, and Serrano hams, he put away all thought by concentrating on the building right outside the driver's window. He focused on each dormer and lintel, each pillar, cornice, and bull's-eye as though he would be called upon to draw a sketch of the grandiose French Renaissance building from memory, and for a while he quelled his mind even if his heart pounded wildly of its own accord.

The driver was one of the pasty-faced clerks from the meeting at the Finlay Theater. He was now dressed in the blue overalls of Carnicería Pons, purveyors of fine meats to the landed families of Havana and suppliers of choice for grand events like the one this evening, the homage to President Batista for surviving the attack on the palace. The collegiate all-star from the meeting sat at the passenger seat up front, also in blue, his overalls a size too narrow for his broad swimmer's back. Morgan wore a tradesman's uniform as well; hidden underneath it were his dinner jacket and the automatic in his waistband. Inside an ice cream carton lay the Speed Graphic camera he'd be carrying as an accredited photographer for the *Havana Post*. Laura was already inside the club, helping her benighted brother in his duties as floor captain while the other members of the cabal were scattered around the location. All were in place, waiting for the moment before the speech when Batista would be felled by a hailstorm of righteous bullets.

At the wooden gate to the parking lot, a soldier in white leggings flagged the van to a halt.

"*Coño,*" whispered the all-star, going for his weapon.

"*Calma,*" whispered Morgan from behind, gripping the young man's gun hand.

"What do you have in here?" asked the soldier, a corporal's twin chevrons on his sleeve, as he pointed his submachine gun at the van.

The driver's face was perfectly blank, years of practice as a complaisant clerk now coming to the fore. He set his hangdog eyes on the sallow-faced corporal, noticed the way the soldier's bones stuck out of his frame, and he knew he had his man.

"What else are we going to have? Meats," answered the driver dryly. "For the *homenaje.*"

"*No me digas*"—don't tell me—said the corporal, drawing in closer, taking a better look at the driver and his companion, a sandy-haired young man. The young man nodded confidently, smiling back at the corporal, gripping ever tighter the butt of his gun.

"What kind of meats?"

"*Filete,* chorizos, *longanizas,* you know, the kind of thing they need."

"Interesting," said the soldier, his face now at the window, peering into the van. Morgan slid down between the crates, pressed his back against the side of the van.

"Imported meats too?" said the soldier, almost casually. The driver smiled, almost imperceptibly.

"Serrano ham too, and some French pâté with tiny cornichons," replied the driver. "You know about meats?"

"Of course I do. My uncle was a butcher in Holguín. I remember very well. Those Serrano hams are *de película.*"

"Clearly they are," replied the driver, letting the line reel out.

"They're so soft, the little slices just melt in the mouth."

"That's right. You can imagine, we are bringing these for *el presidente.* We have nothing but the best of the best. Which is what he deserves, of course."

"Naturally. If it were not for President Batista this country would be under the heel of the *comunistas,* the Jews, and the Masons, for sure."

"*Sí, señor.* So you are from Oriente Province, Corporal?"

"Yes. My old ones have a little *finca* right outside the Preston sugar mill. You know the area?"

"I have passed through it. On the road to Nipe."

"Yes, the bay is about fifty kilometers away. We used to cure our own hams, you know. Around Christmas, when it starts to get cool, the old man would kill this pig, *un carabalí,* a wild pig almost. Very big, maybe ten *quintales* or more."

"Yes, they grow very big very quickly, those animals."

"Yes, tremendous animals. Sometimes with tusks, like boars. They can kill you with that, you know."

"So it is, *Cabo.*"

"All the males in the family, even the little kids, go into the corral with sticks. The pig knows what's coming, six or eight people invading his space. We separate him from the sow and the piglets because otherwise, in his desperation, he might attack them, and that we could not allow. So then the pig would be released out into the corral and we would all jump in, the old man, my uncles, cousins. I was always the youngest, but I was always included because I never felt any fear, you understand."

"Perfectamente," said the driver, knowing he had to bear the tale until the end. In the back, Morgan slid down and wondered what the conversation was about and gripped his own gun, ready to spring out of the van shooting if anyone opened the back doors suddenly.

"So when the pig came out he would race from one to another, grunting and squealing, and every time it would come by, you would strike it with your stick or hammer or whatever you carried in your hand. Pigs can be smart too, and sometimes they would go right for your *cojones,* especially if they smelled that you were afraid. I heard stories of men whose *huevos* were torn off and eaten by the pig before the others had time to pull him off. This is to tell you that this pig killing was no easy business, you understand.

"One time this pig came straight at me, those little pig eyes full of pig smarts. I was the youngest one there but I had no fear, no sir. I took my stick and I struck him right on his snout. He reared and huffed, then I hit him again, and he turned and ran because the thing is, all pigs are cowards, you know, just like men. That's why some people say pigs have souls, even though I personally do not believe it. So then we all drew in closer, making a circle, hitting him every time he would try to go outside the circle, forcing him to run from one person to another, and each time the blows would leave him wobbly. We kept making the circle smaller and smaller, until he had no place left to go, you see, and everywhere he turns he gets another blow, until finally we are all standing shoulder to shoulder and we are all hitting the pig with all our might, until he's finally too tired and dazed and hurting from the blows and he can't move anymore and he falls. Even then you have to keep hitting him because some pigs have been known to play dead, then when the beating stops they suddenly get up and break out into the bush, and there goes your Christmas dinner. So you keep hitting him until he's completely lost all consciousness and there is blood trickling out of the snout. Then one of the women brings the kitchen knife, one with a really sharp edge, and a deep bowl, and then the men all lift the animal and you slice his throat and all the blood comes out, which you catch in the bowl so you can make *morcilla, longanizas,* and other sausages. I always liked to cut the throat. It takes a very sharp knife and the effect is not unlike that of slicing a man's ear. You have to know what you're doing."

"You always do, *Cabo.*"

The two men looked balefully at each other, waiting for the other's next move. The soldier sighed, then raised the gate and waved the van in. The driver turned, grabbed one of the canvas-wrapped legs stamped with the proud letters *Serrano S.A.* and handed it to the soldier.

"Here you are, Corporal. I am sure the fat fish inside will not miss one of these. *Buen provecho.*"

"*Muchas gracias.*"

"*No hay de qué,*" there is nothing to be grateful for.

The corporal walked quickly away to the guard's shack with his prize under his arm, then held it before his eyes again to make certain it was indeed a Serrano and that he did indeed have it.

"*Chico,* all that garbage about the pigs, why did we spend so much time on that, *coño!*" said the all-star. "We have wasted a bunch of time; they are about to set up already."

"The best things take a little more time," said the driver, easing the van next to the service entrance. "There are things that cannot be hurried."

"We should have just shot him down and that was that."

"How ignorant people can be, with university education and everything. They can still be as ignorant as a donkey."

"*Oyeme,* don't you dare call me things like that."

"If the glove fits," added the driver with a sneer as the van stopped.

"What happened?" asked Morgan from behind the crates, in English. The two Cubans looked at each other and stopped arguing in front of the Americano.

"We have a little discussion about soldier," said the all-star. "He talk too much."

"That was good," said Morgan, stretching his stiffened arms, easing his .45 back into his waistband. "A little argument is better than a lot of shooting. Are we ready?"

The driver cast a smug smile of superiority at the all-star.

"OK," said the driver, "we home now."

The driver walked off the van and up the steps leading to the loading dock. His contact, the other saturnine clerk from the secret meeting, was already waiting with a clipboard, looking to all the world like a club employee, the rare calm and methodical Cuban. The two men nodded at each other in silent approval.

The van's back door slammed open as the all-star nervously gestured at Morgan to come out. Morgan walked out of the van backward, carrying a crate of steaks, a cap wedged down to his eyebrows to disguise his fair Yanqui features.

"*Por aquí,* Guillermo," said the all-star, guiding Morgan up the steps.

"What's wrong with that one?" said a man's voice. The all-star and Morgan looked up to see an undercover cop, shirttails out to cover the lump of his weapon at his waistband. He pointed with his unlit cigar at Morgan.

"Nothing," said the all-star. "Why do you ask, Officer?"

"I'm a sergeant, *coño!*" replied the man, sticking the chewed-up drooling end of the cigar back in his mouth.

"Yes sir, Sergeant," said the all-star, looking around for the driver and realizing he and his contact had already walked into the receiving area.

"Don't you go around yessirring me!"

"No, Sergeant, I won't," replied the all-star as Morgan walked past him.

"I want to know why he's wearing a cap in this heat."

"Well, you know, Sergeant, our vans are air-conditioned and we have to go into the freezers."

"So what?"

"Guillermo here has a cold, that's to protect himself."

"I see," said the sergeant. "Also left him aphonic, true?"

Before the all-star could reply the cop swiped Morgan's cap. The two stared at each other for a second, then suddenly Morgan sneezed. The sergeant wiped his face in disgust, jammed Morgan's cap on, and shoved him away.

"*Coño,* get this fucking *gallego* pig out of my face! Just get him inside!"

"Yes, Sergeant."

The all-star, carrying a tray of Camembert in one hand, took Morgan's elbow with the other and guided him into the receiving dock. Morgan sneezed again.

"And make sure he doesn't sneeze on the president's steak," bellowed the sergeant. "If Batista has a cold, Cuba catches pneumonia!"

"Yes sir, Sergeant," shouted back the all-star.

✳ ✳ ✳

128

In the long, high-ceilinged banquet hall, beneath the banners and the bunting, the signs with Batista's picture and the words GRACIAS, BATISTA! and BATISTA, THE HONOR OF CUBA, Laura quietly set the flower arrangements on rows of white-napped tables. She glanced up at the clock on the wall. A quarter to seven. In little over an hour the guests would start to arrive, and still no sign of William.

Had he been captured? Was he being tortured this very moment, even as Laura carefully composed the fragrant bouquets? It was so easy to fall prey to the forces of the tyranny. A tie knotted wrong, a shoelace left loose, anything could arouse suspicion. And if he was captured, how long would he hold out? Until they broke his arms? His legs? Yanked his testicles out with a cord? Drove nails into his wrists? How long? Because eventually most people break. Most people can't resist that kind of pain, that agony, without mercy or end. Calm yourself, Laura told herself, there is no need for this anguish. There must have been a delay. We planned for the unexpected this time; that is why we gave ourselves an hour's leeway before springing the plan into action.

Traffic must have held them up, just as with the attack on the palace. You are being so theatrical. He's just delayed, that is all. Stop worrying and concentrate on your job.

Laura noticed her brother, Wilfredo, down the hall, going over the seating arrangements with the club's social director, a tall woman with brittle yellow hair. But it is strange to be working and it is even stranger to be a revolutionary at work as well. Sometimes I wonder what *papá* would have thought, but then I realize he probably would have approved. He was in the ABC, was he not, with all their cells and bombings and strong-arm tactics. He was always telling us how, when the waterfront was sealed off, he and his friends shaved their heads and armed themselves with iron bars and broke the strike. And he was in his fifties already. He was fighting for freedom then as I am now. Oh, but it is so much sweeter when your own love is in it, when you know it is his arm and his strength and his wisdom that will carry the day.

She noticed the clerk who had driven the van pushing a cart with meats into the hall. She hurried over to him.

"The flowers are in the storage room," he said softly, then wheeled the cart away.

She hustled past him into the kitchen, scuttling around the pastry chefs bringing out the ten-foot-high sugar-and-cream model of the Presidential Palace that would sit as the centerpiece on Batista's table. She dodged the dollies of Veuve Clicquot and Dom Pérignon, then dashed through the bustling kitchen grill, smoky from the hundreds of seared well-marbled steaks, past the racks of fancy glassware and dishes with the gold inlaid crest of the Havana Yacht Club, then down a narrow corridor, winding up in a cool room with tables spilling with cut flowers—lilies, orchids, choryapsis—stopping at a steel-faced door with a refrigerator lock. The clerk with a clipboard was adjusting the temperature on the thermostat next to the door. He saw her and jerked his head at the storage room.

"Do not tarry," he said. She nodded, opened the door, and stepped inside. Rows of hams and strings of sausages hung from steel hooks in the ceiling, stalactites of cured and processed meat. A man in blue overalls, his back to the door, was bent over a carton of ice cream. On hearing the click of the lock he spun around with a gun in his hand. Her heart sang with happiness.

"It's you," said Morgan, bringing down his gun.

"I wait so long," said Laura, arms down, willing herself to enjoy this moment, to relish every second of sparkling anticipation before the unleashing of emotion.

"We were stopped at the gate. There was traffic. God, I missed you," he said, putting his gun on a wooden pallet and opening his arms to her. She ran to him, scattering the carpeting of wood shavings on the floor before her, gliding, almost flying, as she flung herself into his arms.

"Mi amor," she said, and she knew she was histrionic and she knew she did not care, because all the love that coursed through her was life at its fullest, the moment of ecstasy when the individual will melds with the collective consciousness, and she was both the instrument of a larger design and her own woman as well, rushing like a brook to the sea of love. He held her in his arms and lifted her off the floor.

She was light. She had never weighed more than a hundred, and now she was so glad she had never grown to be the tall and graceful woman she'd always dreamed of, because who knows if then he would have picked her up as he did, like a doll or a chalice, bodily, into the air, in her black-and-white maid's uniform? She giggled from the sheer intoxicating happiness of reunion, and he held her up, a prize that he would want the whole world to see. As he turned her slowly around she laughed and showered kisses on his head and then he brought her down and their lips met and they kissed, she breathing life into him and he into her and then they tumbled down to the sawdust and they fumbled for the body encased inside each other's uniform and when he entered her all was alright with the world again. Even Cuba could wait while she felt him inside of her, the wholeness of him splitting her open and the pulsating

joy washed over them in the tangy air of that meat locker in the basement of the proud and fancy Havana Yacht Club.

❊ ❊ ❊

Even as the lovers wooed, Boyeros rode alone in his limousine, absentmindedly watching the city roll by while he pondered the request from
the American attaché.

I wonder how the Americans knew I was sending those Garands and
grenades to the boys in the sierra. Hedging my bets, naturally, but that's
the Cuban way. Still, I suppose there's very little they don't know on this
island. Not that I'm one of those who think they are secretly pulling the
strings to everything, but in this case, they are definitely—what's the
phrase in English, in the soup? No, that's not it. God, it has been a long
time since Yale. Twenty-nine years. I'm surprised I speak English as well
as I do. Of course, some people would say as badly. Be that as it may. In
this one soup, the Americans are all wet.

I don't understand, though. They are supporting Batista but they are
also backing Castro and the boys. It's like they are backing everyone and
no one. I understand, as that British prime minister said, countries don't
have friends, they have interests. But this is almost like two countries.
Two factions in the U.S. government. One is right-wing, for Batista. The
other is left-wing, for the boys. And they both wear the stripes of Uncle
Sam. It's a house divided, isn't it? Of course, we Cubans should talk. Get
three Cubans in a room and you have seven opinions, two per person
and one extra for everybody.

Boyeros caught a quick glimpse of his usual luncheon spot, the Puerta
de Tierra, and of the liveried doorman helping a small, thin, blonde old
woman out of her Fleetwood and into the restaurant. Isn't that Margarita
Coll? thought Boyeros. So she is still boycotting everything about
Batista. She's frozen in the time of Machado. Probably waiting for the
army High Command to fight their way out of the Nacional and put
down the sergeants; he chuckled. But what is worse, being stuck in time
or being of no time at all, like Batista? He doesn't understand that whatever good he might have done with his *cuartelazo* in fifty-two, it's all been
destroyed by his refusal to resign. And these people he has with him!
García, Tabernilla. They just believe in the power of the gun. They're like
that fascist general who said, "Every time I hear the word *culture* I reach
for my pistol." There goes another of their charnel-house carts.

A black-and-white patrol car howled its way through traffic, its overhead light a Cyclops's dreadful eye scanning the street for its next victims.

So now the Americans also want me to back these people in the

Escambray. The same people who couldn't pull off the palace attack now are going to be opening a second guerrilla front near Cienfuegos. I don't understand. They really think they will sweep out of the mountains into the plains and conquer the island? They should remember that the last time Cubans tried that, the Americans intervened and took over. Wouldn't even let General García into Santiago. Do they really think the Americans will let them have a mind of their own? America doesn't want allies, it wants servants. Oh well, no harm in giving them some weapons. It's only a few thousand dollars, and who knows, maybe they'll pull it off after all. That young American, Morgan, is going to be with them, I understand. So maybe then I can claim credit for that with Batista. Tell him he's going to get rid of Castro. I just have to keep giving Batista enough rope and hope that he hangs himself soon. Lord knows we've suffered enough.

I wonder if those boys at the Escambray will succeed. Everybody knows Castro is a communist, so if he wins, unless we keep him contained . . . well, who knows what will happen? But the boys in the Escambray. They would be truly independent, no? They wouldn't even know the U.S. is backing them. Independence. That would be interesting. That would be a rare day indeed. When Cuba is free of all foreign interference, be it from Washington, Moscow, Paris, Peking, whatever. A truly free Cuba. I wonder if it is possible. I wonder if I will ever see it in my lifetime.

Boyeros's limousine glided past the line of army sentries stationed outside the club, machine guns lodged behind sandbag barricades. At the carport, the chariots of the country's rich and powerful debouched their ermined and tuxedoed passengers under the wary eyes of the soldiers and the henchmen.

Bueno, here we are at the farce, thought Boyeros. Let us continue with the art of the possible and leave eventualities to the Almighty. He'll decide what is best for Cuba, I hope. God help us. I hope He does.

✸ ✸ ✸

Down in the locker, Laura buttons up her blouse as Morgan struggles with his bow tie. A moment of blushing silence passes between them, almost as if they were embarrassed by the galloping steed of emotion that they have both ridden and that now, the race at its end, has left their nerves too jangled to speak.

Laura walks up to Morgan, ties the knot under the lump of his gulping Adam's apple.

"Is OK now. *Papá* always have problem with tie too. I help him always," she says, caressing his face. *Ay, Dios mío,* there is so much I have to tell you and I don't know how, she thinks.

He takes her hands, kisses them, then picks up his Speed Graphic, checks the gun under the cummerbund of his dinner jacket, and strides out into the corridor. Laura watches him walk out, closes the meat locker door, and sinks to the ground, dazed by the immensity of the moment, as the room spins, sweat flows, and the explosions go off inside her forehead.

❊ ❊ ❊

Morgan walks down the corridor, the layout from the plans clear in his mind. At the first door he turns right and cuts across the laundry room. A handful of black women, tending the giant washers and dryers, look up from their chores as he strides quickly by. A lost American, they decide, and return to the folding and ironing of the shirts and towels. They have already put him out of their mind by the time he reaches the metal-plated swinging doors leading to the soft-drink storage room behind the kitchen.

Two men in waiter's uniforms, one white, one black, are smoking cigarettes behind the stacked wooden racks of Orange Spot and Coca-Cola. They are on their break, waiting for the dinner service to begin. Later, when the police hold them for three days, slapping them and punching them until they give their version of the truth, they will say only the obvious—one Americano photographer looking for the party, what else! Now the waiters glance quickly at Morgan too, but the camera he's holding makes them relax.

"Mister, dancing over there," says the black man with a quick flash of gnarled yellow teeth.

Morgan goes through another set of swinging doors into the kitchen proper. Dozens of cooks, chefs, and sauciers bustling as they prepare dinner for eighteen hundred people all at once. Filets are slapped on the grill, white sauces whisked for the mushroom dressing, heads of lettuce split and divided for the appetizer. Here, for the first time, Morgan hears music from the ballroom, a tropical beat, a syncopated rhythm with weeping violins. *"Estás en mi corazón,"* you are always in my heart, a proper beginning to the ceremony of *desagravio,* of making up to the president for his having had the misfortune of being set upon by that band of *fascinerosos,* outlaws, who dared to storm the palace in contravention of all civilized behavior, according to the society columnists of *La Marina, El País,* even the Communist-Party-owned *Hoy,* who are there to cover the event in all its glory.

But all Morgan knows now is that his contact is not there. He scans the crowd of kitchen help: apprentices bobbing to and from the stoves; a hubbub of orders being shouted; popping, sizzling, hissing of kitchen work. Then from the back a waiter in a white jacket, bearing a tray aloft, approaches and nods at Morgan. Morgan follows the man as he winds his way down the main alley in the kitchen, stepping on the wooden plank floor, past the sink and the prep counter, past the sauce maker, the bakers, and a cart bearing the replica of the palace.

The waiter ahead of Morgan points to the right at an open door with steps leading to the wine cellar, out of which now staggers a pink-skinned boy with a case of Remy Martin. Suddenly the replica of the palace is wheeled out by two hustling waiters. Morgan and his guide follow it out to the vast ballroom, awash in music, flowers, and the fragrance of a thousand costly scents liberally splashed on the naked necks and shoulders of hundreds of society women.

Morgan stands next to the door, stunned by the show of affluence. The ballroom is a sea of white-napped tables, each with luxurious flower arrangements, ice buckets with champagne, and bottles of gin, rum, and scotch. At the tables sit women in gowns, dripping with jewels and furs, next to florid and sallow and fat and skinny men in dinner jackets chatting and kissing and laughing and biding their time, picking at the canapes offered by the dozens of waiters, all awaiting the arrival of the president, whose thirty-foot smiling image graces a poster above the stage with the caption PRESIDENTE BATISTA, EL HONOR DE LA PATRIA, the honor of the fatherland.

"Go on, take a picture," says a woman next to him. "That's what you're here for, aren't you?"

He turns and sees Violeta Ramírez y Caballero in a lace lilac gown, smiling impishly at him. He picks up the Speed Graphic, anxiously examines it.

"Where's the shutter on this thing?" he whispers.

"On the left. Didn't anybody show you how to work it?" she whispers back.

He shrugs, frames her picture in the viewfinder, setting it against the large poster of Batista so that the photograph will become a study of two faces in perfect compositional opposites. The flash goes off and she smiles for posterity. (This will be found later by the *esbirros*, the hirelings of the infamous SIM, the army's intelligence police, and the alert will go out that Violeta Ramírez y Caballero, the sister of one of the conspirators who died in the attack on the palace, who had repudiated her brother and his communist tactics and was one of the earliest organizers of this *homenaje* to the president, was also involved, and the squad cars will descend on her house in Marianao like baying hounds, but she will already be gone, vanished into the jungles of the sierra or the gilded shores of Palm Beach—but that will be in the future.)

Now, tonight, she turns to the tall Americano and simply asks: "How about a dance, mister? You have to be a better dancer than you are a photographer."

Morgan smiles again, nods, puts down his camera on a nearby table, and takes her out to the dance floor, knowing that many eyes are watching them tonight, the adipose gentlemen in their formal wear, the wattle-necked ladies in their frippery, all thinking there is no way a mere Americano can resist the tropical temptations of a Cuban woman. The ancient watchers are atingle as Morgan and Violeta walk to the head of the room, hand in hand, and she turns and opens her proud white arms to him, her round shoulders embraced by his firm arms, and she sweeps forward, a lilac figure of loveliness, and everyone remarks how well they look together, he tall and blond and strong, and she brunette and petite and seemingly so frail. The smiles of the onlookers broaden as she whispers something in his ear, and they start questioning, Who is the handsome American who has so easily conquered Violeta's grieving heart? (Politics is a terrible thing. He should have never gotten involved. It's part of the times. Such a waste, and he with a wife and children too. They're in New York already. Politics is a filthy business. Thank God for Batista, who looks out for us, but what we really need here is a Franco, to teach these communists a lesson. They will never win, God willing; they can never win. The Americans will never let them. The marines will land here first.)

"Have you seen him?" whispers Morgan as they move softly on the dance floor.

"He just walked in. He's saying hello to all his cronies out front," she whispers, then adds, in a heady mix of perfume and hate, "He didn't have lunch today and he's hungry, so he'll be here soon."

"How do you know that?"

"One of his aides is with us, Luisito. The big man was meeting with ITT people all day about taking over the telephone company. Smile now, here comes your ambassador."

"Who?"

"Quick! What's your name? What's your cover?" whispers Violeta.

"Alexander Williams."

"What do you do? Hurry, he's almost here."

"I'm a . . . a reporter for the *Albany Times.*"

"Albany. That's sweet. I used to date someone from Albany . . . Mr. Ambassador, what a pleasure. It's an honor to have you here."

Morgan steps back respectfully and attentively as a heavyset man with owl eyes approaches them with the air of a communicant at the rail. The thought strikes Morgan that perhaps Violeta has known the ambassador a little too well in the past, but his attention is drawn to the far end of the room, where he spots Laura in her server's uniform, pouring water into the Baccarat glasses at a large table. Almost as if he'd called to her she glances up and their eyes meet across the wide expanse of the ballroom. She stops pouring and holds the cold water jar, beaded with moisture, her wide eyes fixed on Morgan, who also stares back, and the music from the orchestra in the pit reaches its last notes and stops, but that last downbeat floats suspended in the air, a bridge between Morgan and Laura, a connection as true and solid as if they had been pressing flesh against flesh, soul covering soul, until the spell is broken by a wizened old man who grabs Laura's elbow and points at his empty water glass. She turns and pours, and Morgan switches his gaze, and he sees Batista coming into the ballroom, surrounded by his cronies, a few yards behind and to the right of Laura.

"Mr. Williams, I am sure you want to meet the ambassador of your country. He's a very well-known man around these parts."

"Excuse me" says Morgan, turning to face the ambassador, who offers an unexpectedly callused hand.

"Pleasure to meet you, Mr. Williams. Violeta tells me you're a reporter."

"Yes sir. *Albany Times.*"

"Well, I certainly hope you're not down here to write about those rebels up in the mountains, are you? You can see tonight how much the people still love President Batista."

"Yes sir, I can see that. I've been seeing it since I came to the island."

"Well, then, you make sure that your readers are aware of that. I don't care what that *New York Times* fellow, Herbert Matthews, wrote. The Cuban people are very much in support of the president. Just the other day they had a mass rally for him. Half a million people."

"That many?" says Violeta, now also keeping an eye on the progress of Batista through the crowd.

"Certainly. That's what police estimated. Our boys at the embassy toned it down a little, but I'm inclined to go with the higher figure."

Morgan then sees a rail-thin young man with a luxurious head of hair and a generous smile fast approaching their group. Morgan turns to Violeta, then darts his eyes at Batista, moving quickly forward. She raises her eyebrows imperceptibly. It's all up to you.

"Earl," says the young man, "just the man I've been looking for."

"Jack, glad you could make it," says Ambassador Smith. "Senator John F. Kennedy, Miss Violeta Ramírez y Caballero, Mr. Alexander Williams. Where's Mrs. Kennedy?"

"Jackie's in the ladies room, touching up her nose. Now listen, Earl, this is truly beyond belief. At our hotel this morning the—what is it? The Nacional?"

"Yes, that is the name," says the Ambassador.

"There was a bomb this morning! The maid who had just done our room was blown to pieces in the basement. I ask you, is that any way to run a hotel!?"

"Or a country, Senator," says Violeta cattily.

Kennedy gives her a warm smile, but before he can reply the people in the nearby tables suddenly spring to their feet, applauding, as Batista finally walks into the room. Their clapping is a sign for the orchestra to start playing the Cuban national anthem, and the crowd lets out cheers and whistles of appreciation like the rowdiest crowd at the ball park: *"Viva Batista! Viva el presidente!"*

The raucous beat continues even as the short, pudgy mulatto with the deep set-eyes acknowledges the accolade, raises his hand, waving and nodding, confident that once again he has captured the hearts of Cuba just by surviving, because if there's one thing Cubans love most of all, it is a winning survivor. Batista walks on, his presence becoming more palpable as the crowd picks up the words of the anthem "To the fight, people of Bayamo, for the fatherland awaits you with pride. Fear not a glorious death, for to die for the fatherland is to live."

Morgan turns. This is his chance. Up on the stage the two men who will cover his escape, the van driver and the all-star, take their place, machine guns at the ready. Morgan sees Violeta nod her head as though in slow motion, telling him, Go ahead, please, this is the time, the one and only time when the universe will tremble, and it all comes together down to this moment. Morgan reaches for his gun in his cummerbund. At that very moment, just as Batista is about twelve feet away, Morgan sees, even as he's taking out the gun, that Ventura is in the crowd of faithful accompanying the president. It's written all over Ventura's face that the captain realizes what is about to occur, and Ventura too moves his hand as though in one of those slow-motion studies where the horse never touches the ground but seems to fly above the street, all four hoofs in the air.

Morgan then spots Laura, who somehow has made her way to behind Ventura. She has seen what Ventura intends to do and she moves at that moment, flying through the air with her water jar, which now makes contact with Ventura's gun arm and deflects the bullet even as Batista looks to his right and sees the gun in Morgan's hand. The gunmen on stage then move out front from behind the velvet curtain and point their guns over the heads of the assembly of the cream of Havana society just as Morgan finishes taking out his gun and points it at Batista, who's in perfect sighting position. Morgan is a fraction of a second away from pulling the trigger when the senator from Massachusetts, noticing the two gunmen on stage, steps back and, as though prefiguring the fate that will befall him, moves into Morgan's sight line, his head perfectly aligned in front of the barrel of the .45. Morgan knows he should shoot him, then shoot Batista, but he cannot, will not shoot an innocent man, and he jerks away his gun and shoots at Ventura instead, who has already fallen over Batista to cover his master, who now is hitting the ground as a huddle of bodies falls on him to protect him from all harm.

A spray of bullets from the gunmen on stage fills the hall, and Morgan grabs Laura, who's only five feet away, and jerks her up as hard as he can, and she stumbles and follows him as they race for the safety of backstage. The Cuban national anthem is still playing as Laura and Morgan take their first steps up to the dais, and a colonel from Batista's group pulls his gun and fires back at the gunmen onstage. The all-star is hit and falls shouting, *"Viva Cuba libre!"* even as his gun sprays all over the ceiling and the bullets tatter to pieces the giant poster of Batista, which dangles, then drops to the ground.

The colonel fires again but the bullet misses its target and instead lodges itself in Laura's back, exploding with a gush of blood, but Morgan is not aware of it as he runs backstage, then quickly down the escape route along the side corridor, just as he has memorized. He looks back and sees Laura, a few steps behind him, tumbling to the ground. Morgan howls when he notices the wound, and he picks her up and races down the corridor, the white lights turning everything into a world of sharp angles and creased corners, a black hole ahead of him, shouting and bullets behind him.

"Leave me, save yourself!" cries Laura, but Morgan runs on, and it's as though she weighed nothing at all, even though he knows his body is tired and somewhere back in what used to be reality his legs are leaden and convulsed with pain. But Morgan doesn't feel the pain, no, not at all, as he runs through and into the swinging doors of the kitchen. All the kitchen help is at the other end, watching through the glass panes the commotion in the ballroom. Morgan storms in and shouts for everyone to get out, but no one understands him. Two men in suits and guns held high then push through the crowd of kitchen help. They spot Morgan rushing down the steps to the wine cellar, where he races around the stacks of bottles of fine Meursaults, Bourdeaux, clarets and Chablis, cognacs and champagnes, heading for the far end, where a large metal door stands barred and locked.

Morgan can hear behind him the men approaching, shouting, shooting wildly at the bottles in the cellars, which pop open and hiss and stream their precious liquid onto the ground. Holding Laura with one hand, Morgan searches in the box over the cabinet and finds the promised gift. He takes one of the grenades, pulls the pin, and tosses it at his pursuers, expecting to see the storm of destruction around him, but the grenade meekly bounces along the floor, a dud.

The men are now only fifteen feet away, and Morgan can see in their faces the rage and blood lust of the hunter. He pulls the pin on the second grenade and tosses it at the same time that he throws himself and Laura to the ground. A great boom rocks the room and the pieces of metal go hurtling through the cellar, knocking one of the gunmen to the ground and killing the other, his head tumbling down like a ball, stopping next to the unexploded grenade. Morgan picks up Laura, who's blacked out, and heads through the smoke.

A blue Ford is waiting at the head of the stairs. He races up to the car. A thin-faced black man is at the driver's seat, Max Weinberg in the back.

Max opens the door, gesturing at Morgan to hurry. Morgan pushes through carrying his precious wounded cargo of love and he is about to get in when the driver takes out a shotgun and fires at more of Batista's men who are now streaming out of the wine cellar and a bullet strikes Morgan who falls in the back of the car as all goes black and the car takes off in a hail of bullets, leaving Laura alone and bleeding on the sidewalk.

BOOK TWO
The Hills of Freedom

Chapter

1

Children, they are all children, thinks the reporter as he restlessly paces the esplanade in front of the big hut up on the Sierra Maestra. Like children they give and like children they take away. They let you play for a while, but when they get tired they just take the ball back and go home. Rebels or government, they're all the same.

Without realizing it, the young reporter began talking to himself, cursing in the Sicilian dialect his grandfather had taught him back in San Mateo, California. The bearded *rebelde* standing guard by the hut, rosaries and medallions of Saint Barbara slung around his neck, M-3 by his side, watched the peripatetic journalist with great amusement.

Foolish Americanos, always rushing, even when they have to wait. They are an avalanche of motion. What a waste. He should sit down before he has a stroke, in this heat. He'll get his interview sooner or later.

The rebel recalled how the freckled-faced young man with the wavy brown hair had shown up in the rebel-held zone two days before. Armed with a notebook, he was intent, like so many others, on making his name in the jungles of Cuba.

It's like they have an ant up their butt, you know, one of those big red *bibijaguas* that raise welts an inch high. Oh well, he'll learn you can't hurry Cubans. Everything in Cuba happens in its own good time, usually when you least expect it; then, pow, there it is. I wish I had a cigar. Where the hell did I put that *mocho*?

The scruffy guerrilla searched his front shirt pocket for his half-smoked stogie, extracting it with the homage of an acolyte removing the host from the cup. He put it to his lips, lit it with a wax match, and inhaled with great pleasure, then leaned back on his stool to watch a flock of native buzzards, the foul-smelling *auras tiñosas,* spread their six-foot wings over the bristly palm treetops in the rebel camp. I wonder what they're smelling, he thought.

Inside the hut, the leader and founder of the 26th of July Movement, the erstwhile lawyer, student leader, and would-be major league pitcher Fidel Castro, put down the paper that the representative of the Cuban Socialist Party, Carlos Rafael Rodríguez, had brought from Havana.

Castro glared silently at Rodríguez.

These sons of bitches are out to screw me, thought Castro. Like always, they promise one thing then give you another. Don't they know who I am? Don't they know they are facing the forces of history? I'm going to have to teach them a little lesson.

"That is our humble contribution," squirmed Rodríguez, playing with his steel-framed glasses, stroking the goatee that made him resemble some cut-rate Mephisto. He smiled anxiously, well aware of Castro's legendary tantrums. Incongruously, he wore his business shirt and tie with the camouflage pants and combat boots he'd been given after falling into a swamp on the way up to the rebel camp.

"Let me see if I understand you correctly. The party is willing to support our efforts for a general strike on condition that I publicly thank them for their contribution?"

Castro tilted his head forward, a trial lawyer leading the witness down the dialectical path.

"Well, yes," replied Rodríguez, "those are the sentiments of the party. Not that we would seek a position of primacy, mind you, but we would desire an acknowledgment of this historic cooperation."

Rodríguez turned his wide, deep-set eyes on Raúl, Fidel's younger brother, who stood at the leader's elbow, arms crossed, his vaguely Chinese features in inscrutable rest. Rodríguez knew Raúl was a card-carrying member of the party, but that didn't mean much up in the hills.

"As you know, *I* am not a communist," said Fidel Castro, leaning back, feeling proud of himself for having avoided the easy cliché of so many Latin revolutionaries. He burped discreetly his earlier meal of Vienna sausages and chickpeas, cleared his throat. "Which is not to say that I don't admire some of the precepts of Marx, Engels, and, above all, the great Lenin."

"*Sí, Comandante,*" answered Rodríguez dutifully, sitting up straight in the uneven stool Castro had offered him, a full two feet below the leader's own armchair.

"I believe that many of the principles espoused by the party have great relevance to the conditions prevailing on the island. But . . . " He paused, searched for his Romeo y Julieta, then lit it carefully, watching the flame turn the tip to ash before proceeding. "But I don't think this is the time to announce that."

Castro exhaled, the small room filling with the cloying smell of fine cigar smoke.

"I think it would be counterproductive to publicly announce such a marriage of interests," he added, "with the situation with the dictator being the way it is and all. Let me be brutally frank. The last thing we need now, at this point, is for Washington to get confirmation of all the propaganda they've been getting about my political affiliation."

He cleared his throat again, looked out of the corner of the eye at his brother. Neither one of them had ever liked the leadership of the party, and this was the moment they had longed for, to have the top echelons come begging for a place in the new Cuba. He gave a sly smirk, like a store clerk caught after hours in the store trying on women's shoes.

"All the same," he continued, certain that Rodríguez would kiss all necessary rumps to hitch a ride with the revolution, "a revolution like ours, as green as our palm trees, should not be afraid to welcome whatever help might be tendered by whatever party exists in the country. So we will accept all the cooperation that the party of the great Marx, Engels, and Lenin might wish to give us—selflessly, in pursuit of the higher goal of a free Cuba, unchained from all kinds of intervention, like the great Chibás said, be it from Rome, Berlin, Washington, or Moscow."

Fidel grinned once again, let out a series of concentric circles of smoke as Rodríguez pondered his reply.

"Did I make myself clear?" asked Fidel.

"Perfectly, *Comandante*," replied Rodríguez in his breathy, reedy voice, his mind whirring at lightning speed with all the arguments pro and con. Rodríguez knew that Blas Roca, the party secretary general, would be opposed to such a secret alliance as Castro was proposing. Roca would want to publicly stake a place early on in the post-Batista government so that the party might achieve its goal of sole power through electionist maneuvers, backing one or the other revolutionary candidate in the elections that would surely have to be held after Batista fell.

But perhaps if the cards are played right there won't be any elections, thought Rodríguez. We could offer Fidel a structure for governing, an alternative to the corrupt parliamentary system. Fidel certainly is aware of that. Yes, just like he knows that none of the other *movimiento* leaders—Menoyo, Prío, Ray, Artime—will have anything to do with the party.

Well, then, we have no choice. We have to swallow this pill. But this is not a good omen. This man will never follow party leadership. I suppose then we'll have to make *him* the party, concluded Rodríguez. The main thing is getting into power. The rest can come later. Besides, once he's with us, he'll never leave.

"*Bueno, Comandante,* I am ready to pledge myself and all of my efforts on behalf of the revolution. That is why I'm here," said Rodríguez after a moment of silence.

Castro pulled on his cigar and fixed his deep-set Spanish eyes on the Levantine-looking courier. Yes, you say yes, but only because Batista has thrown you out, otherwise you'd still be sucking his dick, *hijo 'e puta.* I remember when you called me a right-winger, a conspirator, an irresponsible gangster. You even got my own wife, Mirta, to leave me, saying I was such a lowlife I'd never be able to provide for her or Fidelito. You and your people hounded me. You, the party of the great Antonio Guiteras; you, who sold out your soul for a plate of lentils at the table of the tyrant. But it's all right. There will be plenty of time later to step on all the *cucarachas.*

"*Coño, chico,* I am so happy," said Fidel flatly, deliberately to let Rodríguez know in no uncertain terms that this was just a tactical alliance. "We should consolidate our forces then, down in the plains, in the cities. Your people in the unions will be giving us their support for the general strike we have planned."

"Certainly, as long as—"

"Good, good. Why don't you go over the details here with Raúl, and he can report to me. I'm sure you fellows have a lot in common, like Cervantes said, birds of a feather."

"*Oye,* Fidel, don't kid around with me," said Raúl, ever sensitive that his brother was maligning his masculinity by calling him a *pájaro,* a bird, queer.

"It's just a trope, Raúl, a manner of speaking," said Fidel, grinning at his dig. "Now go on and do your job. I got to talk to this Yanqui reporter who's been hounding me for days."

Fidel watched Rodríguez leave meekly with Raúl, at last knowing his true place in the scheme of things revolutionary. Castro felt proud of having accomplished in five minutes, and on his own terms, what no other rebels had ever done in Cuba—obtain the support of the Party in a struggle against a sitting government. As Lenin said about storming the Winter Palace, it was surprising how easy it was.

I wonder, thought Fidel, when the time comes, how much support we'll be able to get from Mother Russia to keep the Americans at bay. Like Nasser, like Nehru, like Tito—keep both the eagle and the bear guessing. And giving. In due time I'll have to decide, I know. But for now I'll keep this way down in my pocket. It wouldn't look right; too many people on our side fear the communists. I don't. I know that all they want is power. Just like me. To change the country, to make things the way they should be. We understand each other very well, these commies and me, better than I understand the constitutionalists, those democrats like Sorí Marín and Ray. They think that revolutions can be taken just so far and then stopped, that you only have to break a couple of eggs and wrap it all up again. No señor, a hell of a lot of eggs will have to be broken around here, and the reds have the best eggbeater of all.

"Ameijeiras!" cried out Fidel. The sinewy black rebel, whom Fidel had met in the Isle of Pines prison doing time for selling marijuana, hurried in, eager to serve. As always he was garlanded with chains, medallions, and scapulars dedicated to Oshún, the Santería goddess of love.

"Sí, Comandante!" he replied smartly, putting all his best effort into a formal military greeting. "At your service!"

"Chico, por favor, stop all that military foolishness, I'm not some general in the republican army. Show that Yanqui reporter in, he's waited long enough."

"Sí señor!" replied Ameijeiras cheerily. "He's been cutting a trench out front with his feet, he moves so much."

"Good. That means he'll be happy to see me."

※ ※ ※

The reporter ducked under the low doorway and entered the cramped bohío. Fidel stood over a large relief map of Cuba, which he had spread out over his papers and now ostentatiously examined, as though plotting in his mind the route that the triumphant armies of the revolution would soon take. Fidel looked up, turning his head slightly sideways, so the reporter could catch his best side and report on the length of the aquiline nose, the defiant tilt of the mouth, the Byronic curls.

"Welcome to the free territory of Cuba!" said Castro with what he hoped would be interpreted as a magnanimous gesture. The reporter caught his breath, startled to see that Castro was as tall as he but with the filled-out physique of the amateur athlete. Jesus K. Christ, I finally made it, thought the reporter. I am actually about to interview the son of a bitch. The reporter grabbed for his Hasselbald, even as Fidel postured, cigar in mouth.

"Thank you for seeing me, Dr. Castro," said the reporter, who had been advised to address him with the title used in Cuba for both physicians and attorneys.

Hearing the reporter's Italian-accented Spanish, Castro switched to English. "It is nothing," he said. "To our American supporters I want to say hello. I want to make one thing clear, before we begin. We fight for free Cuba. We are not communists, you understand?"

"*Sí, Comandante!*" replied the reporter, taking picture after picture, feeling already a part of this gloriously romantic revolution, a brother to these Don Quixotes by way of Cortés, who would show a new pathway to freedom to the colorless Western world.

"That is good." Castro smiled, wiping the feathers off his lips.

※ ※ ※

Outside the hut, Rodríguez and Raúl ambled through the rutted main street of the camp, passing by the open door of the shoemaker who was rhythmically pounding a new sole of retread rubber tire on a worn combat boot.

"As you can see, we have to make do with whatever we can find," said Raúl, pointing out the cobbler at the bench stacked full of damaged footgear. From the *bohío* next door they could overhear the high-pitched answers of the peasant children of the area, shouting out in unison: "*A* is for *America*, *B* is for *Batista*, *C* is for *Cuba*."

"And what is *F* for?" asked Raúl's wife, Vilma Espín.

"*Fidel!*" cheered the children.

"Your resourcefulness is striking," commented Rodríguez.

"That is why the financial support of the party will be welcomed by the revolution," replied Raúl.

"You mean the movement," said Rodríguez. "There are other groups besides the Twenty-Sixth of July." He paused, to let Raúl know there were alternatives to the Castros. But Raúl quickly clipped that errant thought.

"They are just brigands. Horse thieves. We, the Twenty-Sixth of July, are the revolution," said Raúl firmly. Rodríguez nodded.

"Yes, of course. I don't know what came over me."

The men proceeded down the path to the zinc-roofed hut assigned to Rodríguez. They discussed the coordination of their forces, the names of the leaders of the different cells in the cities, pledging to set up liaison groups within days. They were at the door to Rodríguez's hut when Rodríguez asked gingerly, "By the way, I was hoping to meet Dr. Ernesto Guevara. I understand he too is a great student of Marxist thought."

"He certainly is. And a gifted military strategist as well. Unfortunately he is out in the field, making contact with our supporters some distance away. We expect him back soon."

"That is a shame. I had hoped to meet him before I returned."

Raúl stood ramrod straight, chin set back, imperious.

"Go back? You can't go back, Comrade. You are here to stay with us until the triumph of the revolution. We will make all our arrangements through couriers. We need you here."

"Oh!" was Rodríguez's sole answer. Stunned, he stared at Raúl for a moment, then shook his head up and down vigorously.

"Of course, of course!" said Rodríguez, thinking, This is going better than I had planned.

"Until we triumph!" said Raúl.

"Until we triumph," seconded Rodríguez.

Chapter

2

William Morgan sat in the shade of the giant pine tree, his 9mm Thompson beside him, watching the struggling column of khaki-suited soldiers snake through the narrow gorge a thousand feet below. For a moment he allowed himself the luxury of commiserating with the sweating troops tramping their way through kilometers of vegetation so thick the sun was only a veil of light. But almost as quickly as he conjured the thought he relinquished it. The fox cannot feel for the hounds, at least not until the baying stops.

He glanced up at the molten sun in the cloudless sky and tried to figure the time, just as Menoyo had urged him to do. Here in the Escambray hills the slant of the rays and the intensity of the light were fatally deceptive, like the waters of the bilarcia-infected stream that looks so clean and tastes so cool and clean after a long march but will empty out your guts within the hour.

Morgan guessed eleven in the morning. He looked at his watch. Nine-fifteen. At least another six hours to Victor's camp.

The one they called El Gato, the Cat, came up to Morgan, Garand rifle slapping at his side.

"*Tú ves?*"—you see?—he asked Morgan, pointing at his eye first, then down at the filing troops below.

"*Yo ver*"—I to see—replied Morgan in the infinitive, the only way he could cope with the dizzying array of tenses in the Spanish language.

"We fight?" asked the stocky, sallow-skinned guerrilla. Morgan shook his head *no*.

"We to wait. Many kilometers to walk still."

"The men, they want to fight."

"Time later. Now we go. OK?"

"OK."

"OK."

El Gato cinched up the trousers of his fatigues and cawed like a bird to the little band of Morgan's followers, his *tigres,* spread out in the shade of the soaring white pines. Five men, all but one *guajiros,* the weathered white subsistence farmers of the Cuban countryside. Like true peasants, they could switch almost instantly from intense activity to total rest, without the jivey nervousness of city people. The moment Morgan had given the order to halt at the clearing, each had sought out a spot to rest, chewing his lunch of boiled yam and gazing quietly at the breathing vegetation all around. Now they all turned their heads, their finely tuned ears recognizing El Gato's call. They got to their feet without complaint or second thought. All except for one.

"Where be Lázaro?" asked Morgan, searching out the big redheaded boy from Havana. El Gato opened his arms in mock dismay, then gave an order in rushing Spanish at Anacleto, the gaunt one who seemed lifted from a canvas by El Greco. Anacleto hustled down a path leading to the nearby creek while the men grinned, anticipating his find. Presently a great howl was heard, as though from an animal in pain. Morgan quickly looked down at the troops below and hoped the sound would not carry.

Anacleto came out of the foliage, his usual sad countenance relieved by a vulpine grin that split his features ear to ear. Behind him stumbled Lázaro, tall, heavy, awkward, sunburned skin matching the dark red of his hair.

"This takes the fucking cake, William!" exclaimed Lázaro in English, buckling up his belt. "I can't even take a goddamn dump in these god-damn-piece-of-shit mountains without getting some bug up my ass!"

"Keep it down, this is not a college dorm," warned Morgan. Anacleto quickly told a story in Spanish that made all the men laugh.

"*Silencio, soldados!*"—silence, soldiers!—snapped Morgan. The men swallowed up their laughter, which lingered in jeering grins. Lázaro flicked his middle finger at them.

"*Niñita,*" someone said. Little girl.

Lázaro grabbed his crotch. "*Esta es mi niñita, ven y bésala!*" Come kiss this little girl!

"That's enough!" hollered Morgan. "Grab your rifle and let's go!"

Grudgingly, Lázaro hoisted the old Garand rifle on his shoulder, all the while cursing under his breath. This is only a test, thought Morgan; there will be many others.

"Vamos," he said, raising his hand. The men followed single-file in his wake down the craggy trail. El Gato looked around to make sure there was no trace left of their presence, no uncovered cigarette butt or fresh excrement, then he took the last post in the troop.

Down below, the last of the remaining soldiers snaked through the jungle. Morgan called El Gato over.

"How many soldiers, you think?" he asked.

"About two hundred," replied El Gato, clambering over a jagged granite boulder. "They will soon turn south for Topes de Collantes."

"Reinforcements?"

"Yes. They are afraid of us here in the hills already."

"How many at Topes?"

"They say three hundred before. Now five hundred."

Morgan remembered the hardscrabble faces of the men at the Segundo Frente's camp when he arrived after leaving Havana. A rifle every two men, little ammo, no training; Eloy Gutiérrez Menoyo rousing their spirits every night by the campfire with talks about the inevitability of victory even as their stomachs growled from hunger.

Forty versus five hundred. And that's just at Topes. How many soldiers throughout the Sierra? Two thousand? Three thousand? All armed with modern weapons. M-3s, Brownings, B.A.R.'s, .57 howitzers, .50 semi-recoil machine guns, the kind of weapons jungle fighters need. The kind we don't have. All we got are these Garands, the few Italian carbines the Directorio passed off to us, and the handful of tommy guns we captured last week. What kind of outfitting is that? We may get there eventually, but this row sure is hard to hoe. Hard and long.

"You said?" asked El Gato.

"I to say if today they to have fear in their pants, tomorrow they will to shit in their pants."

"Without doubt. We will triumph," said El Gato with the easy aplomb of the farmer who knows he can plow the whole field by sundown because he's done so many others like it before.

They walked on down the trail wordlessly, vultures wheeling slowly above them in the cloudless sky. The usual cawing and trilling and whining of the jungle birds lessened as the stifling heat increased, and a drape of soothing silence fell over the green hills. Occasionally they would hear a rustling in the bushes, a *majá,* the fifteen-foot snake of the region, or a *jutía,* the long-tailed tree-dwelling rodent that looks like a rat and tastes like a chicken. But mostly they marched in a sultry silence broken only by the sound of their footsteps and the heavy breathing of Lázaro, laboriously bringing up the rear.

"It may not be easy," Menoyo had told Morgan the night before, folding up the map after pointing out their destination. "Victor is used to having his way; he may prove reluctant to join our forces."

Thin, with his dark beard growing in long curls, Menoyo resembled some arcane priest expounding the truth of John's revelations on the boulders of Patmos.

"But he knows he must come around. We are the future."

Morgan lit the last of the Chesterfields he had brought up from Havana and decided Menoyo was crazy. No one but a lunatic would think that a cattle rustler who's been thriving in the hills for twenty years will want to join a band of starving guerrillas. But then again, if I joined in, why not Victor Cordón?

"He has no choice," added Menoyo, turning up the light from the hurricane lamp in the old coffee-drying shed.

"Fidel is in Oriente, the Auténticos have opened up their own front near Caibarién, we of the Segundo Frente are here. Batista is on the defensive. If Victor wants to be on the side of the winners, he has to come to us."

"That is what I to say?" asked Morgan, swatting a mosquito entangled on the hairs of his forearm, its blood splattering all over.

"Yes. You tell him that he can choose. Or others will choose for him."

"And why he to join *us* and not the others?"

"Because we are here and they are not."

"What else to say? We to have something to offer?"

"Tell him he can remain in command of his own troops. He will be recognized as a captain in our forces, with responsibility for the territory he is in."

"Money?" asked Morgan, remembering the national weakness.

"No money, certainly. We fight for the liberty of our country, we do not buy it."

Morgan thought that was a very gallant but very foolish thing to say; what matters in war is the end result, not the manner in which it is achieved. But then he was just an Americano, a pragmatic Yanqui in a world of romantic Latins.

"Anyhow, we have no money to offer him," added Menoyo regretfully. "Not in the amounts he expects, thousands of pesos. But tell him there is a weapons shipment coming in. Big guns. Mortars. Howitzers. Many submachine guns. It has been promised to us by the Directorio. He will have his corresponding share."

Menoyo pronounced the Spanish for share, *porción,* with the *z* sound of his Spanish childhood, when his parents owned a grocery store in Madrid—before the fall of the Republic, before the civil war that sent them all packing to Cuba, before the family took up arms again in yet another fratricidal struggle.

"When the weapons to come in?" asked Morgan.

"Very soon."

"How soon? We to have no ammo almost. Forty men, no rifles for everyone. Nine men always in camp. I to train but to be of no use if not to have weapons for fighting."

"William, listen to me. It matters not if you have all the equipment in the world, if you don't have the heart to use it. The best-equipped army in the world cannot triumph over a people convinced they are on the side of righteousness. The well-equipped army may win a battle. It may even win all the battles, in fact, but it will still lose the war."

"That is to be impossible," replied Morgan assuredly. "Superior fire-power always to triumph."

"You are wrong, Captain," answered Menoyo emphatically, his long thin arm slashing the air. "Look at China. Chiang Kai-shek had all the firepower, the support of the European powers, control of most of the land mass, and you see where he is right now: hiding in his palace in Formosa."

Morgan shrugged. "OK. I to tell Victor all that then?"

Menoyo flashed a quick mocking smile, lit a rank Superior cigarette, the blond strands of tobacco falling like spangles on his dark beard. Outside in the jungle an owl hooted.

"You just tell Victor he'll get weapons."

"When I to leave?"

"At dawn. You have picked your men?"

"Yes. El Gato, Anacleto, Evaristo, Rabo de Agua, and Octavio."

"All good men. El Gato knows the area well, he can be your guide. There is someone else I want you to take along."

Menoyo stuck his head outside the shack and gestured at a guard, who brought forward a heavyset man in his early twenties. Morgan pulled on his cigarette, puffing up a cloud of smoke to keep the mosquitoes away.

"This is Lázaro Prats," said Menoyo, his arm on the shoulders of the newcomer. "He came to us yesterday from the capital, bringing news. He will be making his way to the Sierra Maestra with some of Victor's people."

"Pleased to meet you, William," said Lázaro in perfect American English, shaking hands with Morgan. "Heard a lot about you."

"Lázaro was studying at NYU until last year, when he came down to join the struggle," said Menoyo. "He has been burned."

"Burned?" asked Morgan, not seeing any wounds on the young man's skin.

"Recognized," said Lázaro, clearing up the misunderstanding. "Cops on my trail. I had to take a powder all the way up here."

"So why he not to stay with us?" asked Morgan of Menoyo.

"Lázaro feels he would be of greater use in the Sierra Maestra with Fidel. He has contacts in the Guantanamo Base that could help secure supplies."

"No kidding. Who?" asked Morgan, finally acknowledging the young man. Lázaro shrugged with the careless air of the man on the inside.

"My brother-in-law works at Gitmo."

"Where?"

Lázaro shifted his weight from one foot to another as though hesitant to remain standing, then shrugged again but no longer with the same feckless attitude.

"In the mess hall," mumbled Lázaro.

"Great. What are you going to get us, a case of Heinz catsup?"

Morgan glared at Menoyo, who removed a rubber band from a rolled up handbill, flattening it open on the table. He laughed.

"*Bueno,* this is entertaining," said the *comandante.* "Look, boys, we are in the Old Wild West! Yee hah!"

Menoyo lifted the handbill. It read, in large script, REWARD FOR THE CAPTURE OF THE *BANDIDOS* OF BANAO.

"It says here that we are *comevacas,* cow eaters, not to mention cattle rustlers," said Menoyo, as amused as a child who's caught a lizard by the tail.

If only there were cattle to rustle, mused Morgan, remembering his own dinner: two pieces of boiled cassava, a small can of Vienna sausage, a tablespoon of condensed milk for dessert.

"They offer fifty thousand pesos for my head. Ten thousand for yours, William. They call you *el yanqui temerario.*"

"What's *temerario*?" asked Morgan of Lázaro.

"Fearless."

"Well, that's not too shabby. Maybe I can turn myself in for some steaks," said Morgan.

"Excuse me?" asked Menoyo in Spanish.

"*Nada,*" answered Morgan. "*Es muy cómico,*" it's very funny.

"Yes, it certainly is."

"Can you to give me it?" asked Morgan.

"Certainly," replied Menoyo, turning over the handbill. "I have too much paper already. I am running a guerrilla base here, not an office, after all. So, Lázaro, good trip and good luck."

"Thank you, *Comandante*."

"That will be all."

Morgan and Lázaro were stepping out into the night when Menoyo gestured at Morgan to return.

"Be careful with him," he whispered. "His father is the owner of the Santísima sugar mill in Oriente. He will get us a lot of aid in the future."

"Lázaro to know about the jungle?"

Menoyo chuckled at the absurdity of the question. *"Qué va,* he knows nothing at all. He was a runner, distributed propaganda. He's never been out of the city.

"A big *bebé.*"

"That's right. But a useful *bebé.* Keep an eye on him."

※ ※ ※

Morgan now looked back at Lázaro, holding the last place in line, green fatigue shirt soaked through with perspiration, wheezing from the climb up the steep trail. I hope he makes it on his own. I would hate to have to carry him.

Down the line the short, curly-haired fighter called Rabo de Agua, Tropical Tornado, puckered his fleshy lips and began to whistle. Morgan did not recognize the melody, but soon all the men, even Lázaro, had picked up on it. Rabo de Agua whistled the lead, while the others played a continuous counterpoint. Morgan recalled his own marine songs, the ditties about Eskimos and whores, and he was amused by the same simple camaraderie, the instinctive way in which fighting men cohere as single unit even if it is only around a whistled melody. I hope they are all like this in battle. If we have to go into battle.

"What to be the song?" he asked El Gato, ducking under the overgrown branches of a flaming flamboyan tree.

"It's a *décima,* a peasant song. The words are by Martí, normally." El Gato gave his impression of a smile, a small upturned tick to his thin lips, which made his expression even more like the sad housebound tabby he resembled.

"Who to be Martí?" asked Morgan. "What other songs he to write?"

"You do not know? Martí is the national poet. Died sixty years ago.

Like us, fighting in the *manigua,* the bush, for independence. It was the Spanish then, and Batista now, but some things, they never change."

"A poet soldier?"

"Yes. As poet, very good. As soldier, very bad. One battle, poof, he dies, riding his white charger. He was a better politician. Organized the Cuban exiles, got the Generals Maceo and Gómez to talk to each other and start fighting the Spanish again."

"I not to comprehend."

"Ay, Capitán, you do not understand us Cubans very well still."

"Perhaps not."

"Perhaps yes. Sometimes we fight the people we should fight, but most often we fight each other better. It's like an illness, you understand? I say this, he says that, we don't agree, and pretty soon it's pow, all blows and slaps, 'I shit on your mother,' 'You faggot, you,' and the rest, no? It's a terrible custom that I sincerely wish we could renounce. Even Martí, after all he did for the cause of independence, he was called Captain Spider because the people were jealous of him and what he had done. You see that bird?"

El Gato pointed out one of the long-necked buzzards slowly turning above them, patiently waiting for prey.

"Buitre, vulture, no?" said Morgan.

"Yes. We call it *aura tiñosa,* the stained raptor. We have a saying. *Si la envidia fuera tiña, cuántos tiñosos hubieran.* That is to say, if envy were a stain, there would be so many people stained. Well, in Cuba everybody is stained. All of us. We are all eaten up by envy. And as you know, envy often makes you do things that you shouldn't."

"You too, Gato?"

"Oiga, Capitán, you listen. I'm Cuban too."

"What you to envy?"

El Gato cast down his eyes, adjusted his knapsack on his shoulders, as if extra weight had been added to his load.

"I prefer not to say, Captain. But convince yourself. Ask around and you will see. Envy is a very pernicious problem in our country."

The men had stopped singing, all lending an ear to the discussion. Evaristo, the thickset mechanic from a little town outside Sancti Spiritus, nodded in agreement.

"El Gato is right, Captain. Here people think that if Johnny so-and-so has this or that, they should have it too. Why do you think I find myself here?"

"Evaristo, I thought you were here because you love the revolution,"

157

teased Rabo de Agua, flashing laughing blue eyes from underneath a mass of chestnut curls.

Evaristo swelled up his chest like a frog before his song, hoisted his weapon in the air.

"This is the proof that I love the revolution. I am here for Cuba. But I hate Batista worst of all. And even more than that, I hate all the Batistianos."

"What they to do to you?" asked Morgan.

Evaristo spit on the ground, then stepped on his green yellow spittle as though breaking the neck of the one he hated most.

"They came one afternoon to my shop, three guys from the SIM. We were working on a car that some people had left for us to fix. Some bullet holes in the body, nothing of gravity. I say, there are always shootings in Cuba, you go and find out who caused it, well, it's impossible, you understand. So these *esbirros,* these hirelings, come in saying that the car had been used in a bank holdup by members of the twenty-sixth of July, and where were the owners of the car? My sister, who was managing the shop, said she didn't know, that the car had been dropped off with a note. The SIM people didn't believe her so they took her in for questioning. *Mamá* went crazy and I moved heaven and earth to get her out. They finally released her after a week.

"You know what those sons of whores had done? Smashed in her teeth. With a rifle butt they'd broken her teeth, then they'd taken them out with pliers, one by one. She was all gap toothed by the time we got her. But that wasn't all they had done. When she persisted that she didn't know who owned the car, they had opened up her legs and into her private parts they poured car battery acid. With a pipe that they just stuck in there. Worse than some animal, even. She was scarred for life. She was no good as a woman.

"We took her to the hospital but the first night she opened up the window and jumped out. She broke her neck and died. The nurses at the hospital said she had gone crazy; she thought she was still being tortured.

"After the funeral, I sold the shop and I got *Mamá* to leave for Miami with my little brother. Then I went to SIM headquarters and I paid some people to tell me the names of the ones who had done this thing to my sister. I went in and talked to one of them, a sergeant. I pretended to be a turncoat, that I had information on a plot to blow up City Hall, that he and his men should show up at this house in the country I told them was the headquarters, and I would show them the conspirators. They were so arrogant they didn't suspect anything. When they came, me and my cousin were in the trees around the house and we opened fire on them. They ran inside and that's where we got them, because what I did is that I set up a bomb so that a fire would explode, and then they're inside and we're outside with guns and nobody comes out."

Evaristo smiled, still savoring his revenge; all the while the men march slowly down the red dirt path.

"So what happened then?" asked El Gato.

"They burned to death inside the *bohío.* Their cries could be heard all over the area, people from the surrounding countryside coming to hear them squeal. It was like a party, almost. The SIM people were begging for mercy, but we wouldn't let them out of the house. I was laughing when I heard them crying, begging for help. Sons of whores, now you want it? And what did you do when Ada María screamed? That smell of burning flesh was the most exciting part. Sons of whores. One of them tried to run out; his clothes were all aflame. We cut him up in two with our machine gun. That was fun as well. The others we turned to cinders. Then me and my cousin we left for the mountains. He was killed in Yaguajay last January, and now here I am."

A brief interval, the smell of death in the noses of the men. Then, "I not to understand. Why is that with the envy?" asked Morgan.

"It was a competitor who called in the SIM on me," answered Evaristo. "He was jealous of our business and thought that would be a good way to get rid of us. But I fixed him good. You should have seen how he screamed when I cut out his tongue. *Hijo 'e puta.*"

"Well done," said Rabo de Agua. "I would have done the same thing."

"Me too," echoed Anacleto, the former schoolteacher with the thick-framed glasses. Even quiet Octavio nodded his head.

"They all got what they deserved," added Lázaro. "Don't you think, Captain? Wouldn't you do that if someone touched your loved ones?"

Morgan nodded, the claws of a pain he had almost forgotten leaping up at him.

"Yes, I too to do the same. Surely."

El Gato refrained from comment, watching Morgan's stunned reaction to the casual viciousness of Evaristo's tale.

I have no loved ones, thought Morgan. I once had Laura, but now she's gone too. I have no one.

Just the thought of Laura was enough to make Morgan wince. He turned and hurried down the path ahead of the group, as if by running away from them he could escape his painful memories as well. The men, bewildered, picked up the pace after their troubled leader.

I don't want to think about her, I do not. I do not want to remember her. Her face, her hands, her breasts, her smile, the way she slumped on

159

the sidewalk when the bullets rained down, the way she kissed me that first night out by the statues in her yard. I cannot think of that. It is wrong and harmful. What good is it to think back to something I cannot fix? The past is buried, and digging up her shadow will not bring me any release. Yes I miss her yes I miss her yes I miss her. I miss everything about her. Her hair. Her smell. Her soft skin. Her smiling eyes. But I won't remember. I don't want to remember. I cannot. I must survive. I must.

Morgan hustled down the path, forcing himself to keep his mind clear, to wipe from it the memory that would destroy him, dooming the little he felt he could do in her name.

"Hey, Willie, slow down, who do you think you are, a marine drill sergeant?" cried Lázaro, on the verge of hyperventilation. "Jesus, you're a ballbuster."

"We have a lot of ground to cover," answered Morgan, talking over his shoulder. He pointed at a swarm of indigo clouds creeping up from the horizon.

"If it starts to rain, we may be delayed more than they expect, and we'll miss the rendezvous. Now hurry up!" Then, in Spanish, at full voice, "The men, to lift their legs!"

El Gato raced up to Morgan, tugged at his sleeve. Morgan looked down into his slanted eyes, full of knowledge and compassion.

"*Capitán,*" said El Gato softly, his small body jerking along at the same pitched flight as Morgan, "we have time. You cannot evade remembrance. You must live with it."

"You what to want to mean?" snapped Morgan, hustling down the trail as though his knapsack was not weighed down with supplies, as though the heat were not stifling, as though his heart were not bleeding.

"We all know, *Capitán*. She was a very valiant woman. Let us honor her memory. Do not stain it with abuse."

Morgan glanced down at El Gato and then looked ahead again. He did not answer. He did not know how to express the pain that racked him, the torture he meant to keep behind the stoic mask.

"I to hear you," he said, peremptorily "and I to tell you we must to hurry. Now to follow my orders!"

"*Sí, mi capitán,*" answered El Gato, knowing it was useless to argue with a man in such a condition. He turned and signaled at the men to break into a forced march, then ran swiftly behind Morgan.

His eyes betray him, thought El Gato, jogging alongside Morgan. He wants to withdraw through action, but he has not reconciled himself yet.

Theirs must have been a great love indeed. But just like an Americano, he does not know how to deal with it. *Qué remedio.* What remedy. We must continue.

So El Gato slowed down the pace and gestured again at the others behind him. They jerked their hands at Morgan, who now hurried down the path, pulling away from his troop. El Gato touched his heart, and they all nodded their heads.

"*Está jodío el hombre,*" the man is really fucked, said Lázaro.

"It is you who will be fucked if you do not hurry up. Give me that rifle; we'll catch up with him soon enough."

Lázaro took off his Italian jungle carbine and passed it to El Gato, who hung it on his free shoulder as though a toy, and the men pressed forward.

※ ※ ※

Morgan hurried down the trail, his feet barely touching the ground, wanting nothing so much as to put such distance between himself and his memories that all of Cuba and the United States would fall in between and still leave enough room for Europe, Asia, the Pacific and Atlantic Oceans, and the rest of the whole wide world.

I should have taken the bullet, he kept on thinking. It should have been me, it should have been me. I have no right to be here. I have no right. No right at all.

Coward, he called himself. Coward. Chicken. *Maricón,* faggot. Yellow. A great big fake, that's what you are. You big piece of—

He tumbled to the ground. He found himself facedown on the red dirt trail, and he had to laugh. I can't even run a straight line and I think that I can fight. What a joke. God, I'm such a joke. I wish I was dead.

Morgan sat on the ground. On a hill down the road he saw the rock shaped like the head of an Indian on a nearby hill. This was the end of their route on the trail, according to Menoyo's instructions. From here on they should cut across the jungle to reach Victor's camp, still a good fifteen miles away.

God, that was stupid, thought Morgan. I shouldn't have run away like that. What kind of example am I giving the men? Some captain I am.

He first smelled the moisture, washing over the hillside like a giant wave, bearing the scent of jungle growth and the slight tang of the ocean forty miles away. A raindrop fell, pitting the dry dirt like a small bomb. Then a second, a third, each drop heavy, viscous, foreboding.

He rose to his knees, ready to pull out the piece of polyurethane that served as his raincoat. A crack of thunder rattled the hills, then a lightning bolt struck the ground like a witch's pitching fork half a mile down the wooded slope. We're in for it, thought Morgan. We're really in for a good one. Where are those guys, anyhow?

Morgan got to his feet, put down the backpack. That's when he noticed the flesh wound in his left calf, blood trickling down into his boot. Stunned, he looked up just in time to spot the muzzle flash of a rifle a hundred yards away in the brush. A khaki-suited soldier behind a royal palm tree was aiming straight at him as another lightning bolt fell and a storm wind howled over the treetops.

Chapter

3

Morgan hit the dirt, shots humming above him, then crawled quickly to the bushes by the side of the trail. Panting, he lay flat, the bullets slicing the ground a few feet to his left. He readied his Thompson, peered cautiously through the long blades of sharp grass.

The shooting stopped. He could see no one, but he heard three distinct male voices, quivering with the high pitch of nerves. One man questioned whether they'd killed the rebel; the other answered he was sure he'd downed the *matavacas*, the cow killer; a third said his gun had jammed, and cursed the cunt of Batista's mother. A crack of thunder. The sky grew black, and heavy drops of rain began to fall, almost timidly, on the expectant ground.

Morgan was grateful for the rain; it would deafen whatever moves he made to escape the ambush. He thought quickly, surveying the situation.

There was no way to tell if the men just a hundred yards away from him were an advance party, or laggards who had gotten separated from the main body of the troops he'd seen earlier that day. He tried violently to remember the map of the area but could not recall if there was yet a third trail that lead directly down to the valley. There was no particular reason why these soldiers should be stationed there. Where was that goddamn Gato?

His answer came to him with the loud bang of grenade explosions and the *rat-tat-tat* of automatic guns down the trail, the stench of gunpowder and cordite mixing with the dirt smell of the rain. There's your reason, you idiot. We've been ambushed.

He considered slithering down the grassy slope feet first to get away from the attackers, then opted for a different tactic. He took off his webbed belt, then threw it about thirty yards away with a bellow. The moment the belt hit the ground, a hail of gunfire sliced it to ribbons. In the confusion he slid behind a felled tree trunk twenty yards away, then eased himself down as far as he could to wait.

A brief halt, then another barrage of gunfire aimed at the remnants of his poor maimed belt. Lighting and a majestic thunderclap as the storm cloud pushed its way through. The rain fell in thick, enormous sheets, like giant waves sweeping over the decks of a struggling ship. The gloom grew deeper, the morning's baking sun only a memory of light.

The firing stopped. Morgan saw, to his relief and excitement, all three men easing out of their hiding place across the road, slowly, tentatively, furtively, tiptoeing their way across. The older of the three, with a bulbous head and scrawny trembling arms, stayed at the edge of the road as backup, pointing his gun at the back of the two younger men, who carefully threaded their way through the grass.

Morgan pressed down on the ground, feeling his weapon a part of his body, the gun sight as sensitive as the whiskers of a cat, waiting for the precise moment to pounce. In that instant of fatal expectancy he was devoid of all thought and mortal regrets. He became the keeper of a gate through which reality eased, unfiltered and immediate, and he knew that it was a faculty greater even than God's, because Morgan did not have to worry about the men's past or future or their families or their souls. All he needed to decide was should they live or should they die, and in that pitiless, exalted choice Morgan was freer than the creator and mightier as well.

But that feeling lasted but a fraction of a second as the two men, in their twenties, with the guarded look of the habitually hungry, advanced into the bushes. Closer, thought Morgan, let them get closer before the firing's done. You have to hit all three at once, so let them take their time.

The men stopped. Did they catch on? wondered Morgan. No. Yes! Yes! They did!! One of them is pointing at the belt and is turning to the other men.

NOW! SHOOT! NOW! NOW!

Protected by the tree trunk, Morgan opened fire on the soldiers. The one nearest Morgan toppled headfirst, gun flying out into the air, while the second man turned and glanced at Morgan with surprise, as though scolding him for tricking them into death, and then collapsed as well.

Quickly Morgan shifted position, rolling over to the far end of the tree trunk, training his gun on the older soldier across the road, who let off a clip of bullets to cover his retreat back into the bush. Morgan knew he had only scant seconds before the man got away, and he didn't even bother to sight and shoot. He grabbed a grenade, pulled the pin, lobbed it across. The soldier was racing for the safety of the tall grass when the impact struck, and he flew twenty feet across the road, propelled by the explosion.

In spite of his wounded leg, Morgan ran at a crouch to the other side of the road to finish the job. It was unnecessary. The explosion had broken the man's neck and he had crumpled like an old, unwanted doll on the muddy ground.

The soldier was carrying an M-1, which Morgan hoisted onto his shoulder, as well as two hundred rounds in his belt, which Morgan strapped across his chest. Gunfire blared again down the road. Morgan left for later the collection of the other soldiers' weapons. He took out the dead man's leather belt, fashioned a quick tourniquet around his wounded left calf, and limped his way down the road.

He spotted his men at a bend fifty yards away, pinned down by a group of soldiers on a high rock two hundred yards up the side of the mountain. The men barely had time to take shelter behind a handful of pine trees by the side of the road when they were set upon. Only the fact that he had strayed ahead of the group had saved Morgan from being down there eating dirt and staring death in the face.

Through the veil of rain Morgan thought he recognized El Gato, crouched behind a tree, firing back at the enemy. From El Gato's left came the report of the other men in the group, shooting from the bush.

Up on the rock, the enemy upped the ante. A mortar shell whistled through the air, landed two hundred yards away from Morgan's men, leveling an old cedar. Rabo de Agua broke away from the grove and, firing wildly, ran for the cover of a cluster of white-frosted *macagua* trees fifty yards away, closer to the rise. Morgan's men, covering Rabo de Agua, unleashed a hailstorm of firepower at the rock, but even then Rabo de Agua barely managed to reach the shelter of the *macaguas,* unable to move an inch further.

A .30-caliber, probably on a tripod, thought Morgan, crouching by the side of the road, fifty yards away from the battle zone. He craned his neck, looking up at the red rock rise behind him, trying to gauge the distance without giving himself away. A few stray bullets grazed his ears. He dropped to the ground.

All at once the pain in his calf returned with the fierce intensity of a dog's fangs in his flesh. With great effort Morgan put aside his pain, drawing two shallow breaths for every deep one, pondering his next move. The soldiers who bushwhacked me were probably the scouts for this group. That means there's another path up there we don't know about, parallel to this one. Morgan looked back, noticed the slight decline leading right to the edge of the road.

I could go back up there and run up the rise, he thought hurriedly, anxiety mounting inside him with each passing second. But if I don't reach the enemy in time, before they straighten out their mortar, they'll wipe out the boys. Besides, they could be expecting something like that. Maybe they set down mines. Even if they didn't, if they see me coming they'll just turn around and pick me off. No, brother, there's only one way out of this, and that's straight up.

He glanced up at the rocky hill in front of him, jutting out at an almost seventy-degree angle from the path. Great, he thought. Now I gotta be a fucking mountain climber too. And in this rain. And with a bad leg. Great. Just fucking great.

Morgan put down his backpack, his captured M-1, and the ammo on the side of the road, moved his Thompson so that it hung down his back, and stared at the wall of rock before him. He forced himself to concentrate on climbing the wall, one step, one grapple hold at a time. Better not look down, he thought as he leaped on a large flat rock that served as a ledge, spotting a side path that would take him some distance up the side of the hill. God only knows if this is going to work. If He cares to know.

He reached the end of the path, then hoisted himself up by grabbing the dangling roots of a sideways-growing bush.

Of course He cares. He always knows, thought Morgan. He knows right now exactly what you're doing. Is that so? Morgan told himself, feeling the rocks sliding under his boots, the surface slippery from the blinding torrents of rain washing down.

Does that mean that He already knows what I'm going to do before I do it? thought Morgan, hugging the face of the rise, the rocks under his feet streaming down, the pain in his calf joined by the clamor for relief of his back muscles and his cramped fingers, desperately sunk like pylons into the loosening dirt for support.

Yes, naturally He knows. He is all-knowing and all-powerful and before you take a step He already knows what road you will take and where you will wind up.

That doesn't sound right, continued Morgan with his mental debate, feeling the world spin around him in pain, the rain streaming through the plastic, running down him like a river, down the torn calf and the screaming arms and the cramped fingers that held him by sheer effort of will from falling sixty feet to the ground.

Down below, El Gato spotted Morgan clinging to the side of the hill and his heart was full of admiration for a man so foolishly daring.

"What do we do?" asked Octavio, next to El Gato.

"Keep firing!" he ordered the men. "But be careful so those sons of bitches don't see him!"

"*Qué cojones!*" muttered Lázaro, loading his Garand.

El Gato kept his eyes on Morgan, who leapt to a protruding basalt ridge on the hill and hauled half his body up, his legs left dangling until they finally gained a purchase, and then he crouched in the rain, looking around for the next turn. This one is a true *tigre,* a mountain cat, thought El Gato. We are indeed fortunate to have such a one leading us, even if the pain in his heart sometimes clouds his vision. He is for us to the last inch of his body.

Up on the ridge the six enemy soldiers waded in the pool of water their foxhole had become. They righted the mortar, aimed it at the grove shielding El Gato and the men. The corporal commanding the group lowered his arm in the rain, the sleeve of his raincoat flapping like the wing of a predator. The shell flew out, striking the top of the trees.

"*Coño,* improve your aim, you shit eater!" cried the corporal to the private first class named Núñez, who struggled with his weapon.

"Next time, *Cabo.* I think I finally sighted them," answered Núñez, looking forward to the hundred-peso reward per dead rebel that General Cantillo had promised the troops.

Crouched on the granite slab, Morgan saw the missile fly by, toppling the top of the pine trees. He had only a few more moments before the mortar shells landed squarely on their target.

Morgan moved with a crabby sideways motion, his face to the dirt, only his elbows propelling him forward. Shaking from the effort and the pain, he covered the final stretch of the rise, finding himself about thirty yards to the right and rear of the soldiers.

He counted six of them, four lying down on the edge of the big rock, exchanging gunfire with Morgan's men, while an officer and a young man with a mortar struggled to right the weapon.

In the end it doesn't matter, thought Morgan, moving his legs in spite of the blinding pain in his left calf. It really doesn't matter at all.

He got ready to spring forward, taking the grenade out of the pocket of his fatigues, hoping this one would not be a dud, as half of the Frente's were. He was removing the pin to toss it when the young man with the mortar glanced behind and spotted Morgan on the mound. The officer, thin and dark, turned to look as well, even as he barked out orders, and two of his gunmen wheeled around, pointing their M-3s on Morgan a scant thirty feet away, but with the storm's final crack of thunder Morgan tossed his grenade in an overhead motion, and the bullets cut the air almost at the same time as the grenade dropped next to the .50-caliber Browning, and Morgan threw himself back on the ground, regretting that he had to take out such a fine piece of machinery but not feeling even a twinge of regret for the soldiers whose limbs were torn by the explosion, which rocked the soggy foxhole with the force of a minor tremor.

It really doesn't matter at all, thought Morgan, preparing to spring up, easing the Thompson off his back onto his hands.

If everything has been predestined, it doesn't matter what we do, he intuited quickly in that moment of lucidity before the final flight of violence. We might as well do what we think is right, because we ourselves can never know. Things will turn out the way He wants them to turn out because it is all in His plans and we truly are only puppets in His hands.

Morgan sprang to his feet. The rain pounded his face like so many bullets.

But am I not a man? Am I not in His image? Am I not free?

Down below El Gato ordered his men to stop shooting. An ominous silence.

Rabo de Agua took advantage of the lull and raced out of his hiding place and crossed the road, pressing his back to the side of the hill, ready to clamber up if necessary. Trembling, he grabbed his gun, jerked his head upward.

El Gato waited in the pine grove, as did the other men, each with his own vision of what the silence could mean. There came the sound of several bursts of gunfire, quick, vicious; then silence again.

Morgan peeked out on the rock, waved, shouted.

"Ya terminar!"—already to finish—he said in his usual, broken Spanish. The men laughed and jeered.

"When the cunt is that gringo ever going to learn Spanish?"

"Did you leave any for us?"

"Oye, what took you so long? Did they make you a cafecito?"

Morgan stood on the lip of the rock, holding up the mortar.

"Es bueno!" It is good! And the sun broke through and warmed the drenched red dirt road.

※ ※ ※

For the next two hours the small group of fighters wended down the soggy trail, slippery at first but soon caked over as the harrowing sun melted away the moisture. At a white pine tree Morgan cut off a low-hanging branch growing in a Y shape, quickly stripping the bark and using it as an improvised crutch.

Soon the mountain trail, with its tall sweeping spires of yellow pine, cedar, and mahogany, gave way to the gentle green hills leading down to the Agabama River, whose slow-moving current shone a dull yellow in the early afternoon sun. Morgan and his fighters moved progressively northeast, aiming to cross the river and meet with Victor's men at the foot of the range that rose in a blue haze miles away.

Terraced fields of coffee, corn, and oranges began to appear, tantalizing in their ripe openness, as though seeming to say, Fighter, stop here, we welcome you. They walked past a peasant's hut, a *bohío*, where the whole family—father in a torn prairie shirt, mother in a long stained dress, and four naked blond boys—gathered to wave and smile. Morgan and his men waved back and trudged on.

El Gato approached Morgan. Looking into his captain's eyes he saw only pictures of cold longing behind the blue orbs.

"Request permission to stop, Captain," said El Gato with a stiff salute.

"Not to have need to salute that way, *Compañero*," said Morgan. "This not to be the army of Uncle Sam."

"*Sí señor*," said El Gato, gesturing at the men to halt. "This is much better."

"That's what I think too. Permission granted. Tell, ah, what the hell, I'll tell them myself."

Morgan leaned on his improvised crutch, addressed the men.

"We're halting for ten minutes. Rabo de Agua, go reconnoiter down the road."

The men smiled, nervous, save for Rabo de Agua, who stood in anxious expectation.

"Well, go on, man, didn't you hear me?"

Lázaro put down his rifle, scratched the side of his neck where a fly bit him, debated whether to tell Morgan.

"Are you deaf, Rabo de Agua? Follow your orders!"

"Ah, Captain," said Lazaro hesitantly, "I don't think he can understand you. You're speaking in English."

"What? Jesus." Morgan opened his hand, slapped his forehead. "*Estúpido capitán*. I to forget the language. You all to be so good the fighters I to think I again in the troops of the Uncle Sam. *Perdones.*"

"No, no, that's all right, don't worry, Captain," came back the response of the men, instantly protective of their leader. El Gato wondered how long would it be before Morgan snapped. He hoped it would be in battle, where the fever of the fight could cleanse him of his lovesickness. Because if it happened during a lull, *ay, ay, ay Dios mío,* it would be a real mess, a real rice with mangoes.

"Ten minutes. Rabo de Agua, to go look enemy down below, to wait for us down there."

"*Sí, mi capitán,*" replied Rabo de Agua, who saluted and took off in a clip, racing down the slope.

Morgan limped to a rock under a cedar tree, leaned back, and closed his eyes. He was asleep in an instant.

Chapter

4

In his dreams Morgan is back in the old yellow wooden house by the sea. Once more a flat, lime-green-and-periwinkle ocean laps against the gray concrete pilings. Scudding cloud castles kiss the horizon, embraced by the pine-forested arms of the encircling bay. Once again he looks away from the ocean, and once again he finds himself in the iron bed in the sparsely furnished room, Max sitting in a heavy wood-and-leather Spanish chair.

"Can you hear me?" Max asks.

Morgan looks down at his bandaged arms, thorax, left leg. He rolls up his eyes to the whitewashed rafters twenty feet above.

"Loud and clear," he says, knowing this is a dream but also knowing, with the inevitability of destiny, that this is what he must answer.

"Welcome back, buddy," says Max with relief. "You've been gone a long time. We thought we lost you."

Morgan sits up, feels the pain not in his arms or his chest or even his legs but in his back, as though all sensation were concentrated on the last vertebra of his coccyx.

"God damn," he mutters as he rights himself, notices the bedpan under his legs, sloshes its foul contents.

"Gimme. I'm used to handling other people's shit," says Max. He takes the pan into the next room. Morgan follows him with his eyes. The living room is sparsely decorated with bamboo furnishings—a bar, a couch, a chair. Max disappears and Morgan sinks back into his pillow. The rackety flushing of an overhead toilet, a squeaky faucet, water rushing out.

Morgan takes a deep breath; his lungs hurt. He spots more details in the room—an old Life magazine, a filched Capri Hotel ashtray on a wooden table next to a wicker chair. He notices the fine mosquito netting draped around the bed and wonders why he missed it before.

Max returns, wiping his hands on a hand towel stamped Sevilla Biltmore.

"Got a cigarette?" *asks Morgan. Max moves away the netting, gives Morgan a Pall Mall, lights it. The taste is harsh, biting. Morgan coughs, hands it back.*

"Where am I?" *he asks as Max puts it out in the ashtray.*

"Varadero, a beach town sixty miles from Havana. We brought you here after the yacht club."

"How bad was it?"

"You're mending. A bullet nicked your left lung; grenade fragments got into your arm and legs."

Max picks up a cup of coffee out of nowhere, sips it, sets it down on the table, then takes a bite of an apple pie, stands up, turns his back on Morgan. Morgan wants to ask a question but he doesn't dare, because in his dream he already knows the answer, even if he can't remember it right now.

Max is standing at the window. He gives Morgan a garbled message, sounding like the faint reception of a distant radio program. Morgan strains to hear.

"Who took care of me?"

"The American Hospital. You really can't go back . . . ten thousand dollar reward . . . coppers from Pinar del Río to Oriente . . . you."

"What about here?" *says Morgan, his words revolving slowly in the room.*

"This is private property . . . Owens Hedge's estate . . . lets us the beach house . . . special cases."

Morgan feels his head swimming. He has always been in bed, looking out at that ocean, always asking questions to which he knows the answers. Max is now lying in bed next to him.

"You know, I will have that cigarette after all." *Max gets up, lights a cigarette, then flies around the room like a toy plane, swooping down to give it to Morgan.*

"Enjoy!" *he orders.*

The smoke wakes Morgan, its harshness a welcome antidote to the anodyne feelings of bereavement. The seconds play on, the tears come as a river flowing to the ocean that is death. Morgan bats his eyelashes. Max is sitting at the chair, apparently normal once again.

"I think it's time you level with me, don't you?" *says Morgan.*

Max opens his hands. "Go ahead, I'm ready."

"Who are you with?"

"Who am I with?" repeats Max once, twice, ten times, his pitch growing louder, shriller; then he answers in Spanish, and Morgan understands every word, even though he knows he really can't speak Spanish, but this is a dream and he speaks it perfectly.

"That's a good question, William. I'm with anybody who can carry out the job."

"Cut the crap. Are you CIA?"

Max gives Morgan a yellow, expanding smile.

"You know I can't tell you that." All at once Max finds himself hauled off the chair, dragged and held by Morgan's one free arm.

"I am tired of this, you understand? You have put me in this situation and I got to find out who's behind this, can't you see that?"

"I can see that," says Max.

Morgan opens his hand. Max flutters away, flying around the room like a peeved wasp.

"I'm sorry," says Morgan. "You did save my life."

"It's OK," says Max, touching his throat, "I understand."

Max lands in the middle of the room, whispers softly.

"An operation . . . State . . . CIA."

"What?" bellows Morgan. "Speak up!"

Max stands motionless in an eerie spotlight as a voice booming from above explains: "You are part of an operation of the agency and the State Department. Your friend Nick was in it as well."

The room becomes illuminated by an oozing yellow light. A white gull flies in through the window, squawks, flies out again.

"How did you know I was at the club?"

"We were following you and Laura. When the police picked up your driver, we took his place at the last minute."

Morgan sees a spot of growing black in the horizon, hears a distant buzzing. The room starts to spin, his eyes feel leaden, his cigarette drops to the ground.

"And Laura?" he asks, needlessly, for he knows the answer already. Max is gone, the room is empty. The voice booms: "She's dead, William. We're sorry."

We're sorry we're sorry we're sorry echoes in Morgan's dream and the buzzing becomes a jet plane moving past the window the racket of the engine rattling the old timbers the pilot waving good-bye at William as the buzzing splits his brain and everything becomes a field of red and everything hurts and he wants to die to end this once and for all.

✳ ✳ ✳

"Wake up, Captain, wake up!" El Gato shook Morgan until the Yanqui opened his eyes and again felt the rending of his troubled heart.

"What passes?" asked Morgan.

El Gato pointed up at the sky.

"Government plane! They've sighted us! Run for the bush!"

⸕ ⸕ ⸕

The lumbering B-26 droned overhead in the limpid blue sky, canting like a vulture riding thermals.

"*Vamos, Capitán!*" said El Gato, helping Morgan to his feet. The two men ran for cover under the spreading branches of a mahogany tree, where the rest of the troop had already huddled.

It's due north by northwest, thought Morgan. It must be heading for Cienfuegos, sixty miles away. What is it doing here?

The plane buzzed in closer, skimming the treetops. No one spoke, as though silence and attention were enough to will the plane back to where it came.

Maybe it doesn't see us after all, thought Morgan. Maybe it's just reconnoitering the area for a future offensive. It doesn't make sense for a B-26 to be out on a search-and-destroy mission, anyhow. It's a bomber, not a jungle fighter. That's like an elephant trying to swat a gnat. Makes no military sense.

Morgan glanced at the men, all rigid with expectation, eyes focused on the aircraft. The giant shadow passed over them, and the men came to life again, smiling, shaking their heads at their silly nerves. Morgan smiled too and raised his hand to keep them in their places when he saw Lázaro move out of the shadows and, in a careless gesture, light a cigarette with a lighter in the burning sunlight, still looking at the departing bomber.

"Get back here, you idiot!!"

The copilot of the B-26, looking over his shoulder, caught the reflected glare of Lázaro's lighter down in the bush. He pointed it out to the pilot, who nodded, then sharply wheeled the plane around.

"To run!" shouted Morgan. "To spread out! The plane goes to bomb!"

The plane banked left, its enormous wingspan almost touching the nearby ridge before setting in and heading for the spot where it had detected the yellow glinting light.

From the air all was quiet and serene. The cerulean blue of the sky was graced with free-form clouds spun off the storm front that had scoured the hills a few hours before, the edge of the cloudlets tinged gold from the reflection of the yellow waters of the Agabama. The pilot could see all the way down to the dark blue of the Caribbean and the far-flung Caballanes keys off the coast of Camagüey. He'd done his training at the U.S. naval air force base in Pensacola and now, as he pressed the button that opened the bomb hatch, he recalled his instructor's constant admonition to keep his eye on the target. I think we hit them this time, he thought, seeing how the bombs made little puffs of smoke on the ground, how his gunman raked the tree line with machine gun fire.

"That's a few less commie rebels," he told the copilot, righting the plane. The copilot grinned, gave him the thumbs-up sign.

Down in the bush, Morgan hobbled as fast as he could, followed by El Gato and Evaristo, behind them the *rat-tat-tat* of the gunner slicing branches off trees, deadwood falling like confetti on the ground. The smell of new-cut pine and the deafening sound of the bombs rocking the ground, trees toppling, rocks hurled skyward by the explosion, the smell of devouring doom.

Morgan was hurled to the ground by the force of the impact. A few yards away he saw the culvert of an old irrigation ditch for an abandoned coffee plantation. He gave a signal to El Gato and Evaristo, also knocked down by the explosion. The men dashed for protection as other bombs fell and the shell fragments filled the air.

Looking up, Morgan saw the lettering of the plane and the flags of the two countries, the American Stars and Stripes and the Cuban lone star and bars, spray-painted on the under fuselage of the B-26.

The plane flew out low over the ridge, wheeled around once more, then righted its course and headed to base, a child called home for lunch after playing out in the field. Morgan leaned back against the cold concrete wall of the culvert, the throbbing of his torn calf all but forgotten in the exhilaration of survival.

Someday I will have to tell someone how this was, he thought, so they will know what our fight was all about. We are making a stand. We are the minutemen of our time.

Morgan took his first few steps out of the harboring shade into the sun. In the aftermath of the bombing, the normal sounds of the jungle—the trilling of the birds, the buzzing of the insects, the gurgling of the small streams and rivulets—nearly all had disappeared in the emptiness left in the trail of the B-26, as though the explosives had gouged out not just the earth but also the continuum of life that flowed all around them, creating a hollow of life and expectations in the jungle.

Morgan noticed the multicolored feathers of two dead pheasants partially covered by the snapped-off branches of a pine tree. He picked them up.

"Dinner," he said, holding up the birds.

"At least we got something out of it," said El Gato, hustling forward. Then he stopped, turned to Morgan with pity in his eyes. Morgan looked ahead.

Under a sliced-off tree branch, blood flowing from his mouth, lay Lázaro, as dead as the birds Morgan carried in his hand.

※ ※ ※

The booms of the explosions filled the air, echoing off the steep walls of the narrow valley. The sound carried down the hillside, leaving vague reverberations among the trees and bushes down the creek in the gorge, all the way to the camp of the outlaw named Victor Cordón.

Cordón glanced up from his game of *tute,* three gilt Spanish cards already on the barrelhead, the mace and the queen in his hand still. He wrinkled his nose as though smelling something foul. His asthmatic companion wheezed, coughed, then said in an Argentinean accent, *"Qué pasa, che?"*—what's wrong, buddy?—in the slang of Buenos Aires.

"They're bombing up in that ridge, *Comandante,"* said Victor, standing up, his sharp raptor's nose flaring open, scanning the horizon like a tracker.

"Sit down, *che,* sit down. The fighting is not with us. That will come in good time. I think I have the *tute.*"

The failed doctor, photographer, and itinerant revolutionary put down his five gilt-edged cards on the barrelhead.

"In fact, I think I won this game," said Ernesto Guevara, chomping on his cigar, as proud of this victory as of all his other accomplishments.

The Cuban army plane flew overhead, the buzzing of its engines a distant murmur of destruction.

Chapter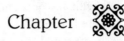

5

"Welcome to the *Creole Kitchen*," said the dark-haired hostess, leaning forward over the counter to show off her shapely bust in the tight white apron.

Glass bottles of milk and wine, a basket of white and brown eggs, and another of brightly colored tropical fruit framed her figure. She was particularly proud of her selection of golden papayas, blue cherimoyas, green soursop, and red bananas, which she knew would make such a striking visual presentation on color TV. True, most of her viewers would not be able to appreciate the subtle effect of that tropical spectrum, since only a few hundred homes in the greater Havana region could afford the high cost of color sets. But those that watched in color were the ones that counted for something in Cuba—the wives of the top businessmen, politicians, and professionals, as well as her own sponsors—and she knew they would appreciate it.

"I'm Nitza Villapol. Today's program will be something special, a wonderful menu that you little housewives will be able to offer your hard-working husband when he comes home. Something *à la française!* First we're going to show you how to make a wonderful dessert, a Grand Marnier soufflé. To go with that, we're also going to be preparing a wonderful but oh-so-easy chicken marengo. And for starters, something that always goes well with the sultry days we've been having, a nice, cool, fast vichyssoise. Yes, it's a totally French menu today, but don't be concerned, you'll be surprised how easy it all can be. But first, here's a message from our sponsor, Patagrás Milk. We'll be right back."

※ ※ ※

In the kitchen of Kuquine, his estate outside Havana, President Batista fiddled with his pots and pans in anxious anticipation of the program's return. He had removed Cuca, the longtime family cook, to the pantry; there she watched and waited, along with the other four kitchen helpers, fascinated by the *presidente's* latest hobby.

It had all begun a few weeks before, during a lull between cabinet meetings on the eternal problem of the rebels in the sierra, when Batista idly flicked on his RCA Victor at the palace and stumbled upon the show. Drawn to the program in spite of himself, he was intrigued by the ease with which the hostess had prepared a stuffed porgy in red sauce. To his own surprise, Batista found himself remembering his early days in the barracks near Manzanillo, when he had had to scramble his own meager omelettes for dinner. His favorite had been *tortilla de papa,* a fluffy potato omelet that was cheap and nutritious, even though he never quite got the knack of cooking it through without burning the edges.

Of course, after the Sergeants' Revolt in '33, he'd moved on to other, more palatable chores, and he had never had to cook for himself again. But this spring, a quarter century after his precipitous climb to power, he felt the tug of the past once more, a discomforting feeling that all glory was behind him. The Cuba that he had created had become an unrecognizable, ungrateful place; and he longed for the days when he had had the prospect of youth and hard work ahead of him. To cook for himself, then, in whatever reduced way it might be, was a way of reaching out to that other, gangly, tawny youth in the tight army blouse and jodhpurs, that lion named Fulgencio who built a golden staircase to power out of a gift for gab and political organization.

Batista now displayed the very same organizational prowess on the counter of his kitchen. He had his mixing bowls, his whisk, his Osterizer, his mortar and pestle, roasting rack, bain-marie pan, deep fryer, Pyrex molds, rolling pin, chopping board, sharpened Wüstholf knives, his salamander, scale, clock, and—in case the cook turned adventurous—his favorite Italian corkscrew and a case of Chianti and another of Chablis at the ready. Strings of French, Italian, and Spanish sausages—including his favorite, the Catalan *longaniza*—as well as dozens of pollards, guinea hens, pheasants, and quail, not to mention sides of beef and pork, were dressed and hanging in the walk-in refrigerator, where sat a butcher anxious to carry out his command. As a final touch, his adjutant, Morales del Castillo, had procured him an extra-fancy toque and a linen apron like the ones worn by the chefs in La Tour d'Argent in Paris, where he'd had such a wonderful duck *à l'orange* back in '46 (or was it '49?), so that now he felt prepared for whatever the hostess threw his way.

Batista picked up his kitchen fork and knife, in his mind's eye already carving out the wonderful chicken they'd cook that day. But wait, what about this soufflé? Soufflé, that takes eggs. Of course, the eggs! Where are the eggs?! He put down his knife, viciously snapped his fingers.

Morales del Castillo instantly appeared by his side.

"*Sí, mi general?*"

"*Oye, chico,* tell the girls to bring me two dozen eggs, separated, and some grated Partagás cheese."

"The cheese on top, General?"

"No, *chico,* on the side! What are you talking about? Don't you know how to cook?"

"Sorry, General. I don't even know how to boil an egg, if the truth be known. That's why I admire you taking up this hobby, señor."

"*Chico,* men always need a hobby, otherwise life is just work, work, work. Besides, you never know what you're going to be facing in life. Maybe we'll all be run out of town and I'll have to be cooking for the troops up in the hills some day, eh?"

Morales del Castillo looked aghast at Batista, shocked even at the thought of such a tragedy. Batista wagged a condescending finger.

"Just kidding, muchacho. You have no sense of humor. Hurry up and tell the girls, the program's about to begin!"

Morales del Castillo turned with the eagerness of the mutt who sees his master returning home, blaring out his instructions to Cuca and her four assistants.

These people! thought Batista. Do they really think I will be among them always? They have no idea how burdensome this job has become. Sometimes I wish I could just walk away, take the next plane to Paris, even if only for a few weeks. Like last summer, for instance. I was all set to take off for Cannes, but these kids in the Sierra just don't want to cut any deals. By my sainted God, the truth is I don't understand them. Don't they know that is the way things have always been done in Cuba? You get upset at the government so you get a few of your buddies together, you go out and make some noise in the *monte,* out in the bush in Oriente or Camagüey or whatever, and after a while you cut a deal and everything goes back to the way it was, only you have a few more pesos in your bank account and a nice house in Miramar or Palm Beach. Prío did it. Grau did it. Carrillo did it. *Coño,* even the communists cut a deal with me. What the hell is it with these muchachos? Bottom line is, I have to call off my trip because I can't very well be off gallivanting around Europe while something like this is happening.

I thought there for a while, after they failed at the palace, that the

whole country was for me again. But something happened. I don't
understand. One day everybody's calling me the protector of the fatherland, of the *patria*, and a month later they're calling me a bloodthirsty
tyrant that feeds on the blood of the people. Oh, I've seen their posters
and their little flyers; I know exactly what this riffraff thinks of me. They
must think I'm truly blind and ignorant not to be aware of what they're
doing, poisoning the national character the way they are. Reconciliation,
getting along, compromise, those are sterling qualities. Cuban qualities.
What kind of extremists are these kids?

I can't quit under these circumstances. Quit? Whoever said anything
about quitting? They're going to have to blast me out of here, feet first,
that's how I'm going to leave office. Otherwise, what kind of example
would I be setting for my children, for Fulgencito and Alejandrito? No,
señor, what we have to do here is tighten our belt and gird our loins.
Anyway, there she is again.

Nitza Villapol came back on the air, her abundant bosom displayed
before the camera as she leaned forward. With one hand she lifted a bottle of beer bearing an Indian head on the label, and with the other, a full
stein crowned with a foamy head.

"Don't forget, everything goes better with Hatuey! It's the pause that
refreshes! But let's save it for the end of the program, shall we?"

Villapol quickly put down the beer and pointed at an array of ingredients set before her on the shiny marble counter.

"This is what you'll need for the vichyssoise. Shallots and onions,
approximately three quarters of a cup of shallots and a quarter cup of
onions, thinly sliced. Also, a tablespoon of butter, a pound of potatoes,
peeled and sliced, a can of chicken consommé . . ."

As Villapol rattled off the ingredients, Batista searched for them, finding everything but the shallots.

"Morales," he shouted, "get me shallots on the double!"

"*Mi general,* what are shallots?" asked Morales del Castillo, again
instantly appearing at Batista's elbow.

"How the hell should I know? I'm new at this. Just get them. Cuca
will know."

"*Sí, mi general!*"

With Castillo scurrying to carry out his commands once more, Batista
turned his attention on the set, trying his fumbling best to follow the
rapid-fire instructions of the bosomy chef.

"When the scallions and onions have cooked in the butter, becoming,
as you can see, almost translucent, is the time to add the peeled, sliced
potatoes and the water."

Potatoes? When did she say anything about potatoes? I didn't hear that.

"Castillo!" bellowed Batista again.

"*Sí, mi general!*" responded the adjutant breathlessly, bringing forth a handful of gnarled bulbs looking like a collection of hairy boar tusks. "I brought you this sweet giant garlic. Cuca thinks it might be as good as your shallots."

"Yes, yes, of course, put them down right there. Where are my potatoes?"

"What potatoes, General?"

"The ones I need! Don't you know I have to have potatoes for the soup! Are you deaf?"

"*No, mi general.* I mean, yes sir!"

"Well, go get them, then!"

"How many potatoes, sir?"

"I don't know. Five pounds, peeled, sliced. Right away!"

"That will take some time, sir, since—"

"Don't argue with me, go get them!"

"*Sí, señor!*" said Castillo, saluting briskly and rushing off.

Now Villapol was at the Osterizer, pouring into the glass cup the cooked grayish slop of potatoes and onions that had been pureed beforehand for the program. She looked centered and content, as though pressing the liquefy button in the blender would grant her instant peace and prosperity.

"Cooking has become so much easier nowadays with all these inventions, don't you think, dear viewers? Why, I remember as a little girl that *Mamá* would spend a half hour with the food mill, doing what we can do in a few seconds by just pressing that little button. Yes, the Osterizer is a very useful tool. You can get your Osterizer at any department store. Or you can get it where I get mine, at Samuel Lipsky Hardware in El Vedado; they carry the very latest lines of these wonderful household aids. All made in the U.S.A., of course. Where else? After all, they are the best. There, I think we are done."

Back in the kitchen, Batista watched with anxiety as Villapol removed the container of pureed potatoes. Castillo dashed forth with a tray full of peeled potatoes.

"Quick, put them in there!" ordered Batista, pointing at the blender. Castillo took several handfuls and stuffed them inside.

"No, no, no, all the way to the top!"

"*Sí, Señor Presidente!*"

Castillo promptly crammed the container to the top, even as the butter in the frying pan started to burn. He poured in the sliced onions, shook the pan.

"What do we do now, General?"

"Turn on the machine, hombre!"

Batista browned the onions quickly. This was something he was certain he could do. The smell of garlic and onions had clung to his fingertips for years even after he could afford his own cook. French recipes couldn't be that much different. After all, this was *cocina criolla,* creole cooking, wasn't it?

Castillo pressed the liquefy button on the Osterizer. In the background, Villapol cheerfully explained the last details of her recipe.

"So now you add the cream and the milk, stir it, and you pour it into a glass or ceramic container. You cover it with cellophane and you put it in the refrigerator to chill."

The Osterizer, struggling to grind the mass of raw potatoes, began to whine and smoke. Batista noticed the signs of distress while he stirred the onions.

"*Coño,* Morales, don't be so stupid, add some liquid to that!"

"Yes sir, General!"

Castillo took a glass, filled it with water, and dropped it into the blender. The blades whirred and gave a mighty blast, and the entire contents of the cup flew up into the air, smashing against the ceiling, white gobs of unprocessed tuber dangling in oozy mounds from the cornices.

"*Coño, chico,* what the hell did you do?"

"Just following your orders, *mi general!*"

The butler, a former corporal from Pinar del Río whom Batista had saved from prison for stealing army supplies, stuck his head in the kitchen. Noticing the mess, he turned with open arms to the tall gray-suited visitor, as though saying, What can a poor servant do? The visitor pointed to his mouth. The butler cleared his throat.

"Mr. Boyeros is here to see you, *Señor Presidente.*"

Boyeros stepped gingerly into the fake French Provincial kitchen with its pasted-on beams, frumpy chintz curtains, and linoleum posing as limestone flooring. Castillo was already up on a ladder, trying to scrape the dangling mass of potato from the ceiling, Batista at the burners and Villapol blaring on the television, while two uniformed housemaids on their knees scrubbed the floor. Batista gazed on Boyeros with an ineffable expression, halfway between surprise and disillusionment, raising a languid hand in greeting, as though abashed to be caught in this predicament.

"It's you, Carlitos," he said gruffly, then turned to watch the set.

"Good afternoon, *Señor Presidente,*" said Boyeros, his words drowned out by the explanation from the TV set.

"History tells us that chicken marengo was born after the victory of

Napoleon, in the town of Marengo, Italy, against the Austrians. This was, oh, two hundred years ago. Napoleon's cook, to celebrate, grabbed whatever food was around, put it in a pot, and as the French say, *voilà!* Well, we're going to make our version of that, a tropical version . . . "

That means we're going to be using half the chicken, twice the spices, and tons of grease, thought Boyeros. Like everything else we do on this island, overdone and overunctuous. Like me, right now.

"Your Excellency has taken up cooking, I see. A very fine hobby."

Batista shrugged the rounded shoulders that gave him the equivocal aspect of a bouffant tropical Buddha. Castillo dislodged the last of the gobs of potato from the ceiling, then, with a hurried bow to Boyeros, exited the room with his grisly catch.

"I don't know, *chico.* Don't you ever find yourself doing things without really knowing why; then, when you stop to think about it, you realize it's because of something that happened a long time ago?"

Batista turned his back on the program, willing to reveal himself to one of the few men on the island he could consider his equal.

"Sometimes, *Señor Presidente,* I think that is our way of telling ourselves to slow down and think about what is going on around us."

Batista frowned, not at all sure he wanted to go down the path that Boyeros was pointing out to him. All Batista wanted was a shoulder to weep on, and instead Boyeros, like some damn Roman consul or something, was pointing out the verities of his situation. As if he didn't know! It's true what they say, thought Batista; great men have no friends.

"Maybe you're right," countered Batista, returning to his pots and pans, refusing to let Boyeros's practicality spoil the warmth of his recollection. "But the last few weeks I've been thinking more and more about our time against Machado, back in the thirties, when I organized the troops."

"Glorious days for Cuba," replied Boyeros.

"Glorious days for all of us," said Batista, laying a hand on Boyeros's shoulder. As always, Boyeros was surprised to realize how violently his heart reacted when Batista treated him as the friend he once was, a companion, in burnished middle age, from the old boon days when so much depended on so few.

"What times those were, eh, Carlitos? Don't you agree?"

"*Sí,* Fulgencio," said Boyeros, carried away by the moment. "We changed an entire nation."

"We changed the course of history, Carlitos, that's what we did," said Batista, his chef's hat all cockeyed. "No one had ever defied the will of the Americans in Latin America until we did it. Sumner Welles was backing Machado all the way to the end. It wasn't until we showed him that we weren't scared of him or the marines that he changed his tune, remember?"

Boyeros nodded, even if in the golden haze of Batista's recollection the facts were twisted to his convenience, for Batista had still been in his barracks in Oriente at that point. It was Boyeros and his ABC people who were out in the docks and the factories, setting bombs and machine-gunning the police, forcing Machado to his knees. But why begrudge him those moments of shared glory? thought Boyeros; we all did what we could for the revolution.

"Those were wonderful days, Fulgencio."

"And the legislation we put through later, in nineteen forty, guaranteeing rights no one else has in Latin America. Even in the U.S. they don't have what we do—forty-four hours' pay for forty hours worked, mandatory arbitration, parental and bereavement leave, all in the constitution!"

And free speech and habeas corpus too, thought Boyeros, suddenly chilled by the enormity of the gap between the halcyon ideals and the bloodcurdling realities of 1958. He discreetly stepped back, causing Batista's hand to slide off Boyeros's shoulder.

"You add the wine when everything is slightly browned," drifted in the disembodied, aqueous voice of that other chef in that other make-believe kitchen.

"And when I leave office, Cuba will be in the best economic shape it has ever been in, too," added Batista, almost as an afterthought, nodding to himself at the wisdom of his decision.

Boyeros's ears perked up, ringing with the sudden hint. Cuba was enjoying an unparalleled period of prosperity. The sugar harvest was sensational, the best in decades; the country had close to $3 billion of American investment; per capita income was higher than anywhere else in Latin America, except for oil-rich Venezuela; there were more telephones, radios, and TVs on the island than anywhere else south of the Rio Grande. It was hard to believe, but in some things, such as the number of doctors and hospitals, Cuba was better off than such developed countries as England, France, and Italy. Boyeros had just turned in the figures to his Canadian bankers when they hesitated to float him the capital he needed to expand his airline. Boyeros himself was enjoying a record-breaking year, both in volume and profits. In short, there seemed to be no end to prosperity. If only the man who had brought it about would step aside so that these other little problems could be dealt with.

"No one can dispute that, Mr. President," said Boyeros, reverting to the courtier's role.

"There, you see, that's what I mean! Look at the job I've done! And to think there are people who want me to step down right away, leaving my job incomplete. I can't do that, now, can I? It's not right."

Batista took the quartered chicken and sank his knife into the pale flesh, slicing the meat from the bone in long narrow strips.

"When the chicken is tender, after about ten minutes, you add the ground pimientos, the tomato sauce, and the whole mushrooms," chirruped the chef once more.

"By the way, I missed you at our celebration in the country club," said Batista reproachfully.

"My wife was feeling ill that night," lied Boyeros. "You did receive our flowers, I trust."

"Yes, but your presence can never be replaced by a floral arrangement, Carlitos. It's people like you who have served us well through the years that have allowed us to carry out our job."

Boyeros involuntarily flinched, realizing that Batista was reminding him of his true station, coconspirator in the bloodiest tyranny in Cuban history. Worse than Machado? Yes, even worse than the old man, thought Boyeros sadly. I helped put you here but I'm going to do everything possible to push you out. Someone has to bell the cat.

"Thank you, Mr. President, but perhaps you should consider your job already finished."

Batista dropped his kitchen fork and spoon with a clatter.

"WHAT WAS THAT YOU SAID?" he bellowed.

He wanted to say, *Et tu, Carlos,* but he forgot the exact words, so he exaggerated the anger in his demeanor. Morales del Castillo, concerned about his master's roar, stuck his head in. Batista waved him away. He knew this confrontation was coming and he wanted to face it head-on, the way he thought he always did things.

"How can you say this to me! To me! To the man who has always looked out after your interests!"

"And I truly thank you, and the good-thinking people of Cuba thank you, but, Fulgencio, it really is time to let someone else take the rudder. I know how upset you are at this suggestion, but you must face the facts. The rebels control a great deal of the Sierra . . . "

"You've been to see them, haven't you? You're dealing behind my back, eh, *hijo 'e puta!*" Batista snarled.

(For a moment Boyeros was back trudging through the backwoods of the Sierra, hacking his way through the bush like a lowly *guajiro* with his

185

escort, suffering through rain and mosquitoes all the way up to the guerrilla camp, to the tall man with the curly beard, thick-frame glasses, and
aquiline nose who grinned and extended a strangely powder-room-soft
hand, exclaiming, "Ah, Boyeros, it was time you joined the forces of
freedom!")

"No, I have not," said Boyeros, shaking his head. "But when I visited
my sugar mill in Oriente I heard all about what they're doing out there.
The point is this, *mi presidente* . . . "

"*Mi presidente,* my dick, you traitor!" shouted Batista.

"No, Fulgencio, listen to me! Colonel Ventura has just been indicted
for the murder of those four youths out by the zoo last year. The State
Department is telling Eisenhower you have to be removed, and there are
four rebel fronts right now on this island! Four! That's more there than
there has been here since the time of Martí!"

"Since the War of the Ten Years, actually," said Batista, stirring his
chicken, strangely quiet once again, but as always eager to show off his
knowledge of any field.

"Fine. Since the time of the Zanjón, then. Every night we get the
radio program from the mountains, Radio Rebelde, Radio Escambray.
Even the communists and the church are officially opposed to you now.
And all the youth has turned against you. At this very moment there are
seventy-five thousand high school students on strike against you. All the
schools are closed! Don't you see what that means!"

"That they're all playing hooky, screwing their girlfriends, I'm sure."

"Fulgencio, please listen to me. For the love of Cuba, this has got to
stop! You will go down in history as the equivalent of Machado!"

Boyeros stopped, afraid he might have gone just one step too far. From
the television, Nitza Villapol droned on.

"Then, as a final touch, you fry these eight eggs, which you carefully
arrange around the chicken just so."

Outside the door Morales del Castillo signaled at the two brawny
bodyguards to be ready to haul Boyeros away at the first sign from the
president. Mere wealth would be no protection for this magnate.

"So what would you have me do, exactly?" asked Batista, almost
purring, turning back to his chicken, stripping more flesh from the car-
cass, whittling the breast down to the gray-white bone.

"You should step down and turn over the presidency to an interim government. Let Rivero Agüero handle it and then hold elections this year.
You will get out with all the glory and the honors. You need a vacation
anyhow, Fulgencio. Who knows, maybe after four years things could
change; these boys could screw up so badly you could run for office again."

"Maybe you're right, Carlos," said Batista pensively. "Perhaps our efforts to contain the enemy have infected our spirit and we have unknowingly adopted his visage, so that in the end we have become that very thing that we fought so long and so hard against."

That's more like it, thought Boyeros, nodding repeatedly. Batista paused, somber, then grinned wildly.

"But I don't think so. I know what I have fought for. A free Cuba. All my life. For an independent Cuba that would not follow the dictates of Washington or Moscow. Look at what we've done in twenty-five years, Carlos. Think back to nineteen thirty-three, when a quarter of the population was literally starving. No schools, no roads, no light. No dignity. Nothing! And now, look around us.

"Havana has the fastest-growing skyline in the hemisphere. People are fed, schools are open—even if those ungrateful university students with their heads full of communist propaganda are agitating against us.

"We were once the playthings of the Yankees; they owned ninety percent of the island. Today they are down to less than a third, and you know we're cutting that back even more. The right way. The legal way. With Cuban businessmen, Cuban enterprise.

"Who was it . . . was it Marx or Engels? *Coño,* I always mix up those two; they're like Laurel and Hardy. Because I studied communism too, you know. But I read it so long ago that I forgot exactly who said this; the thing is, it's communism that will be going into the dustbin of history. Why? Because it cannot support itself. It's an artificial concept, like the mercantile policies of the Spanish crown, which ruined Spain in spite of the riches of the Americas."

"But Spain ruled for hundreds of years all the same," countered Boyeros, caught in the strange quicksilver mind of the chubby, voluble dictator, who never ceased to surprise him.

"Yes, but that was before modern communications technology. See that?"

Batista pointed at the set, where Villapol, having finished preparing the chicken, was wrapping a foil hat around the soufflé mold.

"That is the true arsenal of the West, and the commies know it. History tells us as long as there is free exchange of information, we shall win. It's that simple."

"I see," said Boyeros, returning to his usual skepticism. "Unfortunately I am not as astute a student of history as yourself, Mr. President. But I can tell you that the country will be spared grave bloodshed if you step down."

"But why should I quit?" Batista argued back. "Do you know what I have just received?"

"I'm afraid I won't know until you tell me."

Batista extracted a light blue parchment paper from the inside pocket of his jacket. From the creases and stains Boyeros could tell the president had handled the paper repeatedly, as though he'd read it time and again to confirm its fateful contents—an adder that had already bit into his breast.

"This!" he hollered, brandishing the paper in the air with vigor, like a secret weapon. "This is the reason!"

"And what might that reason be?" queried Boyeros again.

"Castro wants to make a deal with me!" proclaimed Batista. "The leader of the Twenty-sixth of July Movement, the fearless guerrilla holed up in the hills, the bearded one himself wants to come to the peace table!"

"May I?" asked Boyeros, snatching the paper from Batista's hands.

"Go ahead, read it! You'll see what I mean. This was given to me by the representative from Manzanillo, Manuel de Jesús León Ramírez."

"It's authentic?" asked Boyeros, quickly scanning the missive, addressed to the president of the republic of Cuba and signed, with characteristic flourish, by Fidel Castro.

"No doubt about it. He says he will stop fighting if I agree to elections supervised by the Organization of American States and if our troops pull back from Oriente. He doesn't even mention stepping down or that the old judge, Urrutia, be named interim president."

That last bit of information was surprising for Boyeros, who had been told by Castro himself that Judge Urrutia would become the head of the post-Batista revolutionary government. But if this letter was true, that meant Castro was, after all, the same as the other politicians in the country—bullets or ballots, it was always dollars that counted. And I thought he was different, thought Boyeros, almost but not quite regretfully.

"You will accept, I suppose?" said Boyeros, relieved that everything, even Castro, was back to its sad norm.

"Of course not!" snapped Batista, turning on the beater to whip up the soufflé's egg whites.

"Why not?"

"Because it is an obvious desperation move. He knows he is weak and he wants time to reorganize. I'm not going to let him do that."

"But Mr. President, you have no other option!"

"No other option? How dare you tell me something like that?" roared Batista over the sound of the eggbeater, puffy clouds of white spilling out of the bowl.

"As long as I am president," he went on, "I will never surrender! And

I will not leave office until my term is up! In a few weeks we'll be starting a final offensive, and I will wipe them right off the map, you will see.
They'll come down from the mountains on their knees, begging for
mercy."

He paused, savoring already the sweetness of future triumph.

"*Then* I may step down. Although, who knows, I could be persuaded
to remain as head of the armed forces. But we shall see. After all, a man
can only—"

"*Mi general,* the American ambassador is here to see you!" said Morales
del Castillo, striding formally into the kitchen with a martial air. He cast
a snarling look at Boyeros, which the businessman shrugged off.

"Already? I still haven't finished beating my whites!" The frothy
mound of albumen stood quivering on the steel bowl.

"*Bueno,* some other day," said the dictator wistfully, pulling the strings
to his chef's apron and doffing his still-stiff hat. "I just love Nitza Villapol,
don't you?"

"I should think so. We sponsor her program, after all," said Boyeros.

"Of course, I forgot," said Batista, watching with affection the bosomy
chef pulling the golden soufflé out of the oven.

"Do you think that you could convince her to come give me a few
cooking tips?"

Boyeros smiled resignedly. "I am certain she will be more than glad to
give you whatever tips you might want."

Batista wiped some errant flour specks from his pinstripe suit, righted
his tie. "Good, good. Let's do it next week sometime; Marta is going to
Miami then."

"It will be my pleasure," said Boyeros, bowing slightly to the
inevitable. Batista patted his shoulder, then stepped briskly away. He had
already exited when he stuck his head back in the room.

"What was it exactly that you came to see me for?"

"Nothing, *Señor Presidente.* I just wanted to extend my apologies for
not going to your anniversary dinner."

"That's all right. Well, you're an old friend, you're forgiven. You can
always come to the one next year. My seventh anniversary. Seven is a
lucky number, they say."

"Yes, Mr. President, so they say." Boyeros nodded and Batista left.
Boyeros crossed his arms and stared dolefully, blankly at the television,
where Villapol was giving her last instructions to an eager public.

"Remember, the trick to a successful soufflé is never to open the oven
door, because if you do, it will all collapse on itself. You have to let it
cook until it's good and ready, then you take it out. Not a minute before,

not a minute after. Then proceed to enjoy. So, until tomorrow, this is the *Creole Kitchen. Muchas gracias!*"

※ ※ ※

Boyeros crossed the tiled foyer of the Foreign Press Club with his head down, hands clasped behind his back, long legs stepping over four arabesque tiles at a time. He headed for the cedar-paneled bar, hung with mildewy prints of Arabian horses and English hounds. At a corner, thin, stoop-shouldered Herbert Matthews was expounding his views on the rebels for the benefit of the newly arrived correspondents.

"Without a doubt Castro is the most remarkable and romantic figure in Cuban history since José Martí," said Matthews to the five American reporters.

Boyeros asked for his usual gin and tonic, sat at a leather-covered stool, and tuned out the embarrassing farrago of half truths that the *New York Times* correspondent was imparting. By the time Boyeros finished his second drink, Max Weinberg arrived, sweaty and disheveled as always.

"Well?" was Max's greeting.

"He passed the cup," said Boyeros without a trace of irony. He signaled at the waiter for a third round. "It's like that line in that Bette Davis movie, 'It's going to be a rough ride.' "

" 'A bumpy ride,' " countered Max. "I figured as much. It's kind of moot by now, you know."

"How do you mean?"

"We just got a cable at the embassy. The State Department has authorized an arms embargo against Cuba. It's the beginning of the end."

"A matter of months, then."

"Exactly."

"I better call the sugar trust in London," said Boyeros, moving to the cherry-wood phone booth at the far end of the bar. Max asked for a Polar beer, watched Matthews waving his hands in clumsy imitation of a Cuban orator's gestures.

"And to these people who say Castro is a communist, let me say this," went on Matthews. "He has personally assured me that he is not a red, and I believe him. He is a democrat, pure and simple. I know a commie when I see one, and Castro is no commie. By any stretch of the imagination."

Chapter

6

The pit was dug, the body was tossed, the branches cover the lifeless corpse. Only one thing left to do so no beast—from the jungle or the cities—will ever find a trace of the one called Lázaro.

Morgan bends down, flicks on his Zippo, watches the flames spread. Everyone stands transfixed as the fire consumes the body, the blue-green flames of the pyre a hand waving good-bye at Morgan's saddened group; then they all head down the trail again.

The sun begins to set; a bird howls as the weary fighters trek on. When swift night arrives they sit under a tree as the darkness spreads. Morgan closes his eyes, as do they all.

Then all at once Morgan hears the rattling of weapons and a voice that warns, "Don't move or we'll blow your heads off!"

Morgan gets up, stares into the bush where the voice has come from. "Go ahead, relieve me of this," he says, taunting, then falls in a swoon to the ground.

⊠ ⊠ ⊠

In the darkness Morgan hears voices, a strangely accented Spanish one saying he lost much blood, while another, rasping and equally oddly inflected, complains of time lost and insubordination and of a front bearing down on them all. Morgan wants to speak, to say that he lost something much more precious than blood, that no matter how many transfusions he might receive he would never recover the warmth that once filled his veins. He knows he should open his eyes and tell these people holding him, whoever they are, that he is on a higher calling, on his way to an appointed rendezvous, that there is a luminous role he is yet to play and that they should all stand aside and let him through to his appointed rounds. But his speech is gone, the power to communicate cut off at some anterior source, and he drifts helplessly in a roiling darkness . . .

❊ ❊ ❊

The doctor with the wispy beard and vaguely Tartar features, his hair gathered in a long ponytail, tilted his head back in the universal gesture of wonder. The subject of his close physical examination, an American stretched out on the canvas cot in front of him, had already been unconscious for almost twelve hours. Although he had arrested the blood loss, extracting the bullet lodged in the man's left calf, the doctor could not be certain that septicemia had not already set in. The rapidity with which diseases and infections set in in these damp tropical climates never ceased to amaze him, in spite of the fact that the bulk of his practice throughout the years had been in places just like this, miserable little hovels in God-forgotten hamlets stuck in some mountain chain days away from the capital.

Yet that's the way he had wanted it. His colleagues at medical school in Rosario had laughed at him when he berated them for caring more about their own welfare than that of their patients.

"You're in the wrong profession, buddy," they told him. "You should be a priest. We're all in this to make money."

But becoming a part of the ruling elite of his native provincial town in northern Argentina had been the last thing on his mind. He didn't want just to mend tibias, extract tonsils, and vaccinate the snot-nosed runts of the local German farmers as a profession. He wanted to heal the truly ailing, to fulfill the pledge that the old Greek had fashioned thousands of years ago. So after graduation he had set out across the Andes in his Triumph motorcycle, surveying that vast continent of wealth, beauty, and despair that stretched thousands of miles down the macadam roads. Asunción, Santiago, Callao, Ayacucho, Guayaquil, Cartagena—the names of all the cities he visited were pressed flowers in a garland of memories of the dreadful gap between the few rich and the many poor he encountered in his travels. He'd wound up in Guatemala, helping the government of that poor well-intentioned fool Arbenz, and when that had failed, as all well-meaning experiments do, he had traveled on to Mexico, becoming an itinerant photographer in the Zócalo, the vast square in the heart of Mexico City. He had already tried and given up on the Communist Party, and felt a vague stirring for something more glorious, more meaningful and lasting, but saw no way out of his plight until that day when he took a picture of the tall self-confident Cuban who, with the typical swagger of his island people, intruded in his field of vision with a crushing smile.

"My name is Fidel Castro and we're going to win the revolution in Cuba."

"What revolution?" the doctor asked, unaware of anything resembling a revolt in the frightened island that General Batista ran as his private fiefdom.

"The one that you and I are going to make," pledged Fidel expansively. "I am gathering forces. In a matter of months we'll be ready to lead the people to a new era in Latin American history."

"And you think it's going to be that easy, *che?*" said the doctor, using the Argentinean slang for *buddy*. "What do you have that Batista doesn't?"

"History," said Fidel. "History is on our side. We will not fail. This is your chance. Take it now or regret it forever."

And so he embarked on the odd expedition that had landed them in that cane field, strafed by enemy jet planes, all twelve or fourteen or sixteen—he still wasn't sure exactly how many—survivors of the eighty that had sailed out in the pleasure boat owned by former Cuban president Prío. They lost their weapons, their food, their supplies, and almost their lives as they split up into groups to avoid capture upon landing. But the one thing they never lost was that fearless feeling of predestination, that crazy notion that they would triumph, no matter the obstacles.

That is, Fidel never lost it. He was the one—after being hunted for days, surviving by licking dew from the plants of the field and chewing on stalks of sugarcane, hiking ceaselessly through the jungle like a *jutía* fleeing a barking terrier, upon reaching the hills and asking, "Are we in the Sierra Maestra?" and being told that indeed he was there—Fidel was the one who breezily replied, "Then the revolution has already triumphed."

The doctor was not quite so self-possessed as all that. The dampness of the journey had triggered one of his recurring asthma attacks and he'd lain, wheezing and hoping to die, in the middle of a canebrake, hearing the trucks bearing enemy soldiers rumble past down the road a few hundred yards away from his hiding place. Yet somehow he'd dragged himself out, somehow he'd found his way to the hills, somehow rejoined the others, and somehow, in spite of the obstacles, was defeating the enemy.

The doctor said none of this to his patient, of course. The American was still asleep, and in any case the doctor wasn't so certain that he'd understand the long complicated journey of a Marxist revolutionary. So the doctor stepped out of the *bohío* and lit a cigar, staring aimlessly at the myriad stars above, musing on the progress of history and the future of the revolution.

Nothing in the annals of dialectical materialism could assure the doctor that his movement would achieve its desired objective of a people's dictatorship. It was simply a matter of faith—blind, stupid, unreasoning, willful, and obstreperous faith, which climbs mountains, fords rivers, and vanquishes armies. History, like religion, had the maddening habit of being understandable only in retrospect, and while in the throes of change, the agents of revolution could only hope they were truly epigonic of their time. The irony, of course, was that by the time they knew for certain, their bones could be bleaching on some forgotten sunbaked shore. All their tears and sweat and blood as helpless to change the world as the dropping of a cherimoya leaf or the cockle-doodle-doo of that rooster crowing out there in some *guajiro*'s darkened yard. Because . . .

The doctor heard the American stumble to his feet, drag himself to the doorway. Morgan appeared in the light of the new moon like a drunken sailor sweating off some wild spree at the docks, his shirt spattered with the blood of a senseless brawl.

"About time you woke up, buddy," said the doctor, grinning, cigar clenched between yellowing front teeth.

"Who to be you? Where to be me?" asked Morgan, his tongue swollen, the sounds of Spanish almost impossible to pronounce.

"You're in Captain Victor Cordón's camp. Your men are resting."

The doctor extended his sinewy hand.

"I am Ernesto Guevara. You can call me Che."

Chapter

7

Orange flames licked at the outside of the hearth, which sputtered as the rosin in the green pine burst out tiny fireballs. Captain Cordón took a bunch of *palmiche,* the palm tree fruit used to fatten pigs and cattle, and tossed it to the fire. The flames leaped all over the oil-filled kernels and soared several feet into the air. Opening the shutters of his *bohío,* Cordón sniffed the clean air of the early dawn, heard the neighing of the horses in the pasture, the rattle of his cook and lover fixing his morning coffee, and he felt his heart swell with happiness as he did every morning of his life. He was a city boy once, born and bred in Havana, and it had taken him years to get used to the early rising habits of the country after his family sent him to his godfather's farm near Santa Clara. But now there was no other time of day he preferred. The hush of the countryside, smelling of wetness and growth, the stirring of the first few birds, the lonesome moon sinking slowly into the hills like a new bride reluctant to share the marriage bed—life was about to start and everything was new and everything was possible, even winning against Batista.

Cordón took the tin cup of coffee that Pedrito offered and strolled outside his hut to light his first Lucky Strike of the day. A fastidious man in spite of the vulpine face and the rotten teeth that gave him the look of a feral beast at bay, Cordón smoked only American brands, preferring the sweet Virginia broadleaf to the pleasures of the hand-rolled cigars of Las Vegas and Vuelta Abajo. Down in the hollow of the farm he could see the plastic sheeting draped over the slumped bodies of his men, some stirring in the cool blueness of the dying night, others sleeping so soundly their snores were a counterpoint to the warbling of the early morning birds.

Cordón exhaled a mouthful of smoke and glanced over at the avocado tree, where the handful of fighters from the Second Front slept still, exhausted by their grief and their labors. They had lost a man, he was told when he ran into them at the crossing of the two paths; their leader, that Americano named Morgan, was wounded; they were without food, poorly armed, and lost. Yet these were the men Menoyo had sent to recruit him, him, *el capitán Cordón,* for the fight against the tyranny. *Qué ocurrencia,* what a notion, he thought, chortling with contempt. These men think they can defeat Batista, who has fifty thousand soldiers, tanks, jets, and all the rest. *Qué chiste,* what a joke. Nonetheless . . .

Nonetheless what? he asked himself. Nonetheless it is very possible. Look at what Fidel had when he landed. A handful of men who didn't know a creek from a cesspool, who didn't even know where they were standing, and who needed a local guide to show them the way to the mountains. As if they were explorers in dark Africa or something like that. And look how far they've come. Just like the Second Front, which controls even more land than Fidel and his boys. Now both of them are here to court me, the Front and the 26th of July, like two hungry whores after a sailor. Who should I go with? Who should I fuck?

Cordón spat out a pinch of blond tobacco and sat on a small leather-bound stool by the entrance to the *bohío.* He gazed east, where the mauve veil of dawn was being torn by the first spike of sunlight.

Pedrito, his cook and not-so-secret lover, came out of the hut with the captain's breakfast, the typical meal of the early-rising *guajiro: pan con timba,* a piece of spongy Cuban bread with a slice of treacly guava paste. The bread was still warm from the makeshift oven where Pedrito had baked it.

"Be careful, *Capitán,* it is hot!" Cordón set the treat on his lap, took a drag on his cigarette.

"Pedrito, you think it will rain today?"

The cook looked around, sniffed the air like a hound, flexed the muscles of his hairy, slender hands, shook his head.

"Not more than usual, *Capitán.* No cyclones today."

Cordón nodded, remembering Pedrito's warning the day before the hurricane struck last year and how grateful he'd been that he had stayed in camp when the Agabama, swollen with rain, overflowed and swept away the outpost of the *Rurales* he was set on attacking. We all have certain talents and we must give each man his due, thought Cordón. His is cooking, telling the weather, and keeping my bed warm at night. Not a bad combination in a man.

"You think it will be warm?" asked the captain, tossing the cigarette and biting into the bread. Again Pedrito looked around, as though expecting the answer to be told by the ants on the ground or the clouds breaking up in serpentine ribbons thousands of feet up above.

"Yes, it will be very hot. And clear. With your permission, Victor, I must return to the kitchen; the yams are boiling."

"Yes, of course, go."

※ ※ ※

Once Pedrito had gone, Cordón returned to watching the trilling *sinsontes* and *pijiriguas* sounding scales from the trees. So who will we ally ourselves with? he thought. Who will stand the better chance to seize power once the *mulatico lindo* falls? I don't know. I also don't know that I have to choose today. I will have to see what kind of offer they make me. For I cannot be expected to give my support just like that. My people depend on me. I must protect my people. Nothing less is expected of a man like me.

Now Cordón saw, coming out of the farthest hut in the dale, the two men who had been sent to win him over, the doctor and the Americano. Morgan hobbled, leaning on his staff, while Guevara walked by his side with the solicitous care of a trained nurse. What a pair those two make, thought Cordón. And on men such as these the future of Cuba rests. Foreigners, come for adventure and idealism. Poor Cuba.

Cordón was recalling the foreigners who had fought in Cuba's many wars for independence, going back to Narciso López in 1854, when the quick clapping sounds of trotting horses yanked him back from the sands of comparison. He stood, noticed three horsemen fast approaching, the lead and back riders holding rifles while the middle rider, his hands tied to the saddle horn, slumped in the saddle.

Down at the bottom of the hill Che Guevara placed a tentative helping hand on Morgan's shoulder.

"Are you sure you're all right, old man?" asked Guevara in his British-inflected English.

"I'm fine, thank you. I want to see my men," insisted Morgan, cantankerous.

"They are over there, by the avocado tree. But you really should stay in bed and recover."

"I'll recover when the revolution triumphs, God willing," said Morgan, limping down the road.

"God has nothing to do with the revolution. That's just a crutch to avoid personal responsibility."

"Right, Doctor."

"Please call me Che. You are far too formal."

"And you are far too skeptical. Who do you pray to when the bombs are falling all around you?"

"Karl Marx, of course. And I say a novena for Lenin, too, if the bombing lasts long enough. What about yourself?"

"I pray they'll fall on me. Gato, *cómo estar?*"

The rumpled, rancid figure of El Gato came into view, moving out of the shadows still lingering in the hollow. He embraced Morgan, wrapping his arms about him with such strength that Morgan gave an involuntary cry of pain. El Gato stood back, the better to admire his leader.

"*Capitán,* we missed you. We thought you might leave us too," said El Gato, showing his bad teeth for a smile.

"No, Gato, I to be the bad weed, they cannot kill me," said Morgan happily. The two men grinned broadly, like lovers reunited.

"The others, they to be OK?"

"The men are fine, Captain. Still sleeping. You know that I get up with the roosters, but those boys like to sleep with the outstretched leg. I can wake them if you want."

"No, no, not to want. You to eat, to have food?"

"Yes, they have fed us. They wanted us to surrender our weapons, but that is not to be thought of."

"Too many enemies all around," he added, looking askance at Guevara.

"You to know the doctor?"

"Oh, yes, very well. He's already told us we're fighting in the wrong front and that brave men like ourselves should move to the Sierra with Fidel."

Morgan whipped around, glared at Guevara, who shrugged easily.

"I was pointing out the facts, old man. We are the side that is winning."

"Oh, yeah? What do you think we've been doing, playing canasta?"

"I'll admit you have made some progress, but you should face the realities, old man. It's Fidel who personifies the revolution, not your Menoyo or any other Front man."

"The revolution goes beyond any man," replied Morgan. "Too many people have died fighting for this dream for one person to come along and say, It all belongs to me. This revolution is about the people, the will of the people to be free."

"Captain, I grant you the point. But without unity, the struggle will fail. You are not unified, and we are. You really—"

A shot was heard coming from Cordón's hut. The men glanced up, saw a body slump to the ground off the horse, as though to halt the next shot. They hurried up the hill, Guevara giving Morgan a shoulder to lean on as El Gato readied his weapon, covering their rear. By the time they reached the horses, Cordón was furiously pistol-whipping the man on the ground, a Chinese who gave only little simpering sighs each time the gun struck him. A pool of blood was forming around him, oozing from a shoulder wound.

"Tell me, you little Chinese piece of shit, where are they? Where did you hide them?" bellowed Cordón, his lean face contorted by fury.

"That not to be the way to question the prisoner, *Capitán,*" said Morgan, indignant, even as Guevara watched and kept silent.

"Who the cunt asked you to stick your nose in this, Yanqui?" snapped Cordón, pointing his gun at Morgan.

El Gato lifted his rifle and pointed it straight at Cordón's head, finger on the trigger. The two men on horseback then took out their sidearms and pointed them at El Gato and Morgan with the rattle of loyalty. But at that moment Evaristo, Rabo de Agua, Anacleto, and Octavio surged around the group, deliberately clanking their own weapons to warn everyone of their presence. Then Guevara's men, alerted by the shot, rushed down to the *bohío* and positioned themselves around the group, and finally around them came Cordón's own men, all the fighters arranged in concentric circles, fingers on twitchy triggers, waiting for the order that would unleash their firepower in this very Cuban standoff.

Cordón looked around him, noticing the tense faces of the men in their places, the smell of nerves, and death running rampant. He smiled, holstered his weapon.

"Maybe you're right," he said, chuckling. He walked inside his hut, ordering, "Bring that Chinese carrion inside."

The men broke ranks to let Cordón pass, then looked tentatively at one another, none willing to be the first to move. Morgan raised his hand.

"*Bueno,* muchachos, you to go have the breakfast now while we to talk inside. Doctor?"

"Che, Captain. Just call me Che," said Guevara with a sardonic grin, giving Morgan his arm to lean on. The two leaders walked through as the fighters watched warily, slowly bringing down their weapons.

※ ※ ※

"Captain Morgan, I do not appreciate your telling me how to question my prisoners," sneered Cordón inside the hut. "You have no command in this camp."

Morgan shrugged, painfully sat at a footstool. "It to be bad for revolution to torture the enemy. If necessary to kill, then OK. But not the torture. That is not to be the revolution."

"I agree with Captain Morgan," said Guevara, finally speaking up. "We have to behave better than the government soldiers or we will never win this war."

Morgan took one of the thimblefuls of coffee offered by Pedrito, then set down the chipped porcelain cup on the barrelhead where the cards of the game from the night before still lay.

"You two obviously have never fought in these hills before," snapped Cordón. "There is only one language these people understand, and that is force. Brute force. The kick in the rear and the gun between the eyes. Maybe in the city reason can work wonders, but over here this is the miracle worker!"

Cordón brandished his automatic, then kissed it, the grease of the barrel smearing his lips with a shiny sheen.

Morgan felt a deep repugnance, as though watching someone feed on his own green-flecked vomit. That is not the way it should be, he thought. We have to follow laws, we have to be fair, we have to do good. Saying, I don't like you so I'm going to plug you full of bullets, is not the way. We have to do better than that.

He was about to walk out, not willing even to hear why Cordón pistol-whipped the prisoner, when he noticed a luminous clarity in the dark hut and Laura in green fatigues and combat boots sitting by the fireplace, putting her finger to her lips and shaking her head as though urging him to be still and wait for the right moment. The instant he saw her he felt no astonishment or even surprise but just a warm feeling of rightness and naturalness, as though this were the thing that should be, as though in some way he had been expecting Laura to come and visit him sometime, leaving his heart, where she always dwelled, to make her presence known in the outside world.

Morgan glanced quickly around the room, but even as he did so he knew it was unnecessary and that he was the only one who could see her. Pedrito set out a plate of *buñuelos,* sweet-potato fritters dipped in honey, and the riders brought in the Chinese man, who let himself be dragged through the dirt floor and tossed against the hearth.

Laura looked one last time at Morgan, smiling tenderly before leaving in a wake of dust, lifted from the hearth by a sudden gust of wind, motes rising in the air as a shimmering veil of ashes.

Cordón coughed. "Pedrito, will you please clean out this goddamn fire!"

"*Sí, Capitán,*" answered the cook nervously, for he knew firsthand how those fits of fury could change his usually complaisant lover into an animal.

Pedrito took up a tin dustpan and a small rake made of dried-out palm leaves, sweeping up the loose ashes around the fireplace. Cordón ignored him, just as he ignored the Chinese man who now sat quietly against the wall, legs gathered in, head bent down, listening to some far-off message.

"*Bueno, vamos a ver,*" let's see, intoned Cordón, airily dismissing the two horsemen with a nod. He lay his pistol on the barrelhead next to the *tute* cards. The two men nodded back, then posted themselves outside the entrance to the *bohío*.

"So both of you gentlemen want me to join your faction," said Cordón, licking the honey off his fingers. "I want to know what I would get if I join in with either one of you."

Guevara smirked, enormously amused by the blatant selfishness.

"You just tell us what you want, Cordón, and we'll try to accommodate you. Your support is very important to us."

Cordón warmed up to Guevara. Now that is the way to treat a leader, he thought.

"You both know I control this entire area. Here there are no roads, no judges, no teachers here, nothing. This is the forgotten countryside. All the *guajiros* here are indebted to me. I have been their protector against the abuses of the sugar mill owners for many years now. So my little peasants have to know that when I choose a certain side, that I'm doing it for the greater sake of the people. They must know that their voice will not be forgotten."

"But of course, *Capitán,*" countered Guevara with a smirk, "our struggle is to ensure that all the oppressed people of the island have a voice and a defender in the revolution. They are the reason why we fight, so that someday they will receive the full measure of dignity that they deserve."

"How big is that measure?" cut in Cordón, licking his lips, relishing the wildflower-scented honey.

"As big as the circumstances merit it, of course," added Guevara, seeing that Cordón was only too eager to deal. "You will be made *comandante.*"

"That goes without saying."

"And you will remain in charge of your men."

"*Coño,* tell me something new."

"What post would you like in the future government of the people?"

"The governorship of the province. No, wait, to be ambassador to France. Yes, that. I always wanted to see Paris."

Cordón stopped, lifted his shoulders in anticipated pleasure. "The Eiffel Tower, Montmartre, the cancan. Did you see *Gigi?* I went down to Cienfuegos just to catch it."

"I certainly did. A fine movie," assented Guevara, even though the last film he remembered seeing was *Juarez,* back in Rosario.

"Yes. And *Le Moulin Rouge,* with Jose Ferrer, that was good too."

"Ooh-la-la," said Guevara, his sarcasm becoming deadpan support.

Cordón whistled the first few bars of "Poor People of Paris," already seeing himself strolling by the Seine down the Left Bank.

"Maybe I could do both, what do you think? I could be made governor, then also go to Paris as a special representative of the revolution. I could meet, I don't know, Leslie Caron."

"She lives in Hollywood nowadays," suggested Guevara.

"Really? Well, I could go meet de Gaulle. And Winston Churchill. And, I don't know, Adenauer."

"Why not?"

Stunned, Morgan's eyes darted back and forth from Guevara to Cordón, unable to believe the blatant cupidity of their conversation. Morgan felt soiled, as though the two men had been trafficking in some foul substance that rendered the very air in the room unfit for ordinary humans like Morgan—that is to say, in politics.

He looked at the Chinese man. With his pockmarked face, emaciated body, oily hair gathered in a ponytail, and dressed in jeans and khaki shirt two sizes too big, he seemed a waif imprisoned by circumstance. His flat eyes now almost visibly clouded over as he turned his head and silently mouthed some words, as though addressing some figure in the room that only he could distinguish.

(But what Morgan did not and could not know was that José Chang, the prisoner at his feet, was watching the white-robed goddess of mercy rise before his eyes in all her splendor, shaking her yellow rattle, her face caked white with funereal makeup, intoning in classic Mandarin the ode to farewell for births, deaths, and final departures.)

How can I convince this man to join our side? thought Morgan. I shouldn't have to make these offers. Menoyo should have sent someone else. A Cuban, someone who speaks their language, who understands this selfishness masking as heroism. But you have to try, William. It's your duty. And what is that? What you promise to do before God in your heart. The shame is not in the failure, William. The shame is in the not trying. Speak up. Let the ghosts take care of themselves. Speak up.

"We to make you commander in chief of this region and to give you the weapons we to receive very soon," said Morgan, almost biting off Guevara's last words.

"Weapons? What weapons?" asked Guevara, his smirk replaced by the steady gaze of the interested lynx.

"We to receive shipload of Frente guns in next few weeks from Miami. Rifles, bazookas, much ammo. Commandante Menoyo to authorize me to release many of these to you, *Capitán,* if you to come to our side."

Cordón stopped whistling, fantasies of gigolos and male grisettes on the Pont Neuf quickly fading.

"Weapons, eh? That's just what we need around these parts. When do you expect to get them?"

Morgan shrugged. "Next two weeks. Big shipment. By water. From Miami."

"You mean by boat, off the coast."

"Is correct."

"Then you cannot get them without my permission," said Cordón self-confidently.

"Captain, please, you don't control the waters yet," smirked Guevara, "unless you have a fleet we don't know about."

"I control all the roads to the coast and the keys. Either you deal with me or you do not pass."

"No pasarán," muttered Guevara, insolently amused.

"Qué?"—what is that?—asked Cordón, aware that Guevara was in some way mocking him and his men.

"Nothing, it is nothing," said Guevara, effusively waving his hands. "But, Captain, you are not going to surrender your autonomy because of some guns, no?"

"We also have new shipment of boots, *Capitán,*" added Morgan, seeing Cordón's wavering look.

"Boots!" said both Cordón and Guevara, as amazed as if he'd told them ingots of gold were being brought in that yacht.

"Five hundred pairs, in many sizes," added Morgan, knowing that now he had not only the attention but the respect of both men.

"Our boys really need footgear," said Cordón, shaking his head.

"So do our fighters in the Sierra," countered Guevara defiantly, as though to wrest away the yet-to-be-seen cargo.

"I call the shots here, Che! Those boots will come to us!" bellowed Cordón.

"You forget who is representing the people, *Capitán.* We are. And a soldier with no boots is no soldier at all," said Guevara.

"That is your problem, Che. Make do with what you have!"

"Señores, to be sure me to divide, no? Cannot we to establish coordinated front? All for us to fight for a free Cuba, *verdad?*" said Morgan, playing his cards for all they were worth.

"Clearly," said Guevara, "but the leadership must come from the Sierra. There can only be one leader in this fight, and that is Fidel."

"Fidel, Fidel, Fidel!" bellowed Cordón. "I am fed up with everything being Fidel. Does he think he's the only one who's been fighting? Does he think that no one else has been out here for years struggling? What right does he have to want everything for himself?"

The Chinese prisoner laughed, his laughter erupting in a flurry of choked-up chortling.

"You fight like housewives over the last loaf of bread," said the soldier contemptuously. "And you call yourselves revolutionaries."

Cordón stood up, grabbed the pistol, and struck the man across the forehead, the blood flying out in a cloud.

"Shut up! Shut up, you stupid chink!" Cordón jammed the barrel of the gun under the man's chin.

"Do you know what this man did? Do you care to know? He lost me a shipment of weapons! Five hundred Garands I was supposed to get from his Nationalist friends in Formosa. Five hundred rifles! And this man here is stupid enough to let Batista's army take them in Guanajay!"

"We were ambushed and you know it, *Capitán,*" said Chang, the prisoner. "Someone sold us out. We are not responsible."

"Then how come you were the only one left, Chang? What happened to all the other men? What happened to the money?"

Chang spat out a ball of bloody phlegm. "Captured and killed. You were betrayed."

"Betray me! Betray me! Who would dare do that? Who?"

The odd whirring of a plane broke into the room. The men looked at one another, concerned at the sound, as Chang erupted into raucous laughter.

"What's the use, Captain! You hear that? You know what that means? The bombers are coming!"

"That's impossible. I pay them off myself in Santa Clara to leave us alone."

"I told you before, Captain, the rules have changed," said Chang, coughing now on his blood. "General Cantillo is now in charge, and he doesn't believe in keeping anybody safe. Now we're all going to die." Chang laughed again then stopped, as though to catch his breath through the choking of his blood.

"*Comemierda!*" said Cordón and pulled the trigger of his automatic. The gun shuddered in his hand as the bullet tore into Chang's brain from four inches' distance. A plug of gray-and-red matter flew out and Chang collapsed to the floor.

Two of Cordon's men raced into the *bohío*.

"The bombers, *Capitán,* the bomb—"

But they never got to finish their sentence as an explosion blared right outside the entrance to the hut and the blast pierced into the *bohío* like a great fiery hand seeking to regain something it had lost inside.

When Morgan opened his eyes, the walls of the *bohío* were in flames and he was lying facedown on the earthen floor, the body of one of the men slumped next to him, the sound of wild shooting, screams, and the deadly whistling of falling bombs racking the air.

Guevara lay to his left, knocked unconscious by the explosion. Next to him Cordón sprawled alongside the body of the Chinese prisoner. Morgan smelled the rankness of gasoline, felt the crackle of the flames drawing near. He knelt next to Guevara, shook him awake.

"The sons of bitches are dropping napalm. We have to go!"

Morgan managed to haul Guevara out from under a fallen beam and then hurried out of the burning hut. Cordón's guerrillas were firing their rifles fruitlessly, emptying their clips at the giant B-26, which soared above, dropping the projectiles that flared up in whooshing walls of changing flame.

El Gato came running up to Morgan. "They're burning everything, *Capitán!* What do we do?"

"Where to be the boys?"

"We are all on the rise. We have three horses. Please hurry!"

Morgan took a look at Guevara, shook his head.

"I have to get back to the Sierra," said Che. This time he was the one leaning on Morgan for support.

"How?"

"Lend me one of your horses, old man, and I will—" All at once Guevara bent over, wheezing, gasping; his olive-skinned face turned ashen. Guevara gasped for air, falling to his knees, as the B-26 swooped down on the site, dropping yet more bombs. The three men dropped to the ground as the fiery wall of destruction raged five hundred yards down the hollow, incinerating a pine grove.

"Asthma, old man, I can't . . . " Guevara wheezed, trying to gulp down the air that had served him so confidently before.

"Where to be you?" Morgan asked El Gato.

The guerrilla pointed at a ridge a quarter mile away.

"We went over there when we saw the planes approaching."

"All right, then. To give me the hand."

Morgan and El Gato bent down, picked up Guevara, who retched and hacked, even as the other *guerrilleros* continued to fire at the B-26, which now, its deadly mission accomplished, flew back out again.

By the time they reached the ridge, the entire camp was in flames, black smoke rising in pillars against the sky. Morgan looked back and thought he saw Cordón walking around in a daze, pistol in hand, firing at the sky, at an enemy that was no longer there.

Evaristo and the others waited with four horses.

"To help me here," said Morgan to Evaristo, who lifted Guevara bodily on the animal's rump. Morgan hoisted himself up, sat in the hard wooden saddle of the local *guajiros*.

"El Gato, you to return to Menoyo. To tell him the mission not necessary, Cordón to lose his camp, and he should to keep the boots and arms. I will to take Guevara back to the Sierra."

"We'll come with you, Captain," said El Gato, holding the reins of Morgan's piebald.

"No, all of us to draw too much attention. Is more easy for two men alone."

He stretched his hand, took the reins from El Gato. "Ready, Che?"

The *comandante* shook his head yes, gasped, wrapped his arms around Morgan.

"*Adiós, hombres,*" said Morgan, rearing his horse and then setting off at a gallop through the burning fields.

"*Buena suerte, Capitán!*"—good luck, Captain!—shouted El Gato as Morgan rode out of sight.

"*Es un loco, ese,*" he's a madman, said Evaristo, climbing onto his horse.

"*No, es un héroe,*" no, he's a hero, said Rabo de Agua, who looked at his saddled horse then remembered, "*Coño,* I don't know how to ride."

Chapter

8

"The situation is under control, Mr. President."

Batista glanced up from the U.S. Geological Survey map showing every bump, creek, and sugar field in eastern Cuba. Surrounding him in his command center in the basement of the Presidential Palace were the members of his High Command, the men who would lead the way to the restoration of order in his troubled country.

"We will resettle the population of the area, then we will completely surround the rebel forces with a stranglehold. We'll squeeze the noose until all they can do is beg for mercy," said General Cantillo, pointing at the red zones around the Sierra Maestra and the Escambray.

"How many men?" asked Batista.

"Ten thousand," replied Cantillo, his rough-hewn features lit up by the conviction of duty.

"We're calling it Operation Summer. The battalions will go into the jungle, following the same trails that the rebels use. We'll set up perimeters, concentric circles. If they break out of one circle, then the enemy will find itself within another circle. If they still break out of that one, there will be yet a third one. Meantime the air force will be dropping bombs and napalm on them. We've started doing bombing runs on a few camps here and there, and it's worked wonderfully. Maximum results with minimum loss of life on our part."

Cantillo slammed his fist on the island contour, as if already crushing the hated enemy. Batista looked at the map dubiously, noticing how the general had crumpled several of the little red flags in Oriente Province.

Sighing, he glanced at his army coterie, his handpicked choices for the

General Staff, who were anxiously examining his face to come up with their own corresponding emotions.

He had thought of turning this basement in the Presidential Palace into the Cuban war room, and for this solemn, martial occasion he had donned the khaki uniform of the troops, just as in that glorious moment twenty-five years ago when he had charted the country into new waters. Now he couldn't help noticing the graying hair, the greedy grins, the rounded bellies above the waistline of the men around him.

This is a joke, he thought. None of you is fit for soldiering anymore. And I appointed you all, didn't I? I'll bet none of you has had a taste of barracks life in years. Decades. Over there, just the other day, I made sacrifice on the altar to Changó, and he didn't answer. Today I set up this altar to the white gods of war, and I feel they too are turning their backs on me. Now I know how Lincoln felt when McClellan headed his army. Where is my Grant?

"All right," said Batista, "do what you must, *chico*. But no forced resettlement. That sounds too much like the Spaniards, like Weyler in eighteen ninety-five. We don't want to make martyrs out of those people."

"But, Mr. President, that is an essential part of the plan! Otherwise the rebels will continue to receive aid from the locals."

"You mean to tell me that we don't have enough money to give to these *guajiros* so they'll come to our side? *Por favor!*"

The scorn of the sleek filled the basement in long, echoing gales. Batista laughed and everyone laughed, even Cantillo, who realized he'd only have a few weeks—three? five?—to rope in success or he'd be transferred again.

He glanced at his nemesis, General Tabernilla, still shaking his swollen belly from his forced mirth. Tabernilla's byzantine plotting had convinced the president once before to remove Cantillo from the front lines when his reforms interfered with Tabernilla's payoffs. Batista stuck him in Santa Clara until Tabernilla again made a mess of it, thinking only of kickbacks instead of victory. But Cantillo had learned from his time in Santa Clara fighting people like Cordón; now he would apply those lessons against Castro. Once they finished in Oriente Province, they would head back west and mop up Santa Clara. The Second Front over there held more land, but Castro had the press, and more than anything, this was a propaganda war. Cantillo had to show the world that the rebels were running and that the government had the upper hand—and quickly, or all would be lost just as quickly.

"And another thing, *chico*," said Batista, almost as an afterthought. "Please keep a quarter of the troops available to guard the coffee crop and the sugar mills in the area. Don't want to go broke while you take care of business."

Cantillo was stunned but held his tongue. He had to make the best of it, even if the numbers were less than he needed. He'd just have to improvise. And if this plan didn't work? Well, then maybe it would be time for him to start talking to Fidel directly. No use going down with a sinking ship.

"How long do you figure it will take for this plan to take effect, Cantillo?" asked old man Tabernilla.

"Two months. Three months maximum. We shall have them by the twenty-sixth of July."

"That will be good," said Batista, daring to hope that maybe Cantillo, the only decent general in his staff, could pull the rabbit out of the hat after all. He had to. Of course he would.

"A hot summer feast," added Batista.

"That's right, *mi general,*" said Cantillo. "A burning summer."

Chapter

9

The heavy smell of burning sugar woke Morgan up to a sticky dawn. The evening dew had clung to his clothes, and Morgan's sodden fatigues felt as heavy as if he'd been standing in a squall.

Guevara slept still, slumped on the dirt floor in a mass of filthy green clothes, his mouth open, snoring slightly with each inhalation. Morgan rose, walked out of the cave where they had taken shelter the night before. He took a swig of water from his canteen and gazed down at the green valley stretching below. At its far end, a mushrooming pillar of smoke with feet of flame sent out the sickly sweet smell of its combustion.

Morgan's horse, weary still from the burden of two riders for a whole day and most of the night, neighed in not-too-friendly greeting. Friend, I am hungry, the gelding seemed to say; where is my feed, my corn and *palmiche?* The animal pulled at its reins, tied to a low branch of a flame tree, shook its head in frustration.

Morgan ran his hand down the horse's mane, spoke to it in soft, thankful words, telling him not to worry, that soon he'd be with others of his kind in loping green fields with clear water and much pasture.

"We just have to hold on awhile and we'll be there, pardner, you'll see," whispered Morgan, as though afraid that promises made out loud would be harder to keep than the whispered kind. The animal neighed again, seeming to say, What choice do I have? Morgan patted it good-bye, took a deep breath, then headed down to the valley to search for food.

In the chaos and confusion following their flight from Cordón's camp, pursued by strafing planes, dodging the fiery walls of napalm consuming the forest around them, they'd failed to make rendezvous with the 26th of July couriers waiting to take Guevara back to the Sierra. Morgan and Guevara galloped away through the hell of war, hoping that at some point they'd be able to reestablish contact with the rebel forces.

They rode for hours, until it seemed to Morgan the horse could travel no farther with the two of them, its flanks covered with sweat, thick foam lathering at its mouth. Morgan jumped off and, limping, led the animal by the reins, while a wheezing, gasping Guevara held on to the saddle horn. They bought food from a frightened *guajiro* once—bread, guava paste, a shriveled chorizo sausage that they hungrily divided—and they rested, but never for long. It seemed the entire countryside was consumed by the deity of war, as though all the firepower of Batista's army were concentrated on that single spot. Finally, by dusk, they left the fighting behind them, but even then Morgan did not dare stop. Taking a fix on the stars, he traveled east still, down closely forested hillsides, through streams, mudflats, and ravines, until they reached this last promontory, facing north to the great sugarcane plantations of Las Villas. Seeing the caves and deciding to stop in them was all of a moment. A minute after stopping both men and the animal had drifted to sleep.

I hope Che doesn't panic when he wakes up, thought Morgan, walking down the *trillo*, the narrow footpath to the valley below. In spite of their long hike, his left calf felt almost normal, only a tickling of pain to remind him he had a wound that needed dressing.

Morgan came to a break in the path. To his left the *trillo* swept down to a cane field; to the right it veered to a dirt road that skirted the cane field and wound down by the small *bohío* he'd spotted from above. He was automatically going to descend on the dirt road when something drew his attention to the left.

Had someone asked him what it was that caught his eye, he wouldn't have been able to respond, for it was something akin to a silent call, that reverberation of compelling need that turns the father's head before the child falls off the tricycle, that stops the door before it slams into the tiny hand on the frame—an awareness of danger and its concomitant tingle of worried excitement.

Morgan took a tentative step away from the dirt road. Up ahead he spotted someone in white, a slender frame running into the cane field. He gripped his Thompson, dropped to the ground, expecting the attack. The stalks of cane swayed in the mounting breeze, a smell of moisture from the northwest carrying news of an impending storm. A cow bellowed somewhere far off, a rooster crowed.

Moments crawled by, the awareness of danger an icy cape over him.

He scurried on his knees to the side of the path, preparing to run back to the protective cover of the hillside. Just then the figure stepped out of the canebrake, small framed, slender, mane of russet hair falling on her white blouse.

"Laura?" was Morgan's incoherent cry.

She put her index to her lips and motioned at him to join her in the field. Unable to believe his eyes, waves of chills raising bumps in his arms and back, Morgan rushed into the canebrake, following Laura down a narrow trail among the wrist-thick stalks. They stopped at a clearing inside the field, invisible from the outside, sheltered from the wind of the fast-approaching storm.

"What are you doing here?" he asked, tremulous. She again put her finger to her lips, then pointed at the road traversing the field about a hundred yards away. Morgan turned and saw a camouflage green picket truck rumble by, its bed full of army troops, one of the soldiers draped insolently over the back picket, his gun pointing down at the ground. He tossed a cigarette at the red dirt road and stared, almost knowingly, at the sugarcane field, then spit a glob of jade green phlegm.

Morgan turned gratefully to Laura.

"Jesus, how did you know?"

There was no one beside him, the only trace of her presence a faint smell of musk and vetiver. Morgan staggered and sat, staring dumbfounded at the nothing that had been Laura, every nerve and fiber in his body telling him that he had seen her, every thinking cell in his brain shouting out he was going insane. The clouds moved and joined in silent turmoil, and thick viscous raindrops pattered down on the red dirt around the sugarcane.

❊ ❊ ❊

In the cave, the rainstorm's bouquet of freshness woke Che Guevara with a start. He batted his eyes in the gloom, trying to recall how he had managed to steal into a woman's boudoir, so strong was the cool scent of lilacs, until he realized that he had only been dreaming of life back in Rosario and of the afternoons when, bathed and covered in lilac-smelling talc, he'd slide into crisp cotton sheets and snuggle next to his mother's rounded breasts.

Gingerly he took a breath, shallow at first, fearful of triggering yet another asthma attack. Nothing. He took a second, deeper breath. Still nothing. So then he gulped down as much air as he possibly could hold down in his lungs, drinking in the moistness in the cave with the gusto of a drunk gulping down a bottle of wine, the oxygen replenishing the storehouse of energy that twenty-four hours of hacking and couching had depleted. He felt wonderfully alive, thrilling to the urgent beating of his hyperventilating heart.

It's over, he thought. I'm normal again. Or at least as normal as I'll ever be. He chuckled at his own bad joke, sat up, searched his pockets for the ever-present cigar. He extracted a half-smoked *puro* from his rear pants pocket, lit it, and puffed gratefully.

This is the guerrilla's companion, he decided, the fighter's one true friend. He waits patiently for you, thinks only of your pleasure, allays your hunger, and wakens your senses to the world. The cigar, *el puro, el habano.* Of course, at the end he winds up killing you, but isn't that what friends always do, especially among guerrilla fighters? Death comes with the territory. It's only a matter of when you choose to embrace her.

Che got up to pee and noticed, to his amusement, the stiff morning erection of the fully rested man. No wonder I'm thinking so much about the feminine; this boy has to be serviced. It's been a while now, since Aleida went back to Santa Clara. Maybe she'll be back when we return to the Sierra.

The thick shrouds of water came down in jets as though sprayed from a cannon. At the far end of the field the fire had begun to die out, although the cloud of black smoke still hung in the air, reluctant to depart its birthplace. Che noticed a prettily painted *bohío* halfway down the field.

That is an odd place for that *bohío,* thought Che, pulling with relish on his cigar as the long stream of dark morning urine flowed out of him. There are no other houses around here, no *colonos* or even any squatters working the land. It is all sugarcane for many hectares, as far as I can tell. Morgan must have gone there for food. We must be close to Placetas. There we can get in touch with some of the boys from the *movimiento.* That was a narrow escape yesterday. Who knows what would have happened if Morgan hadn't taken me away? All my boys were running for cover. Last time I had an attack like that during a firefight I almost didn't survive. I guess I owe him my life.

Che's stomach growled insolently. He laughed to himself. I certainly hope that Yanqui comes back soon with the food; *ya me duelen las tripas,* my guts are squealing already.

Che emptied the final drops of his bladder to the growing tumult of the storm, then wheeled back inside. A stray lightning bolt landed, to a thundering boom, somewhere in the nearby cane field, illuminating the cavern with its thousands of volts of power. That's when Che noticed, at the far end of the cave, the skull set on the earthen mound, empty eye sockets leering back at him from the recesses of time and circumstance.

⬛ ⬛ ⬛

The rain poured down in great big sheets on Morgan as he trudged down the dirt road, his Thompson tucked under his shirt to keep the ammo dry. Hunger and fatigue weighed heavily on him, the vision of Laura having shocked him to a state of preternatural alertness in which each muscle ache, each stomach growl, was magnified tenfold.

Morgan stopped in his tracks fifty yards away from the *bohío*. The storm showed no sign of slacking in intensity, but Morgan did not feel the rain at all, stunned as he was by the familiar notes of the church hymn issuing from the shack. All at once he was removed from the sticky confines of the Cuban countryside as a low-rolling horizon of fields of Ohio corn spread before him and the steepled frame church with its bill-board reading, JESUS DIED FOR YOUR SINS reared into view, as the music swirled around him and the voices of the faithful rising to the tufted clouds in the heaven, where dwells the all-wise and all-seeing and all-American God.

Thunder boomed once more and the sylvan splendor vanished. Morgan found himself again in the midst of a tropical downpour in a war with no beginning and no end in a country that was not his but where the radiant notes of his childhood faith rang in the warm rain: "Nearer My God to Thee." The words were in sibilant Spanish, and God became a softer, rounder, deeper, and more distant deity, an elderly relation dressed up in the garish colors of the land, unrecognizable except for the same blue eyes peering from underneath the wide-brimmed straw hat.

It *is* a church, God damn it, thought Morgan, hugging the side of the building. He ducked under the roof overhang and peered through the frameless window.

A young blonde woman in priestly black stood at a corner of the building, her arms raised up, leading the ragged handful of swarthy Cuban faces in song. At a nearby lectern, an elderly man in a loose white guayabera shirt smiled and nodded in time to the music. Presently the hymn ended. The old man cleared his throat, picked up his glasses, and placed them, shakily, on the bridge of his long narrow nose. He spoke in the dry but fluent Spanish of the long-established American settler.

"The reading today, brothers and sisters, is from Matthew nineteen, 'And behold, one came and said unto him, Good Master, what good thing shall I do, that I may have eternal life?' "

The young woman beamed at the old man, obviously proud that in spite of his age and infirmity he could still show the path to the Lord. Her expression changed on seeing Morgan, weary, unshaven, dripping wet, staring at her from the window. She became hardened and drawn, gestured with her chin at the back of the church.

" 'And he said unto him, Why callest thou me good? There is none good but one, that is, God: but if thou wilt enter into life, keep the commandments.' "

Morgan walked around to the rear of the *bohío,* painted white with faded blue trim. The smallish door swung open. Morgan stepped through.

The room was a makeshift enclosure, divided from the rest of the shack by a freestanding wall that did not quite reach the ceiling. Morgan noticed a rat scurrying in the rafters, then diving headfirst into the palm thatch roof. He looked down at the lone cross on the far wall, a doorless tattered wardrobe with a handful of men's shirts and pants on wire hangers, a folded army cot, a bookcase with a half set of *Collier's Encyclopedia* and an enormous English-Spanish dictionary, an old icebox, and two leather-and-wood chairs set next to a scratched, rustic table, behind which stood the black-clad girl, arms firmly crossed, head tilted up defiantly.

" 'And again I say unto you, It is easier for a camel to go through the eye of a needle, than for a rich man to enter into the kingdom of God,' " came the crackling words of the preacher on the other side of the wall.

"Usted, qué quiere?" asked the girl in a surprisingly pure Cuban accent, incongruous in the mouth of someone whose very likeness could be found at that moment working the switchboard in Philadelphia, serving breakfast in Cheyenne, or teaching table manners in Grosse Point. *"No tenemos dinero."*

Her thick blond hair in a bun, her thin lips, her round blue eyes, her healthy figure encased in the severe black dress, even her lack of makeup—none of these were as convincing to Morgan that he was dealing with an American as her straightforward attitude, her let's-get-on-with-business manner, even if it was the business of the Lord.

"I don't want your money," said Morgan in English, removing the submachine gun from under his shirt.

"You're American?" she asked, her turn to be surprised. She opened her arms cagily, her eyes drawn to the menacing weapon.

"That's right. The name is William Morgan," he said, extending his callused hand.

The girl glanced down at his hand. Years of democratic training took over, and before she was aware of it, she was shaking it.

"Irma O'Farrell," she said, then quickly withdrew her hand. "What can we do for you, Mr. Morgan? We are poor preachers, as you can see. We have no money or much of anything else. Just lots of faith."

"I'm with the rebels. We are lost."

"You definitely are lost unless you believe in Jesus Christ. Do you believe in Him, Mr. Morgan?"

"Sister, whether I believe or not has nothing to do with it. We lost our way, is what I mean. We're hungry. We haven't had a bite to eat in the past twenty-four hours. If you can help us, fine. If not, I'll keep going down the road."

She looked him up and down in silent contemplation.

"How many of you?"

"Two."

She moved to the old wooden icebox, yanked the chipped chrome handle. "Two I can handle. I guess your soul will have to wait, Mr. Morgan. For now. But I wouldn't recommend you going anywhere else around here."

She took out a loaf of white bread, a jar of Peter Pan peanut butter, another of Welch's grape jelly, the remains of a baked chicken.

"Why do you say that?" asked Morgan, his stomach spontaneously churning at seeing the long-lost food of his homeland.

"This is the land of the Narcisa sugar mill. The owner is one of Batista's cronies. He's had the government send soldiers down here to protect the property."

She set a glass bottle of milk on the table, stood up, rearranged a tendril of wispy blond hair falling out of her bun.

"In any event, the nearest house is two kilometers down the road. Belongs to the overseer. Then there's the big house, the owner's mansion. There are no workers around here right now; it's dead time."

"Dead time?"

She wrapped the foodstuffs in a calico kitchen cloth she brought out of a drawer in the table.

"For a rebel you sure don't know much about Cuba, Mr. Morgan."

"Sorry. I'm learning as fast as I can."

She stopped, looked him in the eye, and smiled for the first time. It was then Morgan realized she couldn't be more than twenty years old.

"Dead time means the harvest hasn't started. During the harvest season, the mill grinds sugarcane day and night. There are hundreds of cane cutters here then, working. That's our usual ministry. Right now all we have are some of the permanent people in the sugar mill, our congregation. My point is, Mr. Morgan, don't go around anywhere else asking for help. They're likely to turn you in. Here you go."

She pushed forward the bundle of food. Morgan grabbed it.

"You won't?"

"No, Mr. Morgan. Render unto Caesar what is Caesar's. And this Caesar deserves to be thrown out. We're all doing God's work. You're doing it your way, we're doing it ours."

✴ ✴ ✴

Back in the cave, Guevara was methodically gathering all the loose twigs and palm tree fronds blown in by the wind and wrapping them tightly into a sheaf. He took out his book of matches. Two left. He lit one, put it to the bundle, but the bundle refused to catch on fire. He took out his last match, lit it, tried again.

"*Vamos, che,*" he said loudly. "Light up!"

This time the husks heeded his call and the improvised torch burst into crackling green-yellow flames.

"*Así se hace,*" that's how you do it, he said to the flames with satisfaction.

He walked back into the depth of the cave; in the half-light he caught a glimpse of a snake slithering into the dark. Guevara raised the flare to light up the painted walls and ceilings.

Lines and symbols jumped out at Guevara, a message from people long ago in a now-forgotten language. He counted twenty-eight circular lines and another twenty-eight black circles, all representing the vastness of the universe in a sketchy cosmic map. Within the larger design, a variety of concentric circles and spirals ending in staircases that led nowhere, serpentine figures slithering into the vastness of time, odd runic crosses and meandering swastikas. The concentric circles, splayed on the edges of the design like constellations around the Milky Way, were made of thirteen black lines, while in the center, four all-seeing eyes of red concentric circles stared unblinkingly into the darkness, the key and origin of this prehistoric marker.

Guevara leaned in close, touched the lines, which smudged off on his fingertips, the paint as fresh as the day hundreds of years before when the native Siboney Indians had drawn their knowledge on the walls of that yawning cavern. The torchlight now illuminated a new find, three other skulls set at the corners of a large imaginary triangle around the mound where the original skull was placed.

Guevara felt both awe and regret at seeing the carefully arranged memorial. He knelt next to the nearest skull, peering into its cavity as through a keyhole to some other, wondrous universe.

"Pobres indios," poor Indians, he finally said, sitting back, in his mind the visions of the lone chief on his rock smoking his cigar watching the conquistadors arrive in their fleet caravels. He turned to the drawings on the wall, then to the brown skulls lying mutely in the dirt.

"Why didn't you send the white men back to their flea-infested land? Had you no idea of the devil that lurked inside them? You should have fought back."

"Who are you talking to?" came Morgan's voice.

Guevara spun around. Morgan stood at the mouth of the cave, his figure outlined against the returning sun.

"History," said Guevara, raising his torch on high. "Take a look."

Morgan advanced into the cave, the calico bundle in his arms.

"I got some food here," he said.

"Good. But this is food too, my friend. The food of thought."

Morgan stood next to the walls, the wavy designs, circles, and spirals opening and closing under the torch's flickering light like a jellyfish waving its long fingers at him. He noticed the long downward slope of the cave floor. It must lead down to a tunnel somewhere, he thought. Maybe if I follow that I'll find her waiting for me on the other side.

"Amazing," was what he said, observing the carefully placed shells on the ground.

"Precisely what I was thinking," said Guevara. "What's for lunch?"

※ ※ ※

Guevara put down the half-eaten sandwich, his mouth full of the cottony, sticky-sweet concoction that clung to his teeth like *melcocha,* the taffy he would buy during recess at St. Augustine's as a boy. He had long ago outgrown the taste for that kind of food, but obviously Americans had not, for Morgan relished the last bite of his sandwich with enormous devotion, licking every last bit of grape jelly off his fingers, then casting a covetous look at the remains of Che's sandwich.

"Please, help yourself," said Guevara. "I'm not that hungry anymore."

"There's some chicken wings too," said Morgan, quickly swiping the sandwich before Guevara had time to change his mind.

"Yes, I will have that instead," answered Guevara. He dug into the bag and extracted a couple of anemic, greasy, yellow wings, which he devoured with the greatest of delights, each wing sliding up and down his mouth like a glistening harmonica.

218

When they were finished they shared the bottle of milk, and then both grew quiet, their hunger pangs subsiding as the golden sun spread its burning mantle on the swaying cane field down below.

"That is a very strange taste, your peanut butter. I had never heard of such a thing," said Guevara.

"It's very nutritious," said Morgan. "High in protein content. Invented by a colored man."

"Truly? What was his name?"

"George Washington Carver. He was the world's expert on the peanut. Said it was God's greatest gift to mankind. A thousand uses."

"Like what?"

"Well, there's peanut butter. Then there's peanut oil. And then . . . you know, I really don't recall. But I know there are. I read that once. Cigarette?"

Guevara shook his head *no*, took out the stub of his cigar.

"I shall smoke this," he said. Morgan lit the stogie for him, a cloud of fetid smoke rising up in the mouth of the cave. The men, relaxed with each other, smiled. Not a bad fellow, each was thinking, prompted by satiety and tobacco. If all communists/Yankees were like him, was their silent, echoing thought.

"A Negro scientist. That is amazing, old man. I thought your Negroes were like our Indians."

"How is that?"

"You know, servants. Bus drivers. That sort of thing. Oppressed people without rights. Cursed to the lowest rungs of society."

"Well, we do have some of that. A lot, actually. But I believe that's a mistake. That sort of thing should not be allowed. Negroes are capable of doing everything that white people do. That's how most Americans view it."

"You are sure? You have been having some problems with your civil rights."

"Yes, but that's all in the South. They're prejudiced down there."

"Perhaps they're just more open about their prejudice, don't you think? If it had been up to the Spanish, they would have killed all the Indians, but they needed them to work. Here in Cuba they all died. Working in the gold mines, from smallpox, other Spanish diseases. All brought on by greed and lust."

"A good Indian is a dead Indian," countered Morgan, flicking off the ash of his cigarette.

"For certain. I have seen your Gene Autry movies, your Roy Rogers and Hopalong Cassidy movies. The Indians are always the bad ones."

"Isn't that the truth?" said Morgan, uncomfortable inside his skin, feeling—not for the last time—that he was being seen as the repository of the best and the worst of America solely because of his birthplace.

"I can't say I'm too proud of what we did to the red man. We slaughtered them, took their land, put them in reservations. I think most Americans know it was wrong, but it was history, you know? What are you going to do now? Besides, the Indians up North were fierce warriors. Comanches. Sioux. Cherokees. They gave as good as they got."

"Naturally," said Guevara, about to launch into a disquisition on Manifest Destiny, a topic that he had studied back during his itinerant photographer days, when he would take refuge from the winter rains of Mexico in the National Library.

"But that's not all we did," said Morgan. "There's always the good with the bad, and when you weigh everything we did, I think the good guys come out ahead. We freed our slaves, we said all men are equal, we gave women the vote. We even said people have a right, hell, an obligation, to rebel if there's a tyranny over them. Nobody else ever said that before."

"What about supporting Batista then? What about Arbenz in Guatemala?"

"That's the fight against communism. The reds are out to take over the world. But I don't have to tell you that."

"Are you asking me if I'm a communist?"

"I don't have to; everybody knows you are. We have a common goal, getting rid of Batista. Once he's gone, all bets are off."

"Bets are off?"

"Anything goes," said Morgan, hoping he hadn't been too harsh on Guevara, remembering his Lutheran pastor back in Toledo, soft brown eyes belied by his stern visage, preaching from the pulpit: Hate the sin and not the sinner, because with the grace of God all is possible.

Guevara rose slowly, with the gravity of someone determined to avenge a deadly insult.

"Come here, my friend," he said, gesturing at Morgan," I want to explain something."

"What for? Where are we going?" asked Morgan, still not quite sure he could trust this particular sinner.

"Please!"

Morgan checked his sidearm, then came up to Guevara, standing in front of the glyphs.

"You see this picture, my friend? This is communism. This is history, and communism is the inevitable march of history."

He turned, the glint of passion in his eyes.

"Just like the Indians came here and painted this, confident that they would last forever, so with the Americans. They come, they build their buildings and their bridges, bring their machines, drop their bombs, invent the A-bomb and the television and the stock market and all the rest, and think that their kingdom will have no end. But so did they, my friend."

Guevara bent down, picked up a skull from the floor.

"Don't you think he had dreams too? Don't you think he did great things too? Perhaps he fought the cannibals who were coming from the east, or maybe he conquered the Tainos out on the west. Does it matter? It matters not at all. It has all been forgotten, like the name of the girl he loved, the children he fathered, the field of corn he planted himself that he was so proud of."

"What is your point, Guevara? You're talking in riddles."

"My point? My point is that America is just a step in the inevitable conclusion of the inner movement of world history toward a community of equal people sharing their wealth without special treatment. Communism recognizes this and seeks to help; capitalism doesn't and seeks to hinder. If you examine the movement of history, you will detect what Marx and Engels and Hegel detected, the gradual unveiling of the world spirit struggling to break free, to manifest itself and create paradise here on earth, not up in the clouds. This is the moment of the United States. It might last another five years or another five hundred, but of one thing I'm certain: in the end your inner contradictions will eliminate America from the map."

Morgan stared at the glyphs, his mind racing from Guevara's frontal attack on his beliefs. There was something askew in that concept of history as its own mover, expressing itself as though it were God, man, or an angel.

"What about Jefferson, then?" countered Morgan, finding his inspiration in the much-abused pages of his sixth-grade civics course book. "What about Lincoln and Washington and people like them? Your history has no heroes, Che, just slaves."

"No, no, listen to me, William Morgan! We are all instruments of the world spirit, and we matter only when we are in the process of helping it to accomplish its goals. Jefferson, Washington, Lincoln, they were great men, yes, but they were great because they knew how to interpret the movement of history. Look at their enemies. Aaron Burr, Benedict Arnold, Jefferson Davis. They did not know how to ride the tiger. The great man was the one that paved the way for the coming of the world spirit."

"What about people like Hitler, then? And Napoleon? Stalin? Genghis Khan? Alexander the Great? There is no morality in your scheme of things then, because otherwise how do you explain people like that? Look at what they did and conquered. They too advanced history. Are they too in the process of what you call this unfolding of the world spirit? Then there is no good or evil, everything is allowed?"

"Those people, they are the *Übermenschen*," said Guevara, grinning slyly as he put down the skull. Morgan had found the hole in his knitting and he had to admit it.

"The what?"

"That is German. It means they are superior. And yes, to them all is allowed."

"That is ridiculous. Who determines who the superior being is? What does he look like, where is he from? And what about values? What about basic human decency? Does that means nothing? Everything is the group, and the individual doesn't count?"

❊ ❊ ❊

"There you are! I've been looking all over for you! Hurry up, the army's coming!!"

Both men turned, astonished, to the entrance to the cave. Dressed still in her black preaching garb, now all muddied from the climb, Irma O'Farrell shook a bag at them with the greatest of urgency.

"I brought you some more food, but you better get out of here on the double. They're onto you!"

Morgan walked past Irma, peered down at the valley below. The army truck he'd spotted before was parked at the bottom of the hill, its soldiers swarming up the trail, moving dots of brown against the lush green landscape.

"How did you know where to find us?" asked Morgan, taking the bag from her hands and glancing quickly inside—more sandwiches, a thermos. He handed the bag to Guevara before taking up his submachine gun and readying it for action.

"I saw you walking this way when you left," said Irma, looking almost embarrassed at her admission of interest. "There aren't that many other places around here that you could hide in. Problem is, everybody around knows about this place, the Cueva del Indio; they think it's haunted. The soldiers came looking for you right after you left. I said I hadn't seen you and I hiked over as fast as I could. I acted real indignant. I told them I was here to save souls, not to make more dead." She smiled, pleased at her own daring.

"Did they teach you that at preacher's college?" asked Morgan, grinning.

"I've picked up a few things myself along the way, Mr. Morgan."

"Who is this?" asked Guevara, his mouth full of a ham sandwich he'd grabbed from the bag.

"Irma O'Farrell, Comandante Ernesto Che Guevara," said Morgan, snapping on his bandolier.

"*El famoso guerrillero?*" said Irma, almost but not quite shaken out of her self-possession.

"*A sus órdenes, damita,*" mumbled Guevara, curtsying briefly as he clutched his M-1.

"Alright, let's go," ordered Morgan. "You stay here until the two of us have left. You know the area better than us."

Irma nodded, followed the men outside into the now burning sun. Che turned questioningly toward her.

"How far is this from Placetas? I'm supposed to meet some *compañeros* there."

A barrage of rifle fire sliced the air around them, raising welts of dust on the ground, bullets zinging past and bouncing against the rocks.

"Down! Down! Drop down!" bellowed Morgan, even as another hailstorm of bullets flew just inches away. Morgan glanced up, spotted a group of soldiers behind some boulders five hundred feet away. He aimed his machine gun at them, fired a quick succession of bursts, preempting their attack.

"There's only two men there on the left!" said Guevara. "Maybe I can go around and get them that way."

Another fusillade broke above them, rending the air into tiny fragments of death. Irma put her face down in the grass, pressing it down in silent prayer until she no longer felt the waves of fear over her body.

"Well, there goes that idea," said Morgan, firing back at the other shooters, to their left, downslope.

Guevara took a look at their position, pinned down left and right, other soldiers swarming up the hillside taking up position.

"Maybe this beautiful lady should say a prayer for us now, because we're going to need it."

Both men fired again at the troops below, forcing them to scatter before they could gather their firepower. Morgan knew it was only a matter of minutes before the commanding officer coordinated the attack and wiped them out.

So this is how it ends, thought Morgan. In some godforsaken God knows how many miles to some goddamn diddly-squat of a goddamn fucking town I finally get to say good-bye. I wonder if she will be waiting for me on the other side. I wonder if there is another side or even a God. No, there can't be a God; otherwise He wouldn't let us go through this, knowing how much we suffer, and still be a God. He can't exist. No, there is no God. No, there is no Laura anymore. This is all there is, this hill and these people I am fighting and this commie and this girl, nothing else exists or has existed. This is the end at last. There is no God.

Down below the platoon commander picked up his mobile phone, bellowing at the base for his reinforcements.

"*Cabrones,* how much time do I have to wait! This is a band of fearsome guerrillas! How many? At least one hundred up on the hill of the Cave of the Indian! Hurry up! No, wait, here it comes. *Finalmente!*"

The loud buzz of a plane broke through the report of gunfire. Morgan looked up to see the broad wings of a B–26 wheeling above him.

"Well, it was good knowing you, *Capitán,*" said Guevara, grinning wildly, slamming another clip into his M-1. "You would have made a good socialist eventually!"

"And you a lousy democrat!" replied Morgan, watching the plane banking, readying for the bomb drop.

"There's a way out!" shouted Irma, now looking up from the grass, bits of vegetation pressed to her face.

"Fine time to tell us!" said Morgan, his voice coming to his ears as though from far away, even as he fired back instantly at the troops below.

"Through the cave! It comes out to the surface about a mile from here!"

"Too late for that!" shouted Morgan as he closed his eyes, expecting the bomb that would blast him to smithereens. Instead a boom, a rattle as though an earthquake, the smell of cordite and napalm, and a yellow wall of flame fell on the soldiers two hundred feet below them, their cries of suffering rising to the burning sky.

"Jesus, he missed us!" was Morgan's first reaction. Then: "Let's go, let's go, before they catch on!"

He grabbed Irma by the arm and propelled her in front of him even as the gunner in the B-26, angry at the near miss, let go a curtain of machine gun fire, slicing the ground in arabesques around them. Morgan's horse, frightened by the firing, finally broke its ties and bolted across the hill, legs loping on the brown dirt. Good luck, friend, thought Morgan watching him, I hope you find your pasture.

Morgan raced through the bush and up the hundred feet to the cave entrance as though pushing through water at the bottom of a fish tank, the air itself an obstacle to his flight until, sometime later—a second, a minute, he didn't know how long—he and the girl and Guevara stumbled into the warmth of the cave as the plane dropped another bomb at the mouth of the cavern. The hillside shook, growled, and sent an avalanche of rocks down from the top of the hill, forcing the remaining soldiers to scramble for safety. The rock slide sealed off the entrance to the cave, trapping the three of them inside as the plane's pilot headed back to Cienfuegos, proud of his mission accomplished.

Chapter

10

The floor of the cave sloped down precipitously, a damp limestone trail leading into an even deeper recess in the earth. From the low ceiling, black-and-white stalactites sprouted like the buried fangs of giants. Morgan held up his Zippo, lighting the way for Irma, who groped in the semidarkness ahead of her. Behind Morgan, a hacking Guevara grumbled down the serpentine path.

"Is it much longer?" gasped Guevara. "This dust and humidity are getting to me."

"It shouldn't be too far," said Irma, stepping over a brooklet to the other shore of a dark unknown.

"C'mon, Che, you can hold on," said Morgan, tramping through the ice cold stream, "or would you rather be outside?"

"Perhaps I should have taken my chances there. At least I could breathe," wheezed Guevara, skipping over the water.

Irma turned down the tunnel and reached its end, a small opening, no bigger than a house window. All three of them stopped to contemplate the hole in silence, their shadows flickering against the wall as the dying Zippo began to sputter.

"We'll have to crawl through this," said Irma. "I haven't been here since I was a kid, I forgot how tiny it is. As I recall, it's about two hundred yards. On the other side there's a cavern with a lake, and beyond that a trail leading back up to the other side of the hill."

Morgan looked dubiously at the opening, then glanced back at a tremulous Guevara.

"You used to do this when you were a kid?" asked Morgan.

"I'd come play hide-and-seek with my cousin Luke," said Irma, hiking up her long skirt. She tucked its ends under the wide leather belt, the remaining fabric falling halfway down her thighs. She got on all fours unself-consciously, showing Morgan a flash of pink-colored panties.

"I was a tomboy," she added, then crawled in through the opening.

I believe it, said Morgan to himself, following her.

They crawled through the passageway, slimy from the growth of innumerable bacteria, Morgan holding his flickering Zippo aloft. No one said a word, each wrapped in his own thoughts of survival and escape, wondering what exactly lay ahead.

Irma stopped before a large boulder at the end of the crawl space. The smooth, massive rock blocked the way as though someone had plugged that channel to prevent it from ever opening again.

"This rock wasn't here the last time," she said, straining against the boulder, her boot-clad feet slipping from under her as she attempted to purchase a grip. "I can't get through."

"Here, Che, hold up the lighter," said Morgan, passing the Zippo to Guevara. "Pardon me, Miss O'Farrell."

Morgan slithered up the passageway next to Irma, pressing his body into hers, feeling the fleshiness of her breasts pushed up against his chest, the warmth of her unscented skin, the ropiness of her muscles pushing against the rock. They were wedged against each other like twins in the mother, waiting to be born. In the dappled light of the failing lighter, Morgan realized the raw beauty of her northern Irish features, the soft golden dew that covered her brow.

"When I say 'Go,' you push with all your might," said Morgan.

"All right," replied Irma.

"OK. One, two, three. Push!"

The two heaved together, bodies in close contact, straining against the stopper of a rock that wanted to block their exit, straining with all their might, their bodies pressed so tightly that they were fused into one being with two heads and two sets of limbs, pushing, straining, until their necks turned red and their temperature rose so high they wanted to tear their clothes off, but instead they pushed mightily against the solid rock, which finally, after an eternity of resistance, gave way and dropped with a noise, somewhere between a sigh and the pop of a bottle, onto the floor on the other side of the tunnel.

"Excuse me," mumbled Morgan, squirming as he crawled out.

"Don't mention it," said Irma, flushed and deeply embarrassed, especially since she'd noticed that the effort had aroused Morgan, who had been pressing his organ—unwittingly, she was sure, but sinful all the

227

same—against her crotch; and the worse part, oh dear Lord, was that she wished it had not ended, but she wasn't about to admit this to herself, much less to anyone else, as she finally wriggled free and pushed herself out of the tunnel as well, both of them tumbling down to the floor of the cavern, panting and squinting, babes in a new world.

The cavern opened before them in a vast hall eighty to a hundred feet high, its ceiling studded with sweaty stalactites. The ground sloped down to a limpid, oblong green pool a quarter mile in length, lit up by its own luminescence, a gleaming body of still green in the otherworldly stillness. At the far end, the hall narrowed to a passageway, from which flowed, calmly and smoothly, the stream that fed the subterranean lake. A sound halfway between a whisper and a hoot echoed in the cavern, which seemed to look back at Morgan and Irma with the same curiosity with which they examined it.

Morgan and Irma stood awestruck, momentarily lost in the eerie beauty of the place. Just then Guevara wrested himself out of the tunnel and dropped with a painful thump.

"*Carajo!*"—dammit—he screamed, the first word spoken in years in that cavern. The sound reverberated as in an echo chamber, triggering a massive, flowing noise.

"Look out!" said Morgan.

Out of the corner of the cave a black cloud detached itself from the ceiling and flew toward them. Morgan raised his gun but Irma pushed it down.

"They're only bats, they won't harm you!" she said, as the host of tiny creatures came at them. Morgan was stunned, then found himself laughing, tickled by the furry wings of the swarm of screeching bats, a stream of underground dwellers colliding against the humans, then reassembling in midair before swooping away into the far passageway, seeking the undisturbed quiet of other, solitary spaces.

After the last straggling beast had swept away, screeching and twitching into the gloom, the three humans walked cautiously down the slippery slope to the lake's edge. As they neared, the water changed color from green to a milky white that sparkled with luminous intensity, alive with odd creatures gathering below the surface. With each movement of the animals, fat white catfish without eyes or fins, the water roiled and sparkled, the lake a shimmering blanket of twinkling light.

"How is this possible?" Morgan asked Irma without taking his eyes off the water, bewitched by its shifting luminosity.

"It's always been like this," she said, gathering a stray lock of blond hair. "We once took a bucket of water all the way to the surface. It glowed on

228

the way up, but when we came out, it was clear. It's the Lord's way."

Morgan knelt down, scooped up some of the lake's milky liquid, which cleared up in his hand, becoming normal translucent water.

"Mollusks, obviously," said Guevara, wheezing, almost disdainfully.

"How is that?" asked Morgan.

"Tiny gastropods that are phosphorescent, like fireflies," said Guevara, his scientific training coming to the fore. "They live in this water, probably have a very good food supply here from plankton and the like. The moment you remove them from their habitat they die; that's why they stopped glowing once you brought them out. You can barely see them with the naked eye. It's a rare phenomenon but it happens in other places in Cuba. What I would like to know is where the light is coming from."

Guevara wheeled around, examining carefully the ceiling of the cavern, then raised his hand.

"There it is!"

He pointed at an opening on the far side, from which a bar of light now spread out in liquid gold.

"The sun bounces off these white walls, then?" asked Irma.

"Exactly. All it takes is one light source. Extraordinary, isn't it?" said Guevara, then he hacked hurtfully. "But please, let's move on. This dampness is very oppressive."

"Look!" said Irma. "What is that?"

Out in the middle of the lake, a shimmering green cloud seemed to gather out of nowhere. The water roiled, great big bubbles bursting suddenly, as though an invisible hand were stirring the surface. A smell of sulfur filled the air. The rock formations on the far side that before had seemed so harmless and natural now turned otherworldly and oddly menacing, resembling ancient warriors frozen in a perpetual gesture of aggression, arms raised, head cocked back, lance pitched forward.

A great wind rushed into the hall, a hubbub of sounds and voices that seemed to carry a message in a language long ago forgotten.

"What is that noise?" asked Morgan.

"People around here say it's the souls of the Indians who died working in the gold mines in this mountain," said Irma. "That's why nobody ever comes in here. They're all frightened of what they hear. Listen!"

Morgan thought he heard shouts and even the barking of dogs in the wall of noise that echoed off the ceiling; then the shouts and cries gave way to an eerie plaintive howl from some suffering soul left to ponder its pain for all eternity. The mist gathered into thick clouds, then all at once the entire hall went dark, the only light the weird phosphorescence of the lake itself.

A small island now rose out of the water, a promontory revealed by the swiftly receding waters. The preserved bodies of three Indians stood on the island, silently staring at the visitors from another world. They were thin, short, and sallow skinned, their noses long and narrow, their burning eyes deep-set, and their foreheads slanted backward in the peculiar shape cultivated by Taíno Indians. The men stood, their arms stretched out, pointing, it seemed, at Morgan, who stood transfixed by the odd spectacle.

"What the hell is going on here?" muttered Morgan, but before he could find the presence of mind to move a muscle, the vision of the men vanished and the great roiling of the waters returned and the island was covered again and the entire cavern turned pitch black. The lake stopped shining and a great wind blew again through the cavern, a cool moist wind that seemed to carry a myriad of voices—howls, screeches, cries of desperation, the cracking of whips, and the shooting of muskets and the wailing and the chattering of teeth, and through it all a word that Morgan could not quite recognize, a word distant yet familiar . . . *salvador, salvador, salvador.*

Then all at once the wind died, the light returned, the water calmed down, and Morgan, Irma, and Guevara found themselves standing once more on the shores of a peaceful underground lake.

Morgan looked around, unable to believe what he had just witnessed, refusing to accept what his eyes had just told him.

"Which way out?" he asked simply, his mouth as dry as if he were in battle.

"Over here," said Irma, pointing at a path of strewn boulders.

"Praise the Lord," she said.

"Hallelujah," added Morgan without thinking.

"I'll say 'Amen' to that," came Guevara's odd rejoinder.

They clambered out quickly through the opening at the far end of the lake, up another narrow passageway again lined with symbols and drawings left by the island's original inhabitants. Rounding a corner, they exited at the back of a cave, which opened to a torrent of blinding light.

They stepped quickly through the detritus of twigs, leaves, and chewed bones lining the dirt floor, and walked out gratefully into the throbbing sun, which seemed to heal them, burning away the traces of the phantasmagorical experience down below.

Morgan noted with satisfaction the rise of the land, the fields of sugarcane, the great brown boulders strewn down the hill, the cottony clouds, the swaying of the graceful palm trees. I am back in reality. This is the world. These are the hills, that is the sky, this is the land, this is true. Just what the hell was it that we saw?

He turned to his companions. Irma had raised her arms, closed her eyes, tilting her head back in silent prayer to the sky, while Guevara slumped down on the ground, shallow breath coming out in spurts, his skin almost green from fatigue.

"What was that word we heard down there?" asked Morgan, realizing with surprise that his voice sounded dry and wasted. Guevara tried to speak but made only a wheezing sound, as air painfully filled his lungs. He waved his hands at Irma, who looked down, her prayers concluded.

"You mean *salvador?*" she asked.

"Yes, that."

"It means *savior,* as in our Lord Jesus Christ."

Morgan stood transfixed, pondering the meaning of Irma's words. Savior? What on God's earth did that mean?

Guevara, having finally found his voice, added a rejoinder.

"No, the word was *sálvanos.* Save us."

"Save us?" repeated Morgan.

"Yes, save us," said Guevara, slowly rising, his torso bent over like an old man's. "But now it's time to save ourselves. Which way to Placetas, Miss O'Farrell?"

"Down the road, ten kilometers."

"*Compañeros,* then let us start," said Guevara, "unless we want to stay here and join the dead in their wailing when the soldiers turn up."

✻ ✻ ✻

On the outskirts of Placetas, a small hilly town dotted with decaying colonial houses on narrow cobblestone streets, Irma made contact with the local 26th of July representative. The man, the town's assistant telegraph operator, had already intercepted several messages between Havana's high command and the troops stationed nearby, giving the description of the wily rebels who had managed to elude the attack on the camp of Capitán Cordón. So when Irma, feet swollen from the long walk, black skirt coated with the fine dust of the road, trudged into the telegraph office and whispered the password, "Sweet tamales," Olvidio García Milanés was more than happy to rise to the occasion.

For years Olvidio had dreamed of just this moment, when his heroic efforts would help the glorious cause of the revolution. The new rebel government might even appoint him head of the telegraph office to personally purge the communications network of the corrupt Batistiano regime, which pocketed half of all proceeds and split the other half with the local *sargento*. That left poor Compañía de Telégrafos Cubanos a paltry twenty-five percent of moneys collected, barely enough to keep up the many kilometers of cobwebbed telegraph wire unspooled all over these isolated hills.

Olvidio rose at once, put up the *Closed for Business* sign, and drove Irma in his creaking Model T to the outskirts of town, where he found Morgan and Guevara in a drainage ditch, playing tag with two children dressed in rags. He picked the men up and drove them back home as stealthily as his clanking, smoke-belching vehicle would allow. He found his wife, tubby, raven-haired Carmela, putting out the posters for the weekly movie she showed in the storefront next to their house, which she had converted into the town's only cinema.

"Look at this, Olvidio," she said, waving a handful of rolled-up posters on seeing the Model T groan up to the stoop. "They sent us Stewart Granger! *The Mines of King Solomon!* We should have a full house for this one!"

"I don't know why can't they send us more Marilyn Monroe. *Niagara* did very well too," said Olvidio, even as he jerked his head inside the car. Carmela walked up to the driver's window just as an army truck rumbled past.

"Oh, you men are always dreaming of the American blondes, what dirty minds you have!" she cried, seeing Morgan and Guevara lying down on the floorboards while Irma stretched out on the backseat.

"That is the way men are, *vieja,* you know that. Besides, that way we'd have two showings and they would both sell out," said Olvidio with the practical experience of the veteran exhibitor.

Carmela lifted a wobbly, tufted arm, pointed at the garage.

"You evil-speaking thing, now go get this car in there and help me set up."

Olvidio meekly drove around the side of the red-tiled building as Carmela raised her voice, making sure the pro-Batista neighbors could hear.

"And Marilyn Monroe doesn't work for Metro-Goldwyn-Mayer anymore, you dirty old man, and I'm glad of it!"

Olvidio hustled his guests past the backyard with its ranging chickens and crowing red rooster, escorting them to an outbuilding lined with shelves and furnished plainly with a cot and two chairs. He cautioned them to be quiet until dark, when the others would come to accompany them to the Sierra. But no sooner had Olvidio closed the door than Carmela came in, wringing her hands in unbecoming modesty, asking if it was true as she had heard from others in the movement that Guevara was a medical doctor.

Guevara, the dirt of the fields covering his features like a second skin, tried to head off what he knew was coming, claiming he had not practiced in a long time. But Carmela was not to be dissuaded and soon prevailed upon Guevara to accompany her down the street, making it sound as though it were his revolutionary duty to attend to a friend's son suffering from a bad case of croup.

"I have drawn a bath for you, *Comandante,* so you will be all nice and clean when you make your visit," she said. "I know cleanliness is supremely important."

"So is good nutrition. And medicine," countered Guevara, wearily accompanying the irresistible woman.

"*Ah, sí,* I know. Tell me, Doctor, is it true that beans can cause diverticulitis?" she asked, long keys rattling from her key ring.

"Not at all, but they do make you fart," replied Guevara in all seriousness, walking out.

"*Ay Doctor!*" was Camela's scandalized screech of laughter and reproach as she closed the building's blue door behind her.

Morgan smiled, then peered out the window at the animal yard behind the house. In the pigpen in the corner, a massive umber-colored sow lay sleeping happily in the mud next to her trough, the only sign of life the trembling of her snout as she snored. During his stay in the hills Morgan had grown accustomed to the odd pig by the *bohíos* of the peasants, scavenging as best it could. They were small, wiry things, no bigger than a small dog but twice as intelligent, carrying in their bones the certain knowledge that, unless careful, they would wind up as someone's impromptu dinner. But this pig was like the porkers Morgan fed as a boy back in Ohio, before his father, in the struggle to avoid bankruptcy, met his fate while balancing the books at his desk.

Morgan shook his head, wanting to distance himself from his own memories, trying to forget the many twists and turns that had brought him to this room in this town in this warm, drowsy afternoon. The past was a country that was better not to explore too deeply. Too many faces, too many failures, with only the cold comfort of a gun as his constant companion.

He turned. Irma stretched out on the cot, fast asleep, her hands involuntarily wrapped around each other in prayer. I wonder how many souls she has saved.

On their trek out of the Cave of the Indian, Irma had briefly told Morgan about her father's family of preachers, six boys born in the

California town of Escalon, children of a renegade Irishman and a Portuguese washerwoman who had found the light in the teachings of Mary Baker Eddy. Her grandfather, an atheist bricklayer devoted to the comforts of Yeats and Glenfiddich, had left her grandmother, who brought up the brood by herself. Drawing on her church for support, she had become a deaconess in Modesto, seeing with pride how her children grew to spread the doctrine to all corners of the world. Irma had an uncle in Hong Kong, another in Mombasa, a third in Brazil, one in Bengal, and another in that most heathen of cities, San Francisco.

Irma's father, the oldest, had chosen Cuba for his ministry, and the island, in its own gay and duplicitous fashion, had chosen him as well. He had met, converted, and fallen in love with a third-grade schoolteacher, Olga, Irma's mother, who convinced him that the greatest need for the Lord's work was in the swaying fields of sugarcane, where life was so hard that his preachings of the word were like messages from another planet.

Irma's mother had died when Irma was thirteen, and Irma had thrown herself into her father's work, preaching the gospel of love and salvation up and down the dirt roads of the island. Their main temple was in Trinidad, and every month they would make the rounds of their churches to bring the light of God's mercy to the needy.

Yet now, sleeping peacefully, Irma seemed like any other American girl, exhausted perhaps by a long day at the cosmetics counter or behind the typewriter, rather than from dodging bullets and hiding from soldiers. Morgan wished that he had some of that peace she seemed to irradiate, that self-confidence which let her fall asleep almost instantly in a new and unexplored place.

Restless, his eye was caught by a collection of tiny plaster madonnas, chipped and dusty, set in a corner of one of the shelves. All of them were white, save for one husky figure with the requisite glow, halo, and stars, but with the unmistakable chocolate skin and flared nostrils of the African people.

Morgan picked up the black madonna, smiled to himself. A colored Mary, how about that? he thought. If Mom is colored, I mean, that means that little Jesus is Negro. Man, wouldn't that get under some people's skin back home?

Morgan moved on down the shelves. Dozens of red leather-bound books, their spine bearing the goldleaf inscription *Constitución de la República*—some dated 1902, others dated 1940. None had been opened, their pages still stiff to the touch. Next to those, well-worn volumes of *El Capital* by Carlos Marx and *La Decadencia de Occidente* by Osvaldo Spengler.

But Morgan's eyes widened when he spotted the next find: rows of film canisters, their titles handwritten in both English and Spanish: *Capitanes valientes, Captains Courageous; Ricitos de oro, Goldilocks; Sin novedad en el frente, All Quiet on the Western Front; Martinica, To Have and Have Not.* Morgan opened the canisters. All they held were scraps, pieces of reels cut off by clumsy editing or burned by the incandescent bulb of their mismanaged movie projector—damaged dreams not worth returning.

Morgan laughed, a laughter scornful of itself, mistrusting, bordering on self-loathing. This is what I am as well, he thought, worthless crap stuffed away in some shitty pueblo. I should be dead. I should have died a long time ago.

I know what this is, he told himself. This is just a bad case of the jitters. This is my nerves playing eight ball with me. It's been hard this last week and I haven't had a break and I think I'm going to need one very soon because my God if I don't I believe I am going to cry for no reason at all but no don't let the tears out no crying allowed not for men like yourself hold it in you're a man you're a Marine God damnit snap out of it!

But in the back of his mind he could hear the dam busting, and the pain of memory rocked him like a blow to his chest. He felt out of control and utterly alone in the world, and all the pain was on his shoulders, and it would never quit.

"Lift your eyes to the Lord, brother, for He will grant you peace," said Irma, laying a hand on his arm.

Surprised, Morgan wheeled around, slapping Irma, who took the blow in silence.

"I'm sorry, you startled me," she said, turning away so she would not see his tears.

"The Lord has the balm for all our sorrows, Mr. Morgan, if only you will come to Him and lay your troubles on His doorstep," she said, sitting next to him, peering intently into his eyes.

"Please don't. I'm exhausted. I don't know what's come over me."

"There is nothing wrong with crying, Brother William. Tears are the way our soul refreshes itself. Tears are the draught of our salvation."

"I have nothing to be saved for."

"Yes, you do, for there is a heaven, Brother William. There is a God, and Jesus Christ was His son, and if you believe in Him you will be cured and your pain will—"

"Stop that preaching nonsense, Irma. What do you know about pain? What do you know about loss?"

"I'm human too, William."

"What do you know? Do you know what I have done? Do you know what I have seen?"

"No, I do not, but I will listen if you will let me."

"You have no idea of what it's like to carry this around, you cannot imagine. Why do you think I'm here? Why do you think that . . . ah, it's no use."

Morgan moved to rise, but Irma held on to his arm with such strength that Morgan found himself pulled down to his seat, staring into the sky blue orbs of this knowing woman-child.

"I forgive you," she said. "The Lord forgives you, William. You should forgive yourself as well."

Morgan bent his head, staring at a tiny red ant running across the stamped green concrete floor.

Irma tugged gently at him.

"Down on your knees, William. You and I are going to pray to the Lord."

Morgan let himself be pulled down to the ground, his knees striking the hard cement floor.

"O Lord," intoned Irma, "please accept this sinner into your fold. For he is a good man, Lord, he fights against the forces of darkness and oppression. Lord, help him be cured of his grief, let him put all that baggage behind him, that pain and suffering that he has carried inside for so long. Let him be your flaming sword, and smite down the evil dictatorship that afflicts this land. Lord, let him be a warrior of the Lord with your grace and strength, in Jesus Christ our Lord. Amen."

Morgan added his own "Amen" and to his own amazement felt relieved, a great weight lifted off his shoulders, a lightness where a millstone had been, and for the first time in his life he thanked God for this surcease. He didn't know, but perhaps he would have welcomed Irma's silent prayer, that this William Morgan, this trembling warrior of Christ, would one day become her husband as the Lord wills it.

A knock at the door. Guevara entered, dressed in a sport shirt and dark pants, beard shaved off and long hair trimmed. He took in the scene, guessed in an instant what had occurred, then reminded himself to have all preachers expelled from the country after the revolution.

"It must have been your prayers," he said, grinning sardonically. "Our ride has arrived."

Chapter

11

The bishop opened his eyes with a start. Without realizing it he had nodded off in the backseat of his Fleetwood limousine. That simply would not do when one was in the situation one was in, taking a message of peace from President Batista to Comandante Fidel Castro. But the early hours and constant struggle were beginning to take their toll on Bishop Mueller. After all, he was no seminary firebrand; he was in his fifties now, and the toils of this human flesh were getting too apparent. The paunch, the goiter, the drowsing at unexpected moments, sometimes—Jesus, Mary, and Joseph help him—even while listening to a monsignor deliver the Sunday homily. But now there was work to do, urgent work to do. He could not sleep, no, he could not! Wake up, wake up, Your Excellency!

Bishop Mueller gazed briefly at the roadblock, where his driver was waving his arms, still arguing with the khaki-suited soldier at the post. The bishop checked his Rolex. Twenty minutes already they'd been arguing, and still no solution. I must remind Father de Dios not to let his temper get the better of him, thought the bishop. It's that Spanish blood in this country; it makes everything come to a boil in an instant.

The bishop, whose family was of good Bavarian stock, felt blessed again that his own character was like that of his Teutonic ancestors— careful, measured, laborious, even, yes, plodding at times. But then that ploddingness was a virtue in a country where everyone's blood was quicksilver, a nation of singing grasshoppers in a world ruled by plotting, plodding ants.

Anger, greed, and lust. In that order, those were the three main capital sins afflicting this country, this blessed island that had never quite felt like home to him. In his years as confessor, time and again he had heard the same plaint: *Father forgive me for I lost my temper and I hit him / kicked her / slapped him / bit her / slashed him / killed him / killed her. Father forgive me for I have stolen / cheated / swindled / taken / hidden. Father forgive me because I kissed him / licked her / sucked him / bedded him / bedded her / bedded them.* The bishop shuddered and forcefully put aside these memories, the lacerating words of debasement and obsession still ringing in his ears even years after the last whispered confession.

Fidel has his faults, too, reflected the bishop. There's that temper of his and that tropical love of luxury. Whenever I see him he always has the best accommodations, the nicest *bohío,* the newest boots, the fattest mattress. And that rifle with the hunter's sight. But he has so much responsibility, those are some of the benefits of leadership, a little padding to cosset the soul. I mean, look at me, I am riding in a limousine, no? That doesn't matter. Lucre doesn't motivate him.

But if it's not love of money, then what? He was educated by the Jesuits, after all, those casuistic opportunists. Could he have some ulterior motive other than Cuba? No, that's impossible. None but a pure man would have taken the risks he took, going off into the wilderness with just his twelve disciples—very much like our Lord, come to think of it—without even the glimmer of a hope of success at the time. It's been the Lord's will that he survive and prosper, and now, with the Lord's and my help, he will triumph as well. Yes, if only these idiotic soldiers let us through.

A flushed Father de Dios strutted over to the limousine, accompanied by a burly sergeant, his belly about to burst from the tight khaki shirt.

"Bishop Mueller?" said the sergeant.

"Yes, my son?"

"I regret to inform you, sir, we have orders to stop your passage into this area."

This is unusual, thought the bishop. Doesn't he know where I come from and whose message I carry?

"Orders from whom, my son?"

"General del Río Chaviano. We are attacking the rebel strongholds and your life might be endangered. My regrets, sir."

The bishop fumed. He wanted to blurt out to this grinning buffoon that he was stopping the progress of peace, that Batista himself had agreed to a compromise, a neutral government that would finally put an end to the bloodletting, that all that was needed now was for the rebels to agree, and that if he didn't let him through, those chances for peace might well evaporate when Batista changed his whimsical mind! Didn't he realize that?

The bishop sighed.

"How long will this situation last, my son?"

The sergeant grinned broadly. He was happy to have blocked, even if temporarily, these fat church capons who were in bed with the rebels anyhow.

"God willing, just a few days until we wipe them out, Your Excellency."

The bishop looked back wistfully at the roadblock, where a black-and-tan Ford was briefly stopped, then let through. He saw the folds of a nun's headdress through the back window of the Ford and briefly wondered what convent she belonged to and why she had not stopped to greet him, as all good and faithful daughters of the church should, but then his attention was drawn back to the ugly matter at hand.

This is the way of the world. The bishop raised his right hand, made the sign of the cross in benediction.

"Thank you, my son. We will come again."

Father de Dios, the hem of his cassock raising a cloud of dust, stormed into the driver's seat, slamming the door behind him.

"Please be more careful with that door, Father," cautioned the bishop. "The gift of the vehicle did not include free repairs. Let us turn around and head back to Camagüey."

"You can't give up on your mission just like that, Your Excellency."

"We will find a way, Father. It is all in God's hands." The bishop paused, then added, "I will call the American consul right away."

✳ ✳ ✳

Up the road from the bishop, the driver of the black-and-tan Ford that had been briefly detained looked confidently at Che Guevara on his right.

"No wonder they let you through, you just look just like my parish priest."

"Thanks be to God," replied a grinning Guevara, his elbow at the window, enjoying the view of the resplendent countryside. He turned to face the backseat.

"And how are the good sisters doing?"

Irma smiled impishly, enjoying the bright young spirit of these men who made a breezy affair out of everything, including the revolution. She even enjoyed the white novice's habit, all flowing, loose, and white, so different from the stern black dress she wore normally.

"I'm fine, Padre, but I think Mother Superior needs a bath."

They all laughed at this. Even Morgan, dressed in the stiff enfolding habits of a nun, had to crack a smile.

"You not to think it funny if *you* to wear this," mumbled Morgan.

"Oh, I don't know, I think it's very becoming," said Guevara. "It brings out the saint in you."

"Wait until we're out of here. You're going to pay for this," he threatened him in English.

"What are you going to do, my friend? Rap my knuckles? Pull my ear?"

"Make you say ten Hail Marys," added the driver, brushing a lock of straight black hair out of his eyes.

"Very funny," said Morgan grimly. "You fellows to be in Las Vegas."

"Las Vegas? Oh, no, we will be in the Tropicana very soon," countered the driver, stepping on the accelerator, the Ford humming as the needle passed the 150-kilometer mark. "Fidel and the boys, that will be the main attraction. A show for all of Cuba, *mi amigo,* you will see."

"I can't wait," said Morgan.

Irma took Morgan's hand. "Don't be sore, he's just teasing you . . . Mother."

They all laughed again. Morgan turned to Irma and drank in the exuberance of her youth, for once freed of the need to preach or convert, enjoying the giddy moment of liberation. He smiled back at her, squeezed her hand. Embarrassed, she let go of his hand and looked away. Guevara, noting the awkward touch, could not help teasing: "Now, Sister, remember the flesh is weak. We should avoid all the occasions of sin."

The driver, who had been distracted by the sight of Irma in the rearview mirror, cursed as he spotted a dun-colored army truck posted across the highway next to a stone bridge. A soldier motioned at the car to halt.

"*Coño,* they weren't supposed to be here!" exclaimed the driver in Spanish.

"What you to mean to say?" said Morgan.

"Our boys checked out this road yesterday and there was only one roadblock. They must have put this one up this morning."

"I not to understand. What to be the meaning?"

"That we don't know who these people are, whether they're freelancers shaking down people going by."

"Or if they got word of something," added Guevara ominously.

Morgan glanced up the road, sizing up the possibilities. Rows of tall pines lined both sides of the road. The trees marched right up against the pavement on the right, but left a clearing of about twenty yards on the left shoulder. An army truck, parked perpendicularly, forced all incoming vehicles to swing to the clearing on the left, where two machine-gun-toting soldiers waited for inspection. Behind the truck, the narrow stone bridge spanning the slow-moving yellow-green waters of a local river.

Even if they slammed against the truck, Morgan decided, there was no room for escape on the right. They would not be able to make it back on the road without being attacked by the two soldiers on the left. They would have to go through the checkpoint, like it or not. They might just wave them through. After all, the soldiers in the last roadblock had done just that.

The soldiers' sly grins as the driver slowed down the vehicle put all of Morgan's senses on alert.

This is a setup, thought Morgan. I can feel it. Someone tipped off the army. We have to break out of here.

But what if I'm wrong? Maybe this is just another shakedown. No, this is a trap. Roadblocks are never this tight unless they know they've got someone. We have to get out of here! But how?

Morgan noticed the driver accelerating.

"You to slow down," he ordered.

"No, hombre, I'm going to ram them and shove them out of the way!" said the driver, his squeaky voice betraying both his age and his nerves.

"No, not to do that. The truck is too heavy; you cannot to move it out of the way. Slow down!"

"No!"

"To slow down!" he bellowed.

"Do as the captain says," ordered Guevara, not liking the situation either.

"You guys are crazy, we're all going to get killed!" said the panicked driver.

"No, no one to die here. Not yet. You to do what I say, OK?" said Morgan.

"OK, OK."

"Though I walk through the valley of the shadow of death," muttered Irma, lowering her head in prayer.

"Amen, sister," said Morgan, drawing the folds of his coif tighter with his left hand, even as his right clutched the machine gun stuck in between the seat and the door.

I was right, now we're trapped, thought Morgan, as the Ford veered obediently to the left shoulder and came to a halt.

"To leave engine running," whispered Morgan urgently before lowering his head as though in prayer. The driver nodded, gulped dryly, his Adam's apple quivering. God damn it, this kid is going to give us away!

"Good afternoon, Sisters, Padre," said the major, smiling, as he walked up to the Ford. That was a lucky blow, he thought, getting word from the movement boys that the Americano was going through here. He bent down, pressed his face into the vehicle, his smile, which had always been his greatest asset, now sparkling like a toothy mask of courtly doom. Yes, there he is in that ridiculous get-up of a nun, just as we were told. It would be so easy to shoot him now, but we're supposed to let the Argentine through. Who is the pretty girl, though? No one said anything about her. She should be fun for a few days.

"*Buenas tardes,*" said the driver, whose own plans for escape were now in peril. This is not the way it was supposed to play out. This was not what we agreed to. Why did Che tell me to slow down? Didn't somebody tell him we're supposed to eliminate this Yanqui? But I couldn't keep going if Che said to stop. Maybe the Americano would have shot me; he's crazy enough for that, I've heard. *Coño*, how did I get myself into this eleven-yard shirt?!

"May I ask where exactly it is that you are going?" asked the major.

A corporal moved to the right of the Ford, rifle aimed causally at the back of Morgan's head. He queried the major with a toss of his head if he should shoot. The major shook his head no.

"We are all going to the Santa Augusta Convent in Camagüey," answered the driver, squeezing the wheel until his knuckles turned white.

"I see," said the major, smiling. "We are sorry to inconvenience you, but there have been reports of rebels in the area. Not that they would ever dare attack the men and women of God, no? And you are coming from?"

"Santa Clara, Major. We went to hear the Mass by Archbishop Arteaga and to obtain dispensation from our vows," blabbed the driver excitedly.

"Really? What vows are those? Chastity, perhaps?"

"No, no," said the driver, panting in between chuckles. "Silence. And retreat."

"Retreat too?" said the major, waving at the corporal to move some distance away. "What about you, Father? Did you get your dispensation already?" he asked Guevara.

"Oh, no, my son, in my country, no one could possibly take that kind of vow. We all love the sound of our own voice too much," replied Guevara with a smile.

242

Hijo 'e puta, thought the major. This is far better than I expected. This is that commie rat who's right at the top with Castro! I don't have to go along with any deal, I can make my own! I'm going to get rich out of this. Very rich indeed!

"You are Argentinean, Padre?"

"Oh, no, we are not so fortunate. I am from Paraguay, a very humble country."

"In truth! *Bueno,* then, allow me to inspect your papers. In fact, why don't you all step outside? You too, Sisters. We should inspect the car as well."

"Why? I was told I wouldn't have to do that," blurted out the driver, trembling with fear.

I was told? thought Morgan, tucking in the folds of his coif, his left fingers wrapped around the heft of a grenade beneath his costume.

"I do not know who might have informed you of that, but I'm afraid that we will have to ask you all to step outside, willingly or not," said the major. He grabbed the door handle, pulled the driver's door open. The corporal yanked open the right rear door, revealing Morgan's submachine gun.

"To run! To drive!" screamed Morgan, simultaneous with a left-hand lob of the grenade, which flew through the window even as his right hand brandished the Thompson, spraying all around.

The driver floored the accelerator as the grenade's concussion reached them, the force of the explosion a boost to the forward motion of the Ford. The vehicle veered wildly, headed uncontrollably for the serried row of pines. At the last moment, just when it seemed they would crash head-on, Guevara grabbed the wheel and jerked it to the right with all his might, the Ford skidding on the gravel, making a three-point turn, then slamming its left fender against the tree trunks.

"Drive, man, drive!" snapped Guevara, while Morgan tore off his headdress and fired his machine gun at the troops, now firing wildly back. Irma bent down, yelled: "Someone give me a gun!"

Morgan tossed his .45 at her. She grabbed it and proceeded to fire back at the troops, who now ran for cover behind the trees.

"LET'S GO, MAN! NOW! NOW! NOW!" hollered Morgan at the driver in English, who understood the urgency of the command even if he didn't speak the language.

"I can't! We're stuck!"

The engine roared as the back wheels spun on the soft mud, unable to get a grip. Morgan emptied another clip at the soldiers, who fled from the attack.

"OK, I'll go outside and free the fucking tires! Translate, Che!" roared Morgan, tearing off his nun's habit while Irma took aim with her gun at the major, now hiding behind a boulder at the far side of the road.

"Cover me!" said Morgan, slapping another clip into his Thompson, tossing the machine gun at Guevara, who grabbed it and fired out the window.

"Be careful!" shouted Irma as Morgan slithered past her out the left side door.

Morgan crawled out, bullets zinging around him, bouncing off the pine trees as the soldiers on the other side of the road regrouped. He grabbed the skirt of his nun's habit, split it in two, stuffing part of it in front of the back wheels, which were throwing off mud like a geyser, covering him from tip to toe. The wheels spun wildly, then caught in the newly found traction, and the Ford tore away, leaving Morgan stranded by the side of the road!

"Jesus Christ," hollered Morgan, "Stop! STOP!"

But the vehicle roared on ahead, heedless of Morgan's cries, even as another hailstorm of bullets fell all around him, driving Morgan to the ground. Morgan lapsed into automatic pilot, acting without thought or plan, knowing just one thing, that somehow he had to escape and some-how he had to rejoin that Ford if he wanted to stay alive. He dashed across the road, zigzagging as the bullets bit the ground around him in mad patterns of destruction, and reached the side of the truck. A soldier leaned out of the cab, fired at him. Morgan gave a great cry and fell underneath the truck.

After a minute, the major on the far side ordered his men to halt their fire. The driver of the truck looked around tentatively, then smirked, anticipating the fat reward. He leaned out of the cab to look down below. Just then he felt a sharp kick to his back and he flew out of his seat, falling facedown in the mud as Morgan slipped behind the wheel, started the vehicle, and jammed it into reverse. The massive double tires of the vehicle crushed the driver to death as the truck slammed into the jeep, pushing it with a great scraping noise off the road into the ditch; then Morgan floored the accelerator and raced out, the sides of the truck raising skeins of sparks as it bumped against the flanks of the narrow stone bridge.

Morgan was racing out of the ambush, a thousand feet from the bridge, when he heard a rumble behind him and a bullet zinged past his right shoulder, tearing out the windshield with a crack. Sons of bitches are in the back! Idiots! If they kill me I'll crash and we'll all die then!

Morgan could see the Ford up ahead, racing wildly, veering from shoulder to shoulder, barely missing incoming cars and trucks. He crouched down, his head barely visible over the dashboard, and floored the accelerator, also steering the truck wildly from side to side.

Up ahead in the Ford, the driver was refusing to slow down, even as he struggled with Guevara for control of the vehicle. Irma grabbed hold of the passenger strap with one hand for balance and, with the .45 in the other, swung down the butt of the gun as hard as she could on the driver's head. The driver gasped, keeled over. Guevara pushed him aside, then managed to slow down the Ford and bring it to a halt. Irma turned, saw the army truck barreling down the road.

"Lord help us!" she said, throwing herself down on the floor, expecting the truck to slam against them, but instead she saw it swing by, Morgan at the wheel, steering wildly, even as two soldiers in the back were aiming their guns at the cab.

"Go after them, that's William! We have to help him!" she shouted. Guevara shook his head.

"You are a real tigress, señorita," he said, then slammed the accelerator and raced after Morgan.

The truck caromed wildly on the road, losing control at a curve, flipping over once, twice, three times, finally coming to a halt in the middle of the highway, a green army giant lying helpless on its side. The soldiers staggered out the back, saw the Ford stop and Guevara come out with his gun. The men threw down their guns and raced away out into the open field, screaming for help.

Guevara and Irma approached the truck. Morgan crawled out, a gash across his forehead.

"Are you all right?" asked Irma.

"I'm OK. We have to go now."

Leaning on Guevara, Morgan hurried back to the car, painfully aware that at any minute the army would again be pressing down on them. They climbed into the vehicle and drove out, then Morgan shouted as they passed by the truck: "Stop!"

"What did you forget?"

"My good-bye present."

The Ford veered around the truck, pulling around it on the shoulder of the road, then stopped on the far side of the downed vehicle. Morgan took out his machine gun, sprayed the truck's gas tanks with bullets, the gas spewing out in a dozen streams, wetting the blacktop. He ran back to the Ford, opened its trunk, took out a flare, lit it, then hurled it at the puddle of gas. The truck exploded in a mighty shudder of fire and smoke, flames rising like tongues of destruction.

Morgan ran back to the car, got into the backseat with Irma.

"Let's go, let's go!!" he told Guevara, then he noticed Irma, in her bloody white habit, still gripping the .45 in her hand.

"Welcome to the revolution, Sister," he said, then grabbed her by the back of her head and kissed her full on the lips. She resisted for a moment, then kissed him back.

"Praise the Lord," she muttered, then threw her arms around him as Guevara raced away down the road, a cloud of smoke rising in biblical pillars behind them.

※ ※ ※

The sun was lying down in fields of purple clouds when the Ford veered into a country road, past grazing fields where zebu cattle looked queryingly at the strange vehicle in their midst. The car stopped at a small whitewashed masonry house where two other cars were already parked.

Inside the Ford the driver was in tears, his right hand clutching a handkerchief to stanch the blood flowing from the blow to his head.

"One last time, are you going to tell us who you work for?" asked Guevara.

"I'm telling you, I don't know what you're talking about," said the driver, his eyes filled with fear.

"Why you to say this not our agreement?" asked Morgan.

"I don't know, it's just something I said. I don't know!"

"Fine. Let's take him inside. Our *compañeros* are waiting for us. They can ask him," said Guevara, sticking the barrel of his gun into the man's ribs.

"Please, I am innocent!"

"A revolutionary jury will decide that," said Guevara, shoving him out of the car.

The three walked out of the car, bloody, dusty, battered.

"Walk ahead of us," said Guevara, "with your hands up."

The door of the house opened. Two men and a woman peeked out.

"*Comandante!*" said the woman, who had the fair skin, dark wavy hair, aquiline nose, and round eyes of the creole aristocracy.

"Compañera Vilma!" answered Guevara.

Just then the driver decided to run for it. He lowered his hands and raced ahead, thinking that in the fast-approaching darkness he'd be able to make his getaway.

"Stop!" shouted Morgan, sprinting after the driver, who skipped over a watering trough, scattering a flock of chickens in his wake.

"To stop!" repeated Morgan, now almost at arm's length from the man, when a shot rang out and the man crumpled to the ground.

Morgan stopped, stunned by the gaping hole in the man's head. At the door to the house Compañera Vilma Espín, the wife of Raúl Castro, put her smoking rifle down.

"That's how the revolution treats traitors," she said to the handful of people around her as an *aura* flew overhead for its last run of the day.

Chapter

12

His hand is on my breast. Should I push it away? But I want it there. Oh Lord, help me! There, he's removed it. Maybe it was accidental. I hope so. But God, I hope not, too. I am so confused.

Who is this man that haunts my thoughts? Why of all people should I feel attracted to him? He's big, dirty, sullen, a man who makes his profession out of killing. No, that's not true. No. He is a revolutionary, a rebel willing to lay down his life for others. Isn't that the greatest love a man can have?

He doesn't know God. Isn't that what you're here for? How can you lead others to him and neglect the one for whom you feel so much? That is nonsense, Irma Louise. You hardly know this man; it's only been two days. Two days and one night of travel and adventure. Yes, that's it, that must be it, it's the adventure, the danger, that makes me like him. Don't you remember when you were little and you used to go deer hunting with Timmy out in California, and how the feeling of danger would make you practically swoon, and the time you two fell down behind the tree and you did that thing? Yes, but the Lord knows I have tried to stay on His path ever since, and that was years ago, and the baby was stillborn, so what's the use of thinking about it?

Where are we now? This trip has taken forever with these rebels, going through these back roads, I guess, although here in the back of this bread truck we can't see anything, really. All I can feel is William next to me, like when we were down in the cave and I could feel him all excited and he pressed himself against me and Lord, I thought I would faint. O Lord, please help me win this man over to you, please let me be the light upon his path. Guide me so I can steer him to you, so that his mighty arm will smite thine enemies like David in the Bible and we can all be your anointed, O Lord I beg of you.

It is dark here and I don't know what to tell her. I can feel her warmth, her skin, the fragrance of her breath. Fragrance. That's a word I don't use much, but I don't know how else to describe it. That sweet smell. Better stop thinking about that. It makes no sense when you're in a situation like this. God, but I hurt. Cramped like this, every muscle is hurting, especially my shoulders, like rivets of pain through my joints. At least it's bread this time, not cold meats like the last time, back at the yacht club.

My fingertips are still tingling from touching her. I really shouldn't have. I had to move my arm, and suddenly my hand was on her breast. I should have pulled it away, but she didn't do anything, she let me touch her. There, she's rubbing against me again. Stretching her legs. We didn't say anything. I guess we're both too embarrassed to be back here like this.

I wonder if those 26th of July people thought we were lovers already. They certainly seem to pair off quickly. It was embarrassing last night, with them at that little house. That Vilma girl after that big black guy. Even after she'd shot the driver just a couple of hours before, they were going at it in the bedroom. How could they be doing it when there was no door and we were all trying to sleep in the living room? I felt embarrassed for Irma. We haven't had much chance to talk. Even now, when we're so close that I can drink in her fragrance, we're still not talking. We can't, of course; it's not safe. But what is safe?

Do I dare? I shouldn't. It wouldn't be right. She is a woman of God. I don't know what she would do. But she is still a woman, and you should respect her. Yes, but how do we ever start anything if it's all out of respect? And what if we die tomorrow? What if when we stop and the doors open, there's some soldier firing away at us and we die?

You sound just like a twelve-year-old trying to justify himself. But it's the truth, William. Life is short. Now you're interested in life? I thought you no longer cared. Yes, that's right, once I didn't. Just yesterday I didn't. Just yesterday I wanted to join Laura; I wanted to pay for what I've done and be finished with all this. But not now. Now I want to keep on living. I want to breathe the air, I want to drink the rum, swim in the ocean, dance slowly with the girl. Is that wrong? Even if it is, I can't help it.

I don't care. I have to bury my ghosts. I can't keep living in the past. When we prayed, when I got down on my knees with her, it was like I had started another life, like she opened another door for me and she stepped through it with me. And if you're wrong? Then she'll tell me so. I have to do it. What's the worse that can happen? She'll say no, push me away. And Laura? Laura. I love you, Laura. I loved you then and I still love you now. I will always love you. But I need her now. I need her life, I need her guiding hand, I need her faith now. Forgive me. Or not. But you are the past, you are Cuba, Laura, and I fight for you. Now I must live for someone else. Stop all that talk. Touch her already. You're not a kid anymore. Touch her. Go on.

Morgan's hand fluttered tentatively in the dark of the bread van, then settled against Irma's right breast again. Irma, startled, gasped, then she let herself relax, feeling the burning passion through his hand, and she put her own hand over his, pressing it down against her breast, without really knowing why, without thinking, really, knowing only that this was good, that this was right, even as her heart raced like a trapped bird's.

He's mine. She's mine. She turned. Their lips met instinctively in the dark. They kissed. No, this can't be happening, she thought, even as she felt him frantically groping at her dress. No, I can't really be doing this, he thought. But the mute strength of life carried them forward, and he lifted her skirt and fumbled with her underwear, and he entered her in the dark. She was wet already. She had been ready for him for a long time, and she gasped and he groaned and they clutched each other, bumping against the soft loaves of sandwich bread around them, the aroma of wheat and yeast enveloping them in a mass of turning life, and they both thought it was crazy, but each bump of the van down the road drove them further into each other, pelvic bones rubbing against each other, until there was no longer any way they could be united any further in the flesh, and then he felt a long released orgasm of agony and longing shudder through him, and she pressed down into him, as though to take in that seed that he was planting in her, to make sure that it would fall on the fertile ground of her body, and when she heard him grunting and felt the warm liquid shooting into her, Irma prayed to God that this would be their child, that it would make a boy child who would grow up to be good and strong and saintly and lead Cuba out of her sorrows, even though she knew prayers like that, born out of sin, were the devil's own, but how could there be evil in what they were doing when she felt so much love for this man, this stranger whom she might no longer see again, and she felt like a shooting star spinning through a mauve sky while below the earth erupted in flames and she turned her head and reached for his face and grasped his mouth and pressed it against hers and this is madness esto es una locura que el Señor me perdone may the Lord above forgive me for this but how do I know this really isn't His plan after all and if there's a price to pay I will pay it for what is there in this country now but turmoil and death and out of darkness there will be light and the seed shall flourish and I will show you the way, O Israel, to that promised land and if there's no promised land it matters not because at least once I had this and I know I will be big with him and I will always carry a piece of the love of this stranger that once crossed my path and fought for the freedom of all and if not on Earth then in Heaven and when the hosts rise before Our Lord on that final day and I will be called upon to answer for my deeds I will simply say I did it for love, Lord, I did it for Your Love.

Morgan and Irma had uncoupled, touching each other tenderly in the dark without words, each wondering which way their road would turn, when the van's doors slammed open. Violent sunlight, a smell of farmland and pine.

"Where are we?" asked Morgan, giving Irma a hand down.

"The Sierra Maestra," said the dark-skinned woman in fatigues, pointing at three horses waiting for them.

Guevara walked out of the van's cab, dressed in the white uniform of La Reyna Bakery. He embraced a long-limbed, longhaired black man wearing a collection of amulets and scapulars around his neck.

"Efigenio, what a pleasure!" said Guevara.

"A sus órdenes, Comandante!" replied Ameijeiras.

The boom of cannons resounded in the glen where the van had stopped. Above them a trail led into the shining green folds of the forest. Guevara turned to Morgan and Irma, rewarding them with the widest smile they'd seen on him.

"Bienvenidos al territorio libre de América," he said. Welcome to the free land of America. "Let's go, Fidel is waiting for us."

※ ※ ※

Compromises, thought Fidel Castro, pulling on his Cohiba Especial, a present from the American journalist Herbert Matthews and a welcome change from the stogies hand rolled here in rebel headquarters in the Sierra. He let out a mouthful of the sweet, potent smoke, feeling it tingle the lining of his mouth and nostrils.

Why does everybody always think I'm ready to compromise? Can't they see that victory is just an arm's length away? Now these fellows from all those other *grupos* insist that we submit to collective leadership, a junta of unity, as though we hadn't been fighting out here by ourselves, in the middle of the Sierra, with all these hardhips. Now they insist, from the comfort of their feather beds in exile, that we are all equal. We are not all equal! The moment they pick up a weapon and come out here to fight with us against the tyranny, then they can talk about equality.

But all of that can wait. What I need now is what this little boy is bringing me.

"*Ven acá, mi hijo,*" come here, son, said Castro to the little bug-eyed, black-haired ragamuffin being led into the room by Celia Sánchez.

"Fidel, what do we tell these people?" asked the operator, cupping the telephone receiver so the representatives of the Exile Front in Venezuela would not overhear the supreme commander's decision.

"Tell them we'll call them back."

Castro mussed the boy's long, straight black hair, eyed his skinny frame, knobby knees, gnarled shoeless feet, remembering his own class-mates at Birán when he was ten and still living with his dour *gallego* father. Castro had always felt personally responsible for the welfare, or lack of it, of the people of Oriente Province. These were his people, many of whom worked for his father's fifty-thousand-acre estate. Many of them had also been robbed and swindled of land by his father as well, so he could never escape the great sense of guilt, that he and his fam-ily—and by extension, the entire country—had prospered because these people had suffered.

"Come with us," he told the boy, moving to what originally had been the study of the rambling wood plantation house, now rebel headquarters.

"Fidel, the boy is famished. He's traveled more than fifteen kilometers without resting," said Celia Sánchez, the only woman in the hills who dared to contradict Fidel, her throaty, raspy voice tinged with reproach. But Castro paid no attention; a mere thing like a child's hunger would not deter him from his plans. He winked at the boy.

"What's your name" he asked.

"Luisito," said the boy, not half as impressed as he thought he'd be by the tall revolutionary leader.

"You can wait to eat, can't you?" said Castro, closing the door to the study.

"*Sí, señor,*" said the boy, ignoring his growling stomach.

"Good, you're like Pelayo. You know who he was?"

The boy shook his head in exalted ignorance. Fidel, never one to miss an occasion for pontificating slip by, launched into an explanation.

"Pelayo was a young boy like yourself at the time of the Moorish con-quest of Spain. Back then the Moors, they were from Africa, and they had conquered practically all of Spain, you see, and the resistance had been driven into the mountains, just like us. So Pelayo, realizing the sig-nificance that his observations would have on the future destiny of his people, used to observe all the comings and goings of the Moorish army, acquainting himself with their tactics, weaponry, and chain of command so that one day he could drive them out and once again lead his country, his *patria,* to the shining halls of freedom and justice."

Castro halted his tale, cut short by Celia's glare of exasperation. The boy had lost interest in the story and walked over to the window, where he stared slack jawed at the view.

"I've never been all the way up before," he said. "Before you *barbudos* came, the overseers of the Lobos always used to chase us away."

"*Bueno,* the times have changed, my son. Soon there won't be a single overseer in all of Cuba," said Castro, thinking to himself. Nor a single family like the Lobos, if I can help it.

The boy pointed at a tiny *bohío* in the green skirts of the mountain several kilometers away.

"That's our house over there! This is like we're right on the edge of the mountain!" he said, still awestruck.

"That's very well, Luisito," intervened Celia, "now why don't you tell Fidel what you saw?"

"Oh, yes," said the boy with the innate gravity of the young and the unschooled. "Two battalions, under orders of Colonel Sánchez Mosquiera and Menendez Martínez, are coming up from the mines of Bueyecito."

Bueyecito? That's only about thirty kilometers from here! thought Castro with some alarm. As always he restrained himself from showing any concern, even to a child or to his most trusted companion, Celia. He never forgot that great leaders have no friends, only followers.

"How did you find this out?" he asked the boy.

"My uncle, he's a squatter near the mines and he sent on the message. He says the forces are going for Santo Domingo."

The boy paused, uncertain whether he'd relayed everything he'd been forced to memorize under threat of a severe beating. Seeing that the big man in fatigues had no more questions, he nodded, then stuck his thumb in his mouth, staring once again out the window. Castro also gazed out, looking blankly at the scenery as his mind examined the implications of the boy's message.

I've already recalled Almeida's column from Santiago and put him near El Cobre. Camilo is now in the center, Ramiro is near Pico Turquino. But this is a new development. This means another two thousand men are coming in to get us. We've already had to pull back; all we have left is about twenty kilometers of undisputed territory. This fucking *operación verano* of this bloodsucker Batista is working, God damn it. But does he know it? Does anybody but us know it? We've had skirmishes, but with our constant retreating, they don't know where or how many we are. That Radio Rebelde has come in very handy, just like the CIA people advised me, to disinform our listeners. But if anybody finds out that all we have is three hundred men altogether up here, we are fucked, that's what we are.

Our sources tell me that seventeen battalions have been sent out against us. That is seventeen thousand men. They have aerial support and tanks, but so far we've held them at bay. Fortunately for us a quarter of those men are out guarding the coffee crop and the sugar mills instead of fighting. Plus Cantillo and del Río Chaviano are both in charge, and they hate each other so much that they almost seem to be countermanding each other. They both want to be the next Batista in a coup after they get rid of us. But first they have to get rid of us, of course, and that will not be so easy. But these two new battalions could definitely cause us problems.

I mean, I can't just pick up and go now, we're settled here in La Plata. We got schools, shops, everything. We're not as mobile as before. And my brother Raúl is up in the Sierra Cristal and Guevara still hasn't returned from the Escambray. *Carajo,* what to do? What would Napoleon have done?

Castro paused, letting the possibilities dance and couple in his mind, then it came to him, as always, as though someone—a household deity or the national demon—were whispering the answer in his ear.

Entrap them. Box them in and let the rivers swell with blood. Even if we lose and have to retreat again, a major engagement is bound to rattle these troops. They're not used to this kind of fighting, anyway. And this is our territory, after all. They can't move a yard without me knowing about it. Just look at this little boy. Runs all the way up here to carry the news. How can I lose with support like that? Of course I cannot. I will engage them, then. Santo Domingo will be Batista's Austerlitz, it's that simple.

"Can the boy get something to eat now?" asked Celia, putting her arm around Luisito, knowing that Fidel no longer had any use for him and would not even realize he was there unless someone reminded him.

"*Sí, sí,* of course, give him a plate of beans and yams. And a pig's trotter, for being a good revolutionary," said Castro, again mussing the boy's hair, before returning to his battle plans, as he stared out the window.

Celia was leading the boy out of the room when Luisito turned and asked urgently, "Fidel, you never finished the story. What became of Pelayo?"

Castro moved from the window, his expression blank.

"Pelayo? Oh, he became a very famous general and he led the triumph of the Spaniards against the Moors. The *Reconquista*. It all began with him."

"In that case, that's what I'm going to be someday too, Fidel," said the boy, squaring off like a young cadet. "I will be a general of the revolution."

Fidel smiled, wreaths of smoke from his cigar wreathing around his ebony curls. He felt tempted to tell the boy that the highest rank in the revolutionary army was major, but he didn't want to shatter his illusions. Besides, someday it might all change.

"I will remember that. What is your full name?"

"Luis Ochoa Marín," said the boy.

"Fine. The revolution will need officers like you, General Ochoa. You may withdraw."

The boy saluted proudly. Fidel returned the salute, then the boy spun around in the best Prussian military manner, marching like a stiff little martinet out of the room, followed by Celia.

Castro chuckled, then hurried out of the study to the living room. He stopped in his tracks, startled by the sudden sight of Max Weinberg, in his usual wrinkled suit, sitting in the long *majagua*-wood-and-wicker couch. Max rose respectfully, straw hat in hand.

"Good morning, *Comandante*," said Max, rising respectfully. "I have good news."

"More money?" asked Castro.

Max nodded, immensely proud of himself.

※ ※ ※

Morgan strolled wide eyed through the rebel compound, Che on one side, Irma on the other, their boots stained red by the clayish mud of the road. People came up to them throughout their walk to greet and embrace Guevara and to flash smiles of welcome. All around was a beehive of activity, far greater than Morgan had seen at Frente headquarters. Over there Eloy and his people had a shoemaker's, a school, a clinic, even a munitions shop, but that was nothing compared to the sprawling town built here in La Plata. The 26th of July had all that plus a dentist, a seamstress, a phone hookup for overseas communications, a cigar factory for the stogies no rebel was ever without, and two radio stations, AM and shortwave. A number of local *guajiros* had settled nearby, their ramshackle *bohíos* ringing the town, which had the look and feel of a boomtown.

Guevara proudly stopped in front of a low palm-thatch-roof building draped in the shadow of one of the many low clouds that traversed the rebels' aerie. Beyond the building lay a ravine, from which rose wreaths of curling mist.

"This is one of the schools we have set up for the campesinos of the area," he said as they dashed under the low roof overhang. "Here they learn their revolutionary ABCs."

Morgan peeked through the open Dutch doors. Several rows of elderly men and women listened as a woman guerrilla, dressed in fitted fatigues, pointed to a blackboard.

"*A* is for *assassin*," she said, "like the forces of the tyrant that oppress us. *B* is for *Batista*, like, well, we all know who he is, don't we?"

All the gnarled old faces in the gloomy room smiled cunningly, breaking into wizened crackling, the gaps in their teeth marking the spaces of lost life.

"*C* is for *communism*," continued the fresh-faced teacher, her ponytail swinging over her shoulder from her emphatic gesturing. "That's the theory of government that says, 'To each according to his needs, from each according to his skills.'"

"Communism? You're teaching these people about the commies?" asked an incredulous Morgan.

"We do have a few dedicated socialists among us," said Guevara, proud of the instructor. "We feel we should not interfere with the content of their curriculum. After all, that would be censorship, which I'm sure you don't approve of."

"I don't approve of propaganda either."

"My friend, what propaganda? She is merely acquainting these people with one of the most pervasive political theories in the world, one that may soon be followed in all countries."

"Not if I can help it," grumbled Morgan.

"Don't they teach these people about the Bible and the Lord's word?" asked Irma, thinking this would be fertile ground for a mission.

"We leave that to the padre," replied Guevara disdainfully. He waved at a passing guerrilla riding a slow-moving mule.

"He's not very well liked, though. He's always trying to marry everybody off, instead of getting himself a good revolutionary mate."

"*C* is also for *Castro*, Fidel Castro, our fearless leader," continued the instructor. "*D* is for *derecho*, your right to your own plot of land, your own tools, and your own horse, without having one of the goons from the sugar mill come and throw you out and take all your things."

"I have a question, señorita," said an old man, his gaunt face as lined as the furrows of the land he had tilled since childhood.

"That communism stuff. Does that mean that if I need two hectares to feed my family but I can only give a box of yams to the government because I need to sell the rest, that I get to keep the land all the same? Do I explain myself?"

"Oh, yes, perfectly, Samuel," said the young instructor, whose last occasion to impart knowledge of any kind had been as assistant volleyball coach at the Sacred Heart Academy in Havana.

"That is precisely what communism means. You only have to give what you can, but you are assured of enough for you to provide for yourself and your family. That's because the government gets rid of excess value and the middlemen who profit off your crops. You have your own plot, the government lends you the tools you need, the seed, all those things. That's part of our agrarian reform program, which will benefit people just like you."

"That sounds good to me," said Samuel, shaking his head up and down.

"I'll believe it when I see it," said an old woman in a patched-up flower-print dress.

"I think we should return to our class," replied the instructor. "Who can come up and write *communism* on the blackboard?"

Leaving the class behind, Guevara led Morgan and Irma down the packed-dirt street. Gray swirls of mist gathered before them, broken here and there by patches of sunlight so piercingly bright that they seemed artificially lit. Presently the clouds would win the struggle and the entire mountaintop would be covered by a wet cloud that drifted through in ribbons, so thick they clung to all the posts and beams of the buildings like freshly spun cotton candy at some county fair. All at once a thin, steady rain broke through, and the three of them hurried up the summit to the ivy-covered plantation house.

This location is ideally protected, thought Morgan. We must be about four thousand feet up. Glancing down the side of the steep road, he saw way below the slow-moving waters of a river. We can't be too far from the ocean, so supplies can come in; or they can withdraw that way if necessary. This would be a tough nut to crack. But how can they carry the war out from here? This area has no strategic value. It's the corner of the island, no major cities nearby except for Santiago, and that's a good hundred miles away. This is a good symbol, but where do you go from here?

At least our boys back in the Escambray are smack in the middle of the country. With a little effort we could reach Havana in a few hours or, failing that, we could split the country up in two. But these guys don't have that capability. This is all show. It's nice for headquarters, but the real action is out there. This is a guerrilla fantasy.

"Do you have a lot of contact with the outside world?" asked Morgan, turning to Guevara.

"All the time," replied the *comandante*. They stood a few hundred feet away from the main house, small groups of people coming and going in a steady stream of visits.

"We have the radio, the telephone."

"No, I mean, do people come up here often like we did?"

One quick look at the rubicund American and Guevara knew all he needed to know.

He's worried about the girl already! thought Guevara. These Americans are really much more gallant than we give them credit for. Don't they know women are stronger, that men live but women endure?

"You want to know if someone will take her down?" asked Guevara, nodding at Irma.

"I'd like that. I'd owe you," added Morgan.

"The first person going back, I'll make sure she goes with him."

"I don't have to go back right away. I can take care of myself," said Irma, upset at Morgan for making decisions for her without consulting her.

"Of course, miss," said Guevara, striding briskly up the wooden steps of the plantation house. "But think of your father. He misses you, no?"

The image of her father alone in their house in Trinidad burned brightly in Irma's mind. He knew she'd gone to warn the rebels, but it had been three days already, and he would be sleepless with worry. She nodded in silent agreement.

Guevara saluted the two guerrillas at the door.

"*Está Fidel?*" he asked.

"For you, *Comandante,* he is always in," replied one of the men.

"Tell him I'm here with a representative of the Segundo Frente. And a representative of God," he added with a smirk. The guards grinned back and dashed inside.

Guevara walked around the porch, gesturing as comfortably as any hacienda owner in the land.

"Good place for coffee growing," he said.

The front door opened. Max Weinberg stepped out, froze on seeing Morgan. Both men were equally stunned, but Max drew on his many years in the deception trade to foist off the moment.

"William Alexander Morgan, you son of a gun, how the hell are you!"

Before Morgan could answer, he hugged him in a tight *abrazo*.

"Hush, we'll talk later!" he whispered.

A great clatter of boots, of doors opened, a chorus of voices, yesses and "of course's," the smell of a Cohiba, a bear of a man appearing at the door.

"*Coño, chico, ya era hora!*"—about time—said Fidel Castro as he embraced his second in command, the two men patting each other on the back with only the slightest glint in their eyes betraying anything other than complete trust and affection.

"So how goes the revolution without me?" asked Guevara.

"*Chico*, without you there is no revolution to speak of," said Castro. "And this Americano, who is he?"

"Fidel, allow me to introduce you to Captain William Morgan of the Second National Front of the Escambray."

Castro's eyes brightened, an eager smile came to his lips.

"*Coño*, did Eloy send you to coordinate our plans?" he asked Morgan, then, without a pause, looked at Guevara. "This one speaks Spanish, no?"

"*Sí, Comandante*," replied Morgan, "I to speak the Spanish. I to speak not too good but I to fight very good."

The men chuckled, but Fidel's mirth vanished when he heard Morgan's next words. "I here alone, no to bring official news of the Second Front. But clearly anything you to say I will take back."

Fidel let out a mouthful of cigar smoke, pondering his words, fashioning the precise message that could deliver him the unity he would need to triumph.

"And this pleasant young lady, is she an American friend as well?" he asked, changing the subject.

"No, Señor Castro, I am all Cuban, from Trinidad," replied Irma eagerly, finding herself carried away by the excitement. "Even my dad, who was born in California, has been Cubanized. We preach the word of the Lord."

"Ah, but this young lady is also a true *guerrillera*, Fidel," said Guevara. "She showed as much courage fighting out of an ambush as any of our best muchachos."

"I see. *A Dios rogando y con el mazo dando*," said Castro—a prayer for the Lord and a cudgel for the enemy.

More laughter. Irma felt her cheeks flush, her heart race. This is odd, she thought to herself. What is it about this man that makes him so appealing? It's the smile of the abyss, she decided. It's danger smiling at you, saying, All is well, even though you could fall in at any moment.

Her eyes flitted from Castro to Morgan and back again, everyone gathering at the door to the house laughing, as carefree as at a social luncheon in Havana. My William is not like that, no, not at all. He is solid and safe, a shelter, not a threat. What are they saying? They want me to go back already!

"Yes, it would be a good idea," agreed Fidel, nodding at Guevara. He waved at Weinberg.

"Max, ven acá."

Max took two steps forward, felt hat in hand, a supplicant at the feet of the powerful.

"You are all acquainted with Max Weinberg. He has been coordinating our press relations in the United States."

Max nodded convincingly, blinking rapidly.

"He will be returning to Santiago right away, so he can give this young lady a ride."

"But I would rather stay," protested Irma. "I would like to see what is being accomplished here!"

"I am certain that Max will be able to tell you on the way down," countered Fidel. "If you do not go with him it might be several weeks before there is transportation again."

"But I—"

"I think it's better if you go, Irma," said Morgan, leading her away by the arm. "Think of your father. He doesn't even know where you are."

Fidel looked down on the couple, stole a glance at Guevara. *Coño,* there is no denying the heart, thought Fidel, even here in the Sierra.

"Why don't you say good-bye to the young miss, Captain, then you can join us inside. Come on in, Che, we have much to discuss."

The two men traipsed inside, a retinue of assorted guerrillas following in their wake. A moment of embarrassed silence passed between the three Americans.

"My jeep's down around the bend," suggested Max. "We can talk on the way over."

They tramped down the rutted dirt road in silence, each subsumed in private thoughts, until Max shrugged, opened his arms in helpless frustration.

"What the hell, guys. *Es la guerra,*" he said.

"Max, is there any pie in which you haven't stuck your thumb?" asked Morgan.

"Not in Cuba. That's what they pay me for."

"Who is they, Mr. Weinberg?" asked Irma, climbing reluctantly into the jeep.

"William and I have a few things to discuss, miss. Would you mind waiting here?"

Before Irma could reply the two men had stalked off, leaving her to gaze at the incoming tower of gray clouds. I should stay with William, but it's true, Daddy must be worried sick. Lord, please preserve him from all harm!

A few dozen yards away, the two men bickered.

"Whose side are you on, Max? What are you doing here?"

"I could ask you the same question. Eloy thinks you died after that attack on Cordón's camp."

"Are you helping these guys too?"

"I'll deal with anybody, William. There's no other way to win."

"Are we going to win?"

"That depends on how much money I can get these guys. You know about Operation Summer?"

"The army offensive?"

"That's right. The Twenty-sixth of July is down to a few kilometers. Unless they pay off the generals to pull back, it's over for these guys. Your group would be the main one left."

"You're telling me I should leave here right away?"

"I'm not telling you anything. We're all in this together. But if I were you, I'd find a way to get back soon. There'll be some supplies coming in a few days; maybe you can hitch a ride out with them. I'll let the boys at the Frente know that you're out here. Anything else?'

"Give me a moment alone with Irma. I want to say good-bye."

Morgan walked back to the jeep, his mind abuzz with possibilities, plans of action, exits, maneuvers—but above all, with feelings for Irma, feelings he wasn't sure he knew how to express.

She turned in her seat, lifted her face up to him. He bent down, kissed her lightly.

"I will see you soon in Trinidad."

"How will you get there?"

"Never mind, I'll find a way. You take care of your dad and wait for me."

"You won't forget me?"

"*Estás en mi corazón,*" he said, his tongue tripping on the emotion-laden words.

"*Y tú en el mio,*" she replied, kissing him quickly.

Max returned to the jeep, climbed in, started the engine. He backed out of the embankment, pointed the vehicle down the road,

"Good-bye, William," he said.

"See you in Havana," said Morgan.

"That's right. One way or another. But a free Havana, let's hope," said Max.

The jeep lurched, crawled down the hill. Morgan watched them leaving for a moment, then ran after the jeep, his boots kicking up clods of red dirt behind him, his Thompson slapping against his side. He ran not really wanting to stop them, but not wanting to let them go, either, chasing after Irma as though after a dream he might never have again.

Irma watched him recede in the distance, becoming smaller and smaller, until at a bend in the road a flank of pine trees hid him from sight, their mist-enveloped branches arms pointing at the swirling sky.

Chapter

13

"The shells say yes."

"*Chico,* are you sure?"

"Fidel, the shells never lie."

Castro looked askance at the white shells spread on the checkerboard. He failed to discern the pattern that Alvaro so blithely claimed to see. Some of the shells lay with their concave side up, others with the convex side up, arranged in a pattern different from the one they had fallen into when he had thrown them down twice previously. Yet in every case Alvaro insisted they received a positive reply from the divinities. It seemed to Castro that the gods of *abakuá* had as many ways of saying yes as a Havana society girl had of saying no.

Still, he was not doing all this just to know the future but for the reputation it would earn him. It was a known fact that one of the bulwarks of Batista's regime, of all governments on the island, was the blessing of the vast, underground brotherhood of Santería. Word had already reached him that the island's college of Santería cardinals, the circle of *babalawos,* were wavering in their support for the pretty mulatto. Odd things had been occurring at the Presidential Palace, goats speaking in women's voices, corpses that walked like zombies and spewed toxic green clouds, hens that lay eggs full of serpents and roaches. Even the *letra,* the forecast for the upcoming year, presaged a period of turmoil and upheaval, storms and disaster. It was up to Castro to inherit the mantle of protector that the black Yoruba gods had wrested away from Batista.

You will see, Celia Sánchez had said, the saints will reveal themselves to you. With them we will have victory firmly in our grasp. Reluctantly he had agreed to this clairvoyant session, half expecting some scarred, grizzled witch doctor wearing a grass skirt to come in banging his drums. Instead she'd brought in this little porcelain-skinned, overweight fox terrier of a man with lacquered fingernails and plump little fingers, whose only sign of otherworldliness was his priestly white clothes and a multicolored African skullcap.

"*Bueno,* that's good, that was just a test," joked Castro. "Everybody knows Major Quevedo is coming over to our side. So ask them if I will be in Havana by New Year's."

"*Ay,* Fidel, you really think so?" blurted out Celia, who'd been sitting quietly in a rocking chair across the room. "That would be marvelous, to walk down the Malecón once again."

"Let us see," said Alvaro, scooping up the shells. He shook them in his hand, then asked Castro to shake the shells as well. Castro did so reluctantly, feeling ridiculous, as though the dignity of his position should forbid such a thing.

"Now toss them on the board."

They clattered down in what seemed to Castro again to be no pattern at all. Alvaro pursed his glossy thin lips like a storekeeper doing mental arithmetic. Nodding, he bent down and extracted a typewritten book from his leather satchel.

Coño, there's always a Bible in all religions, even for *santeros,* thought Castro. Alvaro muttered to himself, looked again at the board, then glanced up, smiling.

"Good news, Fidel. It says you won't be there on New Year's but that soon after that you will be the master of the country."

"That soon!" muttered Castro in disbelief, then chastised himself for his wishful thinking.

"But it also tells the prince, that's you, to beware of the knives of your followers, for many will be killed and the bloodshed could fall on your head. It's a warning that if the prince does not act to stop the slaughter, he will pay a heavy price for it."

"What price is that?"

"He will have no friends, no lovers, no family, no one whom he can call his own. He will be surrounded by people but comforted by darkness, and he will die alone, a miserable death."

"*Coño,* some prophecy you're making."

"It's no prophecy, Fidel, it's the truth. If the prince does not halt the slaughter, the souls of his victims will saddle him for the rest of his life. He will know no peace—I'm reading here. 'At night they will call him,

264

they will knock on his window, waken his dogs, snuff out his candles, rumple his bed. He will lie down with ghosts and will embrace the dust. The bitterness of gall will fill his mouth, and he will not be able to rinse it out. In the end all that he built will be destroyed, and not all the *ebbós,* the sacrifices, the goats and hens and pigeons and rum on earth will stop Elegguá from delivering the prince to his fate.' "

A silence in the dimly lit room of the *finca.* Burnham Wood, thought Celia, remembering the old play Sister Terrence had taught her in high school. Fair is foul and foul is fair, hover through the fog and filthy air, she heard in her mind's ear, recalling the Scottish burr of the sister's native Edinburgh.

Fog had swept up the hillside like the slithering fingers of a hand about to close. A chill crept into the room. Celia moved to close the open window when a great buzzard flew in, smelling of carrion and death, its long, featherless neck stretched out like a striking serpent's tail. Celia shrieked, terrified, while Alvaro dropped to his knees, scraping the floor with his forehead, recognizing the sacred bird of Oyá, the gate-keeper of cemeteries, forsaken wife of Oggún, the god of iron and war.

"Fidel, do something! Get this bird out of here!" screamed Celia.

Castro meant to take out his sidearm, his trusted U.S. Army .45, and blow the bird into smithereens, but he felt a great weight come down upon him, as though a hand were holding him in check while the hideous, foul-smelling creature flapped its awful black wings. It flew around the room twice, then alighted on the crest of a tall black mahogany armoire blazoned with the coat of arms of the former owners of the estate.

The buzzard's bleary, rheumy eyes, coated with a viscous gray film, turned on Castro. It twisted its hideous neck and opened its shit-smeared beak, squawking with foul breath a word that bounced off the walls. For a moment Castro thought he heard the roar of crowds demanding circuses and bread, lions and Christians, weapons to shoot and a slogan to blare until hoarse, and a drumming as of a conga line of millions of dancers drunk on the wine of death while their feet stomped the ground, the earth shaking with the clamor of a people sticking its own beak in its own bowels to pull out the gray-blue innards and fly off with the meal of its own body in its own bloody beak, a nation both Prometheus and the eagle, awash in a tragic tide of fury.

The *aura tiñosa* squawked that awful word twice more, then it flapped its wings again and took off from the armoire to the enveloping sky.

Celia chased the bird out then shut the wooden shutters. A great chill filled the room, the flickering light of the hurricane lamp throwing fantastic shadows on the mustard plaster walls, of things and wars to come.

Alvaro rose trembling, paler than the white clothing he wore.

"Are you OK, Fidel?" asked Celia, seeing how Castro was still sitting motionless, as though chained to the massive wooden chair.

"Yes, yes, of course," he answered promptly, his eyes still large and full of wonderment.

"What was it that the bird was saying? What was it?" asked Celia.

Castro fingered his beard, turned with pleading eyes on his companion, the only woman he would ever trust.

"It said *paredón*," the firing wall, said Castro. He repeated the word for his own benefit, so it would forever remain engraved in his mind.

"It said *paredón*, Celia."

Chapter

14

Morgan saw the plane before he could hear it, the nose of the B-26 peering out from behind the top of the forested ridge, then the gray fuselage soaring into full view as it practically skimmed the treetops.

"To get down!" shouted Morgan. "Quick, below the bridge!"

Morgan and his *guajiro* guide raced across the flooded rice field, trying desperately to hide before the massive bomber swept over them. The nearest cover, an old railroad trestle, lay about four hundred yards away, a distance that seemed to stretch before them the faster they ran, as though the sodden earth grabbed at them with every hurried step. Stumbling, falling, they reached the pilings and scurried down below the old concrete span moments before the plane flew overhead, the foundations trembling from the rumble of the low-flying aircraft.

Morgan's guide, a thin young man with a lantern jaw, stuck his head out, peering fixedly at the aircraft as it flew on overhead.

"To hide, Mario!" screamed Morgan over the noise of the airplane. "If napalm, you to swim!"

But Mario shook off Morgan's warning, turning with a flaming smile. "They're going away already, *Capitán*. They're waving good-bye."

"What the hell?'

"Yes, yes, come see."

Morgan leaned out from under the bridge. The pilot, looking backward at them as the plane pushed on, waved at them from the cockpit the way the engineer in a slow-moving freight train waves at children playing by the tracks.

Morgan looked twice at the markings on the plane, the lone star of

Cuba, the lettering CUBAN AIR FORCE. Yes, that's a government plane, all right. Have we won the war already?

That was the question that kept ringing in Morgan's mind as he and Mario hacked their way back to the headquarters of the Second Front. He had been gone for three months, from late spring to early fall, traveling first to Cordón's camp, then to the sierra in his odyssey with Guevara. He'd stayed on with Castro to watch his forces defeat the army offensive, which collapsed after the battle of Santo Domingo, where three thousand soldiers were trounced by little over three hundred guerrillas.

Morgan knew much had changed, but he found it hard to believe the tide could have turned so decisively during his absence. Yet obviously something drastic had occurred. The roads were no longer heavily patrolled, nor had he seen any of the fighter planes that used to constantly strafe the rebel strongholds. Some collective spirit had turned, shaken its head and said, Enough is enough. But that was not possible. That was not how wars were won. Yet it did seem that it wasn't that the rebels were winning, but that the army was losing—losing guns, losing vehicles, losing the very will to fight.

※ ※ ※

At the first Frente checkpoint, a *bohío* manned by two guerrillas who could not have been a day over sixteen years old, Morgan's peasant guide, Mario, embraced him good-bye, wishing him Godspeed and a quick victory against the tyranny, then scrambled down the hillside again. One of the *guerrilleros,* slender, pale skinned, with the light eyes and long nose of northern Spaniards, took Morgan to a well-fed palomino.

"They are waiting for you in headquarters, *Comandante,*" said the young fighter.

"*Capitán,* you to mean," countered Morgan, easing into the stiff wooden saddle.

"*No, señor, comandante.* Menoyo himself signed the order. You will see. Much has happened while you were away."

"I to see already," replied Morgan, smiling back as he yanked the reins, then trotting up the familiar trail. By the time he reached the ridge and looked down at the flat Agabama River, he spotted what had once been the post of the dreaded Guardias Rurales. The building was burned down to the ground, only rubble left on its concrete slab foundation. Morgan knew then without a doubt that the war was at least half over.

On the outskirts of the falls of Hanabanilla, just past where the river cascades in seven natural obsidian steps, Morgan encountered a road-building crew. The foreman, Rabo de Agua, took off his sunglasses when he saw Morgan, his old captain, unable to believe the Yanqui had come back.

"*Capitán, mi capitán!*" said Rabo de Agua, shaking with emotion, hugging Morgan with all his considerable might.

"Muchacho, to be glad to see you!" countered Morgan, patting him on the back. The road crew stopped cutting the brush and took a cigarette break, watching the spectacle of two grown men crying.

Over a lunch of deviled ham, Cuban bread, and fragrant ripe guavas, Rabo de Agua filled Morgan in on all that had happened in his absence. For one thing, as in the sierra, the army now refused to go into the Escambray. After encounters at Fomento, Guinia de Miranda, and Pedrero, where the Front had decimated the regular troops, the forces of the tyranny kept only to major roads and to the towns during the day. At night even the towns belonged to the guerrillas, the soldiers confining themselves to their barracks.

The Escambray was now a free territory, with more than eight hundred fighting men. A peasant commission had been created to enlist the aid of most of the *guajiros* in the area, and a census was being taken for the first time in fifty years. Dozens of schools had been built; there was a Department of Justice for settling disputes, ten field hospitals, and even a Department of Public Works. He, Rabo de Agua, was in charge of road maintenance.

"There is nothing to be done right now, William," said Rabo de Agua, moving his heavy arms for emphasis. "No fighting. We have won here, and until we decide what to do, we have to do something to keep the boys happy. But now that you're back, maybe there will be some fighting, no? To me it does not make much sense to be a guerrilla at peace in the middle of a war."

"I not to know," smiled Morgan, remembering Rabo de Agua's fearlessness in battle. "Perhaps after coordination with Twenty-sixth of July."

"You just came from there, right?"

"Is true."

"It's strange that they have so many communists, those Twenty-sixth of July people, because I have heard they can be very good fighters. Not too many, but effective. They know how to cut down the mangos," said Rabo de Agua, spitting on the ground. "But I do not understand why they allow the commies in. What did the reds ever do for us? Not a penny, not a bullet. You know, there is this Torres fellow up now; he too has set up his little outfit. I hate them all. They are as bad as Batista."

Rabo de Agua looked up, deep-set eyes filled with malice.

"You think perhaps we can attack Torres just to stay in shape, you know? Wipe out the commies?"

"Not even to think of that," said Morgan. "We are all to fight against Batista, his enemy our friends. We to need cooperation, not fighting."

Rabo de Agua shrugged. "That is too bad. I hate commies, always have. They always back the dictatorship; all they want is to take your money. When the revolution triumphs, we'll get rid of them."

"No!" said Morgan emphatically. "Everyone to have right to opinion. That is democracy, that what we fight. Just not in the government, that is all."

"*Bueno,* we will see," said Rabo de Agua, standing up, taking a deep breath.

"It is time for us to continue to do the work. You have not forgotten the way? For I could send one of the boys to accompany you."

"No, I to remember clearly. What to happen to El Gato?" asked Morgan.

"He is second now to Jesús Carreras, one of the *comandantes.* I am sure he will rejoin you, though. By the way, I have heard of your promotion. Congratulations!"

He saluted formally. Morgan smiled, climbed on his horse, then saluted back.

"At ease, *Compañero,*" said Morgan, who then reared his horse and took off at a gallop.

Rabo de Agua watched him ride up, a trail of dust behind him. I am glad he is back, he thought; we talk too much and fight too little nowadays. This revolution will not be won with talk; it needs more bullets.

Rabo de Agua turned to his four-man crew, still lounging by the ceiba tree.

"Alright, get up, you good-for-nothings! Let's cut the bush for the revolution!"

❈ ❈ ❈

Gutiérrez Menoyo laughed when he read a letter from Castro that Morgan had brought him.

"This man lives in the clouds," he said, placing the missive on the rickety table that served as his desk. "Look at this, even the date. 'Year Five of the Revolution' instead of a normal date and year. Pretty soon he'll be naming the months too, like the Jacobins. Instead of *Germinale* we'll have *Riceale* or *Sugaral.* He's crazy. My brother always said he was nuts; that's why they didn't want him in the student federation."

Menoyo sighed, lit a Pall Mall, raised a slender arm to make his point, with the deftness of the professor piercing a fallacy.

"Unfortunately, sometimes it takes a madman to get things going. If Castro hadn't lit the fire under the opposition's feet, we'd all still be marching, planting bombs, and getting killed in Havana. That is why ours is the Second National Front in the Escambray, because we recognize that Castro and his Twenty-sixth of July Movement was the first to establish an opposition front in the bush against the regime. That must be admitted, I will never deny that. But . . . "

He paused, leaning in closer to Morgan, who sat expectantly across the table.

"That does not mean I am ready to pack it in. That would be a denial of our collective effort, of the blood of our comrades who have fallen to establish control over this area. That would be a sheer betrayal of our principles, and the answer therefore is no."

Morgan felt relieved, because for a moment he'd feared that Menoyo, out of a misguided sense of patriotism, would agree to Castro's directive.

"I to be very happy, Eloy. You to wish I take answer back?"

Menoyo laughed again. "No, muchacho, there's no need for that anymore. We have phone lines nowadays. Some boys from the telephone company joined the ranks, and we've set up a network. I could pick up the phone right now and call Batista, if I wanted."

"I not to think he answer," replied Morgan, grinning.

"No, I don't think he'd take the call either. Don't worry, a formal reply will be drafted and sent to Fidel. In any case, in the second part of the letter he also says that Guevara might be coming out here again to coordinate our forces."

"I not to know that."

"That is how Fidel operates. He asks for total surrender and when he doesn't get it, he offers a so-called compromise that amounts to the original offer. We'll have to see when this fellow comes here. What is your reading of Guevara?"

Morgan paused before answering, searching for the words that would best describe the wily Argentinean, his belief in the rights of the oppressed and world revolution belied by his surface skepticism. He could not reconcile the cynical observer with the devoted revolutionary, and he suspected Guevara couldn't either.

"He is fair and just. If he to coordinate he to leave us alone. In the fight. In the government, I not to know. I do to know this. He to be a good martyr."

"Just what do you mean?"

"He a good symbol of revolution."

"You mean if he's dead," added Menoyo thoughtfully. Morgan nodded.

"Not for us to do," said Morgan, "but if by chance Batista bullet to strike him, he to be the perfect symbol."

"Because he's a foreigner who comes to fight willingly for the revolution when he has no personal stake in it? Because he's willing to give his life for the sake of a country that is not his?"

"Yes, that is what I to mean."

"But that could be you, William, you too would be a wonderful martyr for the revolution. *Our* revolution."

Morgan looked deep into Menoyo's hazel eyes and failed to detect even a hint of mockery. Menoyo was dead serious. Morgan realized there was only one thing to do. He brought out his Colt, cocked it, placed to his temple.

"I to shoot it now or in battle?" he asked.

"No, my friend, put that thing away," smiled Menoyo. "Not now, not in battle, not ever. We do not seek martyrs. We seek heroes. Live ones, preferably."

He stretched his hand, carefully removed the automatic from Morgan's fingers, extracted the bullet clip.

"I think you need a rest," said Menoyo, placing the chrome handgun on a pile of papers.

"I to be fine, nothing wrong with me," countered Morgan, even as he felt his head turn giddy, his heart race, his breathing shallow. Had he really meant to take his own life?

Yes, he told himself, you did. But then, this is all a game of Cuban roulette.

Morgan attempted to concentrate on Menoyo's words, which seemed to him to be coming from the bottom of a fish tank filled with clear oil.

"Alright then. But no more fighting for you for a while. We need you for another job."

Morgan wanted to speak but found his mouth swollen, his words missing. He nodded, feeling reality slowly seeping back into his body.

Menoyo moved around to the front of the table, sat next to Morgan, placed a bony hand on Morgan's shoulder.

"We are bringing the president back to Cuba," he whispered, almost maniacally.

The president? What president? thought Morgan.

Chapter

15

The last constitutional president of Cuba, Carlos Prío Socarrás, stared at the framed eighteenth-century map of the Antilles that he kept in the den of his Coral Gables home, unable to make a decision. All his life he'd avoided moments like this; they were too dramatic, too final, too Spanish for his taste.

This is like Pizarro drawing the line on the sand, thought Prío. Those with me will take the Inca emperor, those on the other side slink back to the pigs and sour wine of Extremadura.

Think of Martí, Prío told himself, riding unarmed in his white steed at the head of the rebel forces. Precisely, he thought. A very brave and very stupid gesture that caused more harm than good. If Martí the martyr unified the quarreling revolutionary forces, think how much more effective Martí the politician would have been outmaneuvering the Americans when they invaded, as everyone knew they would.

Prío sighed, ran for a coffee, and stared out the wide glass door at the rippling cobalt of Biscayne Bay. The sun was setting on the far side of the waters. Along the bay shore, the tile-roofed mansions turned on their lights, twinkling their shifting hellos at the darkness.

My fellow Cubans. I swear they must think they are living in some romantic opera, something by Verdi or Chenier, *Vive la patrie, Va pensiero,* and all that. Just the kind of thing I've always wanted to avoid. That's why I left Havana with my tail between my legs when Batista staged the coup six years ago. I was not going to play the part of the dead hero, holding out in the Presidential Palace, helmet on, with my machine gun and a

273

handful of faithful, while the army blasted the building to pieces. That is craziness. And one thing I'm not is crazy.

Yet.

Yet now I'm about to do something that could be just as foolhardy. To fly into the Escambray and proclaim the Republic in Arms, as the last legitimate president, which I am, against that fascist interloper, which he definitely is.

But that is madness too. Doing something like this will bring all the attention of the world on me, not to mention the full might of Batista's army. Of course Washington says it will recognize me right away, but what if it doesn't? Cuban history is full of broken American promises. Anyone who believes in the word of Washington is a damn fool and will pay a damn fool price.

Prío glanced quickly at the Patek Philippe timepiece twirling slowly on the travertine marble mantel. In thirty minutes they come and get me. And I still don't know if I should go. *Carajo.*

I know I told Boyeros I would do it. His support means I have the backing of the industrialist class, which turned its back on me the minute Fulgencio started making noises about a coup. That was stupid of me. I should have had him exiled in '51 when he gave that interview to the American newspaper saying the country needed a firmer hand. It's those American reporters, he assured me; they quoted me out of context. And I believed him! Well, I wanted to. I had enough problems with Masferrer and all those other gangsters shooting it out on the streets of Havana like it was 1920s Chicago.

Now that it's happening with Batista too, they're coming for me. Too much blood, too much violence. Bad for tourism, bad for the coffee harvest, bad especially for the sugar harvest. The rebels already have burned down a third of this year's sugar crop. If the fighting continues, there won't be any sugar left for the harvest next year. That would be the greatest tragedy. Not since the time of the Spanish has that happened. That's why they're so anxious to have me back. Because otherwise Cuba is going to burn.

I should go, of course. It would be marvelous to walk down the Via Blanca like De Gaulle down the Champs Elysées after the krauts were gone. But let's face it, the Cubans are not the French. They probably wouldn't even appreciate the gesture. Right away they'd start scheming who's going to get what in my administration—who's in Telecommunications, who's heading Treasury, can you get me a job in Education so I can draw a check and not have to work at all? The government as the big tit. Take, *m'hijito,* suck me dry. Like that idiot Grau always says,

Hay dulces para todos, there's candy for everybody. No wonder the country's always in a mess.

Of course, I should talk; I didn't exactly come here starving. But the money I brought I made myself. I did not steal; I just used my good offices. Commissions on government contracts are an accepted way of life and business in the Western world. Even in the U.S. It's just that here they're so much more hypocritical about it. I'd like to know how many presidents have left the White House broke. All of them were millionaires by the time they got out, if not before. Look at Coolidge, Hoover, even that idiot Truman. I'm sure he's got his stash somewhere. It's a fact of life.

Prío sipped his coffee, turned back to his desk. *Coño,* here I am daydreaming again, and I have five minutes before these people show up. The plane is waiting at Homestead; the Front people are waiting; I have to decide.

Clearly my wife doesn't want me to go. I can't say I blame her, either. If it weren't for her injured pride, that she can no longer claim to be the president's wife, I don't think she would object to permanent residence here. As it is, she's here one week, Palm Beach the next, then on to New York, Paris, Rome. She must have a lover stuck away somewhere. Oh well, no harm done. *Ojos que no ven, corazón que no siente.* Out of sight, out of mind. I've always thought that successful marriages are those where the partners turn a blind eye to each other's small mistakes. Only God is perfect, and He died for our sins, so let's make His death worthwhile.

Stop that, hombre. What are you going to do?

A soft knock at the door. Victor, his trusted aide, came in to announce the men from the Frente were waiting for him downstairs. Prío looked in the mirror, liking what he saw—a tall, debonair, patrician leader who exuded smarts and sophistication. He patted down the gray-streaked sides of his hair, ran a quick finger up and down his pencil mustache, his almond-shaped eyes slanting upward from the force of his grin, which cleaved his face with two deep furrows.

I haven't even packed, was his last thought as he moved from the mirror and walked briskly down the hall. He padded down the Tabriz runner on the hallway, his eyes taking in the beauty of all the objets d'art he'd collected in exile. Mere playthings, but they held so much meaning for him. The Degas print, a small bust by Henry Moore, a minor study by Seurat, the brilliant collage by Klee. His eyes fell on the gouache by Roualt at the end of the long hallway, a simple head of Christ the King, full of dignity, acceptance, and painful foreboding. My God, now I understand, he thought. That's Jesus on the way to Golgotha. Jesus on his way to the crucifixion.

He dashed down the stairs as was his habit, which gave him the appearance of a man much younger than in his fifties. He tucked at his shirtsleeves, smiled at the men in the living room. He recognized just one of them, the short, rumpled Americano.

"Good evening, Señor Presidente," said Max Weinberg, rising to his feet. "A new dawn awaits you in Cuba."

Chapter

16

The men rubbed their hands and wiped their dripping noses from the bitter cold, huddling around the remains of the last bonfire for some hope of warmth. The star-strewn sky gazed blankly down on them, saying, Find my secrets and the way will be shown unto you. A lone bird cawed, its cry echoing off the tall cedars and pines bordering the cleared-out airstrip. Morgan shivered in his fatigues, realizing he had become accustomed to the brooding tropical heat. He had finally been Cubanized.

This chill tonight was the deepest of winter, thirty degrees in a thin-blooded country that thrived in the eighties and nineties. Morgan's crew had stared dumbly at the sheets of hoarfrost covering patches of bare ground, unwilling to believe such a thing could happen on their sultry island.

For two weeks they had labored to prepare the landing strip, felling trees with handsaws, mowing long grass with machetes, borrowing a tractor from a coffee plantation to break open the dirt, leveling the field so the Cessna bringing in the president of the Republic in Arms would land safely. Every night for the past four nights Morgan had ordered his crew to light bonfires at the head of the strip and alongside its flanks, to guide the way for the errant plane. Every night they had waited vainly, their hopes dashed by the morning sun that melted the hoarfrost and burned the frigid mist.

The day before, he had sent a telegraph message down to Menoyo in headquarters ten miles away—What if Prío doesn't come? The answer rushed back: Unexpected problems. Wait two more nights in place. The future of Cuba depends on you.

Morgan felt the cold shiver of disappointment blending in with the chilly breath of dawn. He's never going to come. The past is over, we have to make our own future.

The first orange rays of the sun flared over the ridge when the rumble of the Land Rover reached the ears of Morgan and his men. They smiled among themselves.

"The old man never gives up," said Rabo de Agua, his Mongol eyes slanted upward from malice.

"How do you think he got to be the richest man in the country?" replied Evaristo, taking off toward the incoming Land Rover with simian gait, rifle cradled in his arms like a baby.

"Men, to be careful!" ordered Morgan, turning away from the remains of the bonfire, looking at the vehicle halt just a few yards away.

Carlos Boyeros signaled at his driver to turn off the engine, then eased out of the Land Rover, covering the few yards between him and Morgan in a handful of long-legged strides. Dressed in leather jacket, khaki pants, and tall, muddied riding boots, he moved with the self-confident ease of a planter surveying his properties. He nodded at the men, shook Morgan's hand with a vigor that belied his sixty-odd years.

"Morning, William," he said in English. "No sign of him today either?"

"No, Chuck," said Morgan, "looks like this bird is never flying back to the coop."

At first Morgan had felt awkward calling Boyeros by his first name, but the old man had insisted he do so, for it made him recall his youth in Princeton.

Boyeros nodded, rubbed his hands together from the cold, watching his breath condense into clouds. He shook his head in dismay.

"Well, I can't say it's a surprise. He has never had any guts." Boyeros glanced at the lightening sky, giving up the hope that Max Weinberg and the others could convince Prío to be a man and not a gigolo for once. "He never deserved to be president."

He paused, lit a cigar, watching yet another sunrise over the storm-wrecked island he'd tried so hard to heal.

"Mi pobre Cuba," he said to himself, shaking his head.

"Perhaps he to come tonight after all," said Morgan, realizing that Boyeros was more than just disappointed at a political reversal. He seemed to be seriously grieving.

"No, he won't. He's a yellow-belly, William, that's all there is to it.

From now on there's only Batista and Castro to the bitter end. No middle way," replied Boyeros in English.

"Hold on a minute. There's still the Civic Resistance. There's still the Pact of Caracas, the Directorio. There's us. It can't be that easy. Fidel wasn't the only one up in arms. Everyone knows that."

Boyeros glanced at Morgan up and down, almost ashamed of the American's injured pride.

"Yes, there is you. And you should all fight strongly so the world will know there was you, so your story won't be forgotten. But, my friend, in the eyes of the world you will be a footnote. A chapter, not the main event. Castro will win this fight, not just because he's on the side of righteousness, for once in his goddamn life, but because he has won the press."

"What you're saying can't be true," said Morgan, unable to comprehend how two thousand armed men in the Escambray, controlling a territory larger than what the 26th of July held, could be in any position that wasn't of equal authority. "After the revolution wins, we will all be in the government. Menoyo, Ray, Prío, me."

"You and Menoyo and Ray will be in the government. Prío will not; he has just forfeited all his rights to the new Cuba by not having the guts to come here. But mark my words, Fidel will never share power. Not with you, with Menoyo, Ray, even with his own brother, Raúl. Fidel has been preparing for this all his life. He's like Napoleon or Mussolini, men who have no allegiance to anything or anyone but themselves."

"He promised free elections after we win. You don't think he believes in democracy? You think he's a commie?"

Boyeros smiled ruefully, shrugged, slapped the .45 he carried in his waistband.

"This is what Fidel believes in. The power of the gun. He's no *comunista*, he's a *fidelista*. You'll see."

"You're wrong. He tries to pull something like that, we'll all go back to the bush."

"He won't let you, William. He'll remember that's how he got where he is, and he'll cut you off at the knees. He knows how to play, William. He's a pro in a country of amateurs."

"I can't believe what you're telling me. It's impossible. We'll send in the marines."

"Like you?" said Boyeros sarcastically, his heavy gray eyebrows raised disdainfully. Then he turned solicitous, practically paternal.

"Maybe you're right. Look, I don't want to rain on your parade. Go ahead, keep fighting. For all I know I could be wrong. I pray I'm wrong.

But I'm certain of one thing. If someone doesn't stop Fidel, he will crown himself king of Cuba. He'll be Fidel the First. Let's hope his kingdom is brief."

Boyeros walked back to his Land Rover, head down, hands behind his back. Morgan strolled alongside him.

"So what are you going to do?" he asked the old industrialist.

"I'm moving to Palm Beach."

Boyeros slid into his Land Rover, nodded at the driver, who started the engine. He looked up quizzingly at Morgan.

"Are you still a U.S. citizen?"

"I think so. I know we're not supposed to fight in foreign wars, but I figure the State Department will make an exception in this case."

"Perhaps. After all, Fidel wouldn't have gotten this far without their help. Or CIA money. Well, if I were you, I'd start calling your folks back in the mainland. You might have to make a run for it soon after the revolution wins. In any case, take care of yourself."

Boyeros pumped Morgan's hand as though this could be the last time they would ever meet and talk as free men.

"*Tú también, viejo,*" you too, old man, said Morgan, feeling an odd affection for the grizzled captain of commerce.

"Just remember the old saying, William. *Más sabe el diablo por viejo que por diablo.* The devil knows more because he's old than because he's the devil."

Boyeros looked quickly at his driver, pointed at the road.

"*Vámonos, Orestes.*"

The Land Rover rumbled down the steep hillside, back to Boyeros's sugar mill thirty miles away. As Morgan watched him drive away, he thought he heard the old man's voice come trailing through the pines of the thick forest, "See you in a free Havana!" But the words were so faint that Morgan could not tell if he'd actually heard them or merely wished that Boyeros had said them.

After another night of emptiness when Prío's plane failed to materialize, Morgan asked for and received orders to withdraw. He accompanied his troops to headquarters at La Diana, then went on an unauthorized furlough. It wasn't quite an absence without order of leave, because when, after two days, he failed to turn up, all those who knew him well, from Menoyo down to Rabo de Agua, knew there was only one place where the fearless American would have gone, and they all smiled to themselves and wished him the warrior's rest.

✄ ✄ ✄

Trinidad.

The town of the Most Holy Trinity slumbered peacefully when Morgan entered it. A sea of red-tiled roofs, whitewashed walls, cobblestoned streets, wooden bars on narrow windows, peace and calm, as though the civil war that convulsed Cuba had nothing to do with this seignorial town that harked back to the time of the *conquistadores,* a pocket of tranquillity that time and politics had forgotten.

Morgan drove into town in a jeep and clothes he'd borrowed from Boyeros's sugar mill. Dressed as a civilian for the first time in months, Morgan felt awkward, exposed in his new garb. He parked by the town plaza, opposite the army *cuartel.* Morgan figured, rightly, that the one place where a mud-splattered jeep would not draw any attention would be right under the distracted gaze of the military authorities, a portly sergeant and two scrawny corporals more interested in their checkers game than in patrolling the placid colonial town.

Before entering Trinidad Morgan had studied a map of the city, noting the handful of churches, the elevations, the wide avenues leading out from the plaza like spokes from a wheel, the small alleys like capillaries connecting the major thoroughfares. He knew the place he sought was only about fifteen blocks from the plaza, yet even so the twisting alleys with their sudden turns confused him.

Twice he had to ask for directions, once from a group of men playing clackety dominoes in a small courtyard, their cries of *"Doblete!"* and *"Pollona!"* like signals in the jasmine-scented night. The other time a little boy carrying a loaf of bread guided him, taking him by the hand to the corner of the alley and pointing at a small sienna-colored house with green shutters.

"Allá está el templo americano!" said the boy, wide brown eyes flashing guilelessly. Morgan searched for a quarter to tip the boy, but having no money, had to settle for mussing the child's silky hair. The boy grinned at the big man's helplessness and went on his way down the tranquil cobblestoned street.

⊠ ⊠ ⊠

The music rushed out to greet him, shameless in its passion, striding naked to embrace him. Not being a musical man, he could not recognize the composer or the period or the style, but the glowing cloud of notes pealing down flowers of desire and hurtful loss were impossible to misread. He stopped in front of the yellow wooden door, almost overcome by alternating feelings of love and embarrassment, the music so heedless of anything but its own feverish passion that Morgan felt as if he were accidentally looking through an open window at a couple making wild, heedless love.

He glanced at the small sign by the door.

Asamblea de Dios—Assembly of God. Bienvenidos—Welcome.

He lifted the metal knocker and rapped hard three times.

The music stopped. In the silence Morgan heard a distant cock crowing. Presently there were footsteps on the other side of the door, then Irma's silvery voice: *"Quién es?"*

"It's William."

Bolts thrown open, a squeaking of joints, a shaft of golden light bathing the threshold, Irma dressed in black, masses of blond curls falling on her shoulders, her eyes ringed by sleeplessness. She doesn't smile, she doesn't greet or shake hands, she doesn't cry or bewail her loss or rend her clothes in grief. She simply takes Morgan by the hand, pulls him inside, swiftly closes the heavy wooden door.

Years later Morgan would recollect the events of that night, placing them in his mind alongside the moments of transport he had attained with Laura—even then, as always, comparing the one to the other, complementary poles that melded into the figure of the loved one. For all his trouble he could never decide which of the two women he had loved the most, each, in her own way, proving the opposite of what her exterior promised.

Laura, with her sensual features and quick grace, had been an almost ethereal lover who vanished into the swirls of emotion like angels blending their voices into a chorus of praise to the Lord. Yet Irma, whose austere garb promised the dry rectitude of the self-anointed, became as one possessed when making love, a grunting, wordless creature whose every move spelled lust without limits, as though having made up her mind that she would taste the fruit of the forbidden tree, she would sate forever the hunger crying in between her thighs.

That night, as he walked in, guided by Irma's long narrow hand, Morgan had barely enough time to register the disarray in the small house, the sofa bolsters tossed on the unswept flagstone floor, the rumpled issues of *Time* and the *Saturday Evening Post* strewn on the green velveteen covered armchair, the odd empties of Cristal beer and Bacardi Añejo, the overflowing mound of cigarette stubs in the ashtray by the piano. Even after entering the bedroom behind the kitchen, empty save for an unmade bed, a half-open dresser with stocking and undergarments spilling out, and a wooden chair crammed with books, even then Morgan was not totally aware of the emotional abyss into which he'd stumbled. But when Irma, still wordlessly, came up to him and clumsily, awkwardly, but overflowing with desire, pressed her lips against his, guiding his hands onto her breasts, only then did Morgan realize the emptiness that gripped her, the void in her existence that she was trying to fill with his all-too-eager flesh.

They dropped their clothes in haste as though the earth were to end and the only remedy to allay the destruction, to right the world and wipe the specter of death and the singing hurt inside their hearts, were for them to become as one, their bodies joined in a flailing flight. As he entered her, admiring her white, white skin, her freckled nose and breasts, the soft down under her arms and in between her legs, the way her pink nipples stood in attention, Irma whispered words Morgan thought he'd never hear again: "I love you, I love you, God forgive me but I love you. Don't you ever leave me again."

After the first shudder of surprise, the crystalline spasms of delight, when they'd reached the first plateau of what promised to be a long climb into ecstasy, catching their breath before journeying on into physical delirium, Morgan and Irma talked. They talked incessantly, as if they had to tell each other everything, to fill the vessels of knowledge with the outpouring of desire. They answered every question asked and unasked, from how her father had died shortly after she returned from the Sierra to the color of their grandparents' hair to the first time each became aware of their sex and the yearning beast they carried inside. Their first fantasies, their last (and in Irma's case, only) lover, how the smell of orange blossoms and spilled rum excited them both, the way they craved to be touched, caressed, licked, and sucked. Each new revelation was accompanied by a demonstration that led them to further penetration and exploration, release and admiration, in an ever-expanding curve of sexual abandon that became their very world, the entire universe confined by the bedroom's jonquil walls.

But the habits of a lifetime died hard within Irma, and she had him come down off the bed, stained with the fruit of their passions. Naked, they knelt like children beseeching an inattentive lord, and as she bowed her head in prayer Morgan thought she was the handsomest creature he had ever seen, with her tapered back, narrow waist, and wide hips, her full breasts craning forward, her mass of curls like a veil covering her face, her skin gleaming from the sweat of their exertions.

She raised her throaty voice to heaven: "O Lord, we are but sinners in your eyes, yet we have tried to follow your commands, to serve you in that very first commandment in the garden, Be fruitful and multiply. Grant us, then, your peace, and bless this union of your servants Irma and William, so that in your kingdom and by your grace we may find happiness in each other and bring forth the good news to the world, that we are as one, brothers and sisters in the body of your son, Jesus Christ our Lord. Amen."

Irma looked up, corn blue eyes washed with tears. She brushed the hair from her face.

"Kiss me, husband," she said.

Chapter

17

"It's a hospital, all right."

"You mean the patients are still inside."

"Of course. They are perfect cover. They are desperate, these men. They will do whatever is necessary. And so will we."

The white building stood proudly in the piercing winter light, its base wreathed by a bank of fog slowly melting in the morning sun. Built as a sanatorium for tuberculosis patients, the complex rose from a promontory thousands of feet above the valley of Cienfuegos, the second-largest city in the province. Perched, as if on tiptoe, on a spur of the Escambray Mountains, it gave the appearance of wanting to catch in great mouthfuls the sweet currents of air from the Caribbean that swept the region clean.

"Look at it this way, William," continued Menoyo, nervously lighting a cigarette with swift, jerky motions. "This is all that stands between us, the combined forces of the Frente and the Twenty-sixth of July, and the city of Cienfuegos. Remember, the Province of Camaguey has fallen, Oriente is on the brink, and with Che Guevara storming Santa Clara, this is the last redoubt of the regime. If this falls, half the island will be ours. Besides, conceivably, Batista could use the naval base at Cienfuegos to start up another attack, so, one way or another, we have to take it. And the only way to take it is through that hospital."

Morgan nodded, looking again at the proud structure, a monument to the building ambitions of Batista's first presidency. The two *guerrilleros* stood at the window of a *bohío* behind a cluster of white pines in a glen about a quarter mile from the site. They could detect the comings and goings of the soldiers bivouacked in the hospital, the trucks and vehicles stationed around the perimeter, the heavy artillery massed carelessly on the leeward side, as though an invasion were expected up the craggy face of the cliff.

"We need about three hundred men to take building," said Morgan, confident that a daring attack would easily break the demoralized government troops.

"We have more than that, my friend," replied Menoyo with a knowing smile. "We are making rendezvous tonight with the forces of Chomón's Directorio and with the Torres partisans. Altogether we shall have over fifteen hundred men. Is that enough for you?"

Morgan beamed, seduced as always by Menoyo's directness. A daring thought occurred to him, a picture of utter military simplicity.

"I say no to the attack on the hospital, Eloy," said Morgan, wheeling about, his lean tanned features creased by thought. Menoyo looked at the rangy Americano, his blond hair now almost white from the sun, and he thought to himself, Is he going loco on me?

"What do you mean, not attack? How could we fail to press on, with all that awaits us after this battle?"

"Because I have a better plan, Eloy," countered Morgan eagerly. "We have now about a dozen trucks from the army, no?"

"Yes, we captured them but I don't see—"

"Please listen! This the plan. We take five trucks, a thousand men. All armed with the light weapons, greater the mobility. We drive into Havana and take over the city!"

"What?" Menoyo had always admired his *comandante's* daring, but now he began to think maybe Morgan's fearlessness was simply disguised madness.

"Yes, you see? It's a lightning strike."

"You mean a blitzkrieg, like the Germans during the Second World War?"

"That is correct. With the surprise factor, we take the control of the main army base, the Columbia *campamento*, La Cabaña Fortress, the Presidential Palace, all! In the confusion—we go at midnight, two in morning—we do it! Think. The Directorio almost won in fifty-seven, with only fifty men. This time, a thousand men, trained fighters, striking all over the town! One night of daring, we can do it! Havana is only five hours away by truck. We can do it! We can!"

Morgan opened his eyes wide, pressed his hand on Menoyo's shoulder, trying with body language to convey the utter necessity for his plan. He cursed himself inwardly for still not mastering Spanish and hoped that the intensity of his feelings would be enough to put across his message.

"Think of it!" insisted Morgan. "The capital, ours in one blow! We are the first rebel forces in city! We win the revolution!"

Menoyo frowned, angry that fate was showing him the sweet fruit of absolute success only to snatch it away. He felt like kicking, cursing, slapping Morgan for making this proposal now. Now, of all times! Why couldn't he have done it before, when the Front's troops were all united? Then he could have done it, this lightning raid. For it was obviously brilliant, so unexpected that it would surely work, especially now that the bulk of the army was tied up fighting in Santa Clara and Oriente.

A thousand men could do it, no doubt. But Menoyo didn't have a thousand men. The week before, at Guevara's request, he had split his forces. A third to Santa Clara, another third eastward to Camagüey. All he had left was 350 of his own men, not enough to stage the raid. He knew the combined forces would never agree to the Frente becoming the spearhead, entering the capital first and stealing everyone's thunder. No, it could not be done. Not yet. *Carajo.*

"An excellent idea, William, but for now we have pledged to attack the sanatorium here at Topes de Collantes. We must honor our commitments."

"But this is a better idea!"

"Those are my orders, *Comandante!*" snapped Menoyo.

"Sí, señor," answered Morgan, seething in frustration.

"However," added Menoyo knowingly, "once we take Cienfuegos, well then, who knows?"

"Really?"

"Yes, really. Start passing the word to El Gato, Jesús Carreras, and the rest of the staff."

"Havana to be ours?"

"Ours, William. Exclusively ours."

Morgan wheeled out of the room, beaming with happy anticipation. Menoyo called out.

"By the way, William. Your Spanish has improved considerably. You are really beginning to sound like a Cuban."

Morgan beamed. "Thank you. I owe it to Irma. She has been much patient with me. She wants our baby to have a real Cuban father."

"There's never been any doubt about that in my mind, William," replied Menoyo in his Spanish accent. "You are the most native of all of us."

Morgan snapped to attention, dizzy with pride.

"Thank you, *Comandante.*"

"Dismissed, *Comandante.*"

✖ ✖ ✖

Irma turned on the wooden radio on the rickety rattan table and slowly, painfully hobbled back to her rocker on the porch. Though only four months pregnant, she felt heavy and swollen, as if the child were destined to be much larger than normal, an outsized creature already demanding more than others in the womb.

Irma had watched her once-lithe body stretch in ways the books on childbirth rarely mentioned. Her skin became strangely mottled at times, as if a rash were spreading up and down her face and arms, while her legs felt tingly and warm, a thousand needles stuck all at once down her sides. She had no stamina, and for the first time in her life she swooned like the heroine of some Victorian novel. To gather her strength she would lie down and close her eyes, sliding into fitful catnaps, in which she would see the smiling countenance of Desmond, her dead father, gazing fondly at her from a backdrop of tropical lilac clouds, and she would wake up with start.

She was mortified to find that her feet, like her breasts and her belly, had also grown. She had to give up her American shoes with some pain, knowing that they were a measure of the girl she'd never be again. She tried to wear Cuban-made shoes, but their narrow last and stiff leather caused her even more pain, so she gave up on them and simply walked barefoot for weeks, laughing to herself for becoming the barefoot and pregnant wife she thought she'd never be. But when one day she discovered little green worms crawling out of the skin between her toes, she bowed to the inevitable. She killed the worms with a pesticide that turned her toes yellow, and started to wear combat boots, just like all the other women in camp.

My goodness, if it's this bad now, what will it be like when I'm six, seven months along? she thought, rocking slowly in the porch. I will be a constant invalid, and you can't have that in a war. Maybe it would be better if I did leave the country, go see my family in California. But what will I do without my William?

She pondered on this, even as she tried not to think of a very unsettling development over the last few days. She had begun to have her menstrual flow once again. She knew it was not possible, she was certainly and painfully pregnant, so the morning she had discovered the spotting in her underwear she had been horrified, unable to imagine how such a thing could be.

William was away at the time, fighting at the front. Raquel, Comandante Piñeira's woman, advised her that such a thing, while unusual, was not totally unheard of, and perhaps she should consult the camp physician. But Dr. Grajales, a former neuropathic surgeon who had joined the Front out of a deep revulsion for Batista and Castro, was both overworked and out of his depth. His most frequent cure was two aspirin, a shot of rum, and prolonged bed rest, a remedy that worked wonders with battle-weary rebels, who usually just drank the rum, forgot the pills, and slept to their hearts' content. This he also prescribed to Irma, suggesting perhaps she would be better off with a specialist in Havana. She rejected that idea, fearful that once she crossed rebel lines she would be left bereft in the capital, unable to return. So she had kept her morning bleeding to herself, hoping that it was just another of those unexplainable phenomena of pregnancy like hair loss and cravings for pickles and escargots, none of which, thankfully, she suffered from as yet.

Irma had tried prayer, but somewhere after her pregnancy she had paradoxically lost the burning intensity of her faith that made her think her words flew straight to God's ear. After moving into the hills with William, her appeals for divine intervention sounded flat and untruthful, like the nosy neighbor asking for a cup of sugar when what she really wants is to find out, Why all the screaming next door?

Believing that the worst sin was to be a Pharisee and pretend a piety she no longer felt, Irma had simply stopped praying altogether. It wasn't that she had abandoned God so much as that she and He had come, for now, to a painful parting of the ways, each of them wishing the best for each other and waiting, arms crossed, for the other to come running back. She didn't know how much all of this was due to her father's death, even if she did feel that, without his stolid support, there seemed to be no purpose to praying. Hadn't he died in spite of her many prayers? Where is the bounty of a God that takes away loved ones, leaving the survivors grieving in the dark? Since she could not understand, she simply turned away.

In her heart she knew the cause of her lack of faith was her so-called marriage to William, this sinful coupling of lust and obligation that a mere set of bedside prayers could not anoint. She could have asked one of the several Catholic priests in the camp to bless their union, but Irma refused to do so, thinking their powers to invoke divine blessings were negated by their slavish devotion to the man in Rome. What Irma truly craved was her father's blessing, to have him return from the beyond and raise his cracked voice and utter, William, do you take this woman? Lacking that, everything else was inconsequential, yet that very absence only served to confirm the sinfulness of her union, a sinfulness that made the union more appealing, as all sinful things are.

Her lack of prayer was also liberating, such a deliverance from old ties and responsibility that occasionally she became giddy with freedom. At those times, drawing water from the well that served the camp, harvesting the tomatoes she had planted in the yard behind her *bohío,* throwing scraps of bread and pineapple rinds to the noisy chickens she raised, she would smile beatifically to herself, rubbing her belly, as though making a wish that this happiness would last all of her life.

Now from the radio in the porch came snatches of martial music, the first few bars of the battle song of the republic, then the trembling tenor voice of the announcer:

"This is Radio Rebelde, in the free territory of Cuba. The forces of liberation fighting the tyranny have achieved a major victory in the battle for the capital of Las Villas Province, Santa Clara. Yesterday, at around fourteen hundred hours, an armored train sent to combat the insurgency surrendered to the forces of liberation. Three hundred and fifty soldiers and officers were captured as prisoners after a bloody battle near the hills of Capiro, in the northeast of the city.

"Comandante Ernesto Guevara, using tractors from the University of Santa Clara's School of Agronomy, derailed the train and concentrated a barrage of rebel fire on the troops of the tyranny, who promptly laid down their weapons.

"The fighting continues inside the brave besieged city of Santa Clara. Government troops are still occupying five major posts, among them the central police station, the courthouse, and the army barracks. Gallant efforts by the rebel forces have succeeded in gaining control of half of the city in bloody hand-to-hand encounters. In response, the cowardly regime's air force has been bombing the city without consideration for the life and welfare of innocent civilians.

"We have no reports of how many casualties have resulted from this despicable act. In a communiqué from Oriente Province, Comandante Fidel Castro exhorted the rebel forces on to victory, so that now, on the eve of the New Year, the tidal wave of the popular will can prevail and find the road to freedom. Here are a few of the *comandante's* words."

Irma turned off the radio the moment Castro began to speak. She was in no mood for exhortation, and she trusted Castro as little as she trusted Batista. She still remembered vividly the man's magnetic presence in the sierra, when she realized that for a man like Castro there was no reality but that which he sought to create. Castro's words were masks, she felt, promises of honey laced with arsenic, a swarm of angels falling headlong down the bloody alley . . .

Irma realized that she was hallucinating, that the porch was spinning and her father's voice seemed to cry out from somewhere, Look below, look below. She gazed down at her legs and saw the spreading stain of blood on her dress, life's precious liquid dripping down the rungs of the rocking chair. She lifted her eyes, saw the woman of Comandante Piñeira walking by. Irma tried to call out but couldn't find her voice, then tried to stand, haltingly, but her legs failed her too, and she tumbled, gently, as if in a dream, to the strangely padded floorboards of the wooden porch.

⋇ ⋇ ⋇

The rapid clopping of the horse's hooves sounded a drum roll in Morgan's ears as he galloped to his meeting with Menoyo. A mantle of cold stars cloaked the sky over the *bohío*, the amber light of a hurricane lamp glowing through the half-open window. It was the only light in the entire valley, which lay dreamily quiet and damp. A quarter mile above, on a rise facing the ocean, stood the gleaming white hospital, flood lamps illuminating its white flanks.

Morgan feared the worst as he got off his horse, tying its reins to the branch of a sour orange tree. He stepped quickly into the ramshackle hut, saluting the unfamiliar 26th of July guerrilla guarding the door.

Menoyo was at a table with maps and papers, standing next to a bearded, thin, tall man in olive green fatigues. Both officers turned to Morgan, nodding with the quiet somberness of people making funeral arrangements.

"I received your communiqué, *Comandante*," said Morgan, saluting Menoyo. "We expect the muchachos of Directorio and Torres, but we no see them. What is the problem?"

"The problem, William, is that your dear friend Che Guevara, acting with the full approval of Sierra headquarters, is refusing to allow those troops to join us," said Menoyo, almost growling.

Morgan was stunned. He had made all the arrangements for a coordinated attack, splitting his forces in several flanks so that his own men would act as spearheads and breach the enemy defense, relying on the other forces to supply the bulk of the carry-through. Now he would have to regroup his men and hope everyone understood the new plans at the last minute.

"Not only that, he is taking with him the Twenty-sixth of July people who had incorporated into our troops. They are leaving tonight."

"What? How is that possible?" sputtered Morgan. "We have the word of the Twenty-sixth of July. Their word is not to be trusted?"

The tall red-bearded man shrugged, obviously amused by Morgan's righteous indignation.

"Wars are not won in a single battle, *Comandante*," said the man. "Moreover, the troops are needed for the attack on Santa Clara."

"Who is this man, *Comandante*," snapped Morgan, "who sticks his nose in general staff matters?"

"This is Capitán José Suárez," said Menoyo with a gesture that could easily have been converted into a stranglehold in a different place and time.

"The revolutionary troops are now in control of the road to the capital, Major Morgan, and we need every man for the final drive."

"But we need them too! We have to take Topes!"

"I am just carrying out orders here, Major," retorted Suárez. "Let me ask you this. How many men did you have in mind for this attack?"

"About two hundred eighty," answered Morgan.

"Two hundred and eighty. What kind of outfit are you that you need so many men to capture a mere hospital? Do you know that Comandante Guevara at this very moment is investing Santa Clara with only three hundred men? A whole city! You do not need so many men. I am sure you will find another way. Good night."

He saluted Menoyo, who waved his hand in exasperation. At the door to the hut Suárez turned with a sarcastic grin.

"Of course, Major Morgan, if you do not like the situation, you can always call in the marines. I am sure they'll rush right on over for a fellow American."

They could hear Suárez's jeering laughter outside the hut as he and his escort marched back to their horses, mounted, and rode away.

Menoyo tapped his fingers impatiently on the table.

"I should have never trusted Fidel or Che. I, of all people, should have known better. So now they want our troops and we can't have ours back. We are practically helpless! In Santa Clara they have irregulars, they have partisans, they have hundreds of other fighters, not just the regular rebel troops. But here, that is all we have. How dare they! How dare they!"

Menoyo thumped the table, purple with rage.

"How many do we have now?" asked Morgan.

Menoyo glanced down at his papers, as if ashamed.

"Less than two hundred," said Menoyo softly.

Morgan thought quickly, going over in his mind the approach to the hospital, the posts, the roads, the enemy forces between him and a victory so close he could almost touch it. He was not going to allow anything or anyone to stand in his way; no sir, folks from Ohio don't think like that.

"We can do it, Eloy," said Morgan, confidently. "Let me show you."

❊ ❊ ❊

The attack was to begin at midnight.

Morgan and Menoyo had split their forces into three fronts. Menoyo would handle the western flank, Jesús Carreras the easternmost side, and Morgan would bear down on the middle.

At the stroke of twelve Menoyo's men would open fire on the guard-house in the perimeter of the gardens, rousing the bulk of the soldiers, who slept in improvised barracks on the west side, just north of the main building. Using their one bazooka as well as grenades, Menoyo's men were to destroy the trucks parked behind the guardhouse. Simultaneously, a squad of ten men were to spill gallons of lubricant grease on the macadam of the steep winding road, in case any of the trucks or armored vehicles succeeded in escaping. The moment the sol-diers responded from the barracks, Carreras's men were to begin firing, making sure that, once they were out of their lair, the soldiers never returned. Morgan was to save his fire for last, when the surviving soldiers tried to regroup directly south. At that point he would let loose with a barrage, hopefully making quick work of the thing and entering the hos-pital by daybreak—Cienfuegos and Havana next.

❊ ❊ ❊

In the end only 150 men had become available for the attack. Spread out under the pines surrounding the hospital, the men lay flat on the needle-covered floor. With their ponytails carefully laced back, their rosaries and amulets in place, their carbines and M-3s and grenade launchers loaded and ready for the firing, the *guerrilleros* held their breath awaiting the final moment, when the hands of their watches would meet and the slaughter could start.

Morgan shivered, both from nerves and the unusually cold night. From afar he could hear the singing and carousing of the soldiers in the barracks, preparing for the arrival of the New Year.

Poor Joes. Funny that we should be doing this tonight. I wonder if they have any idea what's coming.

He thought back, for a brief moment that stretched to the yawn of eternity, to the earliest days of his arrival in the Escambray and the hard-scrabble group of fighters who had broadcast the seeds of war.

El Gato. Rabo de Agua. Lázaro. Octavio. Anacleto. Evaristo. The orig-inal band. Of all those only El Gato and Rabo de Agua are left, and they're fighting with Guevara in Santa Clara. The others have died. Lázaro in that jungle clearing, Octavio at La Diana, Anacleto in Cubanacán, Evaristo in Camagüeyera. All brave men. All gave their life for their dreams. Funny that I, who wanted to die, have lived instead. Why? I wonder. They had families, children, a country. I had nothing. They died and I, who had nothing, will soon have everything to live for. A child, a wife, a life. And the memory of a love that will not die.

Stop it, William, you're getting sappy. She's gone. It's been over a year. You're a man expecting a child, with a future to live for. A wife. Even if we're not married, a woman who will always love you, who means the world to you. A child again, after all these years.

Still, I wonder, what would have happened had Laura lived? What would my life have been with her? I guess I'll never know. But there's no need to know. I fulfilled my part of the bargain; we're freeing her country. And no matter where she is, she must be proud of me, proud of the thing I've done.

Stop it. Look around you, William. You're on the dirt under the trees, waiting to kill or be killed. Your job is not over yet. No, not yet. But it won't be long now.

The drone of a low-flying aircraft yanked Morgan out of his tense reverie, the broad span of the B-26 casting a malignant shadow over the grounds. Morgan looked frantically at his watch.

Twelve o'clock exactly.

No! Don't start, no, don't! he thought in desperation. Hold your fire, he muttered, wishing for once he had a walkie-talkie. Hold your god-damn fire!!!

He jerked his head left and right, expecting the worst. Out of the barracks on the west side, soldiers cheered the start of the New Year, even as the nurses and staff of the hospital clattered open the windows and tossed out the traditional bucket of water to welcome in the year 1959.

As though in a fevered hallucination, Morgan heard the Cuban national anthem coming from one of the hospital's open windows, then the lilting sound of Guy Lombardo and his Royal Canadians playing "Auld Lang Syne" on a stateside broadcast, then the droning aircraft passed over them, and the enormous bulk of the aircraft sailed away down to Cienfuegos, and it was then and only then that Menoyo's men, wisely, opened fire and the hospital yard shook with the terrible roar of the bazooka shell striking the nearest truck, which exploded with a sharp, rattling boom.

The singing stopped and the national anthem was silenced as the attack increased in ferocity, dozens of grenades now raining down on the parked army vehicles and only the sad-happy sound of "Auld Lang Syne" floating in the grounds, interspersed in between the bombing and the clanging and the loud report of projectile shells and bullets providing their own exquisite form of noisemakers, saying good-bye not just to the old year but to an entire era as the bullets and the whizzing and the fighting were heard throughout the island, even down to the airport at Camp Columbia, where President Batista at that very moment was hushing his wife, Marta, and his children as they boarded the Constellation aircraft that would deliver them from the perilous confines of their native land to the becalmed shores of his neighbor Dominican dictator Leónidas Trujillo.

But the soldiers who rushed out of the barracks knew none of that flight, and the men under Carreras's orders were unaware of it as well when they opened fire on troops half drunk on rum and sweet champagne. When the soldiers retreated, as had been expected, Morgan raised his arm and cried:

"FIRE!!! *FUEGO!!!*"

His fifty men, as if one sole trigger finger, let loose a hailstorm of death that sliced down the running, frightened soldiers, who sought useless refuge behind the box hedges in the grounds before racing back into the hospital building.

The smooth, carefully planned rout became a stand-off as the bulk of the remaining government soldiers, guns blazing, dashed for the hospital, barricading themselves hastily with couches and desks thrown against the locked doors.

Morgan would later learn that the major who handled the rebels' only bazooka and who was supposed to have fired at the hospital entrance to bar such an escape had been one of the battle's earliest casualties, a bullet burning a hole in his throat that took out his larynx and left him to drown in his own blood. Morgan rushed forward with ten of his men, lobbing grenades at the easternmost guard post, disabling the troops there, then took cover behind the concrete retaining wall around the flagstaff in front of the building.

The government troops at the windows and the .50-caliber-machine-gun nest on the roof let rip their own hailstorm of firepower, pinning down Morgan behind the retaining wall for over a half hour. During a brief break Morgan and his men managed to dash over to the half-destroyed barracks, which had been taken over by Major Carreras and now served as headquarters for the attack.

"*Comandante,*" said Morgan, seeing Menoyo for the first time, "we request permission to attack building."

Menoyo nodded as an orderly wrapped a bandage on his left arm, wounded slightly by a ricocheting bullet.

"Of course, William. You need not ask for my permission. Tell me what you require."

"The guns shooting at the building when we storm it," said Morgan, feeling the itch for action burning his insides like an addict craving his drug.

"You are crazy, William. How do you intend to do that with a machine gun nest on the roof?"

"*Comandante*, the building is only two hundred yards away. We have to save the sick people in hospital. If not, the soldiers will use them as the shields if battle last long time."

Menoyo grinned, his badly stained teeth grimacing in a rictus of pleasure.

"Go get 'em, cowboy," he said in English.

Morgan and his men raced out under cover of blinding fire, a hundred guns all aimed at the roof of the hospital, a cloudburst of weaponry that chipped the sides of the building, destroyed the flood lights, and quieted down the soldiers, taken by surprise by such fierce counterattack.

Throwing himself on the ground, Morgan tossed a grenade at the front doors, the pieces of glass and wood flying over him as the explosion rocked the building. No sooner had the smell of gunpowder cleared than he rushed inside, raking the lobby with his Thompson, a raging blaze of fury and destruction. A soldier inside the lobby took aim at the intruder, but one of Morgan's men brought him down with a rush of bullets. Morgan jumped over the bleeding bodies of several soldiers, then crouched behind the reception desk. A nurse, trembling, cried huddled in a corner.

"Not to worry, señora, we are the rebels," said Morgan.

"*Bueno, bueno*," said the woman, wrapping her arms around Morgan. "They've gone upstairs and closed the doors. They're gone!"

Morgan glanced up from behind the desk. His five men, guns held high, rushed from corner to corner of the room, seeking out the enemy. There was no one.

Morgan came out, walked around the toppled bookcases and curio shelves, the desks and couches, his boots trampling on broken glass. He stopped before a mural by the elevator: Batista on rearing horseback, like Napoleon crossing the Alps, pointing with his index finger at the site where the hospital had been built.

Just then Menoyo's voice was heard through loudspeakers in the barracks: "Soldiers of the tyranny, this is Comandante Menoyo of the Segundo Frente. Know that your leader General Batista has left the country for exile. Turn on any radio and the news will be confirmed. Lay down your weapons and your life will be spared."

"Is that true?" asked one of Morgan's men. Morgan shrugged, turned to the nurse.

"Do you have radio?"

"Yes. This way."

She showed Morgan the built-in radio in the lobby. Morgan flicked it on to Radio Reloj. Anxiously, urgently, the announcer read: "Repeating the news. President Fulgencio Batista y Zaldívar has resigned and turned over his office to Prime Minister Andrés Rivero Agüero. The former president is now on his way to a foreign country. Some reports indicate he is en route to Spain, others say his plane is about to land at Miami Airport. So far we have received no official comment from the rebel forces of the Twenty-sixth of July Movement, who have been battling the government for the past three years. And now for a message from Vitalis."

Morgan grabbed the microphone for the building's intercom, pressed down the on button. The radio announcer finished his commercial, his voice booming in the suddenly perfectly still building.

"We repeat the news of the hour. President Fulgencio Batista y Zaldívar has resigned his post . . . "

A group of rebels now rushed inside the building, shouting, *"Viva la revolución!"* The cheering spread through the grounds, the brilliant words resounding throughout the hospital and the island and the world. Batista is gone, long live the revolution!

Morgan lost himself among the men that surged in, exchanging *abrazos* and handshakes. "Next stop Havana!" "About fucking time!"

In the swelling crowd, Morgan found himself embracing a saturnine-looking man who shook his hand with extraordinary emotion.

"William, is you?" said the man in English.

"Yes. Who are you, friend?"

"I am Roberto Ortiz. You not remember? The attack on Batista at the yacht club?"

All at once Morgan recalled—the store clerk, the driver of the meat van.

"Of course. I'm happy to see you," said Morgan.

"Me too! I fight with Jesús Carreras a long time, always I wanted to see you again, no have the time. You listen me! You remember Laura!"

"Yes?"

"She look for you, my friend!"

"What?"

"Yes? She join Raúl Castro in the Sierra Cristal. She is alive, my friend. And you too! Is not life something?!"

A government soldier opened one of the locked doors leading to the upper floors of the hospital, then peeked out, asking timorously: "To whom do we surrender?"

"Comandante Morgan!" someone shouted. *"Comandante!"*

And even though 360 government soldiers now came meekly out, hands held high, trooping down to the lobby to face revolutionary justice, Morgan could think of only one thing—She's alive! Laura lives! Laura lives!

BOOK THREE
After Saint Just

Chapter

1

"Esta revolución no devorará sus hijos."
  —*Fidel Castro*

(This revolution will not devour its children.)

On January 1, 1959, Boy Scouts in uniform were directing traffic on the streets of Havana.

Thousands of young men and women, whose sole authority rested on their rifles and the red-and-black armbands of the 26th of July, the *urbanos,* kept precarious order, stopping vengeful crowds from slaughtering the few known remaining representatives of the old regime who still dared to show their face. The *urbanos,* however, had not been able to stop the wholesale destruction of Havana's hated parking meters, whose revenues had fattened the pockets of the chief of police. Up and down the city, the gutters were full of the remains of the shiny machines—made in St. Louis, Missouri—that symbolized so much of the corruption of the Batista years.

The rebel leadership having proclaimed a general strike, all the businesses and schools were shut down, the entire population of the city thronging the streets for the great big wonderful victory party everyone had been longing for. It was a prolonged New Year's ball, with all of Havana, all of Cuba, reveling in the champagne of revolution, the occasional flourish of bullets sprayed by fleeing Batistianos standing in for the tinkling tones of "Auld Lang Syne."

Morgan tried to join in the spirit of the fiesta but his heart couldn't have been further from merriment. Seeing Havana again only filled him with longing and doubt. Would Irma recover? Would he find Laura once more?

Torn by his two loves, he saw himself with his troops, as if at a distance, entering jeeps with Eloy, El Gato, and a handful of others. They were the first rebels to come down from the mountains to the burning plain, like some long-gone ruler returned to his throne after years of chewing grass and lying with the animals.

Groups on street corners stood and cheered, waving the ubiquitous red-and-black 26th of July banner. Women in balconies threw kisses at them, and children at the large Catholic orphanage by the cathedral clapped spontaneously upon seeing their jeeps, shouting, *"Viva Cuba! Viva Fidel!"*

We should have had a plan for this, thought Morgan. We should have seen that Batista would not last. We let others snatch victory away from us. We won the war but others will reap the glory.

By the time they crossed the Via Blanca, cruising around the Prado, down Muralla to the Presidential Palace, Morgan found they had been preempted. Local members of the Directorio had taken over the ornate vacant seat of power, waiting for Cubelas and Chomón to come down from the hills.

"It doesn't matter," said Eloy, after being told the Frente would not be welcomed in the palace. "We didn't fight against Batista for us to set up a new government. Let the people decide."

"It's not possible, Eloy," warned Morgan. "Life hates a vacuum; someone has to call the shots."

"We'll settle that later, *Comandante,*" said Eloy, returning to his jeep. "Right now I want to see my mother, take a warm shower, and spend all night in my own bed. We shall see what tomorrow brings."

Morgan saw, with painful clarity, what had happened. Once inside Havana, they lost the will to fight. Like a Levantine temptress, the city made the very act of surrendering one of triumph, changing the will and focus of the thousands who poured down from the hills, with their amulets and their scapulars and long scruffy beards and ponytails. Only one man kept his head above the fray, and he was taking his own sweet time on arriving, so that by the time he entered in his jeep—like the chariot driving generals of old—there would be no doubt who had been the proximate cause of the downfall of the tyrant.

Fidel, Fidel, always Fidel.

❉ ❉ ❉

Irma sensed Morgan before he uttered a word. She moved her head and saw him standing at the foot of her hospital bed, still smelling of sweat and grass, bandoliers across his chest, little-boy grin splitting his face into even halves. She felt hazy and relaxed, not from the drugs that kept lassoing her to a down bed of deadened pain, but from an inner light that burst in the middle of her chest and flowed down to her torn womb the moment she saw him. She raised her hand, felt the cottony mouth, the great weights beneath her eyelids. Morgan sat on the bed beside her, holding her hand.

"Everything's fine, darling. There's no need to speak," he said, softly rubbing her long slender palm.

"The doctors, they said—" muttered Irma.

"I spoke to them already, sweetheart. You were touch-and-go there for a while, but everything's going to be fine. You just wait and see."

"I'm sorry, William."

"No need to be sorry, sweetheart. You couldn't help it."

A great wave of revulsion and self-hatred swept over Irma, a feeling of horror reined in only by the narcotics and the tug of love from this wonderful man beside her.

"Was it a boy?" she asked, her mouth feeling as though it belonged to someone else, the words ringing dully from afar.

"Yes, it was."

"Oh, my God. I'm so sorry."

"Don't be sorry, sweetheart. We'll have another one."

"Poor little Alexander."

"We'll have another one, sweetheart. We'll have another little Alex and a little Billy and a Ralph and a Tommy and an Ernest, and so many boys we'll have our own baseball team. And when they grow up they'll be the Havana Kings, and they'll beat the Yankees, you wait and see. Although I don't know if they'll beat the Almendares. That might be asking too much."

She laughed for the first time in weeks.

"Darling, you make me so happy. I hope it turns out like that."

"Of course it will. We won, didn't we? If we did that, we can do anything."

"You really think so?" she asked, once again drifting off to that far shore where the sleeping walk hand in hand with the departed.

"I know so, sweetheart. Nothing can stand in our way. We are the chosen people."

Irma closed her eyes and ordered her mouth to say, It's a sin to even think that, but her lips barely moved and all Morgan could hear was the one word that for him had no meaning because he had never known its opposite.

"Sin," she mumbled, her head turning on the pillow, thin lips falling open to reveal her purplish, doctored tongue.

"Sin," repeated Morgan, then he added, knowing she could no longer hear him. "Sin is all we know, child; sin is all we are."

✖ ✖ ✖

The newsroom of *Revolución* was practically the only place in Havana where Morgan did not stand out. In the last two days he had discovered that everywhere in town the *barbudos,* the bearded ones from the hills like himself, provoked choruses of compliments, hailstorms of handshakes, and rounds of drinks that Morgan, like all the others, ascetically turned down. In a city of more than a million people, where tens of thousands had become overnight revolutionaries, the guerrillas walking the streets with the dazed look of lottery winners were the real article, the true nuggets in a pan of political debris.

But here, in the building that once housed the political organ of the Batista regime, guerrillas like Morgan were the rule rather than the drifting exception. From the receptionist in her fatigues, with the inescapable red-and-black armband, to the editors poring over the news copy, to the reporters waving their pages for pickup or answering phones with the confidence of ultimate winners, everyone seemed a recent transplant from the battlefront.

Morgan was aware that these were 26th of July people, that they had fought in another front under another command for another purpose, yet he could not help feeling a kinship, a camaraderie of arms with these rail-thin, febrile people trying to put out the third issue of the official newspaper of the *movimiento.*

The sharp-featured receptionist, sloe eyes surrounded by rings of insomnia, looked up from her book.

"How can I help you, *Comandante?*" she asked, noticing the single golden star on Morgan's epaulette.

"Excuse me, please. I am looking for one Laura Fernández."

The girl was puzzled for a moment, trying to coordinate the image of the burly Yanqui with her knowledge of the leaders of the rebel army.

"Laura Fernández," repeated the girl, pronouncing it *Lah-oo-rah* instead of Morgan's anglicized *Law-rah.* She turned to a card index file beside her. Finding a number, she picked up the phone, then dialed, motioning at Morgan to have a seat.

"Un momento, por favor."

Morgan remained standing before her, his nerves too frazzled for him to sit. He glanced down at the girl's book, a collection of poems by someone named Pasternak.

"Compañero," said the girl into the phone, "we have here a Yanqui *comandante* who is looking for some assistance. Yes, Carlos, an Americano. Oh, really? I didn't know that. Yes. Fine. *Gracias."*

She hung up the phone. Morgan nodded at the book.

"Is he a good writer?"

She shrugged.

"He's Russian, what can I tell you? Very deep. Do you know his work?"

"No, I have not had much time to read lately."

"Of course, I am so silly. Well, he wrote this novel about the Russian Revolution. Very poetic, but his characters were not convincing. They wanted to embody too much the spirit of their time and they lost their individuality. It was only in the vignettes of ordinary life that he captured the essence of his time. You know, just when he wasn't really trying. Like life, I guess. But his politics were all wrong. He does not recognize the leadership that a cadre can provide for the transformation of a society. A CIA man, I think. But he is a wonderful poet."

A small, slight man in rebel fatigues surged out from the thriving crowd, stepped up to the desk. With his wide hazel eyes and freckled nose, he briefly reminded Morgan of Ted O'Shaughnessy, the MP who had arrested him in Kyoto years before. Without warning, the man threw his slender arms around Morgan in a tropical *abrazo*.

"Comandante Morgan, the victor of Cienfuegos! I am so pleased to meet you!" said the little man, stepping back to vigorously shake Morgan's hand while scanning his features with sharp interest. "I am Carlos Franqui, the editor of the newspaper. We have heard so much about you, about your prowess in the field, your taking of Topes de Collantes, without a doubt one of the most glorious pages of the Cuban revolution. In fact, we'd been meaning to look you up to see if we could interview you for our Sunday section on *comandantes* of the revolution."

"Many thanks," said Morgan, not certain how to handle the effusiveness that flowed from the man. "I will cooperate, but really my life is not too interesting. Many others are better."

"Nonsense," said Franqui, guiding Morgan into the newsroom, "you are a prime example of the kind of international cooperation that we wish to promote in the new Cuba. Please, this way."

"Excuse me?" said Morgan, not understanding what else Franqui had said in the typical hurried speech of Cubans.

"I said," repeated Carlos Franqui more slowly, "that we are in the fore-front of a generational transformation of values that will sweep across the face of Western civilization, *Comandante,* and it is up to us to fashion the intellectual structures that will guide the people along the path of enlightenment and revolution."

"Yes, of course, the revolution. That's why we fought in the hills. But the war, it is over, *Comandante,* " said Morgan, following Franqui down a hallway lined with signed pictures of movie stars on the left—Humphrey

Bogart, Errol Flynn, Johnny Weissmuller—and gilt-framed photos of political leaders on the right—Franco, Mussolini, Napoleon crossing the Alps.

"Hah!" replied Franqui, opening the glass door to a conference room already filled with restless Cubans wired on coffee, cigarettes, and rhetoric. "The real revolution is just beginning."

"OK, very good, but I am only looking for Laura Fernández," whispered Morgan to Franqui, who closed the door behind them.

"Leave it open, Carlitos, there shouldn't be any secrets in a people's revolution," said one of the men in back, puffing on a cigar.

"Besides, his smoke is killing me!" added a strawberry blonde woman with big black-frame glasses.

"Fine, we'll leave it open then," said Franqui, who whispered back to Morgan, "Laura will be here shortly; she went out to get some supplies."

"You are sure it is Laura? Laura the sister of Wilfredo?" asked Morgan, feeling his heart grow giddy, as though pitching down a flight of stairs.

"*Sí, muchacho,* the same, don't worry." Franqui put his arm around Morgan's shoulders. "*Compañeros,* I have here with me one of the leaders of the Segundo Frente del Escambray, Major William Morgan. A good revolutionary and an Americano, to boot!"

"Hey, *Comandante,* how come you're not at the palace with Chomón and Cubelas and all the Directorio people?" asked the man with the fat cigar, a thin-faced mulatto sporting a sly grin.

"We in the Frente fought for the end of Batista," said Morgan, realizing even as he spoke that his words betrayed a childlike faith he did not feel. "Now the people can decide who will govern in Cuba."

"*Comandante,* why did the Frente split up with the Directorio?"

"I do not know all the details. It was a tactical decision of the leadership. I was in the Sierra with Fidel at that time. Fighting," he added, although it was evident everyone wanted to know everything about the politics and nothing about the combat.

"Is it true that you have stolen weapons from the Twenty-sixth of July movement for your own forces?" asked the young blonde by the door.

"Excuse me?" said Morgan, surprised by the accusation. Weapons stolen?"

"Yes, that you are stockpiling weapons."

"Weapons?" said Morgan. "*Armas para qué?*" Weapons for what?

Everyone in the room laughed at Morgan's honesty, amused by the perplexed expression on his face. The blonde in the green fatigues whispered to the swarthy, stocky man beside her, who nodded in agreement. She wrote down Morgan's response in a notepad, with an arrow—for F.

The Great American

A photographer came out of the back room and snapped away as the crowd peppered Morgan with a host of questions—why had he joined the revolution, what were his ideological principles, how did he feel about U.S. intervention in Latin America?—a whirlwind of political queries that Morgan tried to answer as best he could. Yes, he was a democrat who had joined the revolution to fight a horrible tyranny, and of course he was opposed to all kinds of foreign intervention in a country's internal affairs, but all the while he was thinking, What did that have to do with Cuba, and besides, where was Laura? As if reading his mind, Franqui finally raised his hand.

"*Compañeros,* Major Morgan is here for a friendly visit, not an inquisition. We have enough for our purposes."

Ohs of disappointment filled the room, but Franqui insisted, "We can talk with him later, although I must warn you all I hold first rights to any in-depth interview. I think it's time we hold our editorial meeting. We have a newspaper to publish. So, Major, if you will please have a seat."

Morgan walked to the back, found an empty metal folding chair next to a pimply youth with a dimpled chin. He shook Morgan's hand.

"Severo Sarduy," he said. "Welcome to the real revolution, *Comandante.*" And with that the man closed his eyes and fell asleep in his chair, leaning his head on the wall, waking only for the obligatory round of thimble-sized paper cups of espresso a young girl brought in a tray. Sarduy belted his, raised his bushy eyebrows up and down like a flag, then fell right back asleep.

Morgan sat quietly, trying his best to follow the convoluted arguments around the table, understanding all the words but not their meaning, as though there were a hidden text that needed a key or translator.

What happened to our slogans—*Long live free Cuba, Viva el Segundo Frente, Death to Batista?* What do these people want?

He examined their faces. None over forty, most in their late teens and early twenties, in all the motley shades and races of the country. Franqui himself was the picture of a Londonderry dude; his second in command, a short fellow with a goatee and perverse eyes, was a Chinese half-breed who was now invoking the need for a national film institute to promote the goals of the revolution.

It occurred to him that these were not the simple Cubans—if such creatures existed—who parroted lines, postured with rifles, and proclaimed themselves Fidel's faithful followers. These were the wise men in the temple, gathered to slice, quarter, and weigh the body of the fallen regime. They were making the future in this very room, with their talk of reports on agrarian reform, urban malnutrition, confiscated property,

307

corrupt reporters, cultural imperialism, historical wrongs that had to be righted right now, as though the revolution were a tropical flower that blooms, lives, and dies in a day and a night.

This is not what I fought for, thought Morgan. What did you fight for? He remembered his own words, written that day up in the Escambray when the struggle seemed as uphill as the craggy mountains: "Here I can realize the dedication to justice and liberty it takes for men to live and fight as these men do, whose only possible pay or reward is a free country."

But was that really the answer? Or had he fought really out of a sense of guilt, of expiation for the wrong he'd done?

"*Comandante,* the person you were asking for has returned," said Franqui to Morgan, reading a message someone had handed him. "She's waiting for you in the supply room."

※ ※ ※

Morgan stopped a few feet away, hoping that in some telepathic fashion she would realize he was alive and breathing just an arm's length behind her. Hearing her speak in her soft voice, watching the long russet curls still fall like a veil on her shoulders, catching a hint of her scent of verbena and gardenia, Morgan felt transported, suffused with a delirious happiness that made his blood boil with desire. He stood there silently, trembling with longing and lust, absorbed in the intensity of his happiness, feeling as though nothing else had mattered or could matter as much as that small-boned, fine-featured woman before him gesturing at a box of bird feed, discussing with another, plainer *compañera* the best way to capture a dove and make it return, gratefully, to the hand that feeds it.

"But that's not going to be the problem here," said Laura, who stopped talking the moment the other girl nodded at Morgan standing behind Laura. She turned and Morgan saw her face for the first time in years.

"It's you," said Laura flatly, not wanting to notice how Morgan was seething with desire. "They told me you were here."

"We'll talk later," said the other girl, picking up the containers of bird feed.

"Alright, Isabel."

The girl walked past Morgan, nodding her head again in greeting, then darted out of the supply room to the hall.

"Don't forget to ask the Chinese; they know a lot about training pigeons!" called out Laura at the vanishing figure of the girl, who shook her head in assent, then exited down the hall. Laura fixed her quicksilver eyes on Morgan at last.

"You're thinner," she said slowly, biting her lower lip.

Morgan stood before her, feeling an odd itch under his skin, the grave pounding of his blood in his eardrums like the beat to a song he once loved. Although he strained to hear the music, the notes did not flow as they once did before this small slip of a woman, this girl, really, who also stood transfixed in silence, waiting for his next move. Something had happened. Some other obstacle had risen before them, more powerful and insurmountable than death even (for in death you always find solace in the last image of the loved one, while in life disappointment and deception are painted in colors too bright to ignore).

Out of the corner of his eye Morgan saw the stacks of paper supplies, the cardboard boxes and reams of typing paper, the inks, ribbons, and cartridges essential to a newsroom, all arranged in stacks of boxes, like building blocks at a construction site.

"You're thinner too," he said in English, the banality of his own words shocking him.

Is this all we have to say to each other? Will we talk about the weather next?

"Yes, in the mountains, the life is very hard, you know?" she replied, also in English, in the singsong cadence that once drove him to spasms of paroxysm. "But I learned English. I worked for the Radio Rebelde."

"And I learned the Spanish," said Morgan, finally smiling at her hoydenish expression, yet knowing that it was all wrong, that this friendliness was just good manners. Awkwardness filled the silence again.

"How did you know I was here?" she asked in Spanish, her eyes now on the doorway.

"I went to your house in El Cerro. Your little cousin told me. He is grown now, a big muchacho."

"Yes, he grew a lot while we were away."

"I thought for a long time that you dead," he went on, realizing it would be far easier for him to speak in English, yet offering his own weakness in Spanish as a token for a feeling he no longer knew how to express.

"Yes, that is what I was thinking too," she said, playing with a curl that draped lifeless on her shoulder.

"I think of you always," he went on, with infinite anguish, uncertain of what to do or say that would return to him the vibrant creature he remembered.

"I also thought of you. The story of your adventures reached our ears even in the Sierra."

She took a shallow breath as though to say, There it is, take it, let's be done with it this and get on with our life, the country is waiting for us, we are grains of sand in history's tidewater.

Where is it? What has happened here? How can two people who loved each other so much meet and know that everything is wrong? Maybe it's nerves. Yes, maybe that's it. It's got to be that. She can't have forgotten me so soon. She couldn't have felt less than I did, when she was all that life had to offer me. Maybe if I kissed her. Yes, that's it. Maybe if I kiss her it will all come back.

Morgan moved in close, bent down to touch her lips with his. Laura moved her face away, almost as if ashamed, then threw her slender arms around his broad back, hugged him tight.

"*Ay, Guillermo,* so much has happened," she said in the sibilant Spanish of brave dreams and sorry hearts.

"It doesn't matter, sweetheart. You're here, you're alive, that's what counts," he said, continuing their dialogue in their respective languages. He ran his fingers down her silky curls, feeling he was touching the past and the future but not the present, that at this very moment when he held her it was someone else he held in his arms, it was someone else who now started to cry, it was someone else who pushed his face away as he tried to lap up her tears.

"No, don't, it's not right, I shouldn't let you," she said.

"Please, sweetheart, I don't want you to cry."

"What do you care?"

"What do I care? I care for you more than the world, Laura. Not a day has gone by since I last saw you that you haven't been in my thoughts."

She looked up at him, her face a river of tears, an awful pain bursting through that she tried to hide but couldn't, because she didn't know how to cap the torrent of feelings gushing out of her.

"Liar!" she screamed, sobbing, slapping him with a stinging hand. "Liar! Cheat! *Mentiroso!*"

Morgan touched his cheek where the first slap had fallen, his mind a welter of clashing emotions.

"Where were you when I needed you?" she screamed, lashing out at him. "Where were you? Where were you, you son of a bitch, *hijo de puta, maldita la madre que te parió!*"

Morgan was taken aback by her fury, which seemed to spring from some deep well of resentment and despair. He was certain that she had made a mistake, that some envious tongue had whispered things in her ear.

Does she know about Irma? Of course, that's why, she thinks I forgot about her. If I tell her how I feel she'll see how things are, she's really making a mistake.

Morgan tried to hush her, at first with the broad, expansive gestures of a parent quieting down a nervous child, a pat, a hug, a furtive kiss. When she unleashed her anger, throwing objects at him—ribbons, papers, boxes of pens and erasers, a heavy pencil sharpener—he pressed her against his chest, whispering his love even while she raged like a fury.

"No, sweetheart, calm down, it's all nerves. You'll be all right."

"I hate you! I hate you! Why didn't you die in the fucking hills! Get your paws off me, you fucking animal!"

The commotion drew a number of people, their heavy boots resounding in the hallway, the excited hubbub of women's voices asking what was going on, some saying, "Someone should get that man off her." "But he's a *comandante,*" someone else said, then Franqui himself got in between Morgan and Laura, pushing Morgan back as one of the women dragged Laura away, still trying to break free and claw out his eyes.

"I'll kill you myself, you son of a bitch! I'll kill you, I swear!"

The men in the group led Morgan out of the room while the women tended to Laura, who broke into disconsolate tears when surrounded by their questioning chorus. What did I do? Morgan asked himself. What happened here?

Franqui took out a handkerchief, handed it to Morgan.

"Here, *Comandante,* you're bleeding."

Morgan touched his cheek, looked in a mirror. Her fingernails had scratched deep in his cheek, the blood dripping into his beard.

"What is the matter with her? I just talked, that is all," apologized Morgan.

"It's the war. It has been a long struggle for all of us," said Franqui. "Her husband died in Santa Clara, fighting with Che. I think that has really affected her. Perhaps you should leave now. I'll talk to her later. We'll let you know."

"I'm at the Sevilla Biltmore," were Morgan's last words, tentative, sorrowful, as he walked out of the building.

Out in the streets of El Vedado, the carnival atmosphere of a city in the thrall of revolution still prevailed. From all the windows you could hear the broadcast of Fidel's slow procession up the country, passing through Santiago and Camagüey and Santa Clara and now nearing Matanzas, a slow triumphal procession in which the entire country threw itself at his feet, awaiting the word that would start the new era of justice and equality.

But Morgan did not hear. The only thing on his mind as he stumbled down the cool street was why. Why had she rejected him, why had she stopped loving him? He did not know the answer would never be fully explained and that like the sultry air of the land, the beating of the sun, and the sparkling ocean off the coast, it was a natural phenomenon, simply the way things were and would be from then on.

This is what he told himself: It's just a case of nerves, that's all. She'll be back to normal soon. If she loves me we'll find a way. It'll work itself out. She needs time, that's all. Just a little time. That's all she needs, a little time.

And so he waited, and in the waiting found himself a new life by and by.

Chapter

2

It was a French Normandy mansion in the Miramar district, left vacant by one of the departed followers of Batista. Driving by with El Gato on his way to the beach, Morgan noticed the mob trooping in and out of the open doors like a file of ants carrying crumbs back to the nest. On the flowing front lawn, attempting to stop the looting by forcing people to put down their load, even as others retrieved it and ran away with it, stood a helpless Max Weinberg.

"Stop the jeep, Gato!" said Morgan, who almost did not recognize Max, dressed in the national workman's uniform of indigo blue cotton shirt and pants.

The vehicle rolled to a halt next to the statue of a turbaned Arab, occupying the place of the usual black postilion. Morgan, El Gato, and two other guerrillas slowly came off the jeep, making a show of cocking their weapons. On seeing the *barbudos,* the looters—black and brown people who'd been singing as though in some Santería *bembé* to the gods of greed and revenge—stopped in their tracks. A few smart ones put down their booty and quickly slunk away, not wanting to deal with the only authority that counted in the land, a loaded gun.

Max sighed with relief on spotting Morgan.

"I told you someone would stop them," Max told an old black man with Asian features leaning on an old ebony cane.

"Boy, am I glad to see you!" said Max then, extending his hand to Morgan, who did not shake it. Morgan's men fanned out, ordering the looters to put down the radios, the vases, the Coromandel screen, and Spanish paintings they had been so gleefully stealing.

"What's going on here?" asked Morgan gruffly.

"This is Boyeros's house," replied Max, his forehead beaded with sweat. "These people broke into it when they found out he's gone to Miami. They think he was with Batista, but we know better, don't we, William?"

Morgan looked around, his face imperiously cold. He quickly counted more than twenty looters, some of whom, seeing no immediate danger, had picked up their booty again and were walking away with it.

"Fire a couple of rounds in the air," said Morgan. El Gato raised his machine gun, squeezed the trigger. The tearing blast of the bullets was a drum roll to attention. Everyone turned to Morgan, who climbed on the jeep's hood.

"People, listen!" hollered Morgan in Spanish. "This house is now the property of the revolution! We have . . . "

He turned to Max. "How do you say seize?" Max told him.

"We have seized this house in the name of the Second Front of the Escambray! Put down those things or face the revolutionary justice!"

A shirtless strapping mulatto, his left arm sliced off at the elbow, approached the jeep waving his mutilated stump in Morgan's face.

"This is what Batista's people did to me!" he hollered back. "I deserve compensation! This is the people's justice!"

Morgan was momentarily moved by the man's plight until he noticed the shriveled muscles around the maimed arm and the strong right pectoral developed over a lifetime of compensation. Morgan climbed down from the vehicle, picked up a fallen feather duster off the ground, and handed it to the man.

"What is this for?" asked the man.

"To frighten off flies from the shit you tell, hombre. You lost that arm in accident, not torture, many years ago. Now go, get out of here, go, go!" said Morgan, shooing away the man with the barrel of his gun.

Abashed at being found out, ridiculed by the laughing crowd, the man drifted to the edge of the lawn. Looking back, shaking the duster like a weapon, he shouted, "My cousin is with the *rebeldes* too, Yanqui! One day you'll pay for this!"

El Gato raised his weapon, let off a round of bullets right over the man's head. The man shrank his head into his shoulders and ran off, yelping like a frightened cur. Everyone in the crowd laughed again.

"*Compañeros,* this house is now the house of the government," Morgan told them. "Please put everything inside again."

The looters looked at one another, shrugged, then began to return the items to the house with the same alacrity with which they'd taken them out. As they left many shook Morgan's hand, explaining they would have never done what they did—let themselves get caught in the madness of the moment—had they known a hero of the revolution would be living there, and when would he and his family be moving in? Morgan patted them all on the shoulder, saying he'd be moving in soon and no harm done, in a few cases writing down the names of people wanting jobs for themselves or their relatives in the new revolutionary government. Max shook his head in amazement.

"I would have never believed it," he said.

"That's what happens when you appeal to the people's best instincts," said Morgan.

"Sure. As long as you got a tommy gun to make the point."

Max led Morgan on a tour of the mansion, now half emptied of its glittering contents. The old half-breed Asian, who appeared to be a house servant, introduced himself as Manuel, pointing out the places where the looters had run wild, smashing the crystal vases, hauling away the antique Sèvres china, the Lalique lamps, the Christofle silverware.

"The boors even scattered the lock of Napoleon's hair to the wind," said the servant gravely, as if the crowds had desecrated not just a house but an old and famous chapel. "You know Mr. Boyeros had the only lock of the emperor's hair in all of Cuba."

"No, I did not know that," said Morgan, who couldn't decide whether to laugh or cry at such outrageous conduct.

"Fortunately I managed to sweep up most of them off the carpet. But I'm afraid some hairs from Mr. Boyeros's shih tzu got mixed in with them. I don't think anybody will know, do you?"

"I do not think so. I promise I will say nothing."

"Thank you, *Comandante*. You are most understanding of a servant's dilemma," answered the man in all seriousness.

"They took the pictures too?" asked Morgan, noticing the smudged outline of the picture frames on the walls above the ornate furniture.

"No, those were stored by Señor Boyeros. He took the Zurbarán to Miami, but the *Virgin of Remedios* by Murillo he gave to the Marist Fathers. The *Court Jugglers* by Watteau he gave to Judge Dorticós Torrado for his study."

Manuel turned yellow feline eyes on Morgan.

"For safekeeping, you understand. A loan, not a gift. Mr. Boyeros anticipates returning soon."

"Really? How soon?" asked Max, who had so far silently followed in the servant's wake. Morgan was amused by the old man's haughty detachment, hobbling up the sweeping marble stairs, its long Besarabian runner half torn by the greedy crowds.

"There's the crystal chandelier," he pointed out with unwavering index finger. "From the palace of Prince Talleyrand. Señor Boyeros was always very proud of that. Only one of its kind in Cuba, you know. When will he return?"

Manuel stopped at the head of the stairs, regally looking over the plundered remains of his kingdom, the castle whose secrets he alone knew. For once it is mine, he thought; after all these years it is mine, and I cannot hold on to it.

"Take it, Manuel," Boyeros had told him, handing him the keys. "You and your wife can have full use of it until I come back."

"Señor, my wife is no longer with us," said Manuel solemnly, even as he packed the last Thurnbull & Asher shirt into the leather case.

Boyeros had stared, mouth agape, his ties still in his hands, unable to believe what he had just heard.

"What are you saying, Manuel? Did she go back to Matanzas?"

"No, señor. Unfortunately she had a stroke while you were out in the sugar mill in Oriente, and she is gone from us," said Manuel, stiffer than usual, taking down the fine white cotton robe from its hanger in the bathroom. "Perhaps the señor will take his favorite robe as well? I am sure we can find room for it."

That's just the way it should have been, he thought now. What would have been the use of burdening him with the grisly details of Mireya's death, the way she had hacked and retched and gasped for air, the way she passed away while holding my hand in the ambulance? All those years of faithful companionship, waiting patiently for the moment when we'd go back to the farm, away from the city, and I kept telling her, No, no, I can't possibly leave Señor Boyeros; he needs me to run his life. And now, when finally we could retire in peace, she runs ahead of me into the beyond, and Señor Boyeros leaves too, and I am left behind, unable to guard even the relics of our existence.

"Señor Boyeros didn't say," replied Manuel, returning to the hurting present. "But I am certain it won't be long before he returns. Cuba needs men like him, to protect us from our own worst instincts."

※ ※ ※

Later, in the library, Max told Morgan he'd been meeting with members of the Confederation of Cuban Workers in his apartment when Manuel called, pleading for help.

"Didn't even have time to change. I was showing them how this outfit could be made into a uniform for the militia."

"Like the minutemen in Concord?"

"Precisely! That's what I told these people, but they don't know much about American history. It would be a new concept down here, armed militias to defend the revolution. Take power away from the army and give it to the people."

He stopped, smiled, very proud of himself. "The way I figure it, the more guns there are out there, the harder it will be for the commies to take over. Just like back home, right?"

Morgan shook his head in amused puzzlement.

"You're the voice of the people?"

"I remind you that I am Cuban too."

"And a CIA agent."

"One thing doesn't take away from the other. Besides, a lot of us in the company were for Fidel."

"I thought you were for us in the Frente."

"Oh, I was! But you know, anything to get Batista out."

"That doesn't make sense."

"Consistency is the hobgoblin of small minds, William."

"You're not even a real Cuban, Max, you're a Jew."

"That's where you're mistaken. My Jewishness is precisely what makes me supremely Cuban. If you ask in any Cuban family, there's always a Jew somewhere. The first president of the Republic in Arms was a Jew. The greatest businessmen, like the Lobos, are Jewish as well. Some people even say Columbus himself was a Jew, so you tell me. If there's anything that makes me out to be less than the usual Cuban, it's that I'm half American. Somebody treat you different because of that?"

"Yeah, they always think I know everything because I'm a Yanqui."

"Terrible, isn't it? I mean, living up to those expectations?"

Manuel shuffled in, bearing tall glasses of orange soda, which he set on the inlaid jade table before them.

"And just when will the *comandante* be moving in?" asked Manuel.

※ ※ ※

Over the next few days Morgan kept feeling there was something deeply wrong in the country, something that the panacea of victory could not cure. In the drive to build a new order, laws were being discarded, basic human principles of decency and fairness ignored. The only thing that counted was blind allegiance to the revolution. A burning lust for revenge shook the country, as though the tumbrils of today could wipe away the tortures of the past.

At night, when he visited Irma at the hospital, he would watch on television the impromptu executions of suspected Batistianos by so-called defenders of the revolution. Men, women, even youngsters no older than sixteen who had collaborated with the old order were dragged out of their homes and their belongings sacked, while the crowds beat them to death with sticks or the authorities lined them up against walls and executed them. Even Raúl Castro was caught in an act of bloody retribution. As news cameras rolled, a captured army colonel was brought before the maximum leader's kid brother. Raúl slapped the man, then took out his sidearm and fired three shots at the prisoner's head, pieces of the brain flying out in bloody plugs of gray matter. Raúl then turned to the lens and smiled.

"It's the lancing of the pus, William," said Eloy one afternoon in his mother's kitchen. Sipping a *cafecito* and smoking another of his Pall Malls, Menoyo shook his head in desperate acceptance.

"All the ill humors have to come out so the country can heal," he added sententiously.

"Then what is the difference between them and us, Eloy? They did the same thing too!"

"There's a big difference, William. They did it for their own aims, we do it for the people."

"But they are people, too! They have rights!"

"Did they remember the rights of the people they killed and tortured?" replied Menoyo. "Your own Thomas Jefferson said the tree of liberty must occasionally be watered with the blood of tyrants. Well, we had a drought and the tree almost died."

"And now we make it up with a flood of blood? No, Eloy, that is not fair. If these people are innocent? Then what? Oh, excuse me, señores, I made a mistake. Too bad I killed you. No, Eloy, we must be a country of laws."

Eloy smiled sardonically, in unconscious imitation of Che Guevara.

"These *are* our laws, William. Don't you ever forget that."

❊ ❊ ❊

Morgan's feelings of helplessness and disgust only increased after Fidel's arrival in Havana. People hung banners from their balconies reading, FIDEL, THIS HOUSE IS YOURS, while the movement's red-and-black banner waved from all windows and rooftops. On the covers of newspapers and magazines, Fidel's face was ringed with a halo, a redeemer for a country that craved to be saved from itself.

When he entered the city, hundreds of thousands swarmed his jeep, hoping to catch a glimpse of their deliverer. When he walked among them, the crowds parted like the faithful before the prophet. And when he spoke from the balcony of the Presidential Palace—abandoned the day before by the Directorio, which realized it was useless to fight the pull of history—when he addressed his Cubans from the seat of the hated dictatorship, his name was repeated by the gathered faithful and resounded throughout Havana and all of Cuba—*Fidel, Fidel, Fidel*—until the entire country seemed to be delivering itself to him with open blouse and dripping thighs.

When Castro spoke of the reported arms cache of the Directorio, Morgan felt chills run up and down his spine on hearing him repeat Morgan's very same words at *Revolución*. Why should the Directorio need weapons, now that the will of the people was so clear? When the people themselves had imposed their will through the actions of the revolutionary leadership and the rebel army, what was the need for arms? To fight whom? Arms for what?

That night, as the round-the-clock news coverage continued, Castro entered army headquarters, the infamous Camp Columbia already occupied by the popular *comandante* Camilo Cienfuegos. In the middle of his speech he turned, as though apologizing or unsure of his own popularity, and asked him, *"Voy bien, Camilo?"*—how am I doing, Camilo?—and the lanky guerrilla answered, "You're doing just fine, Fidel." At the end of his speech a flock of pigeons were released, and a single turtle dove came and perched itself on Fidel's shoulder, as if drawn there by the spirit of peace and reconciliation—or skillful training.

Morgan knew then without a doubt that his adopted country was firmly in the hands of one man alone and that henceforth there could never be a true revolution in Cuba without Fidel, for he was the revolution personified, all his propaganda efforts finally paying off big. He was history, he was Jesus, he was long-suffering Cuba.

※ ※ ※

Morgan had fallen asleep in the chair next to Irma's bed when the phone rang, waking him. He drowsily lifted the receiver.

"Hello?"

"William? This is Laura. I have to see you."

Chapter

3

Morgan pulled up his jeep outside the entrance to the club shortly after seven. Located in the basement of an office building in the El Vedado district, the nightclub offered a very discreet facade to passersby. Morgan double-checked the address to make sure he was in the right place, then spotted the blue neon numbers next to a set of narrow stairs.

Morgan was just discovering Havana, its kaleidoscope of hidden restaurants, stores, and clubs still a welcome surprise. Like all great cities, Havana had two faces: the loud, garish Las Vegas tart that tourists had known for decades, the fleshpots of Tropicana, Sans Souci, the Riviera, coexisting side by side with the right royal and ancient city of San Cristóbal de la Habana, redone by French-inspired designers of the late nineteenth century and Modernist architects of the thirties. The two cities, the native and the foreign, the slatternly and the plebeian, bore little connection to each other, visitors to one rarely mingling with denizens of the other. The club that Morgan sought was of the latter kind, where few people spoke English, nobody drank martinis, and *turista* was just a word in the dictionary.

A black boy in tatters approached him.

"*Oiga, Comandante,* I'll keep an eye on the jeep for you for a quarter."

Morgan was amused. "To keep an eye for what, muchacho? There is no more police giving the tickets."

The rail-thin boy split open a full set of pointy pearly whites.

"It's the counterrevolutionaries, *Comandante.* They are everywhere, you know. We have to root out those Batistianos. Maybe they'll come back and steal your car if nobody's watching."

"And if you be watching?"

"Obviously I wouldn't let them, *Comandante*. They'd have to take my life first."

Morgan dug in his pocket for a quarter. The boy took it willingly, then gazed firmly into Morgan's eyes.

"*Gracias*. But what I said goes, *Comandante*. They have to kill me first. Like Fidel says, we are building a new country. I'm not going to let anybody take that away from us."

❊ ❊ ❊

Morgan went down the narrow stairs to the entrance under an archway. He pushed through a beaded curtain and entered a different world.

Pale pink neon letters shone against a stark white wall: LA CITA. The date, the appointment, the rendezvous.

The cigarette girl at the counter, a tall thin woman with ginger hair, smiled seductively at Morgan, batting her eyelashes so steadily as to be almost sending signals in code.

"*Bienvenido, Comandante*," she said in a throaty voice, then pointed at another beaded curtain in another arched doorway, the tinkling spare notes of a jazzy piano easing out from the other side.

Morgan walked through, expecting the boozy smell of rum and whiskey, the sweet alcoholic mash that shakes your hand on entering a saloon. Instead he was practically assaulted by a smell of powder, perfume, and peppermint gum, as if he'd entered a girls-only malt shop. The mostly empty tables were reflected off the mirrored walls at the far end of the room, where a grinning, totally bald black man in a tux played the piano to a handful of customers. At the bar, a few lonely women sipped crème de menthes and grasshoppers, staring moodily at their reflection in the Polar beer signs.

The hostess, a honey-colored woman whose green silk dress matched the tint of her wide eyes, led Morgan to a small table with a *Reservado* sign. She removed it graciously, whispered so as not to disturb the pianist.

"Your party will be here shortly; they just called."

"*Gracias*," said Morgan, ordering a scotch and soda, feeling like a blundering bear in the small narrow seats and minuscule table with a single rosebud in a vase, a candle, and an ashtray. Inside the ashtray a matchbox with the words *La Cita* in pink and a drawing of a harlequin mask next to Salvador Dalí's dripping, Surrealist clock.

The pianist nodded at Morgan, eyes twinkling as though he were about to play just for him, then bent over the keyboard, and with the greatest delicacy imaginable, launched into his song.

A few notes, reminiscent of a Scott Joplin rag, then another turn and

Morgan heard echoes of Mitteleuropa, the emotion-laden piano songs of a generation that knew its best days were behind it and the future held only loss, chaos, and blood. The pianist, his bald black pate shining under the spotlight, righted himself up on the bench, smiling like a wistful Satchmo. He sang in a high voice—almost but not quite a falsetto—seemingly about to break from the weight of emotion. Morgan noticed that the few couples in the place stopped their conversation, paying undivided attention to the ballad of painful love.

Yo bien sé que estás herido.
Cien saetas al oído
Te silbaron y traidora
Una fue la que te hirió.
Que te libres solo quiero
De ese dardo traicionero
Que tu vida soñadora
Sin piedad envenenó.

I know well that you were hurt.
A hundred arrows whistled
By your ear, and the traitor
Was the one who wounded you.
I want only your release
From that dart of betrayal
That your life of dreams
Without pity has poisoned.

"Hello, William."

Laura bent over Morgan, kissed him on the cheek, squinted a smile, then sat across from him. As always he felt his heart skip, his ears pound, his skin tingle, his breath come out in sharp, jagged mouthfuls. Laura wore a tailored black dress, a string of pearls around her slender neck, her hair drawn in a bow, her only makeup a coat of gloss on her thin lips.

"I'm going to a reception at the French embassy with Wilfredo later on," she said in Spanish, waving her hand at her dress for explanation. "He's with the Interior Ministry now, did you know? I'm so glad you came to see me, especially after the way I treated you last time. I'm so embarrassed. I hope you'll forgive me. I don't know what came over me."

Where did we go wrong, sweetheart? You know I would do anything for you. I would dance on my children's graves if I thought I could have you again the way we used to be.

"Don't think twice about it," he answered in English. "It was nerves. We've all had a hell of a time."

"*Sí*, it has been very difficult for the revolution. But our job is still not over."

"Really? What else is here to do beside set up the government?"

"*Mucho*. We didn't win just to let things go on the way they were before."

A curvy blonde with cat eyes glided to their table, a picture of purring femininity from her flowing ponytail to her tight red silk sheath to her four-inch stiletto heels.

"Can I bring you something to drink?" she asked in a little-girl voice. "It's on the house, *Comandante*, so order anything you want. Anything." She looked at Laura, smirked, and added, "Of course, if you'd rather order the Piper Heidsieck, we'd be delighted to do that too."

"I'll have a Cuba Libre," said Laura, suddenly cheerful.

"*Ay, m'ija*, with all the drinks there are in the world you go and pick the one we don't have to drink anymore. We are all free already, so let's celebrate, don't you think?" she said, waving large, squarish hands.

"I'll still have the Cuba Libre," retorted Laura, more amused then perturbed by the server's impertinence.

"OK. You want a lime with that, baby?"

"Please."

"And for you, *Comandante?*" she said to Morgan with a full, throaty voice, the little-girl voice vanished, as though to say, Command me and I will obey.

"This drink is OK, thank you," said Morgan. The waitress bent over the table, showing off the top of her breasts as she bent close to the drink.

"That's right," she said. "Excuse me, but I left my glasses home. I'll be right back with your order," she said, sashaying away with a wiggle in her walk.

Morgan smiled until the waitress turned in profile and he saw something suspiciously resembling an Adam's apple in the girl's throat.

It can't be! thought Morgan, watching the waitress place their order at the bar. In the dim pinkish glow of the club, Morgan scanned the faces of the people around him. All at once he realized that everyone he thought was male was actually female—from the suddenly not-so-masculine-looking bartender to the dark-suited gent with the two-tone shoes in the far corner, his girlfriend's head leaning nonchalantly on his shoulder while he played with his *mojito*. Conversely, all the women he had seen and admired—the waitress, the hostess in the green dress standing by the doorway making eyes at him, even the cigarette girl with her strong jaw—all were indubitably of the male persuasion.

Laura chuckled at Morgan's stunned reaction.

"I was wondering how long it was going to take you to catch on."

"Just what kind of place is this?" he mumbled, wanting to bolt for the door.

"The one place where I know no one in Havana will find us, darling," she said, wrapping her fingers around his hand, clutched firmly in a fist. "A transvestite bar. All the girls are boys, and all the boys are girls, and some are both at the same time."

Morgan shook his head.

"Our server?"

"Carolina? Goes by the name of Carlos during the day. Works at the power company."

"And that one?" Morgan nodded at the broad-shouldered barkeep, who winked at him.

"Machito? Her real name is Graciela. She's a receptionist at the phone company. If anybody ever knew about this, they'd all lose their day jobs. That's why it was safe here."

Morgan took it all in, stunned.

"How did you find out about his place?" he finally asked.

"It was one of our drop-off places against the tyrant. You know how Cuban men are; they think if they're around *maricones* that it will rub off on them. Nobody from Batista's people ever bothered us here. Frankly, sexually speaking, I don't think there's that much difference between the revolutionaries and Batista's hirelings. They're both very rigid, you know?"

Morgan chuckled at her bad joke.

"I suppose even the piano player?"

"Ah, no. He's a man, although he does go the other way. His name is Bola de Nieve. A wonderful composer, has a show on TV too. He's been playing here since the club opened."

Bola de Nieve, who had been playing a slow romantic bolero for the few couples on the dance floor, turned to his mike.

"Good evening, ladies and gentlemen. We have the pleasure of having with us one of the top commanders of the Second Front of the Escambray, *el comandante* Morgan," he announced gleefully, then waited a few seconds for the applause to die down.

"In your honor, *Comandante*, we'd like to play you the following song, which I think you will recognize."

Bola de Nieve bent over the keyboards and with a flourish began to play a familiar tune. However, Morgan couldn't identify it, even after he was dancing on the shiny parquet floor. Laura pressed her slender body into Morgan, the clouds of her perfume surrounding him once more.

"I missed you so much," she whispered in his ear, finally saying the words he wanted more than anything to hear. "I thought about you every day in the Sierra."

She clung to him, her lips brushing against his earlobes, the intensity of her words, the warmth of her skin, the longed-for promise of her sex becoming a philter, an intoxicating substance that Morgan knew this time could only lead to a disaster that he gratefully accepted as long as she was beside him once more. In that interstice of time, before her next words came out, Morgan knew he should stay away, step aside, go back to his home and his ailing wife. But just the thought of Irma's patience turned him against her, thinking that anybody who wanted him so badly could not possibly be worth having, before he was overwhelmed once more by Laura's smell, the rustling of her black dress, the coolness of her pearls shining in the hollow of her neck, and he heard the hissing in the grass and the boom of a thunderbolt in the distance and a voice that said sadly, Don't, but he closed his eyes and ears and felt only with that other organ now unfolding between his legs.

She said: "Every night in the Sierra when I fell asleep I dreamed of you."

She said: "Every night we were back in my bed in my apartment and you were doing what you wanted with me."

She said: "Every night I was burning because you weren't in my arms inside of me."

The name of the song Bola de Nieve played on the grand piano came back to him as Morgan drifted up the stairs with Laura out to the darkening street, where the sky had turned violet and the moon hung like a question mark against the umber sky—"Smoke Gets in Your Eyes," he told himself, smoke gets in your eyes as he drove down La Rambla with Laura by his side, her hand on his knee, her head pressed against his neck, showering kisses that felt like needles on his skin.

He knew he shouldn't, but he was powerless to protest as she guided his Jeep back through the winding alleys of Habana Vieja, the old Spanish city that knew him so briefly yet so well in that world that now was gone, a world where he had been both the hunter and the prey, terrifying in its possibilities, which had multiplied with the triumph of the revolution, which in retrospect seemed like the inevitable march of history after all, almost as predestined as his falling in love with Laura all over again, no matter the price.

He knew he should stop, he knew he should ask questions, but as they pulled into the small hotel lodged somewhere in the backstreets behind the baroque splendor of the palace she seized upon him, both hands grabbing him, demanding him with trancelike intensity and he wanted to say stop and he wanted to say tell me where you've come from tell me where you've been tell me why this has become the enthralling dream that drowns me in desire tell me why you hated me and now you love me tell me why you never reached me stop and tell me but don't tell me now not now it can all wait and is this the building?

Yes it is she says and she takes my hand once more and I feel I'm drowning but I'm really walking down the lobby past the leering night clerk and up to the second story the first green wooden door on the right and isn't it strange that these old doors put up by the Spanish are still standing and isn't it strange that these rooms can be so airy and so warm and isn't it strange that there's a little light by the bed and that the print of the Virgin is always hanging on the wall and oh my God yes she's taking off her clothes and now she's taking mine off as well and yes please do yes let me feel you yes sweetheart on your knees yes I'll do you too and the mattress is lumpy and the sheets are scratchy and her legs are riding around my neck and she turns like quicksilver under my hands and my tongue and her hair is like a soft lashing and God I missed you honey and I enter that warm wet world once more and there's a light behind that mirror and I know I'm riding purple lightning and she cries and she hurls insults my way like so many words of love but I just growl and am I in heaven or hell I don't know and I don't care and if I be damned so be it for we will all fall and die someday but until then I'm touching the sky and walking the clouds and the light comes back and God yes I want more more more let me have more more more down on your knees from behind and in the back and slip it here and open up and rain on me and hit me again and let me have let me have let me have let me have.

The old camera whirred noisily in the side room, hacking as it recorded Morgan and Laura on the hotel bed. Herminio, the operator, got close to the two-way mirror once again, incredulously watching the performance. "Like Superman," he muttered, remembering the famous porn star with the two-foot-long penis and the endurance of an elephant. You'd think this guy was black, not just another Yanqui. *Coño!*

He puffed on his cigarette a last time, dropped it to the floor, his own excitement almost too much to bear. He touched himself but decided he couldn't; he was still on the job and he wasn't going to screw that up for a little hand job. Trembling, he took out another cigarette from the pack, lit it with his Zippo.

"*Chico,* don't light the cigarette so close to the mirror, they're likely to see you," said the man's voice behind him.

Herminio turned around, stunned.

"I'm sorry, *Compañero,* I thought we were safe."

The man from the Interior Ministry strolled to the mirror, looked dispassionately at Morgan and Laura in bed.

"We are safe," said the man, "as long as it stays darker on this side. I hope you weren't doing that before."

"Of course not, *Compañero,*" said Herminio.

The man observed the sexual gymnastics in silence for a while.

"That *puta* is something else, *Compañero,*" said Herminio, finally.

"Yes, my sister always liked to fuck," said Wilfredo Fernández, taking one last look at the lovemaking, then abruptly heading for the door.

"Don't forget to send the reels tomorrow morning for safekeeping. This is ammunition for the future. Raúl will thank you for this."

"Thank you, *Compañero,* but I do it for the revolution."

"That's good. We need more patriots like you. We won't forget you."

"Thank you, *Compañero.*"

Herminio stood in attention as the chubby official walked out of the room, as silently as he had entered it.

My sister? wondered Herminio. What the fuck did he mean by that? How could this slut be his sister?

Chapter

4

Irma sat up in bed with a start, jolted awake by the sudden screeching of a bird. In the half gloom of the bedroom she could see through the open doors to the balcony, where the dark feathered creature, perched on the balustrade, cawed as though meaning to wake everyone in the house. Annoyed, without thinking, Irma threw one of her slippers at it. The bird, still squawking, flapped its large wings and flew against the giant yellow moon behind the cypresses in the garden.

Irma laughed at herself, surprised at her own reaction. She realized then that she was about to heal and that the weeks of bloodletting and fatigue were behind her. She glanced at the phosphorescent green hands of her bedside clock—12:30. She rose, put on a terry robe, and walked out to the balcony to retrieve her slipper.

The basalt tiles were cold and clammy underneath her bare feet, and she felt queasy, almost nauseous out of bed. It's the medication. I guess I'm not as well as I thought. She put on her slipper and looked down at the lush garden.

Rows of cypresses stood in hedges at the far end of the property, while close to the house a profusion of tropical trees—browneas, flamboyans, jacarandas—blossomed in multicolored flowers whose fallen fleshy petals covered the flagstone pathways. The full moon shone in the waters of the pool to the left. Beyond that, the tennis court, where Morgan's men had parked an armored vehicle they had confiscated in the last days of the revolution.

Irma could hear the noise of the men down in the kitchen, yellow light spilling onto the terrace and the garden furniture. She heard snatches of their conversation, phrases like *agrarian reform, Fidel must know,* *constitutional guarantees,* even as the clanking of the domino tiles resounded in the stillness of the night. Smiling, Irma chastised herself for the awful sense of dread that had overcome her when she had stepped out onto the balcony.

This is your home now, she told herself; what can happen to you here? You're on your way to recovery. Pretty soon you'll be a real wife to William once again, and things will change. The boys are downstairs, all is quiet, what could be wrong? You little fool.

She took a deep breath, relishing the dewy freshness of the night, the intoxicating smell of the jasmine espaliered against the near wall. She stretched and was about to return to bed when she spotted the man, crouched in the dark behind the jacaranda.

Startled, she hid behind a potted ficus to better observe the intruder. At first she could barely distinguish him, motionless behind the tree trunk, his figure blending in with the shadows so well that for a moment Irma thought she had imagined the whole thing and should simply return to bed. Then the man moved again, slinking out of his hideout with a peculiar movement, dragging a bag on the ground with his right arm.

Irma watched with horror as the intruder slithered onto the flagstone path, the light from the kitchen shining on his hate-filled face, his long naked torso, the useless appendage that had once been his left arm. Irma wanted to scream but could not find her voice as the man dragged the canvas bag out of the shadows and took out a still-writhing animal. The man raised the strangely silent creature against the moon, even as he mumbled unintelligibly to himself. It's a cat, thought Irma, stupefied by the sudden apparition. But why doesn't it scream? What is he doing to it?

The cat struggled to free itself, but the man's strong fingers held it prisoner. Then, in a flash, he swung the cat against the pavement with such strength that the animal lay momentarily stunned. The man's good arm flew out, and from somewhere he obtained a knife, which glinted mercilessly in the cold light of the moon, and he sank the blade into the cat's neck.

Irma screamed, finally finding her voice. The man, surprised, looked up at Irma, and in his wide-eyed demented glare she detected the curse of the devil's brood. He pushed back his lips in an obscene leer, raised the stump of his arm at Irma as though saying, You will be next. Irma screamed again and the man took flight, racing down the path behind the trees.

El Gato and three other men who had been playing dominoes rushed out of the kitchen door, weapons at the ready, their bodies silhouetted from the glare of the patio lights. They stumbled on the body of the animal, then glanced up at the balcony, where Irma now pointed at the far end of the garden.

"He went over there! There he goes!" she shouted as the intruder climbed the tall masonry wall.

One of the men let off a burst of gunfire from his submachine gun, but it fell wide of the mark, and the stalker leaped over and into the safety of the darkness beyond.

Later, after Irma had taken the tranquilizer Manuel had given her and she had returned to bed, Boyeros's old black servant went down to the kitchen to see for himself what had been the cause of so much turmoil. Hobbling in, leaning on his ebony wood cane, still dressed in his striped pajamas, Manuel found El Gato and the others examining the remains of a very large tabby. They had placed the corpse on the kitchen counter, the animal's blood trickling down in a thin stream to the stainless steel sink. The cat had been hogtied and its mouth sewn close with red thread, its eyes gouged out and a garland of dried herbs placed around its neck.

"The lady is still asking for her husband," said Manuel, looking over the ghastly sacrifice. "Does anybody know where the *comandante* is tonight?"

The men exchanged sarcastic looks.

"Same place where he's been every night for the last week," said one, a wild-looking red-haired boy of twenty, "performing his revolutionary duties."

"Yeah, in bed," said a second. "That little *mulata* is driving him crazy."

"Really? Who might that be?" asked Manuel as he lifted the dead animal's leg and saw a gaping wound where the cat's penis had been sliced off.

"Some *chiquita* from the newspaper *Revolución,*" said the red-haired boy. "She must be pumping him—for information, of course."

Morgan's men laughed, except for El Gato, who scowled in disgust.

"What the *comandante* does is none of your business, *Compañeros,*" said El Gato. "You're here to protect him, not criticize him."

The men, abashed, stopped their laughter and looked away, even though the red-haired boy tittered to himself, thinking of yet another clever pun.

"Do you know anything about this?" El Gato asked Manuel. "What does this witchcraft shit mean?"

Manuel took a pair of rubber gloves from the drawer, slowly slipped them on. He shook his head, feigning indifference even though he clearly recognized the curse. In *palo mayombé,* the branch of Santería that trucks with the devil and the souls of the dead, the slain black cat means a blight on you and your family for generations to come. The mutilation of the animal, particularly in its regenerative parts, signaled a lifetime of loss, poverty, and defeat. I will have to call the *babalawo* to cleanse this house, thought Manuel, and hope that the *comandante's* life spirit, his *aché*, is strong enough to ward off this spell.

"I don't know anything about this," sniffed Manuel, neatly wrapping the dead cat in a week old issue of the communist newspaper, *Hoy*. He tucked the flaps of the package in, then turned it over to the headlines: BATISTA'S PILOTS NOT GUILTY OF CRIMINAL ACTS! THE PEOPLE SCREAM FOR JUSTICE!

"I am a Catholic, what would I know of Santería?" he said, dropping the dead cat into the garbage pail. He picked up a sponge and wiped away the blood on the counter.

Outside, the crow cawed again.

※ ※ ※

Morgan stood off by himself on the bow of the ferryboat, smoking a cigarette while the vessel cut its way through the blue-green waters of Havana harbor, the spray rising up at times in great fans whenever the overcrowded vessel ran into a choppy swell. His head ringing from too much alcohol and too little sleep, he held on tight to the railing as the early morning sun draped the pewter-colored buildings of Old Havana with a golden veil.

It's over, he told himself; this can't go on. I have to stop seeing her; I can't do this to Irma anymore. I have to be a husband to her, no matter how I feel about Laura.

The night before he had picked Laura up at *Revolución* after the late edition had been put to bed, the two of them joining a group of the writers and photographers at an old haunt in the Colón neighborhood, behind the broad sea walk known as the Malecón. Surrounded by the loud, gregarious Cubans, Morgan had kept to himself at first, only too conscious of his lack of mastery of the language and more than a little jealous of the constant flow of puns, double entendres, and general sarcasm around him.

Naturally his silence had led the others into making him the target of their jibes, the big Yanqui with the heart of gold, the bananized defender of the revolution, the wayward nephew of *el tío* Sam. Morgan didn't mind the joshing and usually would throw a few digs himself, knowing that underneath it all they were comrades in the same struggle, people who had fought and succeeded and now had the world at their feet. Of course the beers and the rum helped; they made the nightlong procession of whores, pimps, and flaming homosexuals more festive, more enchanting, more typically Cuban in that shiftless, ne'er-do-well sensuality of the tropics.

The problems surfaced only after the fifth or sixth drink, when Morgan's tongue finally loosened. Anything could set off his boon companions, a comment about Richard Nixon, a mention of the American-owned Cuban National Phone Company, Frank Sinatra's singing in *Pal Joey.* Morgan would find himself arguing with the Cubans, as he defended—by default, being the only American present—the things that made America great. But Yankee ingenuity, rugged individualism, and a faith in progress and human perfectibility were not the things that Cubans saw in the United States. Out would come the old warhorses of the Anglo-Saxon white man's burden, the intervention in the War of Independence (which the Americanos arrogantly called the Spanish-American War), Ambassador Sumner Welles and Machado, the sugar quota, Guantanamo Bay, and a host of other things that signified oppression, submission, and the latest popular catchphrase, "American imperialism."

"But the U.S. never had an empire!" he would sputter, to the laughter and jeers of Franqui, Sarduy, Cabrera Infante, Heberto Padilla, and all those who would later mythologize their own version of the revolution.

"What is Puerto Rico, then?" someone would say. "What are the Philippines? What was Cuba itself until just yesterday?"

"We were invited in!" Morgan would go on, trying to argue his way back.

"Yeah, just like the Hungarians invited the Russians in nineteen fifty-six!"

Again more laughter, and Morgan, filled with rum and anger, humiliated and made to feel naive and ill informed, would stalk off from the café. Laura would run after him then, apologizing for her colleagues, who would just laugh some more at the thin-skinned American. Of course they never held it against Morgan; his reaction was totally understandable; in fact, they would have been surprised had it been otherwise. After all, Americans were notoriously misinformed by their government and their schools about anything beyond their own borders.

But to Laura and Morgan those nights at the café were just prologues to hours of further debate and recrimination, as though by endless clashing they could build a bridge between them. And when the insults became personal, when Morgan would curse out all Cubans and Laura would shit on the mother of all Yanquis, when their tempers exploded at her tiny apartment on Obispo Street, they would fall into bed, clawing each other, desperately seeking each other as though the language of sex could bridge their political divide. They would couple like animals and they would howl so loud when they climaxed that the neighbors would bang on the walls and the old lady downstairs would cry, "At least sing the national anthem when you come!"

But then would appear the sadness, the guilt, the despair, the emptiness in the pit of the stomach, and the awful hangovers like the one he was suffering from right now, when Morgan would tell himself, This is enough, I can't do this to Irma anymore, I have to end it right now before it goes any further.

By the time the ferryboat docked at the La Cabaña pier, chug-chugging clouds of blue smoke from its ancient engine, Morgan had made up his mind. I have to give Irma a chance. I'm not even home most nights. Why marry her if this is all I can offer her? I must leave Laura, it's that simple, I must.

Two *barbudos* in fatigues, still wearing long hair, amulets, and rosaries, waited at a jeep by the dock. They looked expectantly at Morgan as he walked off the gangplank, then fired up their engine, greeting him with the know-it-all smile of the Cuban rake, the *tártaro,* the Jack the Knife pose so beloved of the Cuban hipster. Even when he saluted briefly, the men just waved him on.

Morgan climbed into the warm, cracked leather seat. The driver, lanky, with yellow cat eyes, nodded amiably.

"It's been a long time, *Comandante,*" he said, releasing the clutch and steering away from the dock down the macadam road. Morgan held on to the windshield as the jeep rattled over the speed bumps.

"We have met before?"

"Sure, you don't remember? Carlos here in the back and me, we were at the camp of Capitán Cordón when you came down."

"Major Cordón," said Carlos, slant eyed, moonfaced, with a dour expression.

"That's right. *Comandante* Cordón, after we helped take Santa Clara. Carlos and me, we were outside that *bohío* when you almost killed Cordón. Too bad you didn't, you know? He is nothing but a bad weed. I'm sure he's doing all his banditry all over again, only now it's in the name of the revolution."

Morgan thought back briefly to the meeting in Cordón's camp, the bloody clash between them, the raid by the Batista air force, the long trek with Guevara back to the sierra. I saw Laura's ghost in that camp. But it couldn't have been her ghost, because she's still alive. So who was it? What was it?

"It was a stroke of bad luck," said the driver, waving at the guard as they fast approached the forbidding walls of the old Spanish fort. "This country would have been a whole lot better off if that air force had wiped out a few more of our glorious leaders."

"Máximo, shut up!" said Carlos, slapping the driver on the shoulder. "Do you want to get us in trouble with this here *comandante?*"

Morgan grinned, shook his head. "Not to worry, I feel the same."

"You see, Carlos? It's what I'm always saying. The job of the revolution has just begun, don't you agree, *Comandante?* First we got rid of Batista and his followers. Now we have to make sure we're all in this together. One team, pulling the cart, like they say in Camagüey, where I'm from."

"What happens with the others who do not pull the cart?" asked Morgan as the jeep rumbled to a halt next to the sentry post by the entrance to La Cabaña.

The *barbudos* smiled for an answer.

※ ※ ※

"To the firing wall, that's what happens to the enemies of the revolution!" said Che Guevara, his deep-set eyes puffy from lack of sleep. His desk overflowed with tomes of economic research—reports from the Sugar Research Foundation, the Tobacco Institute, the World Bank, the 1952 Census, volumes with titles like *Problems of the New Cuba, Investments in Cuba, FAO World Sugar Economy, Statistic Yearbook of the U.N.*

"We're building a new country here," he said, puffing on his ever-present cigar, serene with the assurance of a mystic in the grip of a vision. "We have to break free from the old ties of economic dependency. We must be self-reliant, like your writer, Hawthorne, said."

"That was Emerson."

"Yes, him too. Anybody who stands in our way will meet with revolutionary justice." He smiled sardonically. "Which is to say, with a revolutionary execution."

"And the justice, where is it to be found in all that?" asked Morgan, rhetorically, he knew.

Che now grinned, his slanted eyes and sparse beard giving him even more the formidable look of a tropical Tamerlane.

"I know that we don't have the same idea of justice, you and I," he said, collapsing on a cot by the desk. "You, my friend, are the product of a bourgeois environment. Your concept of constitutional guarantees, due process of law, and all that don't obtain in a situation as fluid as ours. What we require here is swift retribution. We find them, we judge them, we shoot them. Sort of like the American West, don't you think?"

"Two wrongs don't make a right," replied Morgan testily.

Guevara switched to the queen's English, his voice dripping with scorn. "Really, old man, let's not resort to clichés. At least we don't go around slaughtering Indians. But I forgot, we already had that argument. How is your wife, by the way?"

Morgan was taken aback, picked up one of the volumes of economics on the desk.

"We're not married yet; we're thinking about it. But she's fine, thank you."

"I hear she had problems with that *malparto,* how do you say it?"

"Miscarriage."

"Yes, exactly. But that hasn't stopped you from, what is the phrase? My English is getting rusty. I can't speak it that much. It wouldn't do for people to know I speak the language of the imperialists. Ah, yes, fucking your eyeballs out, no?"

Morgan snapped shut the FAO report.

"You asked me out here to talk about my personal life? I hope not. I hope this was about the executions. Or maybe about the economy, because you're certainly in no shape to talk about morality. Your own wife is still waiting for you in Peru while you're fooling around with Aleida March. People in glass houses shouldn't throw stones."

Che sat on the cot, rubbed his beard. "Well said," he answered, reverting to Spanish. "That's a sentiment Irma or Aleida would appreciate. Funny how we both fell in love with Bible-quoting country girls, isn't it? Both blonde, both Anglo-Saxon. Most curious. Of course, I fell in love. I wonder if you did, too, William? Or do you love that other girl, the one everybody in Havana knows about, this—"

Morgan moved his hand to his holster. "I swear, you say one more word about my private life and I'll kill you."

This reaction pleased Che enormously.

"But, William, don't you see? None of us has a private life anymore! We are all priests in the cause of the people. We can't have feelings like mere mortals." He paused, thought for a moment. "At least not public feelings."

"That is such bullshit. Who came up with that idea?"

"Fui yo," that was me, said Fidel Castro, stepping out from behind the door of an adjoining office. He turned to Che, throwing his arms out in theatrical style.

"Coño, I was waiting for my cue, Che. I was starting to feel like Banquo's ghost."

"Son of a bitch," muttered Morgan, shaking the hand that the supreme leader now extended. It felt large, soft, and moist, as though he had just washed it.

"I surprised you, no? Che told me you were on your way in, so I thought I'd hide out here and see what you really thought of us."

"Fidel, you remember I fought—"

"Speak to me in English, William," said Fidel, lighting, as if by reflex action, one of his large Cohibas. "You know I almost moved to the States when I was young to play for the Senators."

"I know," said Morgan, warming up to Fidel in spite of himself. What is it about this man that provokes this reaction?

"Sometimes I wonder what would have been better for Cuba, to have another star ballplayer out on the diamond or a not-so-stellar *comandante en jefe.* Because at least I know how to play ball. But this governing business, *coño,* I don't know anything about. The worse part is, nobody else does either. It's Fidel this, Fidel that, Fidel the other thing. I've slept four hours in the last two days. Pretty soon if I want some peace and quiet I'll have to go back to the Sierra."

"That's because to most people you are the voice of Cuba," said Morgan guilelessly. Fidel turned to him, beaming, waving his cigar like a magic wand.

"You really think so?"

Morgan nodded. Why deny the obvious?

"Yes, Fidel. You are the leader. But remember, we were all fighters together. You can't forget that."

"Of course I'm not forgetting that. How can I forget your efforts— you, Eloy, Ray in the underground, Frank País, José Antonio, we were all in this together."

Fidel paused, as though to make sure Morgan noticed who was not included in the list—Chomón, Barquín, Prío.

"You boys especially in the Escambray. I understand you were the first here in Havana, but you never gave me any trouble like those bastards from the Directorio who wouldn't leave the palace until I forced them."

He stopped, conscious of his harsh words. Smiling, he laid a conspiratorial hand on Morgan's shoulder.

"Well, let's say I asked them to get out. But that whole weapons business, what a way to start a government!"

Fidel shook his head in amazement at his own problems. Morgan again felt the waves of charisma flowing from Fidel, the odd combination of mock humility, self-consciousness, and high spirits, the way he seemingly took you into his confidence as though you were the only person in the world that mattered to him.

"So, then, why do you fuck it up with your executions?" asked Morgan.

Fidel dropped his hand, as though Morgan's shoulder had caught on fire.

"What executions?"

"The rounding up of the Batistianos."

"Oh, those executions! William, you of all people should know better. It's the code of the Sierra that we're applying. You had to execute a few people yourself back then, didn't you?"

"Certainly, for treason or spying, but I didn't chase after five thousand people and slam them in prison just for being Batista supporters."

"I have to do these things. Look, William, you're an Americano, and maybe you don't remember, but I saw it myself when I was a boy. Back in nineteen thirty-three, when Machado fell, mobs of people descended on anybody who ever said *"Viva Machado"* and beat them to death. Thousands died at the hands of the mob. It's the people crying out for justice, and I have to guide that. If we do it, it's justice, not mob rule. Besides, most of those detained will be let go. We just want to catch the big ones and scare the rest. It's too bad Ventura got away; I would have liked to preside over that trial." Fidel puffed on his cigar, suddenly pensive.

"But we did capture Colonel Sosa Blanco," he said, brightening again. "He's a major war criminal. His trial will start tomorrow at the baseball stadium. I understand it will be a capacity audience. Should be quite a show. But seriously, this whole thing is going to stop very soon. We do have other enemies, after all."

"Who, the communists?" asked Morgan.

"No, no, the reds are useful, they're not a threat. Look, William, I am not a communist. I believe in democracy."

"So when will you call for elections?"

"Soon, soon. This year, I promise, you'll see. But first the revolution must be strengthened, and for that I need your help, William."

"What can I do?"

"I am leaving for Venezuela tomorrow. I'm trying to get a commercial treaty going. While I'm gone I want you to help me get rid of some elements hostile to our revolution. I think you would be ideal to root them out."

"Who are you talking about?"

Fidel paused, as though searching for words. "*El hampa americana.* How do you say? The mob. The mafia."

Chapter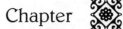

5

"Thank you for coming all the way here to see us, Major Morgan."

Morgan nodded, sitting at the private cabana in the Fountainebleau. All the tourist activity that had died after the revolution in Havana seemed to have simply packed and moved ninety miles north. The poolside swarmed with girls in bikinis, men in porkpie hats making urgent long distance calls, solicitous black waiters delivering cool drinks. An offshore breeze ruffled the ragged tops of the palm trees, the air reeking of coconut tanning lotion, salt air, and cigars. Miami Beach in bloom.

The man next to Morgan, dressed in white linen shirt and gold beltless slacks, glowed with the deep tan of the wealthy and the ungainfully employed. He spoke with the faint nasal twang of New York, revealing a full set of the best dental work money could by.

"We thought it might be better for all of us if our conversation took place somewheres away from big brother," said the man, sipping his Tom Collins.

"Like *Nineteen Eighty-Four?*" said Morgan.

"That's right, Major. Like communism. Like red. Because Fidel is a commie, don't you think?"

"For sure," said Morgan, sipping his scotch and soda, "through and through."

The man smiled magnanimously.

"I'm so glad we see things the same way. Our people thought you would. I hope together we can bring a new day to Cuba, a real revolution."

"I would like nothing better, Mr. Jones."

The man smiled even more warmly, a gracious host welcoming a long-awaited guest.

"You can call me Johnny. I'm sure you've figured out Jones is not the real name. But in my line of work we have to stay ahead of the government, even if only a step."

"I understand."

"The gentlemen I work with . . . " Johnny hesitated, ran his hand through his thick silver mane. "Ah, hell, I might as well come clear. You've heard of Meyer Lansky, haven't you?"

Morgan nodded, waiting to see how much Johnny would reveal. He recalled Fidel's last words before he boarded the jet to Caracas: "William, take it easy at first. Just make believe you got a big problem with me, a personal thing. Say I'm a red, whatever you want, that you want to get rid of me. Flush them out, see who they put you in contact with, that's what we want to know. They'll believe you. They can't conceive that an American would actually be working for Cuba."

"Sure I heard of Lansky, Johnny," said Morgan, playing his part at last. "Who the hell hasn't? What I want to know is, what can you or him do to help us out? Look, Fidel betrayed the Front. We were supposed to be made equal partners and he locked us out of the government. He's got us on the payroll just yanking our dick. That's not what I fought for."

"Hey, I thought you fought for a free Cuba."

"Sure. With me in charge. I got practically nothing out of this, and I want my full share."

Johnny looked quickly at Morgan, deciding if he could truly trust him.

"You know, I like that, William," he said finally, doubts allayed. "Mind if I call you that? We like ambition in a guy. It takes you places. Hell, after you put your ass on the line for those guys and they stab you in the back like that, shit, I'd be sore too. Share and share alike, that's our motto."

"Yeah, well, that's my beef," said Morgan. "We had a deal and he squelched. Now I want him to get what's coming to him."

"Maybe we can help you after all."

A single engine Cessna abruptly buzzed low over the hotel, dragging a Coppertone banner from its tail. Morgan jumped in his chair, grabbing for his gun, until he remembered he was wearing civvies and the war was really over. Johnny was enormously amused.

"Pretty good reaction time there, Billy. I can see how you survived up in the hills."

Johnny glared up at the plane, then cast a hex on it, little and index fingers upraised like horns.

"*Stronzi!*" he muttered, then snapped his fingers. A cadaverous-

looking man with bad teeth and a prominent bulge at the waistband
under his sport shirt came out from inside the cabana.

"Yes, Mr. R.?"

"Lee, could you please find out who was the asshole that authorized
that plane to swing by taking pictures? Last thing we need is for someone to find out Mr. Morgan is here."

"Sure thing, Mr. R. Right away."

The man swiftly returned inside the cabana, picked up a phone,
dialed, spoke in a muffled voice.

"I swear," Johnny went on, "these fucking G-men won't leave you
alone. We're in this together, the government and us, you know. What
the fuck, it's the right hand doesn't know what the left is doing. My
apologies. I realize this could be an embarrassment for you if anybody
finds out you're here."

What the hell is going on? thought Morgan. Is this the U.S.? The government working hand in hand with the mob? "Something more than
that, but it's OK. The Castro people think I'm down in Trinidad looking
over a frog farm."

"Did you say a frog farm?" asked Johnny incredulously.

"Yeah, sure. It's a good source of meat. Frogs' legs. Ever tried them?"

Johnny looked aghast at Morgan, his hooded brown eyes opened wide
in amazement, then he laughed.

"I get it, I get it, it's a joke! Hell, I never knew you guys could be so
funny!"

"You like that?" said Morgan, smiling in return, even if he felt like
smashing Johnny's proud Roman nose.

"It's a killer! Wait till I tell Sal! You're running a fucking frog farm!
That is precious!!"

Johnny laughed some more now, chortling into the white cotton
handkerchief he'd extracted from his back pocket, finally regaining his
composure.

"Fidel Castro is a cocksucker," he said, popping a mint into his mouth.
At a chaise nearby, a Jane Mansfield look-alike looked up from her towel
at Johnny, a quizzical expression on her face. Johnny shook his head *no*.

"You know we helped him out, don't you?"

"I didn't know that."

"We sure fucking did. Some of his people came crying to us, saying
they needed more weapons and more money and more of everything.
Those guys were always asking for more, sort of like my ex-wife, you
know? So we thought about it. After all, what the fuck, Lansky set Batista
up back in fifty-two. I bet you didn't know that either."

"Matter of fact, I wasn't aware of that either."

"Yeah, well, it's not something most people are aware of. We underwrote his Senate campaign. When he took over, we were going to become partners. The government was going to match our investments dollar for dollar to put up the casinos, just like Vegas. We was lucky the son of a bitch kept his word, but you know how it is, you can't trust Cubans. They're real weasels; you never know when they're going to turn against you."

"Boy, do I know that."

"Let me try these names on you. Moe Dalitz. Charlie Tomine. Sam Giancana. Santos Trafficante. Frank Fiorini."

"I don't know any of them."

"I was hoping you might. They're some of the top players in town. Moe's in charge of the Nacional, runs it with Meyer's brother, Jake. Charlie, "the Blade" we call him, he's at the Capri. Hangs out a lot with George Raft, our official host and a hell of a fine actor, if I may so."

"He certainly is."

"Ain't he now? The way he tosses that coin, I tell you, when I was a kid starting out in this business, I used to imitate him. 'Course he's getting on in years now and we have to take care of him. That's the thing, you know, we always take care of our own. *La famiglia,* understand?"

"That's what I like to hear."

Johnny nodded with the deep satisfaction of the self-righteous.

"Good, good, I can tell we're going to have a beautiful friendship here. Now, the other two men, Sam and Santos, they're men of honor. They expect things to happen when they're supposed to, Santos is at the Sans Souci, and Sam, well, Sam is everywhere. He gets a share of all the casinos, clubs. Hell, he's even got a stake in the shrimp trade. OK, the thing is, this fellow Frank Fiorini has been put in charge of all the casinos by Fidel. Now Frank just happens to have a few contacts with the agency, know what I mean?"

"He's a CIA agent?"

"Not so loud! This whole town reeks with spooks. Frankie was the one who had been in charge of supplying all our weapons to the guerrillas out in the sierra. So the word he gets us is that Fidel wants to run us clear out of Cuba. I mean, that's impossible. We are one of the major sources of revenue for the island. I mean, Cuban girls are nice and the weather is fine too, but you can always get all that down here in Miami. It's gambling that draws the tourists to Cuba, and tourism is a major revenue stream for the government. So when Frank tells us Fidel wants us out, I say to myself, That is crazy. Sheer bullshit crazy. We need a reasonable man in there. Because Fidel has this communist thing going, and let me tell you, I hate reds. I love my country. It's the greatest place in the whole wide world, and no commie son of a bitch is going to set up a commie base ninety miles way from us and take our money too, no sir. That's why we're so glad you got in touch with us, because I'm sure we can work together. Deal?"

Johnny extended his hand. Morgan shook it, remarking how strange that someone as smooth as Johnny Roselli should have such a leathery palm.

"Say, do you like pastrami?"

❊ ❊ ❊

"Mr. Morgan, the arrangement is this. We help you to dispose of Dr. Castro and his crew. In exchange, you and the new revolutionary government see to it that our gambling interests are respected. That is all. Does that sound agreeable?"

The short, nondescript old man making the proposition wore a black suit and a white shirt, the lack of a tie his only concession to the tropics. A few stray gray chest hairs peeked out from under the top of his shirt.

Morgan sat next to Johnny across from the old man in a red vinyl upholstered booth. A bowl of dill pickles and green tomatoes lay on the center of the table next to the containers of sugar and ersatz cream. All around them was the din of the elderly Jewish patrons, their "Nech's" and "I've got to tell you's" imported straight from the teeming shores of Jersey and Manhattan. Morgan saw his own reflection in the gold-veined mirror tiles on the wall—a large blond man in loud sports shirt and straw hat flanked by a nut brown fox sitting across from a wizened retiree. The massive air-conditioning system that kept the place the temperature of a vegetable crisper blew a chilly gale straight at their table, turning the skin on Morgan's forearms into gooseflesh.

"In principle, Joe, that's the sort of thing that a new legitimate Cuban government could well accept without too much trouble."

A blue-haired waitress approached bearing a pastrami sandwich, its twin stacks as thick as fists on the white china plate.

"Your pastrami and your Cel-Ray, sugar, as always," said the waitress, Ruby, as per her name tag.

"You're a doll, hon," said Joe, casting a covetous look at the still well-turned calf of the matronly waitress, who quickly walked away in her sensible, rubber-soled shoes.

"You fellows can have all the young girls in the world; it's women like that who keep my blood warm," said Joe, sinking tiny sharp teeth into the glistening mound of cartilage on rye.

"I'm glad you agree with us, Mr. Morgan," Joe went on, speaking through a mouthful of food. "Eventually the person who gets rid of this bearded fellow will find, with our compliments, a nice million-dollar check in his bank account. Or *her* checking account, if it comes to that. Because I always say the female of the species is the deadliest. Ain't that the truth, Johnny?"

"You know it, Joe," said Johnny, shaking his head vigorously.

"Joe, I'm curious as to how your assistance would be forthcoming in this matter," said Morgan, trying to sound as empirical as his companions.

Joe shrugged, the gesture of one who's handled many things like this before—almost always with success.

"There are ways. We could procure a sharpshooter to get him right between the eyes when he's out giving a speech."

"Oh, that would be good!" cooed Johnny.

"Or we could put some poison in his food, so people wouldn't think it was an enemy of the revolution. He gets sick, he dies, who knows? In the confusion, in you go."

"That is brilliant, Joe, just brilliant!" added Johnny.

"I guess you could plant a bomb as well, but that's very iffy. You have to know exactly when he's going to be there, case the place, all that. I don't like bombs. It's a big *tsouris*, it's not worth it."

Joe finished eating the first half of his sandwich, then peevishly took a bite out of the second mound so no one would eat the remainder after he left it on his plate. He finished sipping his Cel-Ray, burped discreetly.

"That was my main meal of the day, gentlemen. Tonight I feast on tea and crackers. Doctor says I should watch my fatty food, but I say, Hey, we all gotta go sometimes, right?"

"Personally I hope they make an exception in my case," replied Morgan.

Joe looked blankly at Morgan, his pale blue eyes blinking rapidly, then raised the corner of his mouth in a rictus of a smile.

"That is very funny, Mr. Morgan," he said.

"I told you this guy was a cutup," said Johnny.

Morgan shifted in his seat, extremely uncomfortable. Nothing he had heard so far was anything he couldn't have come up with himself, had he chosen to. He wanted to know the ramifications of the plot, the conspiracy, who was in on the cabal.

"It all sounds fine, Joe, but how do your people fit into all this? Would you be carrying out all these actions?"

Joe leaned back, slumped his shoulders.

"Maybe I was running ahead of myself," he said wistfully.

"How do you mean?"

"All these plans, I'm giving them to you for free, these ideas. I don't know that I'm in a position to carry out any of them right now."

"But you just said, 'If we do this you do that'!"

"Let me explain my position. We are an organization, and the organization has to take a vote on this. Unfortunately, so far the attitude is, Let us wait and see if we cannot do business with this Castro fellow. Mind you, if it was up to me, I'd be bringing in some of my South Side boys to do the number we need. But the situation right now is not ripe enough for an intervention. Not yet."

Morgan glanced at Johnny, who opened his hands as though saying, Hey, it's not my idea either. Joe took out a large roll of bills from his baggy pants.

"Look, Mr. Lansky, because I know that's your name," said Morgan. "I don't appreciate all the bullshit you've just fed me. I came here sincerely looking for help, and you're handing it to me. Fine. So be it. But remember, when the time comes, I'm going to make sure all your fingers get chopped off at the bone. Thanks for nothing."

Morgan moved to get up, but the old man pulled him by his shirt-sleeve. Morgan turned to see Johnny reaching for a previously hidden .45, even as three other men also rose from different corners of their restaurant, their hands at their waistbands as well.

"Please, Mr. Morgan, please. Sit down. I meant no disrespect. I am merely trying to explain our situation right now. Please. Sit. Maybe we can do business together after all."

Morgan sat down reluctantly, cursing himself for having come unarmed.

"What kind of fancy story are you going to tell me now?"

"Nothing fancy. I want you and me to go bonefishing."

"You're taking me for a boat ride? Just like that? In the middle of Miami?"

Joe smiled sadly. "Calm down, Mr. Morgan. It's not what you think. Besides, what else do people do when they come to Florida?"

* * *

The bonefish tugged at the line urgently, almost wresting the rod out of Johnny's hands.

"Hey, I got me one here! What do I do now?" he hollered. The captain of the boat rushed next to the gangster, urging him to release the reel, let the line out until the fish got tired. Morgan watched the scene from the forward deck, smoking a cigarette, then looked out on the tourmaline sea around the boat.

Three in the afternoon and their contact had not shown up yet. The sun slanted off the shallow banks, turning the water into a pool of liquid jewels. They were somewhere off Little Deer Key, right by the spot in the archipelago where the fingerlings of land at the tip of the Florida peninsula meet up with the great blue waters of the Atlantic. A half mile away the blue-green of the keys turned to the dark sapphire of ocean trenches, a river of blue carrying marlin, spearfish, swordfish, the great creatures of the deep.

It occurred to Morgan that he should feel like one of the characters in the old man's novels, fully alive and excited at his prospects, but the reality of the thing was nothing at all like what the old man had said. Morgan was stunned both by the intense beauty of the keys and the utter boredom that engulfed you out there. That was something the old man never wrote about. All his characters were always doing things, planning, scheming, waxing heroic about what they were going to accomplish. Now, when Morgan had finally reached the point where he had become such a character, all he could think of was how tedious it all was and how easy it would be to become a drunk to wash away the hours of nothingness. *Nada. Cero. Más nada por nada.* And all that. How did it all go, anyway?

Lansky let out a loud snore, his head hanging forward, pressing down on his chest as he lay on a chaise in the shade of the poop deck. Out in the blue distance, a dolphin cut out of the water, its bullet-shaped body springing forth as though propelled by a weapon. A gull squawked. Low-flying terns swooped around the stern, expecting food, while Johnny grunted and cursed as he struggled with his tight reel. A silky soft breeze rose up, teasing Morgan's patience.

Three hours we've been waiting here, and this party doesn't show up, he thought. It's someone who can help you; he's already fighting in the country; he doesn't want us to use his name until he meets with you. Bullshit. If you can't dazzle them, baffle them. These guys must think I'm some sort of yokel that they can come up with all this stuff and I won't complain. But that's all right. They are digging their own graves. One by one we'll eliminate you until all you insects are gone.

A nagging doubt rose up: Then who will be left, William? Fidel and his people. Is that what you want? That's what the Cuban people want. Yes, well, the German people also wanted Hitler. Was that right? For a

German I suppose. Not a Jew. Or a Catholic. Or a Protestant. Or a democrat. Or anybody who wasn't a Nazi.

Look, even if later we turn against Fidel, for now we have to make a common cause. People like these gangsters have to be eliminated. His enemy is ours. For now. Tomorrow, who knows?

But wouldn't it be easier to use their help to get rid of Fidel now, then step into the vacuum and double-cross these people? After all, what could they do? The same thing they're doing now, I suppose. It's a never-ending cycle, isn't it? I win, you lose, you conspire, you win, I lose, I conspire ad nauseam. Maybe it's just human nature. Maybe you just have to accept that this is the way it will always be in Cuba. No, I can't. Too many people have died for us not to be free.

Us? You're a Cuban now? You were free already when you joined. You were born an American and you will die an American, William. Maybe, but I'm also a Cuban now. I've fought too long and killed too many for that to change. No one can deny me that.

Morgan flipped his cigarette overboard, getting ready to wake Joe and ask to return to Key Largo, when he saw the boat approaching. Before he could alert anyone, Johnny, the captain, and the two crew members were already up, scanning the water. Lansky stirred, opened his eyes, warily watched the white cutter heading their way.

The reel sang as the line went taut again, the bonefish picking that moment to pull away.

"Bring it in, Johnny; you've got him hooked," said the captain.

Johnny frowned, handed the rod to the skipper.

"Fuck the fish," he shouted at Joe, more annoyed than concerned.

"We got problems, Joe."

"I'm aware, Johnny," said Lansky, who rose up quickly from his chair, letting out a string of Yiddish curses.

"What's the problem?" asked Morgan.

"Our uncle has decided to pay us a visit," said Lansky, going below.

"Uncle who?" asked Morgan, finally recognizing the telltale lettering on the side of the boat.

Lansky dashed down to the galley, took a notebook from a drawer, dowsed it with lighter fluid, then lit a match. The notebook flared up in black smoke, and his face relaxed. He craned his neck out, pointing his square chin at Morgan standing on the upper deck.

"That there's the coast guard, Mr. Morgan. I'm certain our friends from the FBI are on board. By any chance, are you here on an official visit?"

Joe hadn't finished his sentence before Morgan was slipping down the side of the boat and into the water as quietly as he could.

"Attention, *Mamma Mia!*" blared the cutter's loudspeaker. "Prepare for boarding!"

Those were the last words that Morgan heard for a while as he dove into the water beneath Lansky's boat. Moments later he felt the vibration of the cutter's engine suddenly throttling down, then the bump as the two boats met. Morgan knew that was his moment to gulp down air; everyone would be too busy with the boarding to pay much attention to the surrounding water.

He may have been sent undercover by Fidel himself, but the last thing he or anyone back in Cuba would be able to explain was an arrest by the FBI. Besides which, there was that little matter of his desertion from the army and his escape from Chillicothe. You really can't come back, can you? he asked himself as he peeped just above the waterline, taking in as much air as his lungs would allow. No, not as it stands right now, I guess I can't.

His chest filled like a balloon, Morgan kicked off his shoes, grabbed the keel of the *Mamma Mia,* and propelled himself powerfully off the boat. He had seen a sand spit with a handful of palm trees, bushes, and mangrove about a quarter mile away. He could swim out there if he had enough time. But did he?

He moved powerfully underwater, trying to put as much distance behind him as he could, lashing out at the warm viscous blue-green water until he ran out of breath, but he didn't stop then. He kicked and flailed and struggled against the burning pain that was consuming his lungs, his body racked in the throes of oxygen deprivation. Yet still he swam on until he felt his head giddy and the blue-green water was spattered with purple spots.

Slow, William, slow. Rise slowly, he ordered, his body shaking from the spasms of pain. He drifted up to the surface, took a quick breath, then stole a look back at the boat. No one had noticed. He had swum out maybe five hundred yards, the island still tantalizingly far. Hating himself for smoking, resolving never to pick up a cigarette again, Morgan dove underwater once more.

Back on the boat, Lansky was calmly sitting on his chair watching the captain hassle with the coast guard lieutenant.

"You have no right to board like this!"

"We are perfectly within our rights, Captain, and you know it!"

"Beer, Joe?" asked Johnny, pulling the tab on a Schlitz.

"Don't mind if I do," said Lansky. "Feels like the right time for a brew."

Two FBI men wearing gray suits, white shirts, and black brogues came out from below. A smallish man in a rumpled suit followed them.

"Are you sure he was on this boat, Max?"

Max Weinberg took out a cheap blue cotton handkerchief, wiped his perspiring forehead.

"I know it for a fact."

The FBI agent in charge turned to Lansky, who raised his thick salt-and-pepper eyebrows.

"You and I have got to talk, Lansky."

"I'll have nothing to say until my attorney gets here."

✳ ✳ ✳

Out on the starboard side, one of the coast guard officers suddenly glanced out, certain that he had seen someone in the water. He peered at the blue-green ocean, as still as a rich man's pool, then a bottle-nosed dolphin leaped out, cutting a graceful swath through the air and diving effortlessly back under. Isn't that a beautiful sight? thought the officer. No matter how many times I see them, I never can get used to it. Then the officer turned and headed down into the cabin, tapping the walls, searching for hollow spaces where weapons, drugs, or perhaps even a man might be hiding.

Out on the island, Morgan crawled up the shallow water. He had taken off his loud sport shirt and stuffed it inside his dark pants so as not to draw attention. He moved slowly on all fours up the sand until he was completely out of the water, then ran to a nearby clump of mangrove. Turning, he watched the cutter alongside the boat, officers and agents trooping back and forth for hours of endless discussions. Finally, by the end of the afternoon, the cutter tossed a line to the boat and hauled it away, the wooden yacht splashing merrily in the big vessel's wake.

Morgan waited another hour before stepping out from the cover of the mangrove. His skin was red and blistered, his arms and shoulders a mass of welts from the myriad insect bites, his tongue swollen and caked with salt. He searched the island for coconuts but found none, only more low-lying bushes, mangrove, and the odd palm tree. Most of the island lay just a foot or two above the waterline, the ground soggy and practically impossible to walk on.

He returned to the sandy beach where he had landed, facing the Gulf Stream. He tried to remember where he was exactly and how long it would take him to reach the nearest inhabited land. As he recalled, he was about thirty minutes away from the dock at Duck Key, probably about six nautical miles. He figured he could swim back, if only he could be sure he was heading the right way, otherwise . . .

A pleasure boat, right near where the cutter had boarded the yacht!

Morgan jumped up and down, waving his hands, shouting at the top of his lungs.

"Over here, over here!"

It's impossible, he thought. No one could see me from there unless . . . wait, it stopped? Yes, it stopped. They're waving back! What are they doing? Yes, they're sending a dinghy! Yes, they're coming! Oh God, sweet Jesus, thank you!!

❊ ❊ ❊

The blare of the outboard engine rattled the air as the rubber dinghy pushed into the islet. A black man in white pants and shirt waved him on board.

Morgan scampered through the shallows, jumping on the dinghy. He asked whose boat it was and where it was heading, but the man just smiled, pointed at the noisy motor, then at the yacht, as though to say, All your questions will be answered soon enough. Morgan nodded, grateful for the time to make up his story. He decided he would say he was out on a small sailboat, never sailed much before, had capsized. The boat flipped and sank after hitting a coral reef; if it hadn't been for their help, who knows how long it would have taken him to get out of there? That sounded convincing enough, he hoped.

As they neared the boat, Morgan realized the white yacht was at least seventy feet long, with oiled decks and spotless sides, a perfect pleasure boat for a very wealthy individual indeed. The dinghy came to a halt next to an oiled teak-and-brass ladder. Morgan climbed up. He was met by yet another sailor, a blond Germanic type, also dressed in white, who directed him down the passageway. Morgan tried to start a conversation, but the man replied in some odd Nordic tongue, ending with, "No English."

He led Morgan to a cabin where a luxurious terry bathrobe lay on a wide white bed. The door to the bathroom was open and the sailor indicated with gestures that Morgan was to make himself at home. Morgan nodded. The moment he stepped inside the room, the door clicked behind him. Morgan tried to open the door but it was locked from the outside. He felt the yacht's engine rumble and the boat slip forward, moving away from the island.

"What have I got myself into now?" he wondered, then shrugged and headed for the shower. Whatever it was, at least it was luxurious confinement.

Morgan had finished his shower, slipped into the terry robe, and was towel-drying his hair when he heard a knock at the door.

"Come in," he said.

The gleaming teak door opened. In stepped all six feet, three inches of Carlos Boyeros, the richest man in Cuba until just a few weeks ago.

"Well, William, about time. We've been expecting you, you know."

Chapter

6

The *babalawo* Tiburcio was out in his yard, watering the sacred squash and the beneficent basil, when the bluebird fluttering on the split-rail fence told him there were people looking for him. The old man turned his cataract-covered eyes down the block, sensing someone in need. He put down his tin watering can and shuffled back to the house, kissing the gnarled old ceiba with red bows on his way in.

"*Taíto,* are you there?" came the voice of Yasmín, the youngest of his seven daughters, who had kept the traditions and remained behind to take care of him. She stood barefoot in her stained blue dress, her paste pearl necklace with missing beads hanging forlorn from her neck, gray-streaked hair flaring up like a peacock's tail.

"You go back to sleep, *niña,* I will handle these people," said Tiburcio, fumbling his way into the darkened cinder-block house. Now in his nineties, Tiburcio had only partial eyesight, and that only in the brightest of tropical noons.

He walked into the narrow kitchen, bending his head to greet the sacred stones of the gods at home in their tureens, through the dining room with its Formica table and padded chrome chairs, past the bedroom with the massive oak bed that his father, the slave cabinet maker, had made for his owner, and finally entered the living room.

One of the people he recognized immediately: Manuel, the servant to the cacique Boyeros, the son of his family's slave master. Tiburcio could smell the Chinese blood in Manuel, sharp, cutting, like the shrill sounds of the language of that nation of shopkeepers. Even in a crowded *bembé,* when people were singing and dancing and the sweat of the bodies filled the room with the perfume of holy trances, he could still sniff out the wily half-black, half-Chinese man.

Manuel was not alone. So he had not come to speak to the spirit of his wife once more. Tiburcio heard the rustling of silk and smelled the sweet amber notes of an American perfume. A white woman. From Europe, the U.S.A.? He felt his other senses coming to the fore, exploring the presence of this female. He detected fear and apprehension, but beyond that coating of concern there was curiosity and acceptance, a warm purplish substance that Tiburcio knew was the form of love's desiring, coupled to a sensibility so great he had not encountered its like since the time of President Zayas. Everything told him this woman was old, yet he also knew that her physical being was young, and he wondered whether she knew she was an old soul and whether she was aware of the sad destiny that awaited her.

"*Buenos días,* Manuel," said Tiburcio, nodding at the visitors sitting on the wood-and-cane sofa. "You have brought us a guest."

Tiburcio moved to the side table where he kept the board and cowrie shells for divination.

"*Buenos días, Maestro,*" replied Manuel, with the admixture of skepticism and reverence that was second nature to him. "That's right, you have a female guest."

"An admirer?" asked Tiburcio, cackling,

"Perhaps, after you finish with her," said Manuel quickly.

Both men laughed, even as Irma paled and felt her stomach churning again.

She had not been able to keep anything down for the past three days. She felt constantly nauseated, as though trapped in a boat heaving in a stormy sea. Feeling ill and embarrassed, she wished she had never agreed to come at all. What would her father have said? What would our Lord Jesus have said of these false prophets, these witch doctors, these lowly *brujos?* But in her desperation, Irma was ready to try anything.

Her marriage of two months was failing and she had no idea how to make it whole again. The day she had finally felt well enough to step outside the house, William had taken her down to City Hall, where they had at last made their relationship official—Mr. and Mrs. William Morgan. But after the party at the Havana Libre, with Che, Eloy, Camilo, and dozens of the other leaders of the country, when the time had come to solemnly dedicate their love on the wedding bed, she had proven a poor bride indeed. The moment William entered her she begged him to come out, the pain and the nausea were so intense.

"I don't know what's wrong, darling," she had told him; "the doctor said I could, but it feels like I'm on fire down there." "Don't worry, sweetheart," he'd told her, kissing her like a brother, then spending the night in the guest room across the hall.

That was not the marriage she had wanted; that was not the life she had dreamed of. He had refused to let her satisfy him, even if the only pleasure she would have obtained would be in hearing his cries of joy as he unburdened himself in her hands or in her mouth. Now he was gone again, off on some mission for Fidel that he couldn't talk about, and the house felt like a gilded prison, with the echoes of the lives of so many others who lived there before her, their ghosts almost palpable in the long nights when she walked down the long marble halls.

No one had to tell her William had a lover; she had intuited it weeks ago when he vanished for days on end. Even last week she had offered herself to him but he had declined, saying he was worried he'd harm her again. Go ahead, she wanted to say, break me, tear me open, but don't desert me; it will me hurt less than your neglect. But she had said nothing, only nodding as if accepting his transparent excuse.

Manuel's tale about the black cat, then, and the spell it had cast upon the house found fertile ground in her mind. It must be true; I must be cursed, she thought. The fault lay, then, not within her but outside, in those slums crowded with jealous, covetous people trying to destroy her love. It was madness, she knew, but she didn't care. She needed an excuse, a reason to go outside herself, to go on with her life. What else could she do?

"What does the *niña* want? What is the pain that grieves this child?" asked Tiburcio now, setting down the board with the cowrie shells on the cool concrete floor.

Irma glanced at Manuel, her breath coming out in quick gasps. She wanted to lay herself open but she felt inhibited by the setting, the gloom, the heat seeping into the living room through the wooden shutters.

A large four-tiered altar crowded with statues of saints, flowers, and baskets of food stood against the far wall. Irma would have sworn that one of the plaster saints—Saint Peter, Saint Jude?—moved its head and winked at her just then. From the back of the house she could hear a woman singing, *"Quién será el que me quiera a mí, quién será, quién será?"*— who will be the one who loves me, who will it be, who will it be?—as she banged pots and pans in the kitchen.

"The lady had a spell put upon her house," said Manuel finally.

A ray of lemony morning sunshine splayed on the pale green wall, an M-line bus rumbled by. "Someone is jealous of her possessions and left an *ebbó* at her house."

At this the old man's head perked up from the board, where he'd been carelessly rifling the shells.

"An offering? What kind?"

"A black cat with its privates cut off, a needle through its heart, and its eyes gouged out. It was a terrible sight."

Tiburcio nodded. It was obviously the handiwork of a practitioner of *palo mayombé*. All his life Tiburcio had been forced to cope with the misconceptions that white people held of his religion, believing Santería was witchcraft. They did not realize that Santería was literally the things of the saints, the road to Ollendumare and Olofi, to the creator who made the gods out of stone and mankind out of clay, to the one who is at the center of all things and who wants only the best for his children.

It was the people who worshipped the night, sleeping with the devil in the ceremonies of *palo mayombé,* who had given the righteous followers of Santería a bad name. They killed animals, dug up fresh corpses, flew on the wings of vultures, and became vampires, keeping *ngangas,* or iron cauldrons full of evil spirits, which they invoked by reciting the chants known as *mambos.*

Tiburcio could still remember the panic that swept through Havana when Cuba was still Spanish and he was a young man of twenty-something years. The authorities feared that a secret society of *ñáñigos,* of *santeros,* was kidnapping young children and using the babies for human sacrifices. Thousands of believers had been imprisoned, many whipped, others placed on the rack, some even garroted so they would confess to the conspiracy of devil and snake worshippers. The persecution had ended with the coming of the war and the American occupation. Since then *santeros* like Tiburcio had done their best to convince people that they were not killers, that their religion was one of light and love for thy neighbor.

"What happened to the *ebbó?*" asked Tiburcio.

"I threw it away. I did not want its *ashé* to disturb the house," replied Manuel.

"Well done, otherwise it would created grave problems in the household."

"What is *ashé?*" asked Irma.

"It is the force of life, *niña,* the spirit that lies within all things," said Tiburcio, extending his ropy hand. "When a man of evil sends forth his evil spirits, they can do great harm. Take this."

She opened her hands, into which Tiburcio dropped the divining shells.

"Rattle them and drop them on the board," he said. Irma did as he asked. The shells fell here and there, some with their furrowed side up, others with it down. Tiburcio ran his hand quickly over them, feeling them with the lightest of touches.

Ay! he thought, *ay, ay, ay!*

How could it be that such a sweet and gentle lady would have such an arduous fate! How many times I have tried to understand, and to this day I cannot fathom you, Elegguá, god of the many roads. Open the door so this soul may come through.

"Do you believe in God, *niña?*" he asked, as though afraid of the answer.

Irma thought briefly then spoke the truth as she felt it.

"I believe in Him but He does not believe in me. I believe He has forsaken me."

She paused, looked down, anguished. She rose. "I should go."

"No, please, *niña*, stay. There is much work to be done. Your husband, William, the *comandante*, is in great danger. You must help him find his way."

"How did you know about him?" said Irma; then she looked at Manuel. "Of course, you told him."

Manuel's solemn expression and slow shaking of his head was more than convincing—he had not.

"Your father the preacher is in great pain for you too."

"How do you know this?"

"He says for you to play the *Etudes,* that he longs to hear your playing."

Irma felt chills running up and down her spine, the air in the room becoming cold and stifling, a great wave of fear surrounding her. She tried to leave but found herself sitting back on the couch.

"Don't be afraid, *niña*. Because I don't know myself how it happens," said Tiburcio with a sad smile, absentmindedly scratching the tip of his long narrow nose—the only legacy the slave master had left the family, a nose identical, except for its color, to the one worn so proudly by the richest man in Cuba.

"I have had this blessing since I was a little dirty ass," he added, almost parenthetically. "It has gotten me into a lot of trouble. I can tell you this, *niña*. The shells say you should do a sacrifice. Your husband still loves you but he is lost. He needs guidance from the saints because he is in deep water. Do you understand me?"

Irma nodded, assenting almost automatically, then she shook her head.

"No, I don't believe you. I don't know how you could have learned that about me, but let me tell you this, William is not in danger. William is a leader of the revolution. William has the trust of Fidel and the top people. Everyone loves him and I cannot . . . "

She stopped, realizing that from the back of the house she was hearing the voice of a dead man.

"Irma! Irma, honey, don't be a swell-head!" said the voice in English, with the painfully high inflection that haunted her dreams. "Listen to what the man says."

"Dad? Dad? Where are you?"

She jumped to her feet, the room becoming a sweltering hodgepodge of feelings, sights, sounds—her blue baby dress, her first yellow pacifier, a mess of oatmeal, her father's smile pulling the can of Coca-Cola from the cooler at the beach, the deep sorrowful tones of their church organ, a single phrase repeated over and over, *God's grace is freely given, God's grace is freely given, God's grace is freely given*. The room was spinning, her stomach heaving once more.

"What have you done to me?" she bellowed at Tiburcio. "What are you doing?"

"You sit still, honey, and do what the man tells you," said her father's voice again, somewhere down the house.

Irma stepped out of the living room, heaving Manuel aside when he tried to stop her.

"She can't see it. Don't let her see it!" cried Tiburcio.

But in her madness Irma was unstoppable, even if the floor seemed to a buckle and a cloud of viscous steam rose before her, and she knew it was all impossible and certainly not according to Christian faith, but still she saw it even if she wasn't sure it was truly real or just the imaginings of her feverish heart. She stumbled down the narrow corridor, voices echoing down the hall, the walls warm and supple to the touch like human skin. She pushed on forward even as she felt a current dragging her back, wanting to keep her away.

A green-and-yellow parrot flew by screeching, even as her father's voice ordered her to not come near, because all could be lost forever. But Irma pressed on against the tide and entered the dining room. All at once everything was still. Not a sound was heard, not the buses outside or the radio or even the sounds of the water running out of the faucet in the kitchen, where Tiburcio's daughter Yasmín was doing the dishes.

"Dad! Daddy? Can you hear me? Please answer me!"

Slowly Yasmín turned her head and opened her mouth to speak, but no words of her own came out even as her eyes rolled upward, showing only the white, and a deep-throated voice warned, "Just this once."

The parrot flew back into the kitchen, alighted on its perch, flapped its glossy wings, and said distinctly in her father's voice, "I'll always love you, child," then the bird squawked; but by that time Irma could not hear, for she was already folding, falling down to the floor in a faint, her wide white skirt opening up on the green concrete tiles like the petals of a rose.

✻ ✻ ✻

Laura tapped her fingertips on the thickly padded arms of the well-worn leather club chair. Her brother, Wilfredo, sat silently in another chair beside her in what had been the executive offices of La Gloria Casino until just a few weeks ago.

On the folding screen before them, Laura, more impatient than embarrassed, watched a movie of her and William making love. The scratched film, with its darkened tone, made her think of the famous blue films that Cuba had been famous for, the stag specials where actresses with flaccid breasts mounted priapic men, openmouthed women, or the odd animal or two with equal abandon. The irony was that this particular piece of pornography had been commissioned and shot by the new Cuba, the one that had come to set matters straight, to liberate the country from its addiction to sex, vice, and degenerate democracy.

"I think I've seen enough, Willie," she said, turning her gaze away from the screen. Her brother raised his hand. The projectionist stopped the film in midframe, right as the camera registered Laura interlocked with Morgan in the grip of desperate desire.

"Turn that thing off, *coño!*" she barked.

The projector's light went out, the room dimly lit by the odd rays of sunshine filtering through the heavy flowered drapes. At a gesture from Wilfredo the projectionist exited the room. Laura's brother got up and pulled the curtains open, letting in the rushing sounds of midtown Havana, so blithely going on about its business, convinced a new, better era had arrived.

Laura stole a quick glance around the room, loathing the mediocrity of the bourgeois American tastes so prominently displayed—the stolen Cinzano ashtray, the COME SEE CUBA travel poster, the picture calendar from the Underwater Gardens in Sarasota, the detritus of a class that had aspired to rule Cuba. She asked herself why, if the communists hated the U.S. so much, they aped its ways so thoroughly. Fidel would not do that, she thought; he lives a revolutionary's life in a little apartment with Celia Sánchez in El Vedado. But these people want to be the new Americans.

Look at him now, thinking that wearing rebel fatigues and a beard makes him one of us. *Papá* forgive me, but what a son of a bitch.

"You must be very proud of yourself, spying on people like that, as if it were any of your business," she snapped.

Wilfredo smiled, his face rounder than usual from his scraggly red beard and the pounds he'd put on since returning to Cuba.

"Laurita, everything that affects the revolution is my business," he said with as much honey as he could pour into his voice. He had come to truly dislike his half sister during the time he'd been abroad preparing for the collapse of the Batista regime. He had come to despise all of the 26th of July people, their undisciplined disregard for the leadership of the party. They were feckless amateurs, revolutionaries for revolution's sake.

"How does the fact that I'm sleeping with William affect the revolution?" stormed Laura, further annoyed by Wilfredo's patronizing attitude. "We didn't fight in the mountains to have you guys set up a police state."

"Cálmate, chica," calm down, said Wilfredo, spreading out his hands. "I like William too, but we have to face the facts. He is an American and cannot be trusted. Sooner or later he will turn against us. He's not one of us. He's one of them."

"I don't see that at all. William was out there risking his life while you and your party people were taking lessons in coup d'états from Stalin's brownnosers. As far as I'm concerned he's a Cuban through and through. He's more Cuban than your Che Guevara, who's just an opportunist."

Wilfredo could feel his ire rising, but he struggled to control himself—not that he cared for Guevara either, but because Laura was so intent on creating a scene.

"Why can't you see that this is how things have to be? This has been approved by higher-ups!"

"By whom?"

"By Comandante Guevara, for one."

"In that case Che is not only an opportunist but also a Peeping Tom!"

"And by Fidel himself."

Laura jerked back in her chair, her mind as rattled as if she'd been the unlucky recipient of a sucker punch.

"That's not possible," she mumbled, aware of the enormous self-deception her words betrayed.

"How else do you think that we could have set this up? Who else would dare, Laurita? Look, the *comandante en jefe* has entrusted William with a very delicate mission. We have to make sure that he stays on our side. You could call this movie our insurance policy."

Laura breathed deeply, her mind still reeling. She felt soiled, as though the uniform she was wearing, even the black-and-red 26th of July insignia had been stained by the foulest splattering of a pigsty.

"So I'm to be your Mata Hari," she said, understanding at last.

"You don't have to be so dramatic."

"Alright, then, I'm to be *la puta de la revolución,*" the revolution's whore.

"Laurita, *por favor!* All we are asking is for you to continue doing what you were doing, only do it for us, not just for your selfish pleasure. Do it for the sake of the people."

"I see. Fuck for the sake of Cuba. Is that the only role the revolution has for women, to be whores, consorts, and spies?"

"You're changing the subject. Let's say this is the role that the revolution has for you. For now. The revolution is open to all women. Look at Elena Mederos, the minister of welfare; at Teresa Casuso, our ambassador to Mexico. There is room for everyone and everything. Within the revolution."

"The revolution being whatever the party decides."

"*Chica,* get off this party business. I am here as the undersecretary of the Ministry of the Interior, all right? The fact that I'm sympathetic to the international aspirations of the party has nothing to do with anything. Like Fidel says, this revolution is as green as our palm trees. Green, not red. This is just a job that has to be done, that's all."

Brother and sister fell silent, stared at each other. Into the room floated the cry of a street vendor, riding a wave of salt air.

"*Naranjas!*" Oranges!

"*Naranjas de China dulce!*" Sweet oranges from China!

"And if I don't do it?"

"Well, you know, we can't force you to do anything you don't want to. But . . . "

"But what?"

"Let's say you'll have a hard time finding a job in the revolutionary government after all."

"That's not much of a threat. I've lived without it before. I can do it again."

"And of course we'd be forced to release this film to the press and the television stations. The scandal would not do much good to William's career."

Wilfredo paused, then gave his sister a dry smile, relishing the knife he was about to sink in.

"Or his marriage."

This time the blow was visceral, bile rising up in a foamy plume to Laura's mouth. She swallowed, breathed deep.

"He's married?"

Wilfredo shook his pink cheeks in superb mock irony.

"*Chica*, I thought everybody in town knew. He got hitched in February. And she's pregnant. How could you be so ignorant?"

Laura felt the room closing in on her. She hadn't seen him since he'd left town several weeks before. That William was still with Irma she knew, but she felt it was out of pity for her, that once Irma healed he would leave her and the two of them would be together again. This was the end of that dream. *Sueños. La vida es sueño.* Life is but a dream.

The loud pealing of the cathedral bells came ringing. Three o'clock. Time for the Mass of the dear departed. Down the hall in the converted casino someone raised the volume of a radio, the better to hear the most-requested song in the country, now that the government had outlawed jukeboxes:

> *Según tu punto de vista*
> *Yo soy la mala*
> *Vampiresa en tu novela*
> *La gran tirana.*

> From your point of view
> I am the evil one
> The vampire of your novel
> The wicked tyrant.

"What is it that I'm supposed to do?" said Laura flatly.

Chapter

7

El líder máximo, the maximum leader, lifted the heavy air tank, hoisted it over his shoulders, and slipped his arms through the armholes, strapping the belt tightly around his waist. He had double-checked the rest of the breathing apparatus already and had slipped on the stiff flippers. Now he grabbed his mask from García-Imbert, the French-Cuban instructor who had flown in the latest equipment from Jacques Cousteau's Riviera headquarters. With infinite care the leader spat into his mask, spreading his own saliva with the entranced attention of a child playing with his soiled diaper. Satisfied he had covered every inch of the glass, he placed it on the mask and bit into the mouthpiece.

"*Coño,* I feel like a frog walking around like this," mumbled Fidel, waddling to the edge of the boat.

"That is good that way," replied García-Imbert, "You will feel like a shark when you are in the water."

"If not, at least like a barracuda. Where's my spear?"

"*Voilà, mon capitaine!*" said the instructor, handing the CO_2-powered weapon to the massive leader of Cuba, the man known around the world as the symbol of freedom, youth, and vigor—a new leader for a new age.

Fidel sucked in his stomach while the photographer for *Revolución* snapped away. It wouldn't look right for the national symbol of strength to have a big gut. Of course later he would go over the print sheet with the photographer, selecting the shots that he thought were most becoming, but it always paid to be prepared. Preparation is all. You have to outthink them and you have to outwit them. Like you always do. In the end, no one compares to me.

The yellow buoy bobbed on the easy swells warmed by the clear winter light. Three kilometers away was the jagged coastline around Cojímar, the small fishing village where he had decided to set up the second of what would be many residences around the island. His house, just down the road from old man Hemingway's, was leased from a sympathizer for the commodious sum of one Cuban peso a year. Fidel lifted his gaze and glowered at the horizon. Eighty-eight miles from here lies my true enemy, he thought. This is just the beginning. Let's see who wins this battle of wits.

He turned to an aide.

"*Oye*, remind me to call William Morgan down at his frog farm when I come out."

"Fidel, he's coming to see you this afternoon. You forgot already?"

"Don't fuck with me!" He smiled, squeezed his aide's shoulder.

"I was just testing you, Manolo. See you later. *Allons, m'sieur!*"

He flopped into the water with a great splash, almost losing his mask in the process. García-Imbert quickly followed, alarmed at the great leader's belly flop, worried that something might happen to him while in this, his first scuba dive, and then, *merde,* it was better not to think of that at all.

García observed, to his satisfaction, that Fidel certainly seemed to be in his element underwater. The slight ungainliness that he made up with bluster and brio on land was transformed into a muscular grace that swiftly propelled him through the deep. He followed his trail of bubbles to the coral reef, where Fidel was about to grab a purple-black urchin glistening like an abstract sculpture of wet ebony.

García hurried and came in between Fidel and the urchin, shaking his head violently to warn him off. Fidel raised his hand asking why. García signaled at him to wait. Under the reef a spiny lobster scurried away, seeking the safety of its shelter beneath a coral outcropping. With a swift kick, García glided down and picked up the lobster by its long antennae. The animal, lacking the great claws of its northern cousin, wriggled vigorously in García's hand, trying to sting him with the spine at the end of its tail, which García avoided without too much trouble. He then passed the spiny lobster over the urchin, barely touching one of the mollusk's spines. The lobster immediately turned limp, as the venom at the tip of the spine took quick effect, then the crustacean went into convulsions and stiffened as rigidly as if it had been frozen. García banged the lobster against the reef. Hard as a board. He ran a finger on his throat in a slashing motion. Fidel nodded. That was one signal he understood very well.

By the time the dive was over, Fidel had captured three bonitos, a porgy, and a long moray eel, whose long sharp incisors were no match for the commander's weapon. Fidel surfaced on the boat, shaking his curly head and beard like a large canine airing his fur coat.

"Pretty good, eh?" he said, pointing at the mesh bag with the still-wriggling contents.

"You're the best, *Comandante*," said García, meaning, in all sincerity, that he had never had a student as apt or as quick to learn. But that was not enough for Fidel. His noble Spanish features overcast by a worried gloom, he stepped up to García until their faces almost touched. García wasn't sure if the *comandante en jefe* was going to hit him, kiss him, or both.

"*Oye, chico,* that urchin down there," growled the rebel leader.

"Yes, Fidel, I meant to tell you."

Fidel cut him off before the suddenly intimidated diver could utter another word.

"You have to be very careful. That urchin could have killed you."

"*Sí, Comandante,*" mumbled García, not seeing what was Fidel's point.

"Those things are deadly. You saw what it did to that lobster, paralyzed it like that."

"I know, Fidel."

"If you're not careful, next time I'm going to let you touch it, as a lesson."

"Excuse me?"

At once Fidel was all smiles, wrapping a large muscular arm around the instructor's slender neck.

"I know, you haven't been around lately. You've been in Europe with the *franchutes,* learning how to say, "*s'il vous plaît, marmelade,*" and all those things, so you've probably forgotten how things are around here. But I know these waters, muchacho, and you have to be very careful. Just because you got all that equipment doesn't mean anything. Remember, when we were in the Sierra, the tyranny had all the best equipment in the world, and it did it no good. You have to be alert to the hidden dangers of the terrain. I know these waters very well, so next time, you let me be your guide, understand?"

García felt such an irresistible outflow of sympathy, wisdom, and compassion from Fidel that all he could do was nod *yes,* even as his mind analyzed what Fidel was saying.

He's making it sound as though he was the one who saved me! When I was the one who pointed out the danger to him! But wait, was that what really happened?

The Great American

The photographer for *Revolución* had been snapping away at this image of the *máximo líder* advising the admiring, although obviously befuddled, diving instructor. What a great image, thought the photographer: Fidel pointing out the dangers of the deep because they're Cuban dangers and he knows those better than anyone else.

"What happened exactly, Fidel?" asked the reporter from *Revolución,* who had safely stayed on board during the dive, drinking Polar beer and munching on ham sandwiches. Fidel stuck his chest out as the photographer danced around him, snapping frame after frame.

"*Chico,* it was something tremendous," replied the leader, now throwing his arms expressively around García to show him no harm done, then moving to the edge of the deck, pointing down at the water.

"There are some deadly urchins down there which will stun anybody who's unaware of them. If it hadn't been for me, who knows what might have happened to Enriquito here."

And as Fidel spoke to the reporter, García searched his mind, trying to locate the precise memory of what had happened down below, comparing it to the adventure that Fidel was telling. That's not quite how I remember it, but, yes, it may have happened that way. I don't know, things are different down there.

Abruptly Fidel stopped his account and, grasping the spear with a great flourish, jumped into the water in the middle of his tale. Everyone in the boat was stunned, looked at one another, not quite knowing what to do. García waited a moment, then, realizing that Fidel had dived down, also threw himself into the water. But as he dove down, Fidel was already swimming back to the surface. He had dived forty feet below, without a mask or fins or tank, and dislodged the urchin with his spear, which he now carried aloft like a trophy in the blue-green water. García followed Fidel back into the boat as he climbed in and threw the urchin on deck.

"That's it," said Fidel, dripping salt water and sincerity; "that animal harbors one of the deadliest toxins known to man. If I hadn't stopped Enrique, we'd have a dead scuba instructor right now."

On hearing that, García-Imbert smiled and nodded. Obviously that's just how it happened, he thought. I must be remembering it all wrong. What a brave man Fidel is! How great, powerful, and wise!

✳ ✳ ✳

"*Pase, Comandante,* please step right in."

The bowing, solicitous woman in the green fatigues waved Morgan into the room. An antechamber or living room of some sort on the easternmost wing of the house, the room faced a broad balcony jutting out over a massive outcropping of knife-edge-sharp coral marching all the way to the clashing sea below. On the narrow strip of beach, two rebel army soldiers sat on an improvised bench of empty Coca-Cola crates, machine guns by their side, smoking cigarettes and conversing. A Cuban coast guard cutter sailed over the deep waters, now calm like a pool of Prussian blue oil.

Morgan leaned on the metal railing, taking in deep mouthfuls of the salty breeze. Looking down at the soldiers, he recalled the barred entry to the private road leading to the house, the dozens of suspicious *barbudos* who eyed him warily as he drove in the Jeep. El Gato had to argue with the guards to gain access to the road leading up, threatening them with Fidel's stormy displeasure if the maximum leader's guest, a *comandante* himself in his own right, was not let in at once.

After a hasty call placed on a World War II–vintage field telephone, the captain of the guard raised his hand and the gate finally lifted.

"This shit is worse than with Batista," grumbled El Gato as their vehicle slowly climbed the dusty road to the house at the summit of the hill.

"Shh, *cállate, hombre,*" shut up, man, said Morgan. "There are Moors on the coast," the universal phrase for eavesdroppers in Spanish.

"Those aren't Moors, those are pigs on the coast," retorted El Gato before quieting down.

※ ※ ※

He's very well protected here, thought Morgan. Just like everywhere he goes. I'll bet he has aerial surveillance as well. Yet when he wants to he can be as fearless as any man I've ever known. He seems to be afraid someone will do to him what he did to others, that he'll be paid back in his own coin. But why? What he did was done for the right reasons. Everybody admits that now. Except Boyeros and his boys, naturally. They think he's a commie through and through.

"You don't?" Morgan remembered now Boyeros's incredulous expression as he poured Morgan a frosty daiquiri in a long-stemmed glass aboard his yacht.

"No, I'm not convinced Fidel is a communist, Chuck. Neither were you just a few months ago. What made you change your mind?"

"The evidence, my boy. We didn't have enough of it before and now we do. He's surrounded himself with reds. That Núñez Jiménez who's writing the agrarian reform plan for him, he's a known fellow traveler. There's Raúl, there's Che. Things are different now. I'm sure you've seen it all around you."

"I guess I have. But I've also been asking myself, What is it to be a communist? If you're talking about an oppressive government, denying basic human freedoms, then I am against it. But if being a red means more food for the people, a job for everyone, the government taking care of people without taking away their freedom, well, I don't know if I'm so opposed to the reds, then. Everybody needs a chance, Chuck, and most people haven't gotten one in Cuba."

"Nonsense, my boy. I can show you a dozen people who came to Cuba without a penny and within ten years they were millionaires. From everywhere in the world. Poland, Spain, Italy, China. I even know a few Americans."

Morgan grabbed at Boyeros's suggestion. He carefully placed his drink on the glistening teak table.

"Actually, I wouldn't mind becoming one of those Americans myself," he said finally, after a meaningful pause.

"Well, that can be arranged, as we used to say in Princeton. But don't you think you'll be betraying the people, quote unquote, by becoming rich?"

Morgan merely shrugged, not sure himself at that point if he was playing along or really believing his own words.

"Just because I want other people to get theirs doesn't mean I don't want to get mine too. Besides which, you were right about one thing: the only person who counts for Fidel is Fidel. I hate his guts. He stabbed us in the back, just like you said he would. We have to get rid of him."

"That means you will join us to get him out."

"You bet I will."

Boyeros exploded with cheer.

"Splendid, old boy, splendid! So tell me, what do you want out of this? A job in the government? An apartment on Park Avenue? A villa in southern France? This yacht? Whatever you want, just tell us, we'll meet your price. Just tell us what you want."

Just tell us what you want. That's a hell of a question, Chuck, thought Morgan, still looking out at the ocean from Fidel's balcony. Sometimes I don't know what I want myself. I thought I wanted to see a free Cuba, and now look at me, playing both sides. I thought I wanted to be back with Laura, and now I'm thinking of leaving her. I married Irma thinking I loved her and now . . . that's not true, I do love Irma. And I love Laura too. God. How can anybody love two women at the same time? And Fidel, how the hell do I feel about Fidel? What am I going to do about him?

A rustling of newspapers tossed to the floor, a door squeaking open, the patter of naked feet on concrete tile. Surprised at how well sound carried, Morgan turned to see who entered. A tall white woman dressed only in a green fatigue shirt looked around in the daze of the newly awakened, ran a small hand through a thick head of ebony hair. The moment she noticed Morgan at the balcony, a warm smile of recognition lit up her fine patrician features, and Violeta Ramírez y Caballero ran to Morgan and kissed him.

"My God, William, how are you doing!" she said in her indelible New York accent, gentian blue eyes swimming with laughter. "I haven't seen you since that night at the yacht club two years ago."

"It's been only two years?!" replied Morgan, hugging her, thinking back to the assassination attempt on Batista, the planning, the scheming, the urgency, and the deaths, and the strange love for someone named Laura whose image he would never leave behind.

"It seems longer, doesn't it? But what are you doing here? Of course, of course, to see Fidel. He's still sleeping. He was out till four last night, then this morning he went scuba diving, so he's snoring like a bear right now. But how the hell are you!"

Morgan beamed back, basking in her sunny welcome.

"Just doing great. We set up a frog farm out by Trinidad. We should be harvesting by the end of the year."

Violeta looked at Morgan puzzled, then covered her mouth with her hand, tittering.

"A frog farm? You must be kidding!"

"Not at all. It's a good source of meat, and we can use the skin for purses and stuff like that."

Violeta laughed some more, then restrained herself. "Well, anything to be self-sufficient, that's the slogan nowadays. Excuse me."

She returned to the living room, turned on a lamp stand, then returned to the balcony, shutting the sliding glass door behind her.

"I had to turn off the mike. I didn't want to wake Fidel."

"How's that?"

"The place is wired for sound. If you're out in the balcony, anything you say can be heard in the bedroom. Protection, you know."

"I see. So tell me, how long have Fidel and you two been an item?"

Violeta blushed like a young girl. "Fidel has always been the love of my life. Now that we won, I don't have to pretend anything else. With him in power, all my efforts have borne fruit."

She paused, smiled again.

"Dramatic, isn't it?"

"I'd say so."

"But these are dramatic times, William. We are making history, These are momentous times, like Lenin at the Winter Palace."

There we go again, thought Morgan. It's Russia this, Lenin that. Why can't anybody ever talk about Valley Forge for once?

Violeta went on, enraptured. "This is the revolution of youth and ideals, William. But this is only the first step! What we do today here will be carried around the world, maybe one day even to the U.S. itself!"

"Is that what Fidel tells you in bed?"

Violeta stepped back, shocked. "I beg your pardon?"

"Yeah, I want to know. Is that how he gets you hot, talking about world revolution?"

"How dare you talk to me like that!"

"How dare you! That's not what you and I fought for, Violeta. We talked about defeating Batista and getting rid of his government. Nobody ever said anything about carrying some kind of revolution all over the world. We have enough problems here. You can't force revolutions on other countries. Not unless Fidel is planning to become Napoleon. Or you guys are really all commies in disguise. Are you? Is Fidel?"

Violeta wrapped herself up in her shirt, as though to ward off the chill from Morgan's hostile questioning.

"Of course I am not a communist. With my background, how could I be? As for Fidel, well, you ask him yourself."

"I see. So tell me, is he a good lover? Is he as good in bed as he is in front of a crowd?"

Violeta was tempted to erupt in righteous indignation again, but the very brazenness of the question amused her in spite of herself.

"You know, you are really getting personal there, William. But if you must know, he's really a monster!" She chuckled.

"It's like he's in and out and it's all over. But you know what? At least I know he's my monster and nobody else's. And speaking of Count Dracula. The sun must be going down."

A disheveled Fidel, dressed in baby blue pajama bottoms, lumbered into the room, stretching his arms as he stifled an ursine yawn.

"William! *Coño,* I forgot you were coming! I just laid down for a nap, and see where it gets you."

He shook hands wanly with Morgan, his deep brown eyes alert to Morgan's reactions, his smile as beckoning as the personal liability lawyer ushering a wheelchair-bound client through the office door. He waved Morgan over to the Danish sofa, then snapped at Violeta.

"*Oye tú,*" hey you, he growled, "go get us some coffee. We've got business to discuss here."

"But, Fidel, dear, I don't even know where the kitchen is in this place."

"Just go out to the living room. Celia will show you. Now hurry up, *coño*, I want that coffee today!"

"*Sí, Fidel, mi amor,*" said Violeta primly. She shook Morgan's hand good-bye, whispering, "It's those bennies he's taking, he gets awful jumpy."

Then she stepped back and said loudly for her master's benefit, "Nice talking to you again, William. Let's get together soon."

And without a further word, Violeta Ramírez y Caballero, daughter of Osvaldo Ramírez Sotomayor and Lucrecia Caballero Ponceaga, marquessa of Aguas Dulces and countess of Santa Clara on her mother's side, descended from the founders of Santiago and Camagüey, with homes in Paris, Palm Beach, and Park Avenue, smartly turned around and padded quickly on naked feet out of the room to get Fidel his coffee.

Fidel shook his head, snorting disgustedly. "These women. Just because you go to bed with them a couple of times, they think they own you."

Fidel sidled over to Morgan on the couch, as if by the sheer bulk of his weight he would extract all truth from him. Morgan detected a smell of garlic and Varon Dandy cologne on Fidel as well as another scent that was very familiar yet took him a moment to identify—curdled milk. His breath had the same sweet lactose smell of tiny children and old people.

Everyone in Cuba knew about Fidel's legendary passion for tropical fruit shakes, a love that in barely three months had ballooned the once-lean-and-mean guerrilla fighter. But shakes were only part of his odd dietary habits. He was known to go without eating or sleeping for two or three days, only to then sit at an elephantine feast, where he would devour two dozen oysters, three steaks, four servings of rice and beans, fried plantains, a couple of fried eggs, a piece of chicken or shellfish if he felt like it, plus the inevitable guava shells with cream cheese, and perhaps, to vary somewhat, a *pudín* or a custard, plus his two or three thimblefuls of Cuban coffee and a big fat Cohiba. Morgan noticed the folds of fat spreading larcenously over his waistline. No wonder they call him El Caballo, the Horse, thought Morgan; he's like a racehorse gone to pasture.

"Tell me how those sons of bitches want to fuck us," he said now, draping his limp arm on Morgan's shoulder.

Morgan wriggled away from him on the couch. Fidel waited, confident of eventually getting what he wanted.

"I don't know how to tell you this," said Morgan in English, "but it's really bad."

370

"I am never surprised by people, William, so go ahead. Is the State Department in on this? The CIA?"

"Not directly. Some U.S. government people have approached me, but it's not them. The problem is right here in Cuba. There are thousands of people involved. They're calling it the White Rose, after the poem by Martí."

"It's that big? Who's behind it, then, if not the U.S.? Batista?"

"Trujillo."

Fidel frowned. General Rafael Leónidas Trujillo had lately become the biggest thorn on his side. The dictator of the neighboring Dominican Republic, he had given political asylum to Batista after his escape from Havana. Trained by the Americans, Trujillo had stayed on top since the 1930s through a combination of state patronage and police terror. He fancied himself a nation builder like Bolívar and Peter the Great and had named the capital city of the country after himself, Ciudad Trujillo, and placed a statue with his likeness in every square in every city in the country.

"So what's Chapitas's plan for me?" asked Fidel, calling Trujillo by his familiar nickname, Bottle Caps, for his love of medals and fancy uniforms.

Morgan paused, got up from the couch, walked up to the sliding glass door. If he was ever going to make the jump, this was the time, It would never get better than this.

Out on the water, an oil tanker heading for the port of Cárdenas slowly skirted the shoals of Cojímar.

"I'll tell you, but I want you to do something for me."

"What's that? Just ask me, anything within reason."

"I want to go back to the States."

Chapter

8

"You can't leave us! I won't let you!"

Laura's words were muffled by her hair, which lashed Morgan's shoulders like a whip. Morgan lay facedown, his eyes closed by fatigue and the sweet intoxication of spent love. He realized he must have fallen asleep, for the last thing he remembered was Laura snuggling up to him, her head lying on his chest. He half opened his eyes, saw Laura's slender reflection in the mirror of the Spanish *armario*, her legs straddling his back as she bent over to whisper in his ear while he slept.

"You won't leave us, now or later. No, I forbid it!"

Those were Fidel's words, hissed, not said, by a man who only lost his temper on purpose. Morgan recalled the deadly menace behind the cold order. No one leaves Fidel alive, they implied; I will not be forsaken.

"You can't get off this train," added Fidel with a smile that was born forced but quickly found its way to genuine warmth. "We're not at the station yet. There will be plenty of time for you to pick up your bags later on. The revolution needs you now. *I* need you now."

He paused, then pleaded a guileful grin.

"Besides, William, think of what our enemies will say if you quit on us just a few months after we won. We can't afford that. You're too big now to leave."

"All right, I'll stay," replied Morgan. "But let Irma leave. She would be in danger once our operation starts. This is much bigger than I thought. They probably won't be able to get to me, but who knows what they might do to her?"

Fidel raised a bushy eyebrow, shook his head.

"We don't attack people's families, William."

"You don't know these men, Fidel. They are desperate people. They will try anything. These guys are mobsters and killers, they just don't care."

"I still can't believe it."

"Even if you don't, how effective do you think I will be if I think my family is in danger throughout all this? Irma is pregnant, you know."

Fidel sighed, threw up his hands. "I know. Well, there is no arguing against that. She can go visit her relatives in the States. Doesn't her father's family live in California?"

"How did you know?"

Fidel grinned heartily once more, the wizard making the pigeon vanish with a puff of smoke beneath the red satin cloak.

"We know everything. We have ears and mouths all over this island, ready to whisper all kinds of little secrets, didn't you know?"

Yes, you know everything, thought Morgan now as he stirred, turning his body face up so that he could see burnished Laura and not her smoky reflection. But what do you do with what you know? That's what counts. Information is nothing without interpretation. And how do you interpret us? he thought as Laura bent down and slowly ran her hair over his chest, her right hand going for his rising member, jerking it to full length, as she slowly nibbled her way down his chest to his groin, where she buried her face in devoted concentration. How do you interpret her and me and Irma and the child I will have and what do you make of someone like me who can't belong to either country or either woman and who can't decide if this revolution is the greatest gift of liberty to mankind since Jefferson or the greatest piece of shit since Lenin overthrew—*oh my God yes baby yes I'm coming and yes I love you and what the hell is she doing!*

※ ※ ※

Later, when they again lay in each other's arms, Morgan cupped Laura's head in his hand, her wide eyes staring back at him.

"You not to do that any more," he said in Spanish.

"Why not, *mi amor?*" she replied with a tenderness utterly lacking in her heart. "The anus is one of the most sensitive areas of our body. Sticking a finger or an instrument at the time of ejaculation will bring a man to—"

"Sssh! I do not want to hear! No! Who teach you to do that?"

She moved away from him, sat defiantly erect, her small rounded breasts in proud attention.

"This whore I met at La Cita. She said Prío used to love it, that all powerful men love to fuck and be fucked at the same time. She said the more powerful the man, the more depraved he becomes."

She paused, tossed her hair back on her shoulders.

"I expect to be getting in bed with you and some animals pretty soon," she said, grinning, as though her words were not barbs. Morgan frowned. She took his hand, licked his lips lewdly.

"Or maybe some little boys? Maybe you'd like to suck some little boy's peepee while I suck you off?"

Morgan's slap threw her clear across the bed. Had she not grabbed at the bedsheet she would have landed sprawled on the floor. She touched her cheek, feeling the burn, knowing that the imprint on her cheek would last all day. She slithered back up next to him and taunted him once more, hoping he'd strike her again, hating herself for what she was doing.

"I know. You want me to do it with your wife, right? Now that she's pregnant, think of it! That's four in bed, including an unborn baby. What wonderful perversity, don't you think? I could lick . . . "

She closed her eyes when she saw his hand moving, expecting the next blow, but instead he grabbed her by the hair and pressed his lips against hers, forcing her to be still. His tongue invaded her mouth and she sucked it like a mother's breast, like the last hope she would have to redeem herself. They clawed at each other, and she felt him grow rigid just the way she wanted him, to be weak in his manliness so she could dominate him by his sex, and he would forget his wife and his job and his power, and she would forget her brother and her betrayal, and both of them could come together again in the idealism of an open terror and not the hidden machinations of faceless men. She cried from the unexpected pain as he turned her over and rammed himself into her rectum, feeling the membranes tear and the blood come out, but she welcomed the pain; it made her feel pure, as though by being raped up the ass she would forget the pain that was splitting her heart.

Afterward he cried, big manly tears of frustration and desire, promising he would never do it again, that he was under so much pressure that he couldn't stand the slightest taunt, that Fidel had entrusted him with a job that could make or break the revolution, and that he himself did not know if he was capable of carrying it out. She accepted his apologies and gave him her own. She was too jealous, she said. She knew she was barren and Irma was fertile, and she envied her the gift of life, but all that was behind them now. She gladly accepted her position. She could accept the fact that he would never leave Irma and she would be his lover only.

"There's no need to cry, darling. I understand. Why don't you tell me about this job Fidel has given you, it sounds very important!"

And with those pedestrian words Laura opened up the floodgates of confession, Morgan cradled in her arms.

※ ※ ※

Wilfredo Fernández felt very proud of himself. All the grand old men of the party were gathered at their secret headquarters in Cojímar, waiting anxiously for his report. For once he was more than just a covert communist in the Ministry of the Interior. He was the conduit of new information, vital information, even, that would turn him into one of the undisputed leaders of the party and, if it worked out as he expected, one of the leaders of the country. He would finally fulfill what he always knew was his destiny, to hold the reins of Cuba in his hands.

The grandest of the grand old men, the secretary general of the Popular Socialist Party, the unreformed Stalinist Francisco Calderío, who had adopted the *nom de rouge* Blas Roca, shook his considerable jowls. To him Fernández was an unknown quantity who might be somewhat useful and who for now had to be humored. Unfortunately, anyone who might help the party gain control over the 26th of July people and over Castro himself had to be humored nowadays.

"*Bueno*, Wilfredo. As you requested, we at the Central Committee have made time to hear your report. What is this information about the American *comandante* that could be so useful to us?"

Wilfredo almost shook with excitement, took a sip of water from the glass at the table. Arrayed before him were the faces that up to now he'd seen only in the photographs of party publications: in the corner, with his usual goatee and ironic smile, the assistant secretary general, Carlos Rafael Rodríguez; next to him, the old black fighter of the labor wars and former head of the Cuban federation of labor, Lázaro Peña; Edith García, who once was married to Rodríguez and who was protecting the man who betrayed the survivors of the attack on the palace; Joaquín Ordoqui, Aníbal Escalante, and others, all cloaked with the mystery and wisdom of the party.

"*Compañeros*," he said in a squeaky voice, "this information has been provided to me by someone with the most intimate link to the *comandante*, so there can be no doubt about its veracity. Not only that. Preliminary investigations that I personally have conducted within the scope of my employment at the Interior Ministry, a job to which the party, with its accustomed historical foresight, guided me after my sojourn in the brotherly countries of Eastern Europe, namely Czechoslovakia and Romania, for further training in the means, ways, and methods whereby the inevitable conflict ensuing from the class struggle—"

"Fernández, skip the elementary Marxism," growled Roca, upset at being roused out of his sickbed just to hear a primer on dialectics. "We already know about the forward march of history. Tell us what this information is and what it can do for us."

In his corner, Carlos Rafael Rodríguez stroked his goatee and widened his smile even deeper, amused as always by the contrast between rhetoric and power in Cuba.

"The comrade secretary general means, no doubt, what the information can do for the people of Cuba."

Roca frowned again, shook his head in assent. He didn't like Rodríguez; he was too smart, too weasely, too high society for his taste. He didn't trust him either, always apologizing for Castro and urging cooperation with the 26th of July when everyone knew the party should hold the position of primacy. But protocol had to be followed. A record was being kept, and while it was secret right now, someday it would be opened, and it would not do to seem so imperious.

"Naturally I meant the people of Cuba. The party stands for the people of Cuba, Comrade Rodríguez."

"Of course, Comrade Secretary General. My apologies."

"None needed." Roca turned hungrily to Fernández.

"Well, hombre, so what is the story?"

Wilfredo took a deep breath, let it go, and began to speak as calmly as he was able.

"It's a countrywide conspiracy, *Compañeros.* Agents of the counterrevolution, Batistianos, Americanos, members of the haute bourgeoisie, have approached the American major William Morgan and asked him to overthrow our maximum leader, Fidel Castro, and impose a so-called constitutional democracy. They're calling it *Fidelismo* without Fidel."

"That's absurd," sputtered Roca; "that's like Leninism without Lenin. It flies in the face of common sense."

"My sentiments exactly, Comrade Secretary General," said Fernández, more sure of his ideological footing. "But to those people it seems a viable alternative. They are afraid of the concentration of power in Fidel's hands and what they perceive, rightly of course, as the growing influence

of the party in the revolutionary government. They point to Comandantes Che Guevara, Raúl Castro, Efigenio Ameijeiras, and others who
they say are acting as fronts for party infiltration."

If only that were true, mused Roca. Those *barbudos* just want to use us
to consolidate their power. They have no intention of letting us rule this
country the way it should be governed.

Wilfredo mistook Roca's silence for approval and leaned forward on
the balls of his feet, almost preening, with the self-confidence of giddy
exhilaration.

"This is the plan, as far as I've been able to figure it out. A shadow
government will be formed, ready to step into the vacuum left by
Castro's disappearance. Morgan, using his contact and knowledge of our
líder's activities, will lure him to an office where Fidel will be gunned
down. A number of agents in place will then spring forward at places like
La Cabaña prison, the Columbia army camp, the Presidential Palace, and
will take over the government in the name of the revolution.

"They're calling the movement the White Rose after the poem by the
founder of our country, José Martí. I am certain you comrades remember it."

Wilfredo felt compelled to recite the entire poem in the high-flying
declamatory style of a nineteenth-century performer, upswept brow,
arms flung open wide and all:

Cultivo la rosa blanca
en junio como en enero
para el amigo sincero
que me da su mano franca
y para el cruel que me arranca
el corazón con que vivo,
cardo ni ortiga cultivo,
cultivo la rosa blanca.

I grow the white rose
In June as in January
For the true friend
Whose faithful hand I shake
And for the cruel ones who tear out
My still beating heart.
I grow not nettle or thistle,
I grow the white rose.

When he finished, the entire leadership of the Cuban Socialist Party was speechless, flabbergasted that Wilfredo had used a confidential briefing to indulge in the worst of theatrical excesses. This, after all, was a poem all Cubans learned in second grade. What kind of fools did he take them to be? What kind of fool was he?

Rodríguez, almost casually, asked exactly how many people were involved in the conspiracy.

"Very many, like I said," said Wilfredo firmly. "Possibly up to four thousand."

His reply broke the dam of astonishment and the questions flew.

"What kind of support are they getting from the U.S.?"

"What is the operative date?"

"Who else in the top echelons of the government is involved besides Morgan?"

"Will anybody else be killed besides Fidel?"

"Is the U.S. sending in the marines?"

"Who is paying for all this?"

✖ ✖ ✖

Wilfredo tried to answer as thoroughly as he could each of the myriad questions. In the end he conveyed a portrait of a besieged government whose only hope for survival lay in the hands of the party. At no time did it occur to him that Morgan's part might be that of a double agent, for that kind of duplicity was beyond him. But it was not beyond the wiles of Rodríguez, who had already heard much speculation about the peculiar attraction Morgan held for Fidel.

After Wilfredo had been dismissed and asked to wait in an adjoining room, Rodríguez addressed the party stalwarts.

"*Compañeros,* I believe that this should be reported at once to Fidel. To do otherwise would be not only a crime but even more grave, a mistake."

"Why is that, Rodríguez?" queried Roca, who let a thin smile flower on his lips, feeling for the first time in years that history was on his side. "The sort of chaos that would ensue after the assassination would only further the role of the party. This kind of conspiracy rarely succeeds at its objectives. When all these interests clash, the people of Cuba will turn to the party as their salvation."

"With all due apologies, Comrade Secretary General, but that is wishful thinking, the worse kind a politician can indulge in," countered Rodríguez, smiling apologetically still.

"There you go, quoting Talleyrand again," growled Roca, "as if nineteenth-century courtiers had anything to teach us Cubans."

"I am sorry, Comrade Secretary General, but I was only expressing my own opinion. But to borrow your phrase, I do believe Talleyrand has much to teach us. He represented France at the Congress of Vienna, when the victorious alliance wanted to dismember his country for the excesses of Napoleon's empire. Using only words, he was able to preserve France's territorial integrity when he had no guns, no soldiers, and no money. He saved France for future generations."

Peña lifted his cracked voice, as he had raised it at so many meetings since the founding of the party, in the 1920s. "*Compañeros*, I side with the secretary general. So Talleyrand saved the France of Louis the Eighteenth, a thoroughly corrupt bourgeois regime. So what? I think from a Marxist perspective Napoleon was better for France. At least he truly illustrated the dialectic strides of history better than those louse-ridden apologists of the ancien régime."

Ordoqui, as the party's main theoretician, felt compelled to join the fray. "But, Comrades, please remember that the restoration of the ancien régime was a necessary part of the dialectical process. Marx himself pointed out . . . "

Soon everyone in the room was busy debating the fine points of dialectics as Rodríguez looked on, silently bemused. *Just like Cubans to get lost in a haze of rhetoric. Will we ever learn? Twenty-five years and nothing has changed. The big landowners still own the land, the workers are still subservient to the bosses, the party is still outside the halls of power. That is why the country has always waited for the man on horseback, why Batista lasted as long as he did. And why Fidel is really the answer. He fits the Cuban character, but he has something more. He knows how to make silk purses out of sows' ears. I can't believe what I'm hearing in this place. Is Ordoqui insane?*

"What the party should encourage, therefore, is an American intervention, a massive landing so that, after the U.S. puts down this neorevolutionary putschist regime headed by Castro, because let's face it, that's what the Twenty-sixth of July really is, the people will turn to the party and we can become the standard-bearers of the next revolution. Cuba must become the new Hungary!"

Madness! Sheer madness! thought Rodríguez. *They want to give up the chance we have now to govern for the possibility of a second chance sometime in the future.* Listen to that old bullfrog, to Roca: "I still believe it would be better to allow this plot to proceed so that in one stroke we can restore the primacy of the people's position."

The people's position? Can't they see? It's Fidel the people want. The 26th of July won the war. All we did was hitch a ride with them.

You old farts may be content being relegated to the dustbin of history, but I am not.

❋ ❋ ❋

To Rodríguez's surprise, carefully disguised as always by his ingratiating smile, Fidel was more bemused than irate when he learned of the secret goings-on at the Central Committee. They spoke as they traveled in Fidel's new limo, recently requisitioned from the home of former senator Masferrer, in exile in Miami.

"*Chico,* that is the best thing that could happen to us right now," said Fidel, looking out the window of the Cadillac Fleetwood at the flashing lights of the city.

"How is that, Fidel?"

"Because I have organized the whole episode, that's why. William is working for me, flushing out all these vermin from their hiding places."

"So that explains why Morgan was talking about it."

"Ah, no, not that," replied Fidel, extracting a Cohiba from the cut glass humidor in the backseat. "He was supposed to keep quiet about it. I'd like to see the little cunt that loosened his tongue."

"Excuse me?"

"I said bring her to me. I'd like to meet her before I take off for New York."

This was news as well. That meant Fidel would be out of harm's way while the conspiracy ripened. As always, he knew when to step in and when to step out.

"When will you be going, Fidel?"

"Next week. The American Press Club has invited me, and I've decided to take them up on it. I hope they don't put me up at the YMCA!"

"Will this be an official visit?"

"No, nothing like that. Extraofficial. I'm taking Pepín Bosch, Daniel Bacardí, and López Fresquet from Treasury in case the Americans feel like giving us aid, although to tell you the truth, I don't know what I would do if they did offer it."

"Why is that, Fidel?"

Castro turned his glinting mischievous eyes on Rodríguez.

"Because I think that our destiny lies elsewhere. Do you understand me?"

"Further east?" ventured Rodríguez. "In more, shall we say, fraternal countries and types of government?"

"How well you understand us, Rodríguez," said Fidel, chuckling.

"That's what I've always liked about you. This is just one step, the first step in a journey of a thousand miles."

"How . . . revolutionary popular, Fidel," said Rodríguez, letting Castro know he understood his allusion to Mao Tse-tung's Long March.

Fidel chuckled again, heavily patted Rodríguez's shoulder.

"That's right, *chico.* Paraphrasing Voltaire, if the revolution didn't have the Yanquis, we would have to invent them. We'll never be free as long as we're under Uncle Sam's shadow. But we can talk more about that when I return. Meantime, make sure I meet Morgan's girl," said Castro, as the limo dashed down the Malecón, with its perennial parade of intertwined lovers.

"What shall we do with the source?"

"Wilfredo?" Fidel paused, lit a match, and stared into the yellow flame, as though contemplating a speck of paint to be altered in a canvas only he could see. "Keep him around. I'll find something for him to do."

The limousine swerved by the monument to the *Maine,* then swiftly carried the maximum leader past the boxy skyscraper housing the American embassy.

"You know, one could get used to this," said Fidel as though to no one in particular, while the vehicle entered the narrow streets of Old Havana.

⌘ ⌘ ⌘

The family at the airport lounge stacked its suitcases all around their seats, putting up barriers to preserve their island of departing dreams. The dark-suited father, round faced, with receding hairline and sweaty brow, sat at a corner of the row of chairs. He held in his hand his family's passports and tickets, waiting for the sign from the guard at the gate to enter customs for inspection before departure. The mother, cat-shaped sunglasses disguising the dark rings of sleeplessness, nervously leafed through the pages of a *Vanidades* magazine with Audrey Hepburn on its cover. Two little honey-blonde twins, dressed in white dresses like their mother, sat next to the woman, playing quietly. Occasionally they would turn to their mother, pointing out a chubby little boy dressed in a pinstriped gray wool suit stained with perspiration, chasing after the many revolutionaries storming through in combat boots and fatigues.

"*Pablito, ven acá!*"—come here—said the woman sharply to the boy, who scampered from the *guerrillero* at the gate and returned to the family fold.

The mother scolded the boy, telling him their guns could go off at any time and it was very dangerous to be around those persons.

"But, *Mamá,* they are revolutionaries. They would never fire at us!" said the boy.

"If we're not around them, they won't for sure," said the mother, forcing the squirming boy to sit alongside his sisters.

Morgan saw all that and more as he walked into the airport with Irma. He faced a sea of departing families, hundreds of people with their life's belongings in suitcases—all professionals, all white, all waiting anxiously by the fishbowl, the glass-enclosed lounge next to the departure gates. Above the entrance a sign simply said MIAMI as the only reason needed for their presence.

He led Irma by the elbow past the throng of families, the smell of apprehension filling the room with a vicious bouquet.

"I really wish we didn't have to do this," said Irma in English, just steps away from the Pan Am counter.

"Sweetheart, you've never been to California. This way you can meet your dad's relatives and see how things are out there. I've always heard San Francisco is a very beautiful city. A lot like Havana, in fact. Weather's different, of course."

"But I don't want to go!"

"You'll like it, you'll see." Then, whispering: "Baby, we already went through all this. You know it isn't safe for you here."

"But I've been in the war, I've been in the Sierra, I'm not afraid!" She whispered as well, her words crackling with resentment.

"This is different. We're not playing by the rules anymore."

"When did anybody? I want to stay here with you!"

"No, and that's final! You are going now if I have to drag you into that plane myself!"

Morgan stepped up to the counter, where the reservations clerk gave Morgan a brisk salute.

"You flight is ready for boarding, *Comandante,*" said the girl, cheeks flushed from emotion on seeing Morgan's uniform.

"It's not for me, it's for my wife," said Morgan, quickly grabbing the ticket.

"In that case, *buen viaje, Compañera.*"

Irma did not answer, giving only a forced smile in return. As the couple departed, the clerk noticed how sharply the major was holding his wife's arm, as if afraid that she'd run away from him. What a strange woman, thought the girl. I would be more than happy to go anywhere he asked me. She must be American. Those women are so independent.

"Next," said the girl, smiling pleasantly in anticipation of her date that evening with Esteban, her fiancé.

✳ ✳ ✳

At the gate to the tarmac, Morgan pressed his lips against Irma's. In his haste and his worry she thought he was saying, Off with you, God damn it, get out of my life. She closed her eyes, and for a moment her whole time with Morgan flashed back into view, from their meeting at her father's mission to their last spat, that morning, when she refused to pack for her trip. She opened her eyes, brimming with tears.

"Just one month," she insisted one last time.

"You have my word," he said, and he embraced her, and this time she felt happy, this time she felt his spirit had gone into her, and as in a vision she saw that this separation was only a brief trial and that soon they would be reunited down to the time of their death. She touched her belly, barely rising again from the life she harbored inside.

"I want my baby to be born here, not there," she said. "I want a little Cuban boy."

"You'll be back long before it's due. Now go on, the plane is waiting for you."

He gently pushed her to the DC-3 as the big propellers of the plane started up, a stewardess at the top of the rolling stairs waving at them to hurry. Irma walked backward, still facing Morgan, threw him a last kiss.

"Don't forget me!" she said, but the roar of the engine drowned her words. Morgan stood at the gate, already waving at her from the other shore. She turned and hurried to the staircase. When she looked back he was gone.

✳ ✳ ✳

She saw him again when the plane coasted down the runway and she muttered a brief prayer to a God she felt didn't care for her any longer. Morgan was at the railing of the observation deck, El Gato by his side, both men waving great white handkerchiefs, and she felt her heart explode with joy and pride and worry.

Lord, I know I haven't spoken to you in a long time, and I don't know if you really exist anymore, but if you do, please watch over him. Keep watch over my William and guide him to his destiny in peace.

She broke down crying. The stewardess came, hugged her for comfort.

"I love him so much!" she found herself sobbing to the surprised stranger.

Puzzled, the stewardess gazed out the porthole window and saw a giant poster of Fidel plastered over an old Polar beer billboard.

"I know, *querida,* we all love him too," said the stewardess, patting Irma's shoulder.

※ ※ ※

Down at the airport lounge, the little boy in the pinstriped suit came up to Morgan and El Gato.

"Excuse me, *Comandante,* but do revolutionaries go to heaven?"

Morgan stopped, amused by the boy's boldness.

"I think some go there. Why, my son?"

"Because then when I die I want to go to hell, so I'll never see the likes of you," sneered the boy, his face contorted with hatred. Morgan, momentarily stunned, saw the boy then run back to his family and tearfully embrace his mother. Morgan walked over to them.

"He's your son, señora?"

"Yes, he's ours," said the father, anxiously. "What happened?"

"We were going out and he stopped to say something."

"Pablito! What did you do? You were bothering the *comandante?* I'm going to kill you!" said the father, yanking the boy away from the mother and swatting him with the palm of his hand.

"No, no, please, do not do that!" said Morgan, aware that all the other families had their eyes on them. "I only to want to know, why he does he hate the revolution so much?"

"He doesn't know what he's saying, *Comandante,*" said the father, deadly pale. "It's just that we're leaving the country and he's nervous, that's all. Like all of us. But you shouldn't have opened your mouth!" said the father, slapping the boy once again, as the boy cried and the mother yelled at her husband.

"No, no, please do not punish. It was nothing," said Morgan. "Tell me, why do you leave Cuba?"

The father took out an Irish linen handkerchief, dabbed at his damp forehead.

"Well, *Comandante,* the situation is like this. I work for the Esso refinery and I was offered a new position in New Jersey, so I thought it might be better to transfer while I can," said the man, carefully observing Morgan's reaction.

"But why not stay? The country needs professional men like you!"

"Well, frankly, *Comandante,* we are afraid."

"Afraid? Afraid of what?"

"That the government will take over everything, *Comandante,*"

"Why is that?"

"With all due respect, *Comandante,* we think there are too many communists in the government. Like they say, excuse me if this offends you, I'm sure this doesn't apply to you, really, but they say you are all watermelons."

"Watermelon? I do not understand."

"You mean you haven't heard this?"

"No, please, tell me."

The man paused, licked his suddenly dry lips. "It means that you are green on the outside, like your rebel uniform, but you are all red inside."

"Like the communists?"

The man nodded, then hung his head in abject fear, even as his wife shot him a glance full of daggers.

"I'm sorry, I didn't mean to offend you, this is just what some people are saying, I don't know personally . . . "

Morgan waved a hand, shook his head. "Do not worry, this is a free country, you say what you want. Tell me, please, the government took something from you?"

"Me? Oh, no, not at all. I'm not a landowner. I'm an engineer. We had no possessions except for our house, which we sold."

"Then why leave?"

"Because, *Comandante,* what happens if the government takes it?"

Morgan laughed at the absurdity of the man's fears. On seeing this the entire family smiled, then joined in the chuckling, which was picked up and repeated by all the families, who now all started to laugh as well, all the white, well-meaning, middle-class families fleeing before the doors shut tight on them.

"What is your name, hombre?"

"Juan Pablo Mendoza, *Comandante,* at your service."

"I am Comandante William Morgan, Juan Pablo. I assure you that the communists will not take over. If it happens, they have to kill me first, understand?"

"*Sí, señor.*"

"Go, enjoy the U.S.A. But please come back soon. Cuba needs people like you. *Buen viaje.*"

After shaking hands with everyone, including the little boy—who cowered behind his mother—Morgan walked out to a round of applause from the future exiles. The moment he walked out the door, the families fell silent and turned their gaze once more on the glass-enclosed waiting lounge—their hopes already set on the shores of Miami.

Dear William,

Where are you? I am scared, my love. I long for you, I crave your touch, but you're not around. You have sent me halfway across a continent to the farthest shore of my father's homeland. But it's not my country. I belong in Cuba, darling, next to you, under a warm evening sky full of stars of hope.

San Francisco is a cold and damp city, its buildings washed white by the freezing rain. The sun shines weak in the afternoon and I turn in my bed to catch its rays.

I lost the baby. One afternoon walking on Clement Street with my cousin Margaret, I felt that oozing sensation again. Margaret says I screamed, I don't remember. I must have fainted, just like a stupid woman. All I remember is waking up in a stretcher hurrying along some corridor. Margaret and Leon, her husband, were running alongside me, with a good-bye look in their eyes. I promise you, I wanted to die right then, I knew it was all over, that our baby had returned to the void where he had sprung from, and I wanted to go with him too. I'd like to say that it was my love for you that kept me alive, but it wasn't like that at all. I'm sorry if you think that means I love you less. I didn't feel I had the strength to keep on trying.

Somehow they saved me. The doctors removed one of my ovaries, which means now I only have half the previous cargo of life for you on my return, if ever. Do you still want me? Will you still love me? Will you still think me your wife? I'll understand if you don't.

386

I feel cursed. Perhaps my father is behind this. Maybe he's in that place beyond the grave and he told Jesus, Punish that girl for turning away from you, Lord, and he heard his plea. Maybe I'm imagining the whole thing. These things can be explained scientifically, you know. Besides, I don't fear God anymore. What else can He do that would hurt me worse than He has done already? There can be no worse punishment than knowing you are doomed to never hold in your arms the fruit of your love.

I love you so, darling. There is nothing that would please me more than to give you this child. Will you forgive me? Can you forgive me?

Please let me know. Even if you write to tell me to stay away, that you have found another woman who can give you the children you want, I want you to tell me, even if the pain were to tear out the little life I have left in my wasted body, please let me know. No matter how great the pain, it would be worse if you never answered, if all you did was turn away from me.

I know I'm rambling, but this is a fool's confession. I adore you, sweetheart, for what you are and for what you want to do. For the happiness you have given me and for the hope that has let me live this much so far, for myself, for Cuba, and for all the world, thank you.

Either way, my darling, know that you are always in my heart. I await, trembling, the news of my death or my salvation at your hands.

God bless you, William Morgan.

Your wife,

Irma

Morgan put the letter down on the bed. He had read it and reread it, it seemed to him a hundred times, all without knowing what to reply. Once again he sank into the bed cushions, which Irma had slipcovered with old lace, breathing in her perfume, drinking in the pain of their separation. Again he wondered if he had done the right thing by sending her out of danger but also out of his arms. The longer she stayed in the States the more he craved her and the lonelier he felt.

The white buildings of San Francisco, a city he had never seen, appeared before him like the towers of a prison to which he'd cruelly sent Irma, while he hid the key that could open the gates to her freedom. All it took was a letter, a single call, and she would fly back to his side, doing whatever his bidding was, with a devotion that he found incomprehensible.

But it had gone beyond that. The news of her miscarriage made him feel guilty, responsible for the sudden departure from life of the creature the two of them had fashioned in a night of passion and compromise. Now that guilt mingled with the pangs from his conscience over his affair with Laura, robbing him of all initiative.

It was obvious that she knew of his affair with Laura, and he couldn't face up to the reproach of his own soul, weighed down by the cargo of guilt it harbored. He wished he could be heartless, able to juggle both women in his life without feeling he was giving the better piece of his heart to one and leaving little for the other. He wanted to be like a Cuban, who keeps mistress and wife in two separate spheres, each with her own duties and her own joys. But he was destined to be the good American, always struggling with his conscience and his heart, trying to do right in a world where self-interest was the rule. He wanted to make his whole life cut from the same bolt, unwilling to stitch together a patch that would salve his honor and let him go on living without regrets.

How could he do right in a world that turned away from love, honor, and duty, that rewarded venality instead of honesty, that struck down mercilessly those who sought to balance charity with devotion? He was lost, at sea in a welter of mixed emotions. He knew there was no way out except to face his fears.

He sat at Irma's marble-top dressing table, surrounded by the evidence of her existence—the flasks of French cologne, the ribbons for her hair, the scallop-edged silver frame with the picture of them on a boat down the river Almendares.

He picked up the white phone, stared at his reflection in the smoky mirror, body stiff and at an angle, as though to ward off an impending blow. He dialed the overseas operator, placed the number, waited for what seemed like hours as the phone systems coupled under the vast ocean. The line rang far away, in a place where the rain falls in frigid sheets and the wind howls in from the Golden Gate.

She answered.

"Hello," said Irma dully.

"Hi, sweetheart," said Morgan, his hopes at the end of that long cable all the way to San Francisco.

"William? Is that you?" she said, her voice brightening into something warm and honey gold.

"*Soy yo, mi amor,*" he said.

"Oh, darling, I've been expecting your call. I don't know what to say. How are you?"

"I'm alright, I guess. How are you is the question."

"I'm fine. The doctors released me yesterday from the hospital, that's why I'm here at Margaret's. Everybody's out of town at the farm in Sonoma. I was getting ready to go up there for a few days to rest, but darling . . . ?"

"Yes, sweetheart?"

"I can be on the next plane to Havana if you want me. Do you? Do you still love me?"

"Yes, I love you still. I always will."

"Do you want me back?"

El Gato stormed into the room, waving a newspaper with banner headlines.

"William, it's grave news!"

Morgan wheeled around, annoyed by the interruption.

"What is it?" he growled, not realizing he was still speaking in English. El Gato didn't understand his words but it didn't matter, the intent was clear. He shoved the newspaper in Morgan's face.

"Mira, mira!" Look, look!

"Hello? Hello, William? What's wrong, darling?"

Morgan picked up the copy of *Revolución*. In great six-inch headlines: FIDEL RENUNCIA!

"William? Talk to me, darling. Do you want me back?"

Morgan picked up the phone, spoke hurriedly.

"Baby, I just got some bad news here. I think you better stay in California a while longer."

"What's the problem?'

"Fidel just quit the government."

❋ ❋ ❋

Morgan called Eloy, who referred him to Che, who in turn sent him on a flurry of calls and visits that wound up at Celia Sánchez's modest apartment on Once Street in El Vedado. There, surrounded by his usual coterie of female followers, bodyguards, and assorted *barbudos*, Castro sat in the tiny kitchen, smoking a cigar and sipping an apple drink. Morgan recognized Carlos Franqui, Manuel Hart, Violeta Ramírez among the entourage, all of them enraptured by Fidel's disquisition on Mirabeau's mistakes at the Constituent Assembly during the French Revolution.

"He should have proceeded further as the Jacobins wanted and confiscated also the assets of the crown, not just those of the prelates. That's because he was in the pay of Louis the sixteenth and was conspiring for a constitutional monarchy. Ultimately, of course, the monarchy had to be abolished because that's what the people wanted. But perhaps the *grande peur,* the great fear, and the Committee of Public Safety with all its excesses would have been unnecessary if Mirabeau had acted otherwise."

"But Fidel," said Manuel Hart, the minister of education, "do you really think a true revolution could have been possible without the Reign of Terror?"

Fidel pulled on his Cohiba, shrugged. "That is a question we will have to answer, won't we?" He spotted Morgan braving his way through the crowd, then waved his cigar at the mass of his followers to make way for the American.

"I look for you all day, Fidel," said Morgan smiling, shaking hands with the newly resigned premier.

"Well, seek and . . . you know the rest. Listen, people, go outside and get some fresh air. William and I have to talk some business."

Within minutes they were alone, Celia serving them ice water in flower-painted tumblers before clearing out of the kitchen. Morgan stared at Fidel's famous face, the Roman nose now lost in the ever-growing folds of flesh and tendrils of curly beard. Castro grinned conspiratorially, wiggled his bushy eyebrows as though to say, What fools we mortals be.

"I'm worried, Fidel," said Morgan quickly in English, in case someone should come in unexpectedly. "What does your resignation mean?"

Fidel flicked off his grin, moved his broad hands expansively, shooing away a political fly.

"*Chico,* it's just one of those things that had to be done."

"Quitting is one of the things you have to do?"

"It's just a strategy. I'll explain everything tonight during my speech at CMQ. Look, it's no big problem, there are many ways to skin a cat. This President Urrutia is becoming a very big pain in the ass. I'm prime minister, but he wants to call the shots. He's talking all the time about communism and Bolsheviks, and I'm tired of all the struggling. He is not, what you say, a team player. Well, I'm picking out a new team for the new season. What news do you have?"

Morgan shook his head in admiration. Fidel's sense of brinkmanship was impeccable, his desire for total control becoming more apparent every day. But to what purpose?

"In that case, maybe I shouldn't be here either, Fidel. I don't like commies either."

"Ah, but you are different, my friend. You have a right to be of a different opinion. You fought with us in the Sierra."

"You mean only the *barbudos* have a right to criticize?"

Abruptly, Castro turned bitterly stern. "No. *Nobody* has the right to criticize the revolution. Everything within the revolution, outside the revolution, nothing. We have too much at stake."

Just as suddenly, Castro was all light and smiles.

"Why, are you turning against me like Urrutia? Because, *chico,* you're in a wonderful position to do some real damage. Imagine if you were really against me!"

Both men laughed at the absurdity of this notion. Then, "What did you find out?" said Castro, all business.

"I'm meeting with this guy named Santos Trafficante tonight. You know who he is?"

Castro frowned. "A gambler?"

"Right. He runs the Capri."

Castro bristled. "I hate gambling, I hate gamblers, I hate the mafia! They have laughed at us and owned us. I am going to destroy them!"

"That's just what he's afraid of. He heard I was working with other people against you, so he's having me over. He's going to give me a quarter million dollars to remember him when you're dead. That's in cash, by the way."

Castro shook his head in wonderment. "Imagine that! *Vaya,* William, by the time this ends you will be a millionaire. In cash! What will you do with all that money?"

Morgan saw the steel beneath the jest, threw open his hands.

"Why, give it to the revolution, of course! What else?"

"Good!" was Castro's quick reply. "Bring it by tonight. We can use the money."

※ ※ ※

The parking attendant at the door of the Capri snapped to attention when Morgan's Jeep drove up the curved driveway. The boy, tall, olive skinned, with the chubby cheeks of the pampered middle class, swung open the door to the hotel.

"Welcome to the Capri, Comandante Morgan," he said in English. Morgan beamed at being recognized by name.

"How did you know it was me?"

"I have read all of you, *Comandante.* There was no other American like you in the Sierra."

"I fight in the Escambray," said Morgan, annoyed at being pegged with the wrong front.

"Oh, no, it says so right here, *Comandante,* look," said the boy, whipping out a comic book from the back pocket of his satin striped pants. He opened the magazine, showing it to Morgan.

In a quarter-page panel drawn in garish colors, Morgan—or a shirtless comic-book-hero version of Morgan, wielding two blazing machine guns—mowed down a host of army soldiers, who ran like frightened rats from a dun-colored hill. The caption read, *Major William Morgan, the hero of El Charquito, single-handedly drove away a battalion of crack troops of the tyranny.*

El Gato, standing next to Morgan, snickered when he saw the illustration.

"I never knew you were so macho you could scare away a thousand men all by yourself, *Comandante,*" said El Gato.

"Shh, hombre, let me read!"

The next quarter panel showed Morgan hailed heroically by Castro, with Che, Camilo, Raúl, and others gazing fraternally at their glorious companion.

"For his gallantry, the maximum leader Fidel Castro Ruz raised him to the rank of major, the highest available in the rebel army."

"What's your name, kid?"

"Salvador Pérez, *Comandante.*"

"How come you have this, Salvador?"

"I collect the stamps, you know? Stickers. They give us the book and we—how you say?—stick the stamps on top. You know, yours is very difficult to get. Is for collectors almost. Not that many printed."

"I see. Maybe it's just as well."

"Why is that, *Comandante?* Everybody should know about you. I only wish I too had been in the Sierra with you and Fidel."

Morgan grinned sympathetically at the boy and for a moment experienced an overpowering feeling of déjà vu, that this interchange had occurred once in the past but that then he had been the young man and someone else had been Morgan.

"You want to know why? I'll tell you why. *Es muy bonito pero no es verdad.*"

"Excuse me, not true, *Comandante?*" said the boy, as astonished as if he'd told him Batista had saved Cuba from anarchy. "But I pick it up at the INRA, the Institute for Agrarian Reform! How can it be wrong?"

"It's not true, kid. Read the history," said Morgan. "*Vamos,* Gato," he said, turning away and heading into the hotel.

"But, *Comandante,* this *is* the official history!" cried the boy in anguish one last time, almost begging not to have his dreams shattered.

❋ ❋ ❋

The deep blue plush carpeting of the lobby, as new as the rest of the low-slung building, still smelled faintly of formaldehyde. A dark-haired man in a green sharkskin suit abruptly stopped Morgan and El Gato before they reached the front desk.

"Major Morgan?" asked the man in a rounded New Orleans accent. "Would you mind accompanying me to the manager's office? Some friends of yours are waiting for you there."

❊ ❊ ❊

Morgan walked out of the manager's office with an attaché case full of greenbacks, exhilarated by the success of his plan. Santos Trafficante had proved to be just as gullible as all the other mobsters. Fidel was right. They were unable to conceive that an American would really be doing all this for Cuba and not be looking out for his own interests. They didn't realize that for this American, Cuba was his best interest. In one fell swoop Morgan would be able to root out not only all the right-wingers who were out to destroy the revolution but also all the mobsters who had thought Havana was just another town in their pocket.

Hell, no, we're not Las Vegas and we're never going to be. He walked down the aisles of the mostly empty casino, actually feeling sorry for the few luckless souls still tossing dice or moving their chips to the numbered slots of a fake fate. Don't they know the game is rigged? Don't they know the house always wins down here?

El Gato, who had been waiting some distance away, came up to Morgan, shaking his head.

"Urrutia just resigned. Right in the middle of Fidel's speech, would you believe that? They had it over the TV. Couldn't take the criticism."

"I was expecting something like that," said Morgan, walking fast, as though afraid someone would come up to tell him Trafficante had changed his mind about the money after all.

"I wasn't," said El Gato. "It's not good news, *Comandante*. That means the commies will be all in control."

"No, they do not have control. We still have a chance."

El Gato snorted. *Our only chance will come when we get rid of Fidel, he thought. When will you see that is our only chance, Comandante? Instead you go around, chasing illusions. If only I could make you see.*

A few pallid gigolos flounced around the casino bar, chattering aimlessly as they nursed their one drink, keeping an eye on the door, waiting for luck to step through. El Gato stopped briefly to check out the only going game in the place, a spirited baccarat competition between a balding German tourist and a sallow-skinned croupier with a pencil-thin mustache and an ice cold stare. The house folded, the German pocketed his chips. El Gato scurried after Morgan, already walking through the pneumatic doors to the bracing salt air of the Malecón.

"What were you doing in there, Jefe?" asked El Gato, looking at the attaché case firmly lodged under Morgan's arm.

"Sweeping Cuba clean for my children."

El Gato nodded, not wanting to point out the obvious, that childless men shouldn't concern themselves with a paternity they may never have. But then, he had probably meant it as a symbol. Aren't we all children of the revolution?

"Where to, *Comandante?*"

"To find Fidel."

"Again! I spent all afternoon doing that already! Maybe we should get a government car, a nice Cadillac like Fidel has, no?"

"No. This Jeep is good enough for us *barbudos,*" said Morgan. "Please drive and do not make the bad jokes."

"*Sí, Jefe.*"

※ ※ ※

They searched for Castro until the early hours of the morning, scuttling from place to place, following the trail of celebration now that Fidel had won the war of words with Urrutia. From Celia Sánchez's apartment in El Vedado to Fidel's suite at the Havana Hilton to Violeta's house in Marianao, everywhere Morgan and El Gato drove they ran into cheering and dancing crowds, all of Havana jubilant over the new political muscle of the masses.

The bodega owners, the bus drivers, the little housewives, the teachers, and the doctors, all who felt the revolution had been threatened by Urrutia—and it was threatened because Fidel had said so, and Fidel did not lie—everyone knew that their word was now the law. Because when Fidel had asked the handpicked audience at the TV station, "What shall we do with this man?" their cry had come through loud and clear: "He should quit, he should quit!" And if he wanted to slash his veins at the palace, so much the better. And now that Urrutia had slipped away, he and his wife dressed in painter's overalls, to ask for political asylum at an embassy, the crowd tasted blood. Rabid revolutionaries, organized by the newly formed blue-shirted militia, organized impromptu rhumbas and conga lines in Cayo Hueso, Jesús María, El Cerro, La Víbora, and Santos

Suárez, in all the crowded, nervous, working-class neighborhoods where for the first time the people dared to think that they held the reins of power.

Finally, by one o'clock, Morgan asked El Gato to drive him to Laura's apartment. El Gato turned to see if Morgan meant what he had said. He recognized the light of lust in the man's eyes, nodded, and drove silently to Old Havana.

"Tomorrow, pick me up here at eight," said Morgan after El Gato dropped him off in front of Laura's building. "I have a breakfast with Eloy."

"*Sí, Comandante,*" said El Gato, giving him a brief salute, then driving off, remembering that old saying of his mother's, *Más jala un par de tetas que una junta de bueyes,* a pair of tits pulls harder than a team of oxen.

Morgan walked up the narrow steps, tired and tingling with excitement. He had not seen Laura in weeks, and now that he was about to succumb to precious temptation, his heart felt like exploding out of his chest. He still had the key to her apartment, so he let himself in. Opening the door, he heard Fidel's speech still going and wondered whether Laura had finally bought a television set. He realized his mistake when he walked into the living room.

Castro was on the balcony facing the courtyard, addressing the residents of the building in shirt and underpants. Out of the kitchen Laura came out wearing a flimsy nightgown, a glass of milk in hand.

Morgan thought he heard a loud noise, then realized, an eternity later, that it was the glass of milk that Laura had dropped to the floor. Castro turned, saw Morgan, but continued with his speech a while longer.

"I wasn't expecting you," said Laura, embarrassed, wrapping her arms around herself.

"No, you wouldn't," said Morgan, painfully aware that the glass was not all that was broken. From the hi-fi, a few bars of *Tosca,* Callas muttering, "*Davanti lui tremava tutta Roma!*"

Castro came over, smiled, hugged a motionless Morgan.

"*Lo jodimos,* William," we fucked him.

"*Sí, Fidel, jodimos,*" numbly repeated Morgan.

Somehow Morgan handed him the money Trafficante had given him, and somehow he found the presence of mind to mumble good-bye and to stumble down from the apartment. The marble steps rose like an infinite stairway in a dusty print, and Morgan raced down them, hoping that it was all a nightmare, that he would find himself running up and down the stairs as in the nightmares of his childhood, and that he would wake up and Laura would be in his arms again.

But the stairs ended at the street and the nightmare did not end, for it was reality. The street tilted, the light from the Spanish lightpole casting grasping yellow fingers on the cobblestones, and Morgan felt ill. He held on to the side of the building until the nausea subsided and a single powerful thought filled his mind, ringing with the truth of a thousand Bibles—I will kill Fidel Castro.

Chapter

10

Eloy nodded at Morgan from the far end of the reviewing stand at the Plaza de la República. The handful of revolutionaries who controlled the destinies of the nation were gathered to render tribute to the one who by sheer will had bent history his way, the man whom the million people in the broad esplanade awaited eagerly, their impatience breaking out in a rhythmic conga beat:

"Fi-del, Fi-del, Fi-del!"

Raúl Castro, commander in chief of the armed forces, stood on center stage next to the lanky, ever-smiling Camilo Cienfuegos, who wore his cheerful good nature like a halo. Vilma Espín stood some distance from the center, next to Celia Sánchez. José Naranjo, Serafín Ruiz, Pedro Miret, Raúl Roa, all the yes-men of the cabinet who had replaced the old liberals sacked the month before, were there too, along with the old Sierra hands, Ameijeiras, Hart, Franqui, Matos.

Morgan nodded, shook hands and slapped backs with all of them, all happy, all victorious. Even Che Guevara abandoned his usual sarcastic pose and gave Morgan an *abrazo*.

"Wonderful day for all of us, isn't it, William?" he asked, his breath smelling of cigar and asthma medicine.

"A better day there cannot be," answered Morgan, thinking, If only you knew.

Oltusky, Cubelas, and the other Directorio leaders were stacked at the far end. Next to them, the leaders of the Front, Eloy, Jesús Carreras, Morgan.

Eloy's wide hazel eyes looked questioningly at Morgan. They had met

397

just the night before at Eloy's house to review their plot strategy. They embraced.

"How is it going?" asked Eloy, whispering.

"All is in place," answered Morgan, a grin as wide as the Ohio sky.

"They arrested Max Weinberg last night," said Eloy, still grinning. Morgan was stunned.

"I get him out after this, I promise," he said.

"I know you will," said Eloy.

The men turned away from each other, careful lest their embrace be seen as the conspiratorial lock it truly was.

The new president, Osvaldo Dorticós Torrado, walked up to the microphone. The portly socialist attorney and former commodore of the Cienfuegos Yacht Club stood out in his black suit against the wall of olive green uniforms behind him. The military band at the foot of the steps sent forth the opening martial horns, then the full call to arms of the national anthem.

The entire plaza rang out with the singing of the crowd, a cry of joy so deep that the words seemed to fly around the world, crying out, We are here, we are Cubans, we are free!

Dorticós waved his hands at the band below to stop, once the anthem was over, then took out a lacy handkerchief to wipe his florid, sweating face. He pressed his lips to the CMQ mike.

"Ladies and gentlemen, in response to innumerable requests, we are happy to announce that Fidel has agreed to continue as prime minister of the nation!"

The crowd broke out in a delirious yell, all their hopes fulfilled, their happiness so thorough it eclipsed the many pleasures of the flesh. Fireworks flared against the sky, an airplane overhead dropped rose petals on the crowd, coves of pigeons swept freely through the burning air.

"And now here he is, the once and future leader of the revolution, our captain, our comrade, the guide and inspiration of the people of Cuba, the one and only maximum leader, Prime Minister Fidel Castro Ruz!"

Fidel broke through the crowd of *comandantes*, who, along with the rest of the crowd, applauded wildly at their hero's comeback.

Morgan clapped as well, feeling in his heart his divided loyalties, admiration for the ideals but abhorrence of the reality of this revolution. His heart grew cold when he saw Laura, as smartly turned out in her fitted fatigues as if wearing a Dior. She stood right behind Castro, wanting to be in his shadow, away from the other women of the revolution, as though to herald her closeness to him, her total and unreserved devotion.

The crowd cheered and clapped and danced and shouted themselves hoarse, screaming slogans—*"p'alante y p'alante, y al que no le guste, que tome purgante"* (Forward and forward, and if you don't like it, go take some purgative)—while Morgan coldly plotted what would happen if he were to take out his .45 to shoot Fidel through the head. Would he have time to do it? Or would he get shot down first?

I would die, of course, but we all have to die sometime. The question is, Who would inherit the empire? Who would take over? And how many people would be killed if I slay him here in the sight of the nation?

"Viva la revolución!" shouted Castro.

"Viva!" replied a million people as if with one voice. In the dizzying sun, the half million *guajiros* brought in from the countryside for the occasion in cars, trucks, and automobiles unsheathed their machetes and waved them above their heads like swords, ready to slay whoever would threaten their dream, whoever would seek to extinguish the flame of revolution they labored so long to light.

"Fidel, Fidel, Fidel!" they shouted.

Castro, smiling broadly, shook his head like a father whose child will not stop praising him to the skies. He turned to his cohorts, shrugging his shoulders good-humoredly as though to say, Aren't they great! He caught sight of Morgan and called him over.

Now's the time, thought Morgan. I'll shoot him before anyone realizes what I'm doing. Then I'll kill Laura, and everyone will think it was jealousy. There will be no purge, no slaughter, just the three of us dying in the flames of passion. Yes, that's it. Do it. Here's your chance, set this country free!

Morgan deliberately bumped against a chair, discreetly unbuttoning his gun holster. There, it's loose, all I have to do is whip it out. Just like a cowboy. Wyatt Earp. Wild Bill Hickok. Tom Mix. Two shots and the world will never be the same.

Everything slowed down as if in a movie, as Morgan approached Castro, the sounds of the crowd and the glitter of the flashing blades in the background.

Morgan was ten feet away, then Che stepped out of the way, then he was six feet away, and Camilo smiled at Morgan. Then he was three feet away, and Morgan's hand moved down to his holster and he was about to grab the chrome-plated .45 when Raúl turned and fixed his gimlet eyes on Morgan and in those narrow Asian slits Morgan saw the future of Cuba without Fidel and heard Fidel's warning "If you think things are bad with me wait until Raúl takes over" and he saw the bleeding ambition in the younger brother's eyes and the veiled desire for someone, anyone, to rid him of his brother so Raúl could take over like Stalin after Lenin. Morgan moved his hand away and instead draped his arm on Castro's shoulder. This is not the time. Find a place to eliminate the brother too.

Fidel whispered to him above the din, "That thing with the White Rose, wait a couple of weeks. We have to get all the *guajiros* out of town so they won't go crazy."

"Whatever you to say, Fidel," said Morgan, burning with desire for the day when the plug would cleave through the wide forehead and the venom that was Castro's brain would ooze out.

"That's what I say," said Fidel, who then turned and winked at Laura before returning to the rostrum to face his maddened nation.

"*Democracia directa!*"—direct democracy—he shouted, and the machetes flashed in the sun and the screams shook the very buildings.

Morgan looked at Laura. She stared back at him.

"This is for you," she said, kissing him full on the lips, then stepping away to snuggle next to Castro.

For me? What does she mean, this is for me? She loves me after all? This can't be! What is going on here!

"*Revolución! Revolución! Revolución!*" came the cry of the people.

The buzzing of the cicadas swarmed over the still August night, almost drowning out the static-laden message blaring from the radio transmitter.

"Forward, Henry, forward!"

Fidel Castro grinned at the cackling speaker, waved for Morgan to reply, then pantomimed at a handful of rebel soldiers outside the hut to fire their rifles in the air. A fusillade of shots rang out. Morgan pressed the on button of the stand-up microphone.

"This is Henry!" said Morgan, deliberately breathless, in his heaviest American-accented Spanish. "Our men are advancing but we cannot do it all alone!"

More shots, sprayed wildly at the up-to-then peaceful lemon grove outside the runway of the Trinidad airport. Fidel Castro, almost giggling, shouted, "Down with Fidel! Down with Fidel!"

He ran outside, maniacally exhorting the puzzled troops to pick up the cry. Soon all two hundred militia and guerrillas posted around the runway erupted in the same faked shout of defiance: "Down with Fidel! Down with Fidel! Death to the communists!"

Grinning at Fidel's antics, Morgan pressed down the on button again, making sure the other side would hear the unusual background noise.

"We need help!" he shouted. "We have captured Trinidad but we cannot stand alone! Send in the Dominican Legion! Please come soon!"

"Don't worry, Henry," answered a second man, his words distorted by static. Morgan stopped smiling the moment he heard him. "We are coming to the rescue! How bad is your position?"

"I cannot talk! I must fight the enemy! Come soon! *Viva Cuba libre!*" said Morgan, turning off the transmission.

"*Viva Cuba! Viva Batista!*" came another voice over the radio. Morgan turned off the set, lit a Pall Mall, then wheeled around in the squeaky wooden chair.

"They arrive in half hour or so," he told Castro, who stood in a corner holding his bulging stomach, convulsed by fits of laughter, surrounded by a handful of faithful.

Laugh while you can, *maricón,* thought Morgan. Your turn is coming sooner than you think.

"That Trujillo must have come all over himself when he heard that," said Castro, guffawing some more, then finally controlling himself. "*Bueno,* let's go, boys, before these boys call again and I shit in my pants from laughter."

He trooped out with his retinue, scornful laughter trailing behind him.

Eloy remained behind in the transmission room, with his usual, dour, El Greco look. He shook his head in disgust.

"This is a piece of shit," he said. "I feel like a whore. Do you realize that was Luisito on the box?"

Morgan nodded. Luisito Pozo, the son of the former mayor of Havana, had been one of the early coordinators of the Directorio in Havana under Batista and a personal friend of Eloy's. Desperation clawed at Eloy's face.

"*Coño,* at least Fidel promised he won't execute them. What a stupid jackass that Luisito is, God damn it!" said Eloy, bitterly. He stormed out of the room. Morgan stared after him in silence, listening to the call of the cicadas fill the night with the sound of anxious love.

This was what they had all been working for the last six months. Within the hour the circle would be closed, the remaining leaders of the White Rose conspiracy caught in Morgan's well-tended trap. Ten thousand people had been picked up in raids throughout the country that day, from the tiniest hamlet to the top addresses in Havana, Santiago, and Camagüey. Morgan had handed Castro the opportunity he'd been looking for, a means to uproot the remaining conservative opposition within Cuba. Those that weren't ensnared would be forever discredited as right-wing extremists, advocates of foreign invasions, followers of fascist tyrants like Trujillo. From now on all Castro needed to do was watch his left flank, and there he had plenty of support.

Morgan picked up his tommy gun, strolled out of the shack, looked down the landing field, then up at the blinking stars under the burning summer moon. Survival is the key. Survive to fight another day. But for what? And for whom? A wrenching thought assaulted him. Is this the way all revolutions end? Everyone out for himself until the biggest fish wins in a sea of blood? It wasn't supposed to be like this. We didn't fight to end like this. No? What did you fight for?

Morgan didn't have to look far to find his answer—there she was, down in the hollow under the mango tree, snuggling up to Castro. As if she knew he was thinking of her, Laura waved at Morgan. He nodded, then walked down the opposite way, where El Gato sat with his *tigres,* the loyal Morgan troops. They stood to salute. Morgan gestured at them to remain seated.

"In a half hour the Cuban cat eats the big fish coming down from the sky," grinned Morgan, slapping El Gato on the shoulder with a happiness he couldn't even dream of feeling.

"*Sí,* William, we will strike a big blow for revolutionary justice," replied El Gato intently. Their eyes met and both men knew the other was lying.

"Come over here, Gato," said Morgan, taking his trusted aide some distance away. The men walked next to a royal palm, its ragged top swaying in a soft breeze.

"All the preparations are in place?" he whispered. El Gato nodded.

"We have buried all the weapons in El Banao, near our old headquarters, just like you asked. Two hundred machine guns, ten thousand rounds, grenades, all. We are ready, the men and I. All you have to do is give us the word."

"Fine, then. The moment he falls, we will all run for the hills, *entiendes?*" El Gato revealed his golden eyetooth in a sudden grin.

"Not even water is clearer," he said, happy to return to the fray.

"*Bueno.* Be alert. I give you the signal when the time comes."

Morgan strolled away, chain-smoking Pall Malls. El Gato watched him warily, a wave of concern threatening to send him into the eddies of doubt.

I have to believe that he knows what we are doing, thought El Gato. He has never failed before. I don't think he would fuck up the whole thing so late in the game. We should have asked Eloy to join us, though. But perhaps he is right. Perhaps it is better that we do it all by ourselves. Eloy has grown soft, he believes too much. You can only believe in a few things if you're a fighter. Your God, your country, your leader. Everything else weakens you.

El Gato returned to his men, all equally thoughtful in the quiet before battle. One of them offered him a warm Pepsi. He shook the bottle to release the gas, then took a long swallow. Is he aware of what he will have to do? thought El Gato. I wonder. He must. A man in his position must have no compunctions. He does what needs to be done. After all, tonight the head is chopped off. They are all here tonight. And they will all die. Fidel, Raúl, Camilo. Only Che and Ameijeiras are not here, and who is going to follow them? No one.

El Gato again experienced the familiar tingling in his loins, his member slowly rousing itself in anticipation of a kill. Many a time he'd gone into battle with an erection as hard as his weapon. Tonight promised to be the same thing. It is wrong, he thought. He crossed himself, kissed the gold medal of the Virgin of El Cobre he wore around his neck.

Death is not lust. It is a sad affair, and nothing a real man should get excited about. I should be able to control it. When all this is over I will go to the sanctuary in El Cobre and I will walk the whole length of the church on my knees for my sins. When this is over I may even join a monastery. This life has little meaning for me, save for my gun. But that may not be for a while. And this restless dick of mine tells me there will be much bloodshed before I can don that habit. God help us. And God help Cuba.

Under the mango tree Castro told jokes about his days in the Sierra, to the delight of Camilo, Raúl, and the others who guffawed at the old chestnuts. Morgan eased down a path to the other side of the lemon grove, stopping at a rocky mound overlooking a lazy gray brook. Up in the sky, the low, yellow moon seemed another lemon pinned to the vast foliage of fast-moving clouds. A bird sang in the dark, the sweet tang of citrus flowers laced the air.

"William?" A woman's voice, the patter of steps down the path, the rustle of leaves pushed aside.

Morgan's heart skipped a beat. He would recognize that voice as long as he lived. In the darkest cave or the coldest nightmare, she would be the future lost, the past recaptured. He noticed the bird stopped singing, as though jealous of its rival.

Laura walked up to Morgan, ninety-eight pounds of desire and despair, love and betrayal. She stopped just a few feet away, cheeks flushed, as though she'd just finished a perilous race. She played with a lock of her hair, folding it and twisting it, eyes bright in the moonlight. I could stretch out my hand and she'd be mine again, thought Morgan. It would be that easy. And that wrong.

"Yes?"

A cold monosyllable, a blast of the northern air Laura knew she would never feel. How can I tell him? she thought. How can I explain the sorry mess of my life?

"I saw you walking out here all by yourself and I thought it would be better if we spoke," she said in Spanish. "We haven't had a chance to talk since—"

"Since I found you in bed with Fidel." He finished the sentence in English. He was surprised at his control over the hounding pain vibrating within him.

Laura stepped forward, touched Morgan's face.

"*Ay,* William, please try to understand!"

"Understand what? How you willingly became another notch in his bedpost?"

"It's not that way."

"That's how he has you, Laura. He wants total control. He fucks you."

"Don't use that word."

"He fucks you just like he fucks everybody around him. Man, woman, and child. He has to call all the shots. He has to possess you totally. He's got to be God, don't you see?"

Laura didn't answer, her heart singing with grief on seeing William's anger. I do see, *mi amor,* she wanted to tell him, but you two are two kinds of love. He is everything and you are a man. He's beyond us, William. He is our ghosts and our future and our ambition and our desire. How could I not go to bed with him if he asked? I could not deny him anything.

He's not a mere mortal, he's of the stuff gods are made of. He's our Mars and our Apollo, our Mercury and our Bacchus, our hero, our leader, our shining light. He's the one whose hand tills the soil, reaps the harvest, and lights the sky. He's Cuba, William, come to us in human form for everyone to love, and you—you, my poor darling William— you are just a man. You are a good man, a great man, even, but you are just a man.

You are not one of us and he is, don't you see? You will always be the great American, but you will never be one of us.

"You don't mean that much to him," Morgan went on, "but you meant the world to me."

"And your marriage?" she asked, wanting to find a way out.

"That was my only weapon, don't you see?"

"No, I don't."

Morgan grabbed her by the shoulders, brought her just inches away from him.

"Listen to me, Laurita. I knew what you were doing when I first met you. I knew you were using me, but I didn't care, you see? It was a good cause, a cause worth fighting for, and I probably would have done it even if we hadn't slept together. But that was beyond you and me, the things the two of us did. What I felt for you was real. I didn't care whether you thought you were using me. My love for you was real, my pain for you was real. And then you vanish after I think you're dead, and then you show up after I'm with a wonderful woman, because I won't deny what she's worth, either. What am I supposed to do? That's why I married her, because I was afraid that my love for you would drive me to that act of cruelty against someone who had only given me love. Don't you see, I had to marry her! Not because I loved you less but because I loved you still! Do you understand me?!"

Laura nodded *yes,* a trickle of tears coursing down her smooth cheeks. Morgan felt her breath on his face, an intoxicating perfume from the past. Love me still, it promised, love me always. He let go of her.

"I suppose I should be grateful to Fidel for taking you away. But he's using you too. You should have gone with someone who cares for you, not just the greatest user this country has ever known."

"But he does care for me, William! He cares for all of Cuba! He is our hero! He is Fidel!"

And tonight he dies, Morgan wanted to say, but the buzzing of the arriving plane broke through the shell of their emotions. They glanced up at the hills. A twin-engine cargo plane flew low, burdened with the promise of a thwarted past. El Gato ran up to them, out of breath.

"They're here, Jefe! They're looking for you!"

Morgan raced back through the lemon grove ahead of El Gato and Laura, as if rushing to meet his destiny, hurrying to the one moment he had been born for. He leaped over boulders, sidestepped low branches, scurrying down the muddy path with only one thought in his mind— our time is here, our time is now!

The twin-engine C-46 now hovered above the runway, slowly banking south, a noisy buzzard of doom. Morgan raced down to the shack, where a frantic Eloy gestured at the radio.

"Where the cunt have you been, William? They won't land unless you give them the go-ahead!"

Castro, Raúl, Camilo all huddled around as Morgan sat at the wooden chair.

"Here is Henry! Here is Henry! Land, chariot of liberty!"

The transmitter crackled, then the voice of Luisito Pozo was heard again: "We read you, Henry. We will be landing presently. The first step for liberty has been taken. *Viva Cuba!*"

"*Viva Cuba!*" replied Morgan, looking at the crowd, who picked up the chant, *Viva Cuba, Viva Cuba, Viva Cuba,* even as Castro and his High Command turned red from glee. Morgan snapped off the mike.

"*Bueno,* you shit-eating shitheads," he cursed in his most profane Spanish, "what the fuck you do here? Go hide! Hide!"

Castro and his men scurried out. El Gato glanced quickly at Morgan, tugging at his ear to signal his readiness. Morgan nodded, walked outside.

"I better talk to these muchachos alone; they are expecting me," he told Eloy, who was deploying a handful of loyal Second Front men around the runway. In the lemon grove, about two hundred men crowded in the darkness, guns at the ready. Fidel hid under the mango tree at the north end of the main runway.

"Are you certain you want to risk it? What if they smell a rat?"

"Not to worry, that means they have smelled me!"

The lumbering plane drones on down, its giant propellers shattering the tropical night. It touches the runway, then sets all its wheels down, screeching wildly as its brakes are applied, sliding to a halt at a spot where Morgan ordered an old Jeep placed as a barrier. Perfect, thinks Morgan. He is only 150 feet away. We won't miss this time.

Again cries in the dark—"Death to Fidel!" "*Viva Cuba!*" "*Viva Batista!*"—all led by Castro. They can't hear that but it doesn't matter, thinks Morgan, swiftly approaching the plane. He's always after the effects, the theatrics. He should have been an actor.

⌗ ⌗ ⌗

The hatch door flings open. Morgan watches as through a camera lens, at a remove. All is tainted with the clean deceitful light of the yellow moon pinned on the sky above the hills. Morgan thinks, This will be how I die, this is the end of it all.

A man in priestly cassock and collar steps out: Monsignor Luis Cervantes from Asturias, the local head of the Opus Dei and Batista's former confessor. Like the chaplain with Columbus, he sets out with a cross aloft, blessing the sacred soil of Cuba.

"Padre!" says Morgan, embracing the priest, who hugs him back with the faith of the deceived.

"My son," exclaims the monsignor, moved to tears. Other figures gather to move out of the plane. Morgan speaks quickly, there is little time to waste.

"Is the president with you?" asks Morgan, hoping that his dreams will be fulfilled and the two tyrants can be eliminated in one stroke.

"No, Henry. President Batista wanted to accompany us, but his youngest son is ill again and he couldn't leave him in his hour of need," says the padre, reeking of garlic and wine.

"And Masferrer? Did you hear from him?"

"Rolando will come in the next few days, God willing."

So Masferrer gets away, thinks Morgan. The murderer of Mariano will never be ours. Fine. We'll make do with what we have.

"The bazookas?"

"They are in the hold. We have brought twenty men and all the ammo you need."

"Luisito!" exclaims Morgan, on seeing Pozo coming out.

Morgan turns to the Front guerrillas, about to give the order to El Gato, who has posted himself a few feet away from Fidel. Stepping away from the priest, Morgan raises his left hand to his ear and moves his right to his holster. A flash of green catches his eye—a figure scurrying to the mango tree at the last possible moment.

"NO! NO! STAY AWAY!" bellows Morgan in English, seeing Laura crouch next to Fidel under the branches.

"FUEGO! DISPAREN!"—SHOOT! FIRE!—someone screams in the bushes.

"STOP! STOP!" shouts Morgan, but no one can hear his cry. He sees himself moving slowly even though he knows it's all going fast, much faster than he can imagine. The priest drops to the ground, holding his silver cross on high like a shield to protect him. From inside the plane the invaders fire back at the massive onslaught of firepower surging in waves of red sparks from the lemon grove. Under the light of the yellow moon, Morgan sees El Gato raising his machine gun.

"DON'T DO IT!" he screams again. "NO SEÑAL! DON'T MAKE ME DO THIS!"

But El Gato, like a good soldier, knows only he must carry out his duty. Time slows down to a syrupy substance. Morgan can hear each separate report from each separate gun, the cicadas still humming in between the shots, the grunting of the soldiers in the bush, the hurtful cries of the wounded invaders, a man painfully calling for his mother, the rattle of a clip emptying in the sultry night, the faraway weeping of a country that asks itself what has gone wrong. And he sees with detailed precision El Gato pointing the barrel of his gun at the tree where Fidel and Laura are crouched under the branches and he can hear the spring of the safety catch clicking open and El Gato grunting as he prepares to pull back the worn dull black trigger and Morgan sees his own two hands grabbing the handle of his .45 as he stands with his heart a field of ashes and he steadies himself and fires a moment too late for El Gato has pulled the trigger and the red tongues of death have spit out the first rounds from the guts of his tommy gun spraying the mango tree and the two frightened figures who cower under the branches. El Gato falls, the wound in the left temple opening up to a gap the size of an apple as a stream of blood and cranial fluid and grayish matter flies out in a fallen arch and El Gato's gun tips upwards and sprays wildly at the blinking stars which seem to wink down and say everything's alright don't worry everything's alright.

"Alto al fuego! Alto al fuego!" finally is heard, the order given by Camilo, who stands up next to Morgan, forcing the men by the strength of his conviction to put down their weapons and to stop the senseless surprise attack. But Morgan doesn't hear, doesn't care. He has walked to the top of the runway where the body of his friend lies crumbled, the faithful soldier who had saved him so often from his own well-deserved destruction, and he knows there is nothing he can ever do that will begin to make amends for what he's done. He turns and walks like an automaton to the leafy mango tree, where Fidel has stood up, bathed in blood.

"A doctor! Someone get a doctor!" orders Fidel. Dozens of people rush to his side, screaming all around him.

"Are you all right, Fidel? Are you OK?"

"It's not for me, *coño,* it's for this girl; she was gravely wounded."

Morgan flies to Laura's side, drops to his knees, sees the tiny fragile body, the gushing of blood from the row of gaps in her chest, the russet curls turned crimson in the light of the yellow moon.

"Laura! Laura, sweetheart, talk to me!" implores Morgan.

She turns her head slowly, her spirit already swimming to the far shore, but she recognizes Morgan and attempts a smile. A gush of blood flows out her throat and washes down her slender throat.

"Viva Cuba!" she gurgles, then her eyes shine in a peaceful grin.

"NO! NO! COME BACK TO ME! DON'T GO!" bellows Morgan, shaking her now-lifeless body, trying through sheer will to return life to the one that he loved so much. Hands pull him away from her, strong arms hold him back. He watches Camilo come over, look at Laura, tenderly close her eyelids.

Morgan finds himself out by the edge of the field, staring at the yellow moon, the lone survivor of a world that failed, while the invaders are led away in trucks under the watchful eyes of the *barbudos.* An arm embraces Morgan, a familiar voice whispers in his ear.

"They were heroes of the revolution, William. They will never be forgotten," says Fidel. Morgan nods; the swelling nodes of pain have taken over his voice. (But not Fidel, no, his voice will never stop; like Robespierre he will be gagged the day of his execution.)

"We will put them all on trial on television. We'll show the world the evil they were trying to do, the great things we accomplished here." He paused, filling himself with the gravity of his words.

"The world will long remember what happened here and those who gave their lives in the service of freedom."

Fidel looks down the field, notices Camilo waving at him.

"I have to go. I want to get rid of these stinking clothes. See you in Havana," says Fidel, giving Morgan one last squeeze on the shoulder, then walking away.

"YOU SON OF A BITCH!" roars Morgan, wheeling around, reaching for his .45.

The holster is empty, the gun lies discarded out on the field, out there by the ghostly, deadly plane. Morgan laughs, then collapses on the runway, crumbling like a puppet with its strings cut off.

He sits on the macadam, rocking himself, all alone, in the glare of the yellow moon.

The runway lights come on, a guard at the shack turns on the radio, the lilting melody of *"Me lo Dijo Adela"* by the Orquesta Aragón croons out.

You've won, Fidel, you've won.

Chapter

12

They came for him before dawn, stomping their boots, rattling the old Spanish keys to the dungeons of La Cabaña. The prisoners in the neighboring cells, the ones with the *P* on their back for *prisionero político,* straightaway began their daily chant, taunting their jailers: *"LIBERTAD! LIBERTAD! LIBERTAD!"* FREEDOM! FREEDOM! FREEDOM!

They had kept him isolated for weeks, so he felt no need to vocalize his own stubborn patriotism. It was better to save your strength, stay on top of the game through ingenuity and concentration. So he sat on the dirt floor, shooing away the brown rats that scurried through his blanket every night, overturning his slop bucket, licking his food bowl, nibbling at his fingers and toes.

He gathered the filthy cotton blanket on his shoulders and leaned against the ancient brick wall, waiting in the darkness. He could smell the briny morning mist of the bay slipping through the narrow barred window up by the ceiling. The moonless, starless night was almost over, the blazing sun of August would soon shine through. He wondered whether he'd ever live to see the outside of those walls again.

The iron cell door clanged open. Marks, the red-haired American jailer, swaggered in, swollen gut pouring over the webbed belt of his fatigues.

"Let's go, buddy, it's Christmas," said Marks with a whiskey breath.

He didn't move; he didn't ask where they were going. He had been trained—to show concern was to give them the first opening. He had heard of the mock executions, the unlucky prisoner voiding his bladder and bowels, expecting death, only to open his eyes after the salvo to the jeers and catcalls of the firing squad. The prisoner, reeking of his own waste, would be taken back to his cell, the same charade going on for days until the day when the bullets were finally real. Was that about to happen to him now?

"C'mon, you really want to stay here another day? Aw, what the hell." He turned to the Cuban guards. "Pull that shit up, now!"

The Cuban guards jerked him upright, handcuffed him behind his back, blindfolded him with a thick piece of medical adhesive tape, then shoved him out of the cell. He stumbled, hit a wall, felt the blood gushing out of his forehead.

"*Coño,* man," shouted Marks in his fractured Spanish, "not that shit. Later, they to say, we torture. We no torture in Cuba, *coño!*"

The Cuban jailers laughed. One of them pressed a cool bandage smelling of peroxide to the wound. Dazed, the prisoner stumbled blindly through the corridors, the jailers cursing out the prisoners, promising them beatings, hosing-downs, dog bites, and no food, but the prisoners would not quiet down. Their chanting bounced off the walls that had housed those who fought against Batista, against Machado, against the Spanish, and so on, through the centuries, in the never-ending cycle of oppression and revolt, a cry so ancient and so new that the bloodstained letters on the walls never had a chance to dry in four hundred years of oppression: *LIBERTAD! Libertad! Libertad!*

They packed him into the back of a laundry delivery van, amid bundles of newly washed clothes fragrant of soap, starch, and lye, smelling as sweet to him as a bouquet of roses, because he knew then he was not going to die. He dozed on and off for the rest of the trip, glad to be somewhere away from filth and fear. His throat parched, his shirt soaked with perspiration, he held his bladder for hours, unwilling to besmirch the cleanliness that embraced him. Once or twice he thought of his wife and his children and his mistress, but he pushed those thoughts away too. Live for the present. No expectations. Desire can blind the will.

Hours later, after having been parked in the blazing sun near a highway, the van moved again. They traveled for a short distance, then the door opened. Someone snapped off his handcuffs. Morgan's face was the first he saw once the blindfold was ripped off.

"I couldn't let them do it to you, Max," said a clean-shaven Morgan, smiling warmly. "No matter how big a prick you are."

As if a spell had been broken, Max Weinberg heard the whirring and buzzing of the planes in the crowded airfield. The fuselage of a parked Pan American Airways plane stood tantalizingly near, only a few hundred yards separating Max from the flying comforts of home. A blue-suited stewardess, hat at a cocky angle, descended down the rolling metal staircase. Max watched her approach, feeling an enormous hunger for the safety of her flaxen hair, her long slender legs, her sky blue eyes.

Someone from the group of *barbudos* accompanying Morgan gave Max a small cloth suitcase. Morgan himself pressed a roll of hundreds on Max's palm.

"To tide you over," said Morgan. "Just in case there's nobody waiting for you in Miami. Have a Mai Tai on me at the Fountainebleau, OK?"

Max took the case, trying to clear his mind for the trip he thought he would never get to take.

"Did they treat you OK?" asked Morgan.

"As well as could be expected. I thought every morning would be my last."

Morgan grinned again. "This *is* your last. In revolutionary Cuba."

The stewardess drew near, a vision of Hoosier tranquillity.

"We're ready for you, Mr. Weinberg," she said, her smile revealing the perfect teeth of American orthodontics.

"He's going right now, miss," said Morgan, giving Max an *abrazo*. As the two man hugged, Morgan whispered, "Come see us again soon," then broke away to observe Max's reaction. Max shook his head in assent, ran his hand through his thinning brown hair.

"Thanks for the memories," said Max, who then took the stewardess's arm. "Miss, lead on, if you please."

Morgan and his men watched Max strut proudly away with the tall blonde, a defeated but unbowed general withdrawing with honor from the field of dubious battle. He slowly ascended the staircase, stopped at the final landing next to the entry door. He looked about him as though to survey one last time his birthplace, now casting him aside in a puzzling whirlwind of history. He snapped to attention like the best of all possible soldiers, squaring his shoulders, his hand flying out to his forehead in a formal salute.

"*Viva la revolución!*" he shouted.

Morgan's men snapped to attention as well, returning the salute.

"*Viva la revolución!*" they shouted back.

The stewardess hustled Max inside, closing the hatch door. In minutes the Caravelle taxied down the field, heading for the home of the brave. Morgan stood on the runway, watching the plane take off and head out into the clouds gathering over the Florida Straits.

Chapter

13

*V*iva la revolución.

The last words that Max uttered haunted Morgan for the next few weeks, throughout the long, drawn-out public trial of the invaders, the endless interviews and photo sessions, the speeches he and Eloy gave all over the country.

At times, sitting in the television studio floor, watching Fidel conduct the interrogation of the captives, Morgan would feel strangely removed from the proceedings.

He knew he was at CMQ's Studio One on L and Twenty-third Streets in the heart of Havana, watching from up close the grilling of the prisoners, hearing at length about his own participation in the scheme—the money collected, the weapons seized, the grand plans Trujillo and Batista had for Cuba once Castro was defeated. But Morgan also felt he was elsewhere, in a living room in some dusty home in La Víbora, watching the show surrounded by friends and family who demanded death for the invader. He also felt himself in some suburban Ohio den, over the *Huntley-Brinkley Report,* watched by some pipe-smoking father who glanced at his tow-haired son fearing he'd be fighting in Cuba someday; in the office of some lonely senator in Washington, sipping Haig & Haig on the rocks and wondering how this would affect the 1960 elections; and in a bedroom somewhere in San Francisco, where Irma stared wide eyed at her William, giving a gasp and crying for joy at seeing him alive.

He was in all those places except the one that he should have been in, his home in the Miramar district, with his wife and the hope of a new beginning. He was the nowhere man and he knew it, no matter how many times Fidel draped his arm over his shoulders and called him a Cuban married to a Cuban, no matter how many times Camilo would swing by to take him to a game of basketball or dominoes. His center had died and his will to live had died with it as well.

Yet, he smiled on, giving the usual interviews to the *Reader's Digest, Life, Look, Coronet,* the *New York Times, Time* magazine, CBS, NBC, ABC, all the American press clamoring for an interview with this unlikely hero. He concocted a glamorous past for himself. A paratrooper, a judo, gun, and knife expert, a man capable of killing you with one finger. None of it was true, but the way he saw it, none of what he did was true anymore. It was all a great farce perpetrated on Cuba and the world. He was one of the golden boys, one of the saints of national liberation. It was all a bitter lie, but it was lies the world wanted, and it was lies that the world got.

Then it was all over, just as suddenly as it began.

The press moved onto other quarry—the OAS conference in Chile, the return of Che Guevara from a world tour, the raids by counterrevolutionaries on a sugar mill in Pinar Del Río. His band of *tigres,* his die-hard followers, dropped away, and in the end he was left only with Boyeros's old servant, Manuel, in the big house in Miramar. He was the news of August, forgotten in the *vendavales* of September. That's when he finally picked up the phone and asked Irma to come home.

She too had changed. Her stay in the land of her father had paradoxically made her even more fervently Cuban than before. Away from the clouds of conspiracy, from the daily question of which job would next be taken over by the communists, Irma had swallowed the notion of the revolution as a cleansing force for good in Cuba and the world. Morgan could scarcely believe his eyes when she walked out into the terminal at the newly renamed Jose Martí Airport, dressed in the olive green fatigues of the rebel army, the black-and-red armband of the 26th of July Movement—which no one bothered to wear anymore—strapped firmly on. On her head she wore a great white *guajiro* straw hat with a picture of Fidel pasted to the upturned brim.

He waved her through customs, they kissed. Even her lips are someone else's, he thought. She stepped back, blue-gray eyes riotous with glory.

"Hello, my hero."

"Hello, my love."

"I never want to be away from you or Cuba again," she said in Spanish.

"I'll never let you go again."

She embraced him, the picture of Fidel on her hat's brim grinning back at Morgan. She took her husband's arm, let herself be guided out to the sidewalk. Almeida, the army chief of staff, had procured a DeVille limousine for them. Irma looked on dubiously at the symbol of capitalist wealth.

"Isn't this a little ostentatious for a *rebelde?*"

"We're the new class, sweetheart," said Morgan, regretting his own doublespeak. "We represent the people, so this is all in the name of the people. Hop in."

Morgan was stunned when she removed her hat. Her long golden tresses had been shorn, leaving her with a close-cropped haircut no longer than a boy's crew cut.

"You like it?" she asked, running her fingers through the corn gold stubble. "I feel so free!"

"But why?"

"A new era, darling. We're creating a new country and we need new ways of being. We have to start afresh. A new man, a new woman."

Morgan shook his head, frustrated, then pressed the button raising the glass divider between the front and back of the limo.

"Irma, you must believe this," he said, taking her hand. "It's all a lie. This is all a show. You can't believe what they're telling you."

"I'm afraid I don't know what you mean, William," she said looking into his eyes. "Aren't you the hero of Trinidad? Aren't you the man who saved Cuba from the return of Batista?"

"Yes, but don't you see, it's all been a mistake. They're out to take over everything."

"Who?'

"The communists."

Irma looked at him surprised, then broke into laughter.

"Of course, of course. This is all a joke, right? You're pulling my leg. Oh, sweetheart, I wish you would pull every part of my body!"

She crawled over Morgan, pressing herself against him, kissing his face, his neck, his shoulders, grabbing his back, his legs, his crotch.

"It's been so long. I've missed you so!"

"I missed you too, but I'm not lying, I'm telling you the truth!"

"We'll talk about it later, I know we will. But love me, William, make love to me now!"

The driver took a quick look in the rearview mirror and smiled as he saw the bare flesh, the thrashing of limbs and body parts.

Coño, what a *revolucionaria!* thought the driver. If that's the way it's going to be, *viva la revolución!*

416

✖ ✖ ✖

Irma wouldn't listen to him.

Fidel is no communist, she would say. He would never allow the revolution to be miscarried. This country has seen too many injustices, she would add; you're mistaking social progress for socialism. It's because you're American, she would conclude; you think everything must be black or white, communist or capitalist. There is no big conspiracy; this country will never turn red.

Morgan could only watch as Irma was swept up in the revolutionary fever that swept the country. With salaries doubled by government decree, rents frozen, and free education and medicine now within reach of all, Cubans felt as though some rich uncle had left them a long-awaited legacy that would satisfy all their dreams.

Even the trial of Huber Matos, the *comandante* in charge of Camagüey, failed to excite her into changing her position. Matos had been arrested and charged with sedition simply for resigning his post, following the appointment of a Communist Party member to run the agrarian reform—and thus the government—in the province. Fidel himself, trembling with anger, had flown to Camagüey and arrested Matos in person. Matos had allowed himself to be detained without firing a single shot, and in a trumped-up trial was sentenced to twenty years in prison, even though no evidence against him was ever found.

"Nobody leaves the revolution, William," she said, sipping on *yerba mate,* the South American drink made popular by Che. "Remember that. Tragedy always follows those who defy the will of the people."

"So what will you do when they come for me?" he asked her.

She put down her chipped Sèvres cup. "Why would they? You're a hero of the revolution. You saved Fidel."

"The question is, What will you do when they come for me?"

"Are you conspiring?"

"And if I were?"

She stared back at him, unable to believe that her husband would willingly go against all that they had created.

"I refuse to deal in hypotheticals," she said, getting up from the table. "I must go to my literacy meeting."

She placed her cup on the stainless steel sink, then returned and gave Morgan a kiss on the cheek. Her hair had grown back a coppery color, in short and nappy curls that gave her the disconcerting appearance of a *mulata* with ivory white skin.

"I know you wouldn't do that. You're teasing me, that's all. I'll see you tonight."

Morgan watched her exit the house, dressed in the olive green fatigues she now was rarely without. She cut across the old-fashioned rose garden and slipped into the baby blue Oldsmobile given to her by Minister of Education Manuel Hart for heading the literacy campaign in Havana Province.

We are all parasites, he thought. We are all living off the blood of the people. But this is what they want! No, what they want is Fidel. We're just along for the ride. As long as it lasts.

✳ ✳ ✳

He tried to think as little as he could during those days. He busied himself down at the frog farm, surrounded by ponds and spawning pools and scads of tadpoles destined to be devoured, he hoped, by the Cuban consumer, once the country learned to appreciate the odd amphibian delicacy. But mostly he brooded and he drank, not to excess, but enough to blunt the pain.

At home in the afternoons he would stare numbly at the television test pattern until the regular programming began. He grew to be very fond of that pattern. It did not ask him questions, offer advice, or expect anything out of him. Its comforting tone and half-scale grays and whites were simply there, the announcement of a show that was about to start.

That was the fun, of course, the programming that would follow, the almost daily fare of subtitled Warner Brothers classics: *I'm a Fugitive from a Chain Gang, The Public Enemy, Yankee Doodle Dandy, Juarez, The Treasure of the Sierra Madre,* and naturally, that great unparalleled masterpiece, which someone at CMQ must have been crazy for, as it showed at least once a month: *Casablanca.*

Sometimes, nodding off from the beers and the whisky, he would open up his eyes in the middle of the movie, finding that some burst of gunfire or some character's urgent cry for help had penetrated his dreams and rescued him from his stupor. Other times just the opening bars of the score would be enough for him to wake up and sit glued to the old Admiral, relishing every word of slang and every pungent slur, every sharp twist of the English language that had once meant home to him. At times like that he would be proud of being American, as the scrappy Warner Brothers characters, living on the edge, braved their way through a world where all the cards were stacked against them but where, through luck and pluck and sheer honest courage, they overcame the odds and achieved a triumphant, if not always a winning, end.

Then the movies would end and the tedious inanity of the government programs would begin: news from South America, interviews with smiling peasants, arts programs where what was hot in Moscow and Vladivostok had replaced the fashions of New York, Los Angeles, and Miami. But even those were preferable to the times when Fidel commanded the airwaves.

Foreign policy, cattle raising, the sugar industry, the depth and location of the country's nickel deposits, the exact configuration of the Vuelta Abajo tobacco fields, the enormous wealth to be made from commercial fishing, on everything Fidel was the island's top expert.

Not enough coffee to meet the country's needs? Well, let us plant coffee bushes around Havana, for the bounty of this island is so great that anything will grow anywhere. Not enough milk because we slaughtered our prize Holsteins when we nationalized the cattle ranches? Then we shall import zebu cattle, which are even more revolutionary since they come from that Third World brother country, India. Not enough meat? We shall all breed rabbits then, in our balconies and backyards, and we will export the surplus to those poor countries who lack the far-seeing leadership of Cuba.

And everyone would applaud—for there was always an audience at the studio dying to cheer the *líder supremo, el comandante en jefe, el gran caballo,* the great horse who would lead his people to greener pastures. And in the newspapers the next day there would be announcements of cabinet appointments to develop the new policy announced last night by Fidel, to ensure Fidel's vision became crystalline reality.

Of course the coffee plants would shrivel and die because the soil was poor and the bushes never tended; the zebu cattle would give even less milk than the few scrawny native cows still left; and the rabbits would never thrive, since there wasn't enough food to feed the rabbits to begin with. But by that time Fidel would be on to other topics, reclaiming the salty swamps of the Zapata Cienaga to plant rice, or diking up the deep-trenched ocean south of Cuba as the Dutch do the North Sea, or using *bagasse,* the remains of the sugar cane after the harvest, as fuel for industries based on oil and hydroelectric power. There were always plenty of dreams, and if one followed the other fast enough, no one would ever notice how the last one had died a miserable death.

And so Morgan slept while Fidel spoke, waiting for the bell that would spring him from his slumber, knowing he was in a fantastic land unlike any his somber compatriots up north could have imagined.

Yet all sleep ends eventually. Morgan's wake-up call came around December, shortly after Fidel abolished Santa Claus for being an imperialist symbol and replaced him with Don Feliciano, a bearded *guajiro* in guayabera, straw hat, and long machete.

It was late at night. Morgan tossed about in a rum-induced nightmare, chasing a ghost down the narrow cobblestoned streets of Old Havana, when the bedside phone rang.

Dazed and confused, Morgan reached over and picked up the receiver. "Hello? *Qué pasa?*"

"Am I to speaking with the Comandante William Morgan?" asked a woman in English. Morgan could not place the voice although it was instantly familiar. A snatch of music drifted over the line.

"Apaga eso!"—turn that thing off!—snapped the woman at someone nearby. The music died down.

"Alló? Comandante Morgan?" queried the woman again.

"This is he speaking," said Morgan.

"My name is Mónica Farrés."

No wonder he recognized the voice. Mónica was the most popular singer on the island, the toast of revolutionary Cuba, with her ballads about mad love and tyranny, her voice almost as ubiquitous as Fidel's.

"I have a longtime friend, he wants to meet you for autograph."

Morgan glanced at his clock. Two-forty. Irma muttered something in her sleep, turned on her side.

"Well, that's very flattering, Miss Farrés, but I am not in the habit of meeting strangers in the middle of the night."

"Maybe you know my friend. He say he's a king."

"A king?"

"Yes. His wife, she die crazy in Belgium. Maybe this will make you cry too, no?"

Morgan sat up, startled. Was it possible?

"Where are you?"

Morgan recognized the address once he parked the blue Olds down La Rambla. He walked down the same narrow stairs to the entrance under the archway and stepped through the same beaded curtains lifted from some dry goods store in Provence. Once inside, only the name had changed, La Cita becoming La Pareja, the couple.

Mónica, tall and arresting in a formfitting white dress, stood up from a bar stool. She shook Morgan's hand.

"I am so glad to meet the hero of Trinidad!" she said in warm Spanish.

"I am surprised you remember."

"Cómo no! If not for you, the revolution would have ended right there. Come, please tell me all about it." She signaled at the bartender. *"Tony, un Cuba Libre para el señor."*

She sat next to Morgan, liquid brown eyes fluttering in adoration.

"Bueno, but I drink scotch."

"You'll like this drink, buddy," said the bartender, a short man with thinning hair and an outsize nose, setting a glass of rum and Coca-Cola on the counter.

"Jesus, you *are* back!" whispered Morgan at Max, who nonchalantly flicked a dishrag over the counter.

"La vida da muchas vueltas," life has many turns, he said, then added in English, "Sometimes even U-turns."

"Comandante, please excuse me, but I must sing my last couple of numbers, very special. You will stay, no?"

Morgan nodded. Mónica stepped down to the floor, shook a few hands on her way to the stage. She stationed herself next to the pianist, was soon joined by a guitarist and a drummer. A few notes as prelude, then an unusual song, "Autumn Leaves," sung in flawless French.

"Isn't she something?" beamed Max, wiping clean a highball glass. "She owns this place. Of course, we at the company had to lend her a few bucks to get it, but she's already repaid us. Man, it's nice to be back in Havana!"

"You're nuts! What are you doing here?"

Max grabbed the bottle of Bacardi, poured another splash into Morgan's glass.

"Let me freshen this up for you," he said, pointing with his eyes at a tall man in a black suit who walked by the bar. He waited until the man had taken a seat at the far end of the room to watch Mónica with deliberate casualness.

"That's a G-2 agent," said Max, lighting Morgan's cigarette. "I don't think he knows who I am. He's probably following you, William. I assume you know your phone is tapped?"

"I thought so. What brings you here?"

"You," said Max, barely moving his lips. He examined a glass for an invisible spot then sloshed it again in the sink.

"Me?"

"I came to pick you up tomorrow. You and your wife. We want you to come over and help us prepare."

"For what?"

"The invasion."

"Excuse me?"

"We're setting up an expeditionary force, training in Honduras right now. The old man gave thumbs-up the other day. You can be military leader. Interested?"

"I don't know."

"I do. You don't have much time left. They don't trust you."

"I haven't done anything!"

"You don't have to. You're American. They're just waiting for the chance to slam you in jail. Why do you think they're tailing you?"

"I see."

"We're having a boat out in Tarará tomorrow. Ten o'clock. Kilometer marker fifty-one. Just give those guys the slip and we'll get you both out."

"There's one problem."

"What? These women with their lipstick!" said Max, loudly. Then, softly, "Quick, laugh!"

Morgan chuckled, as though he'd heard one of those wonderful observations that only the intoxicated can truly appreciate.

The man in black walked up to the bar. Morgan smelled the Aqua Velva, the stale odor of garlic.

"El servicio, dónde está?" he asked.

"A la derecha," answered Max, pointing at the men's room as he stared at the man's pockmarked face. The man nodded *thank you* then walked down the hallway.

"Wanted to get a good look at me, the son of a bitch," frowned Max. "OK, so what's the problem?"

"My wife wouldn't come. She believes."

"What? At this point she still believes in the revolution?"

"Very much so."

Max shook his head. "You have a problem, all right. You could kidnap her, of course."

"That wouldn't do any good."

"No, I see your point."

The two men stared at each other, then smiled and looked away. Mónica finished her set; the man in black returned.

"I have an idea," whispered Morgan.

"What?"

"Mañana, my friend, *mañana* I'll tell you," said Morgan, leaving a ten peso tip so the G-2 agent could see how grateful he was for having been so thoroughly entertained. Mónica walked up to him.

"You're not leaving already, are you, *Comandante?"*

"The time, it waits for no one," he said in Spanish, then took a napkin and scribbled quickly on it.

"This is for your friend. Sorry he did not come."

"Yes, life is like that. *Adios, Comandante."*

They kissed on the cheek and Morgan strode quickly out of the room. Within seconds the black-suited man did likewise. Max picked up the napkin.

"What does it say, *mi amor?*"

"It says, 'For my Cuba, everything. Comandante William Morgan.'"

Chapter

14

Irma was surprised the following morning when, on coming down for breakfast, she found William fully dressed in rebel army uniform. He was sipping a *café con leche* at the sink, looking more alert than she had seen him in months.

Is he back? she thought. Is he out of his funk?

"Well, to what do we owe the pleasure?" she said, kissing him on the freshly shaven cheek, taking her place at the wrought iron table in the arbor by the kitchen.

Morgan followed her outside, watching as Manuel poured her a chamomile tea.

"We're taking a little trip today, Irma, just you and me."

"Really? I had told the *compañeras* at the ministry I'd meet them for lunch."

"I'd like you to cancel if you can."

"Why is that?"

"I want to show you the real face of the revolution."

❈ ❈ ❈

Morgan thought she would oppose his plan, but to his surprise, she quickly agreed to accompany him after a series of quick calls to her colleagues at the literacy campaign. What Morgan did not realize and she did not tell him was that for months she had been waiting for just this very show of concern on his part.

More than anything in the world she had wanted to be by his side upon her return from California. Even her devotion to Fidel had been a misguided attempt to show Morgan that she was more than just a wife, that she was really a kindred spirit. Irma had been unable to understand why he hesitated to bring her into his life, why he dawdled by the television set all day or hid in the frog farm for weeks. But now, finally, he seemed to have snapped out of it, becoming like the Morgan of old, the kind, adventurous man she had known before the triumph of the revolution.

Doesn't he see? she thought as they drove out to the docks. Is he really that blind to think that I have changed so much that any government is more important to me than he is? Doesn't he realize I was doing it out of spite? Doesn't he know I'd follow him anywhere?

"Where are we going?" she asked as they parked by the pier.

"We're going to La Cabaña."

"Are we going to see Che?"

"No, sweetheart," he said as he walked her to the ferryboat. "Che has moved to the National Bank. We're going to see some of the people Che locked up."

※ ※ ※

Irma wanted to ask more questions but grew quiet at being surrounded by dozens of women with children, lugging large parcels of food and clothing. For a moment Irma was puzzled, but soon their purpose became clear as the women spoke of their husbands, brothers, and sisters, all detained in La Cabaña prison.

"I tell you, my husband Roberto, he never lifted a finger to help those counterrevolutionary *gusanos*," those worms, bewailed a thin, caramel-skinned woman with bulging eyes, sitting next to Irma. The woman glared at Morgan, who looked out at the bay, seeming to pay no attention. She raised her voice, as though to say she was not scared of his green-shirted authority. "He was always a good revolutionary!"

"*Ay chica,* then why did they put him in? He must have done something!" queried a shorter, stouter woman down the stained pinewood bench.

"Because he likes to listen to rock 'n' roll, that is the only reason," replied the first woman, her teeth bared in contempt.

"I don't understand, *vieja,*" said the neighbor. "What does music have to do with antigovernment activity?"

"That's what I would like to know myself. He was just singing 'La Bamba' when that monster who heads the Defense Committee on our block, Paquín, swings by and arrests him. Later he says he was singing, 'I am not Marinello,' you know, like the old communist, instead of what the song really says, *'Yo no soy marinero,'* I am not a sailor."

"*Santa María!*" said the neighbor, crossing herself. "And so what happened?"

"Ten years they gave him. Now how am I going to raise Carlitos without a husband, eh? Come here, *niño.*"

A long-limbed, frizzy-haired youngster climbed off the railing and dashed to the woman like a homeless bird.

"Now what am I going to do, eh? You tell me. You tell me!" The woman raised her voice at Morgan, then broke into tears as her boy and her neighbors comforted her.

Morgan looked back at the woman, then fixed a cool, expressionless gaze on Irma for the longest time. He moved to the bow of the boat, stepping around the children sprawled on the dirty wet floor. Standing silently at the railing, he lit a Pal Mall with his Zippo.

Irma looked at the woman, amused yet horrified. To think that someone might be detained for singing a popular song was both stupefying and hilarious at the same time. But that the same person might actually receive ten years for that was beyond belief. The woman must be lying. Yes, that's it. Or it's some mistake. Yes, that must be it, some bureaucratic confusion that will be righted as soon as the proper authorities find out. That's not what the revolution was all about, no, not at all.

A Jeep, driven by two surly blacks in the blue uniform of the militias, waited to transport them inside the prison. Irma turned worriedly to Morgan on their way to the vehicle.

"What that woman said on the boat, it can't possibly be true, can it?"

"There's thousands of cases like that, Irma, and thousands more that are worse every day. We may have bread but we have no liberty."

"But how can that be? How is it possible?"

Morgan laughed, replied breezily: "That's the nature of the beast. Just you wait, there's more still."

She grabbed him by the arm, jerking him close. "No, please, don't do this to me."

"Do what?"

"Take my dreams away."

Morgan looked down, caressed her brow wrinkled with worry. "I'm sorry, sweetheart, but there are no dreams left in Cuba, not unless they're ordered by the government."

"Does Fidel know about this? I'm sure you could call and tell him."

Morgan gave her a look of indescribable compassion. "Irma, this is exactly the way he wants it. Save some tears for later. You'll need them."

"What are you talking about?"

Morgan looked at the waiting militiamen lounging insolently by the jeep.

"Muchachos, thanks for coming!"

They grunted, the older of the men turning on the engine after Irma and Morgan climbed into the backseat. The vehicle groaned, jerked forward to the high-walled prison.

"What happened with Carlos and Máximo? They were here last year when I came to visit Che."

The men looked at each other, laughed in cheerful complicity.

"They're still here," said the driver, scratching his scruffy head, to the great amusement of his companion.

"Yeah, but now they're on the other side, you know what I mean, *Comandante? Galera* twenty, that's where you'll find them."

"*Galera* twenty? What to be that?"

"The political prisoners' wing, *Comandante*. Isn't that where you're going?" asked the driver, squinting at Morgan through the rearview mirror.

Irma was in tears when they left the stifling confines of La Cabaña. Inside, in a cell jammed with sweating bodies and reeking of human feces, they had seen the drawn face of Major Rogelio Piñeira, one of the original members of the Second Front. His common-law wife, Ana, had saved Irma's life during her miscarriage in the Escambray. He had admitted to conspiring against the government and had been sentenced to death. Today was his last day, and Ana and her four children wailed throughout the visit. Ana implored Morgan to save him, getting down on her knees and kissing his boots to find a way to spare Rogelio's life.

"Help us, William. You have the ear of Fidel. Please have his sentence commuted!"

Morgan had shaken his head and cried with them too. He had already asked Fidel. The sentence was irreversible.

"The government will guarantee you, his widow, a pension and a house. Your children will receive the finest education," said Morgan. "Nothing else I can do."

Irma saw the pain in her husband's face, and she knew he was sincere. She knew too that her dreams of a free Cuba had again been shattered. All that remained was the long struggle to a new victory.

"There must be something you can do, William," she said, once in their car back in town, where they knew no one could hear them.

"Not for him. It is too late. But maybe I can do something for others. With your help."

She looked at him, took his hand.

"Thank you for trusting me."

"Thank you for having me back."

And so that night, when the amphibian landing craft pushed ashore in Tarará, under the very nose of the patrolling Cuban coast guard, Morgan had his answer. Max, implausibly attired in a black wet suit, was accompanied by two ruddy-cheeked men of beefy build.

"We don't have much time. Are you coming?" asked Max.

"No, I'm staying. But she's going with you."

Irma stepped forward, dressed all in black as well—shirt, trousers, boots, her hair gathered in a bun.

"Tell your boys I'm going to open up a new front in the Escambray. The first front this time. We're going to need weapons and money. I've got some supplies put away, but it won't be enough for what I want to do. And we're going to need money, lots of it. We'll pay it all back, but for now we're going to have to bribe our way through. As long as the dollar is still good down here. Give Irma the money. She can bring it back when you drop her off."

Max smiled at the blunt talk, then gave Morgan a quick *abrazo*.

"No guarantees, pal, but I'll see what I can do for you in Washington."

"Tell them we'll coordinate when the invasion comes."

"I will."

"Now you better scat before the coast guard shows up."

Morgan and Irma stepped into the water, the sloshing tide swirling around their legs. They kissed one last time.

"You remember the code?" he asked.

"My aunt Electra is better, when I call."

"That's right." He stopped, not knowing what to say, so he simply told her what was in his heart.

"I love you. You're the best thing that ever happened to me. Now get out of here!"

"I love you," she whispered as he clambered up the coral reef and vanished into the darkness. "I love you," she repeated as the boat buzzed away into the luminous night. "I love you," she said as she sailed away to Miami in the speedboat, and she knew it was both for him and for her country that her heart ached and that she couldn't find a way to separate the two of them, even if she tried.

Chapter

15

Morgan never felt more alive than he did during those febrile months of preparation. With each shipment of weapons and each suitcase of cash, he was opening up yet another breach in the fortress, laying down another charge that eventually would blow Castro and his crew out of the pages of Cuban history.

He returned to his old haunts in the Escambray, to Cubanacán, Banao, Hanabanilla, to all the thickly forested gullies and ravines where once he had struck deadly blows for freedom. Gone was the numbing torpor that had kept him glued to the television, sucking life out of a bottle. For the first time in years he knew he was doing good, and in so doing he was making amends for his past. He was making up for Laura and El Gato and so many others who had died through his weaknesses or his failures. He knew that history, fate, God, whatever you choose to call it, the strange entity that moves men on the board of life, was acting through him, and like the *hashshashin* of old, he knew for a certain fact that he was the sword of that force.

He also never felt closer to Irma. Now she was totally, completely, undisputedly his, and their two beings were perfectly molded to each other. She became his confidante and advisor, the steady voice of reason that kept him on course, reining in his temper and allowing him to continue with their life as before so no one would be the wiser until the final moment of rebellion.

Even the farmers in the area opened their doors to him. The agrarian reform plan that they had pinned their hopes on had not granted them ownership of the land, which was to be held in the name of the people by the government. The *guajiros* realized they had merely exchanged one landowner for another, that the burden of servitude was still upon them. So when Morgan and the handful of *tigres* that he had recruited began to show again in the hills, they welcomed them back like long-lost brothers.

Only Eloy refused to join in, claiming the timing was wrong.

"They've done surveys, William," said Eloy. "Seventy-five percent of the population thinks Fidel is like Jesus Christ. That's three out of four. How in God's name can you fight God? This is not the time. You should wait."

They were in Morgan's backyard out in Miramar, strolling by a grove of cypresses. Morgan picked up a stick from the pavers, snapped it in two.

"That's how much I care for public opinion. If we had waited for public opinion, Batista would still be in the Presidential Palace. We to have to act now. Every week they think of something else to nationalize. Look at the government. There's not one democrat left in there. They took all the TV stations and the newspapers, no one said a word. And Huber Matos got twenty years."

"But at least Fidel didn't execute the invaders," countered Eloy. "He made that promise and he kept it."

"One out of thousands. What about the elections? When he came in he said in six months, we'll have elections for sure. Now, here we are, a year later, he's saying four more years."

"I'm sure he'll keep his word. If he doesn't, we will do something about it. Then. Not now. What you're doing is premature."

"It is not. Now is the time. We should learn from Lenin," he added sarcastically.

"How is that?"

"The true revolutionary leads the way. He's in the vanguard. We must relight the torch of freedom in Cuba. Are you with me?"

Eloy took off his black-framed glasses, his hazel eyes swimming with tears.

"No, William, I cannot be with you this time. But don't worry, I will not betray you."

The men embraced.

"And during the invasion?" asked Morgan suddenly. "You will fight with us?"

"If the invasion were today, William, I must tell you I would be with Fidel again."

"That is not possible!"

"Yes, because at least Fidel is Cuban. An American invasion would be nothing but a repeat of our long and tragic history of U.S. intervention."

"And a Cuban invasion? Next year?"

"*Ah, bueno,* that is flour from another sack, like they say," replied Eloy. "Maybe then we'll fight together again."

"We will fight again, *Comandante.* I know we will."

※ ※ ※

So Morgan stored more weapons and recruited more people to his cause, establishing links with other groups, like the MRRR, the Movimiento Revolucionario de Rescate, headed by Manuel Artime, which had begun a campaign of urban terrorism.

But time was on the side of the government. With every passing week the country lurched further down the road to totalitarianism. Government mobs burned opposition newspapers. Blue-shirted militia singing the "Internationale" broke up memorial masses at the cathedral for the victims of communism. The Agrarian Reform Institute took over all the sugarcane fields. The government nationalized all foreign companies—Texaco, Woolworth's, Coca-Cola, the nickel plant, eighteen distilleries, sixty-one textile mills, sixteen rice mills, eleven movie theaters, the state spreading its tentacles throughout so that no corner of private enterprise could exist for long before being choked to death.

※ ※ ※

One morning, toward the middle of September 1960, Max Weinberg got out of his rented Falcon carrying a box of Cuban pastries in one hand and the *Miami Herald* in the other.

CIA deputy head of station in Miami since his release from La Cabaña, Max was in charge of more than five thousand paid operatives in and around the city, the busiest such station in the entire world since the time of the Berlin airlift.

He carried one dozen guava and one dozen meat pastries for his usual Friday morning meeting with the representatives of the Frente Revolucionario Democrático, the umbrella group that the agency had sponsored and pressured the Florida Cuban exile community into accepting. There had been problems with the internal unity of the front, and Max was hoping that Tony Varona, the former prime minister, who relished these pastries from El Carmelo, would be able to hold it all together.

Max entered through the sliding glass doors of Avionics International, said good morning to Mercedes, the receptionist.

"Who took my spot in the shade, Mercedita? There's a black Chevy parked over there."

"I don't know, Max," replied curly-haired Mercedes in English, always trying to improve her diction. "When I arrive, it was here already. Maybe a customer, no?"

Although a CIA front, Avionics also carried on a legitimate and highly profitable business on the side. In fact, it was so profitable that at times it proved a nuisance for headquarters, which had no idea what to do with the money it earned.

"I certainly hope so. I had to leave my car in the sun, and the air's not working. Let me know if they leave so I can move the car, OK?"

"OK."

Max looked forward to turning on the air conditioner full blast and glancing through the headlines before Tony arrived when he noticed someone already in his office, going through his filing cabinet.

"Excuse me, but what the hell are you doing with my stuff? This is a private office, mister!"

The man now slammed the cabinet door closed and straightened out to his full wiry frame. Max looked up at the lean face above him. He dropped the *Herald* but managed to hold on to the box of pastries.

"Jeffrey Dunphy," said Max levelly, not quite believing his old Havana section chief was actually standing there in his full six-foot-five glory.

"Donuts, Max? Really, you shouldn't have," said Dunphy, seizing the box. Max sat on the guest chair almost by instinct while Dunphy sat on the edge of the desk and opened the box.

"Oh, it's those sticky Cuban things. You can have them. I hate them."

Max took back the box, put it on his lap.

"You look surprised, Maxwell."

"Maximilian."

"I forgot. You didn't think my assignment to Brazzaville would last, did you?"

"I was hoping," said Max, finding his voice.

"We all make mistakes. I made mine with Batista. You are making yours now. So, how is Mónica? Does she miss me?"

The face of his mistress crossed Max's memory. He recalled that brief interlude before Batista fell, when Mónica had left him for Dunphy, who promised he would take better care of the child. The boy was now in the La Salle Military Academy in Miami, waiting for his mother to skip across the waters any day now, courtesy of the agency.

"She doesn't talk much about you."

"That is too bad, because I am looking forward to meeting with her when you bring her over. You know she's a Castro operative."

"That is not true, Dunphy. I don't know what you're talking about," said Max with some trepidation, suddenly realizing that Dunphy could be right. That would explain why the G-2 showed up so quickly the night they met at the club, why Max had such a hot tail he couldn't stay in Havana for more than twenty-four hours. What does that do to William? he wondered.

"Look, let's not argue, Dunphy," Max went on. "I'm glad you're stateside, Africa is no place for a white man. Where are they assigning you?"

"Right here."

Max's heart grew cold. In a flash he saw what was coming, but he knew he had to go on with the performance.

"Here? Well, we don't have a need right now for someone in your grade, but I'm sure we'll work something out, if you don't mind losing some seniority."

Dunphy smiled phlegmatically, took out his pipe, tamped it down, procured a wooden match, and lit it. A cloud of apple-scented smoke filled the room. It's true, the golem is out of the basement, thought Max. *Qué tsouris, coño!*

"You don't get it. I'm taking over for you, Maxie, you double-crossing little kike."

"You can call me anything you like, but I've always been straight with you and the agency."

"Really? I find that hard to believe, considering that your father was a member of the Cominterm."

The walls shook, a gong went off somewhere—his heart, Max realized with wrenching anguish.

"I don't know what you're talking about."

"Oh, yes you do. Your old man was Nikolai Shlyaprikov, one of the first Soviet agents in Latin America. Advisor to Mella, Roa, that whole gang back in the twenties. He'd changed his name to Morris Weinberg by then, but he was with the reds all the same."

It's a bluff. It must be a bluff.

"Of course we don't visit the sins of the father on the sons. But back in Langley we thought it curious that you never mentioned that kind of thing. Not that we would have picked you if you had told us, so I can't say I don't understand you."

"I can prove you are wrong."

"I certainly hope so, for your sake. The Bigots are mighty peeved that this lasted so long. You know, Richard, Jesus, and the rest of the boys."

Max swallowed, found a stone stuck down his throat.

"I'm off immediately," said Max, finally understanding.

"That's right."

"What about operations? We're about to launch a front in the Escambray, and they're expecting weapons."

"You mean your little friend William Morgan?"

"He's got a thousand men under arms already. He's just waiting for the word *go.*"

Dunphy exhaled a great cloud of apple smoke.

"Off the list. Unreliable. He could be a double agent again. Did it before, you know."

"He's on the up-and-up; his skin is on the line."

"Then I guess he'll just have to find a way to save it all by himself. He betrayed people before. Very bad form. We'll just stick to Tony and his Frente Democrático boys. Like FDR might have said, they're SOBs, but at least they're *our* SOBs."

He paused, glared at Max.

"You just can't trust a turncoat, don't you know?"

※ ※ ※

Morgan never knew what happened to Max. One day the messages he sent him from the transmitter near Topes de Collantes were not returned. For a week straight, every night he dashed off the same words, "Grandma, Gladys has a cold, what should we do?"

Silence, crackling of the ether, vast indifference. Then one night, a reply: "The hospital closed its doors. Grandma is dead."

Morgan released the button on the mike, composed himself, then answered: "The family sends its condolences."

He walked outside, standing under a swaybacked pine, watching a bank of gray clouds scud against the gleaming white sliver of a moon. He felt a chill in the high altitude, but he knew it was more than the late hour or his frazzled nerves—it was the realization that he was alone.

Whatever he hoped to accomplish, he had to do fast, before the government swung its troops into the area. With the American aid he was expecting, he had intended to set up a complex ring of booby traps in the roads leading to the hills. But with only two barrels of explosives and no detonation fuses, that plan would have to be scrapped. Still, he had collected enough weaponry to set up his front; his men were trained and ready to set out for the bush once more. He only hoped that somewhere down the line he would be able to coordinate with the upcoming invasion. Yet he wondered, What happened to Max? Will I ever see him again?

※ ※ ※

"I'm afraid, William," said Irma. They sat on the red satin bedspread in their room, a map of Cuba before them, two knapsacks full of clothing and toiletries.

"Don't be," said Morgan. "This government won't last. When the invasion comes, we'll link up, and soon we'll be back in town again."

"What will you do now?"

"Alert all the *comandantes* and invite them to join us."

"How will you do that?"

"Ameijeira's wedding on Friday. I figure all the people I want will be there. They'll know my signal. That night we leave."

She broke down crying. "I can't help it, I'm frightened." He kissed her wide brow.

"There is nothing to fear. God is on our side."

Is He really? thought Irma. Or are we just thinking He will bridge over our terror? And if there is no God? What will we do?

"William, there is something I have to tell you."

He stopped packing, turned to her, shaving kit in hand.

"Yes?"

No, I can't tell him. What if I lose it again? This time, he may not be able to bear the pain. And neither will I.

"I love you."

He walked over to her, embraced her.

"I love you more than my life, sweetheart," he said. "If anything happens to me, you run, understand?"

"Yes."

"Run to the nearest embassy and ask for political asylum. Don't wait and don't bargain. If they're coming for you this time, they're coming for good."

"I'll remember."

He pressed her hand against his chest.

"This heart is all yours now, Irma. Once I shared it with someone else, but that was an illusion, you understand that?"

She felt the tears springing from her eyes, burning, unbidden.

"I know."

"You do?"

"I saw her once. At a reception somewhere. Tiny, with masses of red hair and coppery skin. There goes Major Morgan's lover, someone said, not knowing who I was."

"You know that it was all a lie."

"I know. I also know that what happened between you two happened long before you met me."

"And you were not hurt?"

"I was. But I am your wife, William, and I am still here. I am pledged to you and you only. You are everything to me. You are my soul and my salvation. You are my country, William. And you are mine, sweetheart."

❊ ❊ ❊

Morgan examined the small green frog-skin purse. I'm certain Ameijeiras will like this, he thought. There's never been anything like this here.

Compact, yet stylish, the purse was the epitome of fashion, the perfect example of the kind of product he had once hoped to promote as a source of income for the country. Only a handful had been made, but in the future, when freedom returned to Cuba, it could prove a profitable enterprise.

He considered wrapping it in gift paper, but at the end merely placed it in a black hatbox and strolled out of the house. It was already mid-morning and Irma slept still, the bedroom door closed. On his way to the Oldsmobile he noticed Manuel clipping the roses, basket in hand. He waved hello at his faithful servant, got into the Oldsmobile, and drove away, thinking that once Fidel was gone, as he soon would be, they'd turn the house over to the old man.

He's certainly worked hard enough for it, and we'll have plenty of other places to choose from, thought Morgan, bearing down L Street to the ornate Ministry of the Interior.

Morgan noted with distaste the blaring billboards above the Malecón. Literacy campaign and water rationing posters had recently displaced the ones for Mercedes-Benz autos and Philip Morris cigarettes, giving Havana the atmosphere of an impoverished Eastern-bloc country. Bad slogans and worse art. How can anybody live in a country like this?

He pulled in front of the ministry, parking in the special lot reserved for functionaries and leaders of the revolution, and walked quickly, as was his custom, down the broad sidewalk in the morning sun. Another limpid blue sky, tufted clouds on the horizon beyond Morro Castle. He stopped for a moment to look at the glistening bay a handful of blocks away. Tonight after the reception we leave for the hills, he thought. I have never seen Havana so beautiful.

He entered the inlaid-marble-floored building, saluting the young, new militia guard who moved to stop the obvious gringo in *comandante* uniform. But an older guard, once a member of the now dissolved 26th of July, saluted Morgan briskly and let him pass to the ornate elevator. "That's the American *comandante,* William Morgan," said the old-timer.

"The hero of Trinidad. He foiled the invasion from Santo Domingo."

"Really? What invasion from Santo Domingo? That's not in my history books at the university."

"It must be, you just didn't study it. He was also in the Second Front," added the veteran, before moving to another part of the hall.

An American *comandante* with Raúl Castro, thought the young guard. How curious. I'll have to look that up.

Morgan carried the box under his arm when he walked into Ameijeira's office. The gaunt mulatto looked up from his desk, parted his prominent lips.

"Qué tal, Efigenio?"—how are you?—said Morgan.

But the words Ameijeiras said were unlike any Morgan had expected, at least not that day.

"Arrest him!" cried the police chief. Six armed soldiers surged from an adjoining room, rushing Morgan, throwing him to the ground in an instant.

"Take that box out of here, it might be a bomb!" shouted Ameijeiras.

"What are you doing? It's your wedding gift, stupid!" cried Morgan.

"Slap the handcuffs on him!" ordered Ameijeiras, standing up behind his desk, his long curved nose pointed down like the beak of the *jomeguí,* the Cuban magpie—Ameijeira's street monicker when he was a pot-peddling pimp under Batista.

Morgan struggled vainly as the six men placed the cuffs, then hoisted him bodily off the ground.

"What are you doing? I am a *comandante* of the rebel army!"

"Even more reason to be ashamed of your treason," said a well-known voice. Morgan spotted Fidel and Che Guevara coming from the adjoining room.

"What are you saying?"

"We have evidence you have been conspiring, William," said Fidel, "that you are planning to take up arms against the government."

"Says who?"

"I say it!" said old Manuel, shuffling into the room, his features distorted by the universal mask of greed. "I am the witness! I have seen you and heard you conspiring many a time!"

"Good. That's all we need to hear for now," said Castro. "Take him away, muchachos. We'll deal with him later."

"Will I get the house like they promised me, Fidel?" asked Manuel.

"Of course, muchacho," said Fidel. "The revolution always takes care of its own."

"His wife is also involved, Fidel. Don't forget her."

"*Coño, chico,* you're right." Castro turned to Ameijeiras. "Send someone to pick her up right away."

"Where should I put them, Fidel?" asked the police chief, more used to dealing with petty criminals than top conspirators.

"In La Cabaña, *coño,* where else? We'll talk later."

Che Guevara shook his head, as if embarrassed by the vulgarity of the actions he witnessed, regretting the entire scene.

Morgan did not care. All he could think of was his Irma, his sleeping, pregnant—he was sure—Irma, defenseless in bed.

"IRMA!" he shouted, as though his voice alone could warn her.

"IRMA! IRMA!!" he hollered with all his might.

"IRMA!!!! IRMA!!!!!! IRMA!!!!!!!!!!!!!!!!"

❈ ❈ ❈

Years later Irma would say that her husband's cry was evidence that love is not bound by the laws of physics or reason.

She had tossed and turned all morning, in the half-conscious state of pregnant women who find themselves hosting a life that seems to demand more than they can give. She was dreaming of her father for the first time in months, and she squirmed at the sight of him, feeling sinful and unclean. They were back at the mission, only now it was set not in swaying fields of sugarcane but deep in the heart of Havana; in fact, the ramshackle building had somehow been transported to the Plaza de la República. Her father was leading a congregation of millions of souls of all colors and races, singing a hymn that she could not recognize or follow. The sign on the board gave the hymn number, but the hymnbook did not carry that hymn, and her frustration mounted, for she knew she was supposed to be leading the congregation in song, but she could not find the words.

She cried and begged someone to show her where the hymn was, but no one would listen to her, until finally the congregation grew quiet. Her father looked at her and opened his mouth. She tried to hear but she could not make out his words over the howling of a siren. Finally one word rang out clearly, only it was not her father's voice but Morgan's, a shout of anger and desperation.

IRMA!!!!!!!!!!!!

She opened her eyes, sat up in bed. The howling of the siren came closer, then stopped right outside her window. She got up, glanced outside. Two police squad cars had pulled up in front of the house. The doors of one of them opened, and Manuel came out with two militia guards. For a moment she thought Manuel had been arrested, then it all became clear—they were coming for her.

Not even stopping to put on clothes, she grabbed her purse and ran down the marble staircase to the first floor. She raced barefoot from the living room right as the door was kicked open by an overanxious guard, Manuel standing at the threshold with the key in his hand.

I have to get away! I have to escape!

She remembered Morgan's words and recalled that the Brazilian embassy was only six blocks away. They could grant her asylum, she would be safe there. If she could only get there! She ran out through the kitchen, stubbing her toe on the door stop, bending down without thinking to grab her toe for the pain. That reflex reaction may have saved her, for a policeman going by the back of the house looked in the window at that very moment and, not seeing her, ran around to the front.

Irma, hobbling from her bleeding toe, opened the back kitchen door and stepped out into the patio, only to be confronted by a young guard, who pointed his machine gun at her with trembling hands. Irma panicked for a moment, then realized the guard was a boy barely of shaving age, fifteen or sixteen, and that his wide brown eyes showed even more fear than Irma felt in her heart.

"Stop right there!" he ordered.

"No, please, let me go! I haven't done anything!" she pleaded.

"You're an enemy of the revolution!"

"I'm just a pregnant woman! Please let me go!"

The boy was about to call for help when Irma opened her purse, tossing out ten- and twenty-dollar bills.

"Here, here, take this money, just let me go!"

The boy looked at her, then looked at the money. It was more than he had seen in a long time, and it was dollars. He hesitated. Irma placed the purse carefully on the ground.

"Here's the money, here's the purse. You keep it, just let me go. OK? OK?"

The boy didn't answer, his eyes riveted on the money and the purse. Irma could hear the others crying out inside the house, "She's not here! Check outside!" I have to risk it, she thought. I have no choice.

She stepped back carefully, backing away from the boy, their eyes still on each other, then she turned and ran. The boy raised his gun, then he too heard the thumping of boots closing in, and he dove for the money, stuffing his pockets with the cash. By the time he looked up, Irma had dashed to the far end of the property and was climbing the ivy-covered wall. She wavered for a moment on the edge, then jumped out of sight.

Chapter

16

For months, while waiting for the trial in La Cabaña, Morgan kept asking himself when would they start.

He knew all about their games, from holding people's heads under water in toilet bowls until they threatened to drown, to having them run the gauntlet naked while being smashed with rifle butts, to placing you in the infamous *gavetas,* the drawers, cramped cells where you could not lie or stand but were kept naked and contorted while guards up above peed and poured water on you at all hours. He had not heard of the other refinements of the socialist art of punishment, as practiced in the Boniato and Combinado del Este prisons: inmates forced to clear latrines with their tongues or left to stew for days dunked in vats of human feces. But had he heard of it, he would not have been surprised, either. He was only too conscious of the fact that the brave new world hailed by Pablo Neruda, Jean Paul Sartre, and Allen Ginsberg—the myth of Cuban revolutionary humanism perpetrated later by Carlos Fuentes and Gabriel García Márquez—that those fantasies stopped at the entrance to the jail cell and, more precisely, at the threshold of the bloodstained *paredón,* the execution wall.

He had no doubt that he would be executed. Sorí Marín, the former minister of agriculture who had also risen up against the government, had been captured and also expected no mercy. Captain Manuel Beatón, who had attempted to set up a rebel stronghold in Raúl Castro's old redoubt of the Sierra Cristal, had been shot summarily when captured. Others with even less involvement had also been executed. Death, then, was certain. The only question was how it would come.

That was why he felt encouraged, on hearing the news from Key West over a smuggled transistor radio, that the boys he had trained in the Escambray, the hardscrabble farmers who wanted only to own their own piece of land, were fighting the government troops. He would never know that it would take five years before the rebellion he sparked was finally extinguished, that the government would win only after burning down entire mountains, relocating tens of thousands of people, and removing the name of the Escambray from the geography books of the island so no one would ever remember the heroic deeds of those men.

Bravery, then, not foolhardiness. That was the reason he was holding fast. So he told Che Guevara when the Argentinean came to visit after a six-hour trial during which Morgan was not allowed to say one word or present a single piece of evidence on his own behalf.

"Sorry we could not allow you to speak," said Guevara, offering him one of his foul stogies. "You might come up like Fidel, give a speech like he did after the attack on the Moncada, and we'd be stuck with another 'History Will Absolve Me' piece of shit that would be the theoretical foundation for another rebel movement. No, William. We learned our lesson well."

The men laughed, the absurdity of their situation leavening the entire scene with a mirth an outsider might never have understood.

"Why did you treat me so well all these months? I mean, you fed me regular, let me exercise, mingle with the other prisoners."

"Believe me, it wasn't easy. Raúl wanted to put you on the rack, and Fidel almost let him. I had to remind them of what you did for us back then, with Trujillo."

"I thought revolutionaries didn't know the meaning of gratitude."

"We do, when it benefits the revolution."

"I think I will take that cigar after all."

Morgan bent down to light the Partagás, the yellow flame of the waxen match flaring up, burning the tip of the cylinder to a thick gray ash.

"I'm going to miss you, Che. We never did talk much after the revolution, but with me you were always a straight shooter."

"There is no need for that."

"How do you mean? I'm going to be executed, aren't I? It's a foregone conclusion."

"Not necessarily. I am here to offer you a deal, William. Cooperate. Tell us who your allies were. Help us to capture them and we'll let you escape."

"Escape? To where?"

"To the hills, the U.S. Anywhere you choose. People have been

0

known to escape from here. I know. I used to run this place, remember?"

Morgan puffed on his cigar, then shook his head *no*.

"Sorry. The only deal I could accept would be if you fellows trade places with me. You and Fidel and Raúl and the whole crew."

"Don't you want to see your wife?" insisted Che. "Don't you want to grow old with her, bring up your child, have others, maybe, in some place safe and secure?"

Morgan looked fixedly at Guevara, then walked over to the barred window of his cell. Below, the flat yard and the bullet-scarred *paredón*. Morgan turned back to Guevara.

"No. You want to know why?"

"Please. I'm anxious to hear your death song. They say we all have a particular one just for us and that it is uniquely beautiful. Let me hear it."

"What kind of man would I be to my family if the price of my own liberty were the death and suffering of thousands of others? I did that once, and it was wrong. Because that is what we're talking about. I live, they die. That is an unacceptable trade. Yes, it's true some lives are worth thousands, even millions of ordinary lives. Martí, Michelangelo, Mozart. But that is not for us to decide; that is for history to decide. No, my friend. I go to my end knowing that I have done absolutely the right thing, that for once principle has triumphed over expediency. I am a dead man already."

Morgan paused, then frowned as if forgetting some bothersome detail.

"Perhaps I was already dead by the time I came to Cuba and it's only been here that I have had, even if briefly, a full measure of life."

Guevara clapped slowly.

"*Bra-vo! Bravísimo!* Spoken just like a Cuban."

"I am Cuban, Che. I have become Cuban. Fidel himself said so a long time ago."

Guevara gave Morgan a last quizzical look, then stood up.

"I'm afraid you're right. I'm not, you see. I don't think I'll ever be a good Cuban. That's why I don't see much of a future for me here. Pretty soon they'll be packing me off to socialist exile, to visit trade fairs and make idle chatter about political art. That's what they've done to Chomón, you know. They sent him to Moscow. *Qué vida, che!*"

They hugged, then Morgan made the sign of the cross in the air.

"Get thee behind me, Satan!"

"I'm going already. If you change your mind, I'll be at the execution. So will Fidel and Raúl."

"I doubt it."

"Yes, that's what I told Fidel, but you know how he is. He thinks everybody is like him, always out to make a deal."

Che knocked at the steel plate door; the guard yanked it open with a groan.

"By the way, don't worry about your girl. She's on her way out of the country already."

Morgan stood, shocked, smiled. Gratitude for the devil.

"Thank you."

"It's alright. You saved my life once. A life for a life. Or a life and a half."

Guevara stepped out, the door banged closed. Morgan sat down, shaken by the news.

Irma lives! She lives! All the time he had been imprisoned, the lack of news about her whereabouts had been almost impossible to bear. But now he knew she was safe, on her way out of the country. It was all done, then. Except for one last thing.

He walked to his cot, lifted the mattress, opened a piece of paper folded into a square no bigger than his fingernail, then searched through a hole in the cotton matting of the mattress, finally extracting a pencil stub. He sharpened it with his teeth and sat down to compose his last letter.

My darling Irma,

This is the last you will ever hear from me. There is so much I want to tell you and so little time.

Outside, the moon is hidden and the troops are readying for my execution. Know this, that I have loved you more than my life and that I have chosen death rather than dishonor.

Tell my child what his father did. Let him always remember the fight for freedom we undertook and the price it cost us. Make him grow strong and proud of who he is, the best of two different worlds.

As for you, my angel, your face will be the last thing I see before my final sleep, your arms the ones that will enfold me when the bullets do their work. I think of you and I hear the music of our love, strong and reckless, rushing forward to meet me at my final hour.

Until that moment when we embrace again in that place where lovers love for all eternity, I will always be,

Desperately yours,
William

An hour later, when the wind from the bay had died down, he heard a knock. The door opened, a priest stuck his head inside.

"Would you like to say your confession, son?"

"*Bueno,* padre, you will take the confession of a Lutheran?"

"Yes, if you think God will hear you."

Morgan smiled. "I will soon find out. Please come in."

The priest stayed with Morgan for a half hour and came out in tears, moved, he said, by the courage of the man inside. He carried in his pocket the much-folded last letter of Morgan's.

The guards arrived, handcuffed Morgan, took him out to the good-byes and acclaim of the other prisoners, who again cried, again with all their heart, again to no avail:

"LIBERTAD! LIBERTAD! LIBERTAD!"

This doesn't seem real, thinks Morgan as he walks down the clamoring corridor. I am walking to my execution just like Maximilian in *Juarez*. But this is what it's all about, isn't it, William? Life *is* a black-and-white film. The hero may have his heart in the right place, but that doesn't mean he'll live. Sometimes real heroes have to bite the dust. And like it.

❈ ❈ ❈

The spotlight shines down on Morgan, blinding him. A row of six riflemen stand before him. In the shadows he vaguely discerns the big-hipped figure of Raúl, the wraithlike profile of Che, the tall, beguiling presence of Fidel, cigar in his mouth.

One of the guards heaves him against the *paredón*.

No, this is not a Warner Brothers flick. There they always blindfold you, they give you a cigarette, a last request. Here they just want to kill me.

❈ ❈ ❈

It doesn't matter.

I *am* a Warner Brothers hero.

"Down on your knees!" someone shouts behind the spotlight.

"I kneel for no one!" answers Morgan.

A shot rings out, blasting his left kneecap.

A second shot, to the right knee, forcing him down.

"God damn you, Fidel! God damn you!" shouts Morgan, for he has recognized the voice and seen the figure, rifle with telescopic lens at the shoulder.

A fusillade of shots. Most miss, but one slams him against the wall, another pins him to the ground. Morgan is still alive, still defiant.

"Death to Fidel! Death to communism!" he hollers.

A short, bearded man, a rebel army captain, runs forward, machine gun by his side.

"*Hijo 'e puta!*" he shouts.

He stops before Morgan, points the tommy gun, pulls the trigger.

The entire clip empties into Morgan's chest, the bullets cutting the aorta, the carotid artery, the spinal cord, shattering his body but never his defiance.

"*Viva Cuba!*" Morgan manages to shout still.

The captain takes out his sidearm and empties the .45 into Morgan's brain, the pieces of skull and gristle flying out in a halo from his head.

And at that very moment, in a flight to Sao Paolo over the wine-dark Caribbean Sea, Irma feels a kick, the creature in her womb stirring as though it knew that hundreds of miles away, against a bespattered bloody wall, his father was dying for a principle, for the right of a nation to be free, for an end to the suffering and the ever-spinning wheel of torture that breaks the backs of the Cuban people.

Viva Cuba libre.

Alex Abella is a Cuban-born novelist and screenwriter raised in New York City. His last novel, *The Killing of the Saints,* was a *New York Times* Notable Book. A former foreign correspondent and television and newspaper reporter, he now lives in Los Angeles.